People Like Us

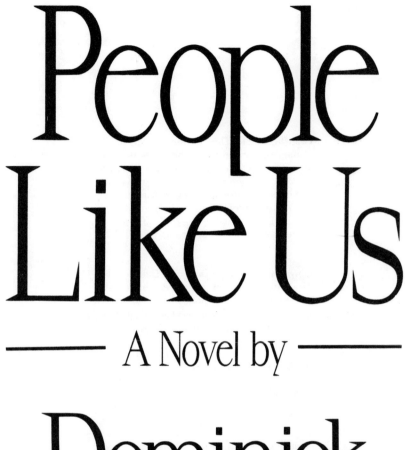

People Like Us

— A Novel by —

Dominick Dunne

Crown Publishers, Inc., New York

Portions of this book have appeared in *Vanity
Fair.*

Published by Crown Publishers, Inc., 225
Park Avenue South, New York, New York
10003 and represented in Canada by the Ca-
nadian MANDA Group.
CROWN is a trademark of Crown Publishers,
Inc.
Manufactured in the United States of America

Book design by Dana Sloan

Library of Congress Cataloging-in-Publication
Data
Dunne, Dominick.
  People like us.
  I. Title
PS3554.U492P46 1988   813'.54   88-353
ISBN 0-517-56879-9
10   9   8   7   6   5   4   3   2

To Virginia Dunne Finley
with love

People Like Us

Prologue

IT WAS half after one, as Ezzie Fenwick always called it, in his rococo manner of speaking, on the Tuesday noon following Black Monday, and the midday social frenzy at Clarence's was at its peak, with every table filled to capacity, as if a financial catastrophe had not taken place. The bar, where those who couldn't get tables waited patiently until after the personal friends of Chick Jacoby, who owned Clarence's and ruled Clarence's with an iron hand, lunched and lingered over decaffeinated espresso for as long as they wanted, no matter how many people were waiting for tables, was three deep. Black Monday. Black Monday. Black Monday. It was the topic of conversation everywhere that noon.

Ezzie Fenwick was securely seated in the window table, the very smart restaurant's very best table, except on the rare occasions when the First Lady came to lunch, or the King of Spain, and the Secret Service advised Chick Jacoby that the window table was far too visible from the street, in times like this, with mad people about, and insisted on moving them into the unfashionable second room, where Ezzie Fenwick would never be caught dead sitting.

The previous day the stock market had fallen five hundred and eight points, and there was panic in the city, especially among the speculators and the nouveau riche. There was also a smug satisfaction, only covertly expressed, that the new billionaires of New York, whom no one had ever heard of six or seven years ago, and who now seemed to control the financial, charitable, and social life of the city, were publicly hurting. Herkie Saybrook reported to Justine Altemus that one of the Zobel brothers, of Zobel Brothers, had been seen weeping uncontrollably at his desk over his enormous losses, ha ha ha, and might have to apply for a federal bail-out. Sims Lord reported that Milton Sofiar, whose personal fortune had been depleted by between three hundred and five hundred million dollars in a single day, had attempted suicide, although not seriously, and had been admitted to Harcourt Pavilion at Manhattan Hospital under an assumed name. The joke of the day was that the only winner on Wall Street the day before was Elias Renthal, who was in prison and barred from trading on the stock market forever, ha ha ha.

Ezzie Fenwick, who knew everything about everyone, was, as always, surrounded by adoring ladies in the very latest of fashion who laughed and laughed each noon at his witty accounts of what had happened the night before at whatever party he had attended. Ezzie reported to Lil Altemus, who was born a Van Degan, and Matilda Clarke, who was the widow of Sweetzer Clarke, and old Cora Mandell, who was society's favorite decorator, that he had dined the night before at the billionaire Bulbenkians, and that Reza Bulbenkian gave an ultimatum to his new wife, Yvonne, that her spending spree simply had to stop. Yvonne Bulbenkian, he explained to Lil Altemus, who sometimes pretended she didn't know who people were, when she knew perfectly well who they were, used to be Yvonne Lupescu, when she was the constant companion of Constantine de Rham.

Reza Bulbenkian, who was the richest of all the New People, as the Old Guard called them, now that Elias Renthal was in prison, was smarting already from the bad publicity engendered by Yvonne's allowing their new limestone mansion on Park Avenue to be photographed by the *Times Sunday Magazine* in the same issue that featured a cover story on the homeless of New York. He begged Yvonne, even before the officers of his company begged him to beg her, to desist from her extravagant spending habits. How could he, he reasoned with her, fire a thousand of his employees, in an economic cutback, when Dolly De Longpre, the society columnist, was reporting in her column that Yvonne had spent a hundred and fifteen thousand dollars for a lynx coat and was planning to fly to Paris, on the company jet, for a private view of the new Lacroix collection, not to mention her noisy bidding at the auction of the Van Gogh irises, which had raised eyebrows, even before the crash.

"She's so frightfully common," said Matilda Clarke.

"The stories I could tell you about her," said Ezzie, his hand to his heart.

"Oh, tell, tell," said old Cora Mandell, who knew that Ezzie only needed to be urged a bit.

"Laurance knew all this was going to happen," said Lil Altemus, getting back to the crash, because it did not interest her to discuss people like the Bulbenkians. "Laurance has been saying for some time that the market was at an unsustainably high level." Lil Altemus

2

quoted her brother, Laurance Van Degan, more than any other person in her life. She spoke with the ease of someone whose fortune had remained intact throughout the recent financial panic. "Laurance got out of the market a week ago, and, of course, I did too, and so did Justine."

Although they all liked to say that they had gotten out of the market in time, or that their losses were only on paper, as if they didn't matter, Rochelle Prud'homme, of Prud'homme Products, makers of cordless hairdryers, pulled Chick Jacoby aside to tell him that she was canceling her dinner dance for one hundred and forty people that she had booked the restaurant for several weeks earlier, and Chick Jacoby, who had already ordered fourteen pink moiré tablecloths and a hundred and forty pink moiré table napkins cut and hemmed by the seamstress around the corner, looked crestfallen. Jamesey Crocus, the specialist in fine French furniture, arrived at Clarence's for lunch with the distressing news that the auction of fine French furniture that morning at Sackville's had been a major bust, with most of the ormolu-encrusted pieces not meeting their reserve prices. And Maisie Verdurin, the art dealer, looked particularly peaked behind her smile, although she had as yet told no one that two of her most important clients had reneged that morning on Post-Impressionist pictures that they had agreed to buy.

On the very rare occasions that Ezzie Fenwick removed the dark glasses he invariably wore, you could see that he had one peculiar eye, rather like a poached egg in appearance, that looked off in a different direction entirely from his other eye, and it made you believe him when he said, as he often did, in his nasal voice that all his friends could imitate, "I never miss a trick. When I'm walking on Fifth Avenue, I can tell you what's happening on Madison and Park." So none of them was surprised when Ezzie interrupted Lil Altemus, who thought she had his full attention with all her inside information about the crash, to say, "My dears, you will not *believe* who just walked into this restaurant."

No one appreciated social drama the way Ezzie Fenwick did, and he was beside himself with joy when the reclusive Ruby Renthal, so long out of sight, and the just-released-from-prison Augustus Bailey walked into Clarence's at that moment, without a reservation. Ezzie's companions, and everyone else in the front part of Clarence's, where all the good people, as Ezzie called them, sat, turned to look at the curious duet who stood quietly just inside the door waiting for Chick Jacoby to hurry forward to greet them, albeit with furrowed brow. Chick Jacoby spent the latter part of each morning seating his luncheon tables with the artistic precision of a stage director, as aware as Ezzie of the ever-changing marital, financial, and social statuses of his regular customers, and last-minute changes, such as this one now, upset his sense of divine order. But it was, after all, Ruby Renthal who was upsetting the divine order, and the businessman behind the perfectionist in him knew that Dolly De Longpre would surely print that the unusual couple had lunched at Clarence's in her column the next morning if he seated them prominently and then got to the telephone in time to beat Dolly's deadline.

"For heaven's sake," said Chick, who could scowl and smile at the same time, pushing his round-rimmed glasses up on the bridge of his nose with his long forefinger.

"I'm a country lady these days, Chick," said Ruby. She spoke in the deep throaty voice that people used to remark on in the days when she was the most discussed woman in New York.

"She looks beautiful," said Cora Mandell, who had decorated the Renthals' famous apartment.

"Good-looking suit she has on," said Matilda Clarke.

Lil Altemus did not look at her. She could neither forget nor forgive that Elias Renthal's despicable financial manipulations had sullied the name of her brother, Laurance Van Degan, causing him to have to resign as the president of the Butterfield, which broke his heart, and she was sure caused the slight stroke that had moved his mouth to the side of his face.

"You watch," said Ezzie, in his nasal voice, to Lil and Matilda and Cora. "Chick will move Lord Biedermeier and Constantine de Rham over to his own table, as if he's giving them a big treat, and put Ruby and the jailbird there."

"What possessed us to come here?" asked Ruby.

"I haven't a clue," said Gus.

"Did you see Loelia?" asked Ruby. Ruby didn't have to tell Gus that Loelia Manchester used to be her best friend.

"And Matilda, and Lil, and Ezzie, and Cora," replied Gus. "And Lord Biedermeier and Constantine de Rham. Nothing seems to change."

"There was a time when I found all this very attractive," said

4

Ruby, looking around, as she put her napkin in her lap, but not meeting anyone's eye. "There's Maisie Verdurin over there. I bet she's not selling many Post-Impressionist paintings today," said Ruby. Maisie Verdurin had probably never had a client who had made her as rich as Elias and Ruby Renthal had, with the accumulation of art they had collected.

"The first time I ever met you was at one of Maisie Verdurin's parties," said Gus.

"Oh, I remember. I was a nervous wreck that night. Dressed all wrong. Bright blue sequins. I bought it in Cleveland. Said *cunt* by mistake to Maisie, and she looked at me like she was thinking, Where did this girl come from? Then I ate the artichoke with a knife and fork."

Gus roared with laughter. "You sure changed quick."

Ruby smiled. She was the most elegant lady in the room.

"Was it awful in prison?" she asked.

Gus shrugged. "I knew when I did what I did I was going to go to prison. For me, it was just part of what my life was supposed to be. And I wrote a book there."

"Ezzie Fenwick always said you were going to write a book. He said you were always listening."

"For once Ezzie Fenwick was right."

I

EXCEPT for July and August, when everyone was away from the city, Maisie Verdurin, the art dealer, entertained in her Park Avenue apartment at large monthly dinner parties that had become so significant a part of the social life of New York that even people in the subways, at least those people in the subways who read the social columns, knew her name. In her interviews, as a hostess of repute, Maisie Verdurin often talked about society today being made up of people of accomplishment—the doers, she called them—and she had only words of contempt for the highly pedigreed few who rode through life on inherited wealth and social perfection. What she could not, simply could not, stand, ever, was to be bored, she often said, and the kind of people who came each month to sit on her sixty gilded ballroom chairs placed around eight tables—six tables of eight, two tables of six—set up in her drawing room, dining room, and library, were guaranteed to provide the kind of conversation that could never, ever, bore.

All the Cézannes, Van Goghs, Picassos, and Monets on her green moiré walls were for sale, and her dinners, which her detractors claimed she used as tax deductions, were a way of doing business and bringing together the political, financial, media, and literary figures of New York into her Rigaud-scented rooms.

Maisie infinitely preferred her own dinners to other people's dinners, but on the occasions she was asked back by the people she had invited, she sometimes called Augustus Bailey to escort her. Gus Bailey, a perennial spare man, obliged if he was free, and their conversations, in taxicabs on their way to and from the dinners, were always monopolized by Maisie, who rarely expressed any curiosity about Gus's life. She knew that he had a California past; she knew he had been something or other in films at one time; but neither California nor films interested her, in the way that Wall Street financiers did, or arbitrage traders, or real-estate entrepreneurs, whose first step on the road to riches was the acquisition of art, and she simply assumed Gus's agreement when she sometimes asked, "Aren't you glad to be away from California?" Gus was glad to be away from California, but

7

not for the reasons Maisie supposed, which had mostly to do with what she called a singleness of theme, the movies, in dinner-table conversations "out there." Maisie also knew that Gus had a wife in California, with money, called, improbably, Peach, whom a lot of people knew, but that sort of information was of less interest to Maisie than the facts that Gus Bailey had a good dinner jacket, could keep up his end of the conversation, and didn't have to be whispered to by the butler to remove the finger bowl and doily before the *crème brûlée* could be served.

Maisie took Gus to Rochelle Prud'homme's party at Clarence's to launch her new line of cordless hairdryers, which Gus hadn't wanted to go to, but there he ran into his old friend Nestor Calder, a Brooklyn-born novelist of note, whose latest book, *Judas Was a Redhead,* was on the best-seller list.

"I liked your new book, Nestor," said Gus. "It'll make a terrific movie."

"They don't make movies of books anymore, Gus. They make mini-series of books. One of the studios is interested in making a mini-series of it," answered Nestor. "But they don't want me to write the screenplay, and I'll only sell it if I do write the screenplay."

"It seems to me I've heard that song before," said Gus.

Nestor laughed.

"How's it going, Gus?" asked Nestor Calder. They had once worked on a film together.

"Oh, okay," replied Gus. When anyone became personal with Gus Bailey, he replied in as few words as possible.

"How's Peach?" he asked.

"She's okay."

"Do you hear from her?"

"Sure."

"Give her my love, will you?"

"Sure."

"I'm going to be in L.A. next week to meet with the studio," said Nestor.

"Peach will want to hear from you," replied Gus.

Even after they were divorced, people who had been their friends still thought of Gus and Peach Bailey as a couple. Gus and Peach, people would say. "Do you remember that night at Gus and Peach's house in Malibu?" Or, "I still think that Gus and Peach's black-and-white dance was the prettiest party I've ever been to." When friends would meet Peach in California, they'd say to her, "How's Gus?" Or, if they ran into Gus in New York, they'd say, "How's Peach?" as if they were still one when they hadn't been one for nearly as many years as they had been.

"Are you involved with anyone, Gus?" asked Nestor.

"No."

"I'm not being snoopy, you know."

"I know."

"It's just that you never talk about yourself."

"I talked nonstop all through dinner."

"You talked nonstop all through dinner about all those people you write articles about."

Gus's friends, like Edwina and Nestor Calder, teased Gus because he went out to dinner every night. Some nights he went out with writers, like the Calders. Some nights he went out with movie people he knew from his Hollywood days. Some nights he went out with people in society, who called him up after they read the articles he wrote, or had their social secretaries call him up. "Mrs. Harcourt wondered if you could dine on Wednesday the twenty-first, black tie," they would say, in voices every bit as grand as those of the people for whom they telephoned. Mostly he listened to what his dinner partners had to say, for he was an excellent listener, giving them his full attention, whether they were witty or dull, intriguing or boring. It seemed to make no difference to him.

"What do you see in all those people you're always having dinner with?" asked Nestor.

"I like to listen to them talk," answered Gus.

"When does that guy get out of prison?" asked Nestor, changing the subject and lowering his voice.

Gus didn't have to say, "What guy?"

"Two years from now," he answered, quietly, wanting to withdraw from the direction the conversation was taking. There was a part of Gus's life that he did not discuss with the people with whom he spent his time, even a friend like Nestor Calder, who spanned both his old life and his new life.

Nestor whistled. "So soon, huh?"

"So soon."

"What was his name?"

Gus hesitated, as he always hesitated when the name came up. "Lefty Flint," he answered.

"Does it worry you?" asked Nestor.

"Yes," said Gus. "It worries Peach too."

"THE *NERVE* of that Edwina Calder," Maisie Verdurin said indignantly in the taxi on the way home. "She said she didn't like her seat at my last party, for the Vice President and his wife. Can you imagine?"

Gus, who liked Edwina Calder, didn't reply, but Maisie didn't expect a reply.

"She said that I never seat her at what she called one of the *good* tables, but that I always seated Nestor at one of the good tables. So I said to her, 'After all, Edwina, Nestor is a first-rate writer, and people want to talk to him.' "

"But Edwina is so beautiful," said Gus.

"Beautiful girls are not what my dinners are about," Maisie answered haughtily. "My dinners are about conversation. I think it's a waste of time at one of my dinners when a man flirts with a pretty girl, like Bernie Slatkin does for instance, when there are such marvelous things being said at every table. It's called missing the point of the evening."

Maisie always spoke possessively about her dinner parties, as creative output, in the way that a poet might speak about "my poems," or an author might speak about "my novels," and woe to anyone who displeased Maisie, for banishment from her list was the consequence. After each of her evenings, she dissected her guest list: who had pulled his weight in conversation, who hadn't, whom she had given too good a seat to, whom she had not given a good enough seat to, and who would never be invited back, no matter what.

One of the things about escorting Maisie Verdurin anywhere, Gus discovered, was that the end of the evening came at exactly the point where she was delivered back to the canopy in front of her apartment building and into the safekeeping of her doorman. There were no invitations upstairs for a nightcap, and all the things that implied. It was not ever necessary to follow her out of the taxi to her doorstep.

With her sables wrapped tightly around her, she dashed for her own door with only an over-the-shoulder reminder of her next dinner.

"You're coming to me on the twenty-fourth, remember."

"Okay."

"You didn't write a thank-you note after my last dinner," she added.

"I sent you flowers instead," said Gus. "I felt I was beginning to repeat myself with my notes."

"Don't send me flowers," said Maisie. "I never go into my living room except on the nights I have parties. Just send me a note. I save them all and put them in a scrapbook."

SINCE Gus Bailey had moved to New York from Los Angeles and begun writing articles about famous people for a fashionable magazine, Maisie Verdurin, who had an eye for new people, had begun inviting him to her dinners and, through Maisie's dinners, he met other people who began inviting him to their dinners, and soon he was what is known as on-the-circuit in that group of New Yorkers who went out to dinners every night.

However, as Gus's literary reputation was not commensurate with that of Nestor Calder's, for instance, who was year after year on the best-seller lists, he was more often than not assigned to a table in Maisie's library, which was generally conceded to be a less desirable location for seating than her adjoining drawing and dining rooms. When confronted, Maisie stoutly denied that this was so, but the less celebrated wives, husbands, lovers, and escorts of the celebrated were usually placed there, seated beneath a Tissot or a Bombois, while their mates of the evening dined in the drawing or dining room beneath a Monet or a Manet.

"I'm on my best behavior tonight," said Edwina Calder to Gus, kissing him on both cheeks, when he walked into Maisie's drawing room for the cocktail hour. "I'm in Dutch with our hostess, have you heard? She'll probably seat me in the kitchen tonight."

Gus laughed. "Where's Nestor?"

"He's out in Hollywood," said Edwina.

"He told me he was going to write the mini-series of *Judas Was a Redhead*," said Gus.

"He went to see Peach," said Edwina.

1 1

"Peach never tells me anything."

"What are you writing about now, Gus?"

"Oh, some gigolo who got all the money off a rich old lady," replied Gus, shrugging, dismissing the story as not important. "And then I'm going to do a story on a society walker who got murdered after taking a rich lady home from a party."

"I liked your article on Faye Converse," said Edwina. "She was always my favorite movie star growing up. Do you think she's really off the sauce for good?"

Rochelle Prud'homme, who made her fortune in hairdryers and was sponsored in her social rise by Matilda Clarke, advanced into the room in tiny little running steps, her left hand beneath her pearls, clutching a panel of her couturier dress. Known in New York as the Petite Dynamo, Rochelle stood barely five feet tall, and was known to be one of the best bridge players in the city, a passion she indulged in when she wasn't running her industrial empire or going to parties. She waved little waves to acquaintances, held her cheek to be kissed by friends, and smiled perfectly for the flashing strobe light of a reporter doing a feature story for a new magazine on the world of Maisie Verdurin. "Otherwise, you know, I *never* have reporters at my parties," said Maisie to each guest, "except Dolly, of course, but Dolly is a friend." Dolly De Longpre, beloved by all, never missed one of Maisie Verdurin's dinners, no matter what, and filled whole columns with Maisie's guest lists, who was there and what they wore and all the sparkling things they said at Maisie's tables, even though Maisie was not, by her own admission, in society at all, at least in the sense of old family and old money.

"Biarritz was a disaster," Rochelle said to Maisie. "Rain, rain, rain, and the worst people you ever saw. Not a soul one knew."

"Ain't she grand? Listen to her. Nestor swears her real name was Roxy Persky, and she was three classes ahead of him at Erasmus High," said Edwina Calder to Gus.

"Whose real name?" asked Gus.

"Rochelle Prud'homme."

But Gus Bailey's attention had been drawn to someone else entering Maisie's drawing room. He heard Rochelle Prud'homme conclude to Maisie, "You're coming to me on Thursday the nineteenth. I'll send you a *pour mémoire*. Princess Murat is coming to town." *Pour mémoire* was French for reminder, and Rochelle had taken up French, along with bridge, with a passion.

"Oh, I'll remember," said Maisie.

It was the appearance in the room of the tall and bearded Constantine de Rham that occupied Gus's attention. De Rham made a gesture of kissing Maisie's hand by raising it toward his lips and then dropping it. Maisie dressed for her parties with expensive care, and de Rham, who noticed such things, complimented her on the handsomeness of her pearl-encrusted bodice. Maisie, more used to business tycoons than French aristocrats, was charmed by his courtly manners. Whether entering a party, or a restaurant, or a theater, there was always someone present who whispered to someone else, "There's Constantine de Rham." In years past, when playboys were still in fashion, his escapades and exploits had filled the international gossip columns, but a fatal car crash outside of Paris a half dozen years earlier had ended his days as a romantic figure; his beautiful young companion, the daughter of a French duke, had gone through his car's windshield when he was speeding home in the early hours of the morning from a ball at a country estate. It was a part of his story and always took precedence over the other dramatic circumstance of his life, the death of his wife, the immensely rich Consuelo Harcourt de Rham, Adele Harcourt's daughter, who had died falling down the marble stairway of their house on Sutton Place, after returning home from a party she had not wanted to attend.

"There's Constantine de Rham," said Edwina.

"I know all about Constantine de Rham," replied Gus.

At Constantine de Rham's side was a young woman dressed far too elaborately for a Maisie Verdurin dinner in a revealing gown of gold lamé, with diamonds in great quantity on her wrists, ears, neck, and bosom. Her blond hair was combed straight back and coiled silkily in a bun at the nape of her neck, giving her the look of the wife of a South American dictator.

Maisie's drawing room was now filled with guests. Waiters carried trays of drinks and hors d'oeuvres, and passage from one side of the room to the other, which seemed to be Constantine de Rham's intention, necessitated a circuitous routing. Followed by his young companion, he edged his way sideways between Maisie's white brocade sofa and the coffee table in front of it, murmuring charming apologies to Dolly De Longpre and a quartet of seated guests, like a person taking a seat in a theater after the curtain has gone up.

Dolly De Longpre, glamorous and voluptuous, dimpled and pink-skinned, barely acknowledged Constantine de Rham and went on with her own conversation. "Seating can make or break a party," she said. "And Maisie Verdurin has a genius for seating. She agonizes over her *placement*."

A painting by Monet of water lilies had been hung over Maisie's fireplace only that afternoon, in anticipation of the arrival of the immensely rich art collector Elias Renthal, whom no one in New York yet knew, except Constantine de Rham, who had brought him to Maisie to start his collection. Reaching his goal, Constantine de Rham held his black-rimmed spectacles like a lorgnette and leaned toward the pink in the center of a water lily, as if it possessed scent. "Ah, ravishing," he pronounced admiringly to Maisie about the painting, and she smiled modestly about her acquisition.

"Isn't the pink marvelous?" asked Maisie.

"Like the inside of a seashell," agreed de Rham.

"It's the pink that has so intrigued Elias Renthal's new wife, you know. If he decides to buy it, it's to be the color of the walls in the drawing room of the Renthals' new apartment that they just bought from Matilda Clarke."

Constantine smiled a superior smile, including Maisie in on this joint superiority, over people like the Elias Renthals of the world, who looked on art as an extension of interior decoration. "What an impressive group you have gathered, Maisie," he said, looking around the room.

"Your friends the Renthals have still not appeared, and I don't intend to wait for them when the butler announces dinner," she replied, taking his arm and leading him around the crowded room to introduce him, knowing that, as hostess, paths would be cleared. Maisie always gave a thumbnail sketch of each guest's accomplishments when she introduced him or her. "You'll be at my table, Constantine, between me and Rochelle Prud'homme. You know Rochelle, don't you? Prud'homme Products? Cordless hairdryers? Home permanents? One of America's most outstanding women. Plays such good bridge. And I'm counting on you to draw Elias Renthal into the conversation. He's hopeless at parties, I understand."

They walked past a group of laughing men whom Maisie always

called "my bachelors," although they were the same group of bachelors who sat nightly on gilded chairs in the dining rooms of Lil
Altemus, or Loelia Manchester, or Matilda Clarke, when she was still
giving parties, or any of the other hostesses of the city, balancing out
tables where widows or divorced ladies of quality sat. There was
owlish-looking Jamesey Crocus, who knew more about eighteenth-
century French furniture than anyone in New York, people said, and
always pushed his round black-rimmed spectacles up on his nose
with his forefinger as he talked excitedly about collectors and collecting, his favorite topic of conversation. And Nevel, just Nevel, which
was Leven spelled backwards, who designed dresses for most of the
ladies in society, and always counted how many ladies in the room
were wearing his elegant gowns. And Freddy Winslow, about whom
people said such terrible things, who bought and sold estate jewelry.
And Count Motulsky, whose mother was one of the de Brown sisters
from San Francisco, who taught French to Rochelle Prud'homme and
sold porcelain at Sackville's.

"I always expect the lights to dim when Constantine de Rham
walks into a room," said Gus.

"He doesn't seem like Maisie's kind of guest," said Edwina.

"Who's the Evita Perón look-alike trailing behind de Rham?"
asked Gus.

"That is Mrs. Lupescu, or Baroness Lupescu, as she sometimes
calls herself, but it's a bogus title. Constantine de Rham calls her
Yvonne," replied Edwina.

"Are they lovers?"

"So it would seem."

"She's showing a lot of tit for a Maisie Verdurin party," said Gus.

"I don't know where to look first, at her tits or her diamonds,"
answered Edwina.

"Why doesn't anyone speak to her?"

"She has what's called a dicey reputation."

"Ah, the plot thickens."

"May I present Constantine de Rham," said Maisie, when she got
to where Gus Bailey and Edwina Calder were standing.

De Rham held out his hand to be shaken, but Gus did not take it.
Instead, he nodded at the tall man but still did not take his hand. De
Rham, overlooking the slight, turned away, as Maisie led him on to
the next group.

Gus wondered that Maisie, so obsessed with people who "do things," could treat in such a special manner a man who had done absolutely nothing with his life, except marry an heiress who had died before she even came into her inheritance. After her daughter's death, Adele Harcourt cut her son-in-law in public, and thereafter he was no longer invited to the sort of parties he had been used to attending. He continued to live in the house he had inherited from Consuelo, and there were rumors he sometimes used it for nefarious purposes to make ends meet.

MAISIE'S efficient secretary marshaled the guests to their various tables. "Senator Marx, you're over there, next to Justine Altemus, in the short blue strapless dress, beneath the little Renoir. You know, don't you, Justine Altemus is Laurance Van Degan's niece?" And, "Oh, Mr. Fenwick, you're next to Mrs. Renthal, who doesn't know a soul, but her husband is the richest man in Cleveland, and Maisie's counting on you to make her feel at home, if she ever shows up, that is."

It was just at this point that Elias Renthal and his young wife, Ruby, entered Maisie's apartment, flustered by their lateness. Elias was stout and not tall, with broad hands and broad chest, suggesting physical strength, and his presence was such that people turned to look at him. His glance, which was described as terrifying by the people who worked for him, was open and expectant in Maisie's drawing room, where he was unsure of himself. Social life was as yet an unknown quantity for him, but he had been told that casual talk at New York dinner parties could be an important source of business information for him. His third wife, Ruby, years younger, with whom he was besotted, was pretty but not smartly dressed in a gown of bright blue sequins, and her hair was arranged in an unbecoming fashion.

Except for Constantine de Rham, to whom Elias nodded, and Rochelle Prud'homme, the Renthals seemed to know no one in Maisie's rooms, although all the businessmen present, like Emil Jorst and the Zobel brothers, knew who the very rich Elias Renthal from Cleveland was. His purchase of the ailing conglomerate known as Miranda Industries for six billion dollars, using relatively little of his own money, and then liquidating it, had netted him a profit of three billion dollars in only sixteen months, a widely heralded transaction that was thought to be the most lucrative leveraged buyout ever, making the heretofore unknown Elias Renthal a financial celebrity.

"I'd almost given up on you," said Maisie, rushing to greet the latecomers. If the Renthals had not been the possible purchasers of the Monet water lilies, asking price six million, but negotiable, Maisie, who insisted on promptness in her guests, would certainly have been less charming.

"I'm sorry we're so late," said Elias. Loyalty to his new wife forbade him telling Maisie that Ruby had changed her dress and hairstyle three times in the previous hour. "I don't think you've met my wife. Ruby, this is Maisie Verdurin."

"I'm so pleased," said Maisie. "The painting is over there, and I'm mad to have you look at it. Constantine de Rham *raved* about it. But the waiters are about to serve."

"Plenty of time to look at pictures," said Elias.

"That *is* the color pink I like, Elias," said Ruby, looking across the room at the Monet.

"I hear Elias bought you the Palumbo pearl," said Maisie to Ruby, as she took her to a table in the library, after directing Elias to her own table in the drawing room.

"Yes," said Ruby, holding out the pearl, which hung from a chain around her neck.

"How marvelous."

"It's very, uh, useful," answered Ruby, unable to think of a more appropriate word.

"I've put you next to Ezzie Fenwick, who's the best friend of all the famous ladies in New York, but be careful what you say to him, because he repeats *everything*. And Gus Bailey on the other side. He writes all those magazine pieces on famous people. I hope you'll enjoy yourself."

"Augustus Bailey?" asked Ruby.

"Yes. Everyone calls him Gus. Do you know him?" asked Maisie.

"No," replied Ruby, quickly. Maisie could tell that Ruby was nervous and wished that she were sitting with her husband.

"Is this your first New York party, Mrs. Renthal?"

"Yes."

"I so admire your husband, the few times I've met him," said Maisie, who always admired financiers, especially financiers who were starting collections. "He knows what he wants in art and goes after it, although, I must admit, sometimes he scares me to death if things don't work out. He does swear a bit, doesn't he?"

"Oh, honey, he doesn't mean anything by that," said Ruby, waving her hand dismissively at the thought. "If I hadn't understood that *cunt* meant *sweetheart*, this marriage wouldn't have lasted out the first year."

Maisie, startled, looked at Ruby with an astonished smile that plainly said, "Where was this woman brought up?" Depositing her at her table, she said, "Your seat's here," and returned to her own table.

"Your husband's shorter than I thought he would be, Mrs. Renthal," said Ezzie Fenwick.

"My husband is very tall when he stands on his wallet, Mr. Fenwick," replied Ruby.

"Hmm," said Ezzie. *"Touché."*

Gus Bailey, seated on Ruby Renthal's other side, smiled at her and introduced himself. For an instant, Ruby looked at Gus, as if she might have known him.

"Where'd you get that dress?" asked Ezzie, squinting his good eye at Ruby's bright blue sequins.

"Cleveland," replied Ruby.

"I thought so," said Ezzie.

IN THE library, where she was also placed, beneath a tiny Tissot, young Mrs. Lupescu was displeased that she had not been seated at Maisie's table in the drawing room where Constantine de Rham and Rochelle Prud'homme and Elias Renthal and Justine Altemus had been seated, and said audibly to her dinner partner, Bernard Slatkin, an anchorman on the television news, whom she had never met before, that Mrs. Verdurin had seated her at the C table in the C room. Thereafter she maintained a haughty silence, and lit cigarettes throughout the meal, to the distress of Matilda Clarke, who loathed smoking and constantly waved her napkin in the air to clear away the smoke.

Gus Bailey observed Mrs. Lupescu through the white anthuriums of the centerpiece, while his dinner partner on the other side, Matilda Clarke, the widow of Sweetzer Clarke, who died when he fell off his horse fox hunting, drunk, and left her in bad financial straits, talked into Gus's ear about their mutual friend Evangeline Simpson, while patting the back of her pageboy hairdo with both hands.

"Evangeline's drunk all the time, Gus. Hiding Jack Daniel's in her Lazlo bottles, that sort of thing. I took her to Smithers to detox and dry out. No one has to tell me anything about Smithers, God knows. I took poor Sweetzer there enough times, but Evangeline wouldn't stay, or they wouldn't have her, I don't know which, and I don't care anymore, for that matter. If you could have seen the way she behaved, to *me*, her oldest friend."

Gus listened, as he always listened when people told him things at dinner parties, which they always did. He planned someday to write a book about these people who went out to dinner every night, and talked and talked and talked about each other, who was rich, who was broke, who took drugs, who drank, who had cancer, who was having an affair with whom, who was getting a divorce, who was straight, who was gay. There was very little they didn't know about each other, and very little they didn't discuss about each other.

"Odd, don't you think, Maisie having Constantine de Rham to dinner?" replied Gus.

Matilda Clarke, used to conversational shifts at dinner parties, abandoned Evangeline Simpson as a subject. "He's a new acquisition of Maisie's. I think he introduced her to this ghastly common Renthal man who bought my apartment and is trying to assemble an art collection in ten minutes. Maisie probably pays Constantine a finder's fee for digging up these new billionaires."

"Hmm," said Gus, signaling to Matilda that Mrs. Renthal was on his other side.

"Constantine's very cultured, you know," Matilda continued. "And he's awfully amusing to sit next to at dinner, Gus. I bet you don't know the name of Talleyrand's chef at the Congress of Vienna, but Constantine does. Or the name of Sebastian Flyte's teddy bear in *Brideshead Revisited*. Constantine does."

Across the table Yvonne Lupescu, who had already pronounced Maisie's veal "mystery meat," now declined the cheese. "I hate brie breath," she said to no one in particular, although Matilda Clarke kicked Gus under the table to listen and signaled Ezzie Fenwick by pointing to Yvonne with her eyes.

"She just won't do. She just won't do at all," said Matilda, holding her hand in front of her mouth, as if she expected Mrs. Lupescu to read lips. "Constantine must be out of his mind."

"Hmm," said Gus.

"Will you look at the way she's overdressed," said Matilda, tying and untying and then tying again the sleeves of a cashmere sweater she had tossed over her shoulders to protect herself from the icy blast of Maisie's air conditioner, even though it was nearly winter outside. "When I was giving parties, when darling Sweetzer was still alive, and we still had the big apartment, I always had my secretary call my guests on the morning of the party and say, 'Mrs. Clarke is wearing a long dress tonight,' or, 'Mrs. Clarke is wearing a short dress,' so that all the women would be dressed alike. I mean, look at this woman. She looks like she's going to the opening night of the opera in Istanbul."

"Rather hard to pinpoint her nationality," said Gus, studying Mrs. Lupescu's ample mouth and wide-apart eyes.

"Oh, Peruvian, maybe," said Matilda, giving it some thought. "Or Corsican, possibly, and maybe more than a tinge of Albanian tossed in. What Sweetzer used to call a mongrel."

"Pretty, though."

"Shows too much gum when she smiles. Ask Ezzie Fenwick about Mrs. Lupescu sometime. Ask Ezzie what she did at the airport in Tangier when she didn't have enough money to pay for her excess baggage." Matilda rolled her eyes. "Nice china Maisie Verdurin has," she continued, picking up the dessert plate that had been placed in front of her and turning it over. "You don't often see the Fitz Hugh border like this. Do you suppose it's for sale? Like all her pictures?" A waiter passing the dessert interrupted her. "Oh, look at this *crème brûlée*, will you! It's far too pretty to break into, but I will. A million calories, that's all."

Across the table, Yvonne Lupescu, unrushed, stared down at Maisie's *crème brûlée* for half a minute before tasting it and then, with a shake of her head, dropped her spoon loudly on her plate. "That's not worth getting fat over," she said to Bernie Slatkin.

As a rule toasts were not given at Maisie Verdurin's dinners, except when a former President was present, or a cabinet minister, so it was unexpected when Constantine de Rham rose to his feet, after the champagne was poured, and tapped his fork against the side of his champagne glass until there was silence in the three rooms where Maisie's guests were seated.

"I would like to propose a toast to our hostess," said Constantine, and, encouraged by several "Hear, hears," in the rooms, he spoke charmingly about Maisie as a formidable force in the art world of New York as well as a hostess of such note that her monthly fêtes would one day be recorded as part of the social history of the city. Maisie flushed prettily. "She has given her talent to her work," Constantine concluded, "but she has given her genius to her life."

No one applauded more enthusiastically than Mrs. Lupescu, as if approval of Constantine de Rham was the thing she most ardently desired, reflecting, as it did, on herself.

"Marvelous, wasn't it, what Constantine said about Mrs. Verdurin?" said Yvonne Lupescu to her table. "That she gives her talent to her work but her genius to her life. Marvelous."

"It was even more marvelous when Oscar Wilde said it originally, about himself," said Gus to Matilda Clarke.

THROUGHOUT dinner, Ruby Renthal, terrified of the sophisticated society-wit Ezzie Fenwick, sat in silence and watched, declining to participate for fear of making another mistake. She understood from his remark that her dress was all wrong, as well as her hairstyle, just from the look he gave it with his one good eye, which she figured out was not the one that went off in another direction. And worse, her table manners, once she realized she was the only one who ate her artichoke with a knife and fork, were wrong. On the several occasions she tried to speak to Gus Bailey, she saw that his ear was monopolized by Matilda Clarke, whose apartment the Renthals had bought, but his eyes were focused on Yvonne Lupescu.

When Gus went down the long hallway to the bedrooms to find his coat, Ruby Renthal followed him. "Mr. Bailey," she said.

Gus turned. "I think the ladies' coats are in Maisie's bedroom on that side, Mrs. Renthal," said Gus.

"Mr. Bailey," she said again.

"It's Gus," said Gus.

"Gus," she said. She looked both ways in the hall, as if to see if anyone was coming, and Gus realized that she wanted to say something to him. He remembered then that she had looked at him strangely when they had been introduced. "Didn't you use to live in Los Angeles?" she asked.

"Yes," he replied.

"My name before I was married was Ruby Nolte. Does that name mean anything to you?"

Gus looked at her, as if the name struck a note, although her face did not look familiar to him. "Help me," he said.

"Does the name Lefty Flint mean anything to you?"

"Oh, yes," said Gus, quietly. The name Lefty Flint, whenever he heard it, caused a violent reaction within him. He walked into the bedroom where the coats were hanging on a rack and turned to look back at Ruby Renthal, who followed him into the room.

"It was in your family that it happened, wasn't it?" she asked.

Gus nodded. Something stopped him from pulling away from her.

"I used to be a redhead. I used to be an airline stewardess too, at least at the time. I went out with Lefty Flint for a while. Then I grew scared of him. When I tried to break off with him, he beat me up. He broke my nose. He knocked out two of my teeth. He blacked my eyes. He fractured my jaw. I thought I would never again have a face I could look at in the mirror."

"Dear God," said Gus. He sat down on the edge of the bed.

"I was in the hospital for ten days, thanks to Mr. Lefty Flint," said Ruby.

"Dear God," Gus repeated.

"Did you ever hear of a lawyer called Marv Pink?" she asked.

"Oh, yes, I know Marv Pink," said Gus.

"Some of Lefty's friends came to visit me in the hospital. They told me if I testified against Lefty, Marv Pink would nail me to the cross. My background is not of the Virgin Mary variety, if you get my point. It would all end up looking like I got what I deserved. Do you know what I mean?"

"Yes, I know what you mean," said Gus. "It's the fashion in the courts these days, blame the victim."

"They paid my hospital bill, and I disappeared. It's something I've always regretted," she said.

"And Flint walked away, scot free."

"I know."

"How come you told me all this? I wouldn't have known Mrs. Elias Renthal was Ruby Nolte if you hadn't told me," said Gus.

"I couldn't believe it when we sat next to each other tonight. You see, I read about what happened in your family a few years later, and I always felt guilty. I felt that if I'd gone to the police at the time, what happened to you might not have happened."

Gus nodded.

Ruby sat down on the bed next to Gus and took his hand. "I'm sorry for what happened to you," she said.

"I'm sorry for what happened to you," replied Gus.

"When does he get out of prison?"

"He only got three years."

"Three years?" she said in disbelief.

"He was a jury pleaser. He wore a coat and tie, and he always carried a Bible. They fell for it."

Ruby shook her head.

In the hallway there were voices as other people began to look for their coats. Ruby jumped off the bed and went to the mirror and started to brush her hair.

"Listen, Gus, my husband doesn't know," said Ruby. "I never told him. A guy doesn't want to marry a girl who's been beaten up like I was. Elias would have thought I was damaged goods, and Elias Renthal is the best thing that ever happened to me."

"It's not a thing I'd ever talk about," said Gus.

"Ruby?" called out Elias in the hallway.

"In here, Elias," she called back.

"What the hell's going on in here?" asked Elias, staring at Gus sitting on the bed and Ruby brushing her hair in the mirror.

"Just getting my coat, Elias," said Ruby.

"Maisie wants us to look at the picture," said Elias.

"Elias, this is Augustus Bailey. My husband, Elias Renthal. Mr. Bailey wrote that article you liked on Laurance Van Degan."

"Pleased to meetcha, Mr. Dailey," said Elias. He shook hands without looking at Gus.

"Same," said Gus, taking his coat. "Nice meeting you, Mrs. Renthal," he added. Their eyes met in the mirror, and Gus walked out.

"That guy's old enough to be your father," said Elias.

"So are you," replied Ruby, still adjusting her makeup at the mirror.

23

"So am I what?"

"Old enough to be my father."

"What the hell is this? We go to our first New York party, and you end up in the bedroom with some guy."

"Oh, calm down, Elias. I end up in the bedroom with the coats, talking to Mr. Bailey. He's a writer. He writes about rich people. One of these days, you and I are going to have to get to know guys like that, when we start moving in this town. And, listen, this dress of mine is a disaster. There's a guy here tonight called Nevel who—"

"A guy called Nevel?"

"Leven spelled backwards. He designed Maisie Verdurin's dress, and the young Altemus girl who's Laurance Van Degan's niece. I'm going there tomorrow, so get out your checkbook, big boy, because he costs an arm and a leg, and I'm going to buy him out."

"Okay, okay. How'd you know this Dailey?"

"Bailey, not Dailey, Elias. If he was from Wall Street, you'd remember his name."

"Bailey then."

"I sat next to him tonight at dinner, and I met him once before in L.A. I met a lot of people before I met you, Elias, and if you're going to start getting jealous every time I run into someone you don't know, we're going to have a boring few years in front of us. Okay?"

"Okay," said Elias.

"Now smile." She put her finger under his chin.

"I'm smiling."

"Love me?"

"Love you." He kissed her shoulder.

"Same here. Now let's go look at that six-million-dollar Monet and see if it's the right color pink."

NO ONE lingered after dinner at Maisie Verdurin's parties; the evenings always ended with the liquored coffee, after which there was a mass exit for the elevator. That night the consensus was that Mr. and Mrs. Elias Renthal were never going to make it in New York, no matter how much money they brought with them from Cleveland.

"How was Mrs. Renthal?" asked Matilda Clarke in the crowded elevator.

"She called her evening dress a formal," said Ezzie. "And she ate her artichoke with a knife and fork."

"Imagine people like that in my apartment. Sweetzer must be turning over in his grave. He grew up in that apartment," said Matilda.

Gus closed his eyes. He felt protective about Ruby Renthal. "I thought she was very pretty," he said, "and very nice."

"Hmm," said Ezzie.

"Gus, come out to the country for the weekend," said Matilda Clarke, when they got out on the first floor. "Rochelle's coming, and maybe the Calders, if Nestor gets back from Hollywood."

"Thank you, but I can't."

"Where are you off to?" insisted Matilda.

"I'm going in the other direction this weekend," replied Gus, smiling at Matilda.

"You're always going off some place mysterious, Gus," said Matilda.

OUTSIDE Maisie's building several homeless people slept on the sidewalk, with packing cases beneath them and over them. On the street limousines were lined up waiting for the departing guests. "They shouldn't allow this," said Ezzie Fenwick, as he gathered Matilda Clarke and Violet Bastedo into the back of Violet's limousine, careful that the long skirts of their dresses would not be caught in the door.

"Can you help me out? I don't have anything to eat," said a beggar, holding his hand out to Ezzie Fenwick as he was about to step into the car.

Ezzie, frightened by the proximity of the young man, put his hand in his pocket and handed him some silver without looking at him and then hopped into the limousine with a litheness that belied his age and girth.

"Did you give him anything?" asked Matilda.

"It's hard to say you have no money when you're getting into a limousine wearing a coat with a fur collar and black patent-leather pumps with grosgrain ribbons on them," answered Ezzie.

The three sat in silence for a moment, while the chauffeur pulled his car out in front of the other cars.

"Let's go hear Bobby Short," said Violet Bastedo.

2

BERNARD SLATKIN knew Justine Altemus by sight for several
months before he actually spoke to her. Justine, the daughter of the
famous Lil Altemus, and the niece of Laurance Van Degan, was a
regular figure at most of the fashionable parties in New York that
Bernard Slatkin, in the first flush of his professional success, had
started being invited to in the last year.

"We've met before," he said to her in the elevator leaving Maisie
Verdurin's party.

"Where?" Justine replied.

"Here at Maisie's."

"I've just attended my last party at Maisie's," said Justine. "Too
crowded, and I don't like having to sit at a table with Constantine de
Rham's mistress. Consuelo de Rham was my mother's best friend."

"It was the party where one of the Zobel brothers bought the
Toulouse-Lautrec," said Bernie.

"Tonight Elias Renthal was buying a Monet," said Justine. She
looked at him. "Oh, yes, I do remember you. You were talking to
Violet Bastedo about corruption in city government. Oh, so serious
you were. And Violet was pretending she was understanding the conversation, which she wasn't."

"Would you like a ride home?" he asked quietly.

"One of the advantages of being a Van Degan, even by indirection,
is that I have a car and driver. Not a limousine, mind you. That's for
the Mr. Renthals of the world. Just your average station wagon, but it
relieves my mother's mind to know I'm not standing out in the street
waving for a cab at ungodly hours," replied Justine. She spoke in a
breezy manner, friendly but distant, with the assumption that great
heiresses possess that the young man knew exactly who she was.

"I thought your name was Altemus," he said.

"It is, but my mother was a Van Degan."

Bernie Slatkin looked at this youngish woman who had now mentioned her mother three times. Her eyebrows were dark and gracefully arched. Her face was unmistakably the face of a well-born

woman, but, somehow, beauty escaped it. "Do you live with your mother?" he asked.

"Same building. Different apartments. Different elevators too," she answered.

The elevator stopped with a jolt. When she accidentally bumped against him, she could feel his erection, even through their coats.

"How about giving me a ride then?" asked Bernie, meeting her eyes.

"As long as you don't live in the outer boroughs," she replied. Then she remembered what she knew about this man. It was the very same Violet Bastedo who told her. Violet, who discussed such things, said he was more than amply endowed, referring to his male member. Violet said it right in front of the waiter at Clarence's while he was serving them their chicken paillard. Of course, Violet had said it in French, but, even so, Justine had been shocked and screeched, "Violet!"

"Just Central Park West," said Bernie.

"Just don't get fresh with me in the backseat," said Justine, wagging her finger at him, in a joking way that covered her shyness. "My driver doubles as a bodyguard."

Bernie Slatkin laughed. "Only my thoughts will be impure," he said.

"Now I know who you are," said Justine. "It's the dimple. I recognized the dimple. You're on the television news."

"And all the time I thought you knew that."

"You see?"

In the car he held her hand and told her about being an anchorman on the local New York news. She made appropriate comments, saying "Fascinating" from time to time, but her mind was on other things. Sleeping with men, or "sleeping around," as her friends like Violet Bastedo called it, was not a thing that Justine Altemus did. She had had the occasional affair—with Toby Walters, for instance, when she was thinking of marrying Toby, and Jean-Claude St. Cloud, one summer in France—but those carnal events were rare, widely spaced in time, and only occurred after careful deliberation on her part. To sleep with a man within the first hour of meeting him was altogether unthinkable, but, at this moment, in the backseat of her mother's car, with a man she had just met in an elevator, whose erection she had accidentally bumped into, it was the thing she most desired in the world and intended to consummate, with no thought of consequence, if he made the request.

It had been a dozen years since her presentation, a small dinner dance at Grandfather Van Degan's house in Syosset, for family and close friends, and then a ball under a pink tent for six hundred, with a list carefully honed by her mother to eliminate all the arrivistes, outsiders, and "New People," as her mother called them, who were being invited everywhere in New York. The hope was, of course, that she would have a year of dancing and parties, and then a year of traveling, meeting all the most eligible young men, and after that would take her pick of the many suitors her mother envisioned would be lined up for the tall, pretty heiress, but it hadn't worked out that way, and Justine Altemus, at thirty, had still not wed.

"Drink?" asked Bernie, when the car stopped.

"Where?"

"My place. Great view."

"Great view right across the park at my mother's apartment."

"Yours, too."

"I'm on the other side of the building."

"Well?"

"I'm going to be having a drink at Mr. Slatkin's, Joe," said Justine to the driver. At thirty she still behaved as if she were twenty.

She was nervous when she entered Bernie's apartment. She looked around at the stark black-and-white room with its floor-to-ceiling windows. "Is this what they call the minimal look?" she asked.

"Like it?" asked Bernie.

"Actually, no," replied Justine. "Now don't look crestfallen. It's just that I've been brought up in rooms of cabbage-rose chintz, as dictated by old Cora Mandell."

"Who's Cora Mandell?"

"Oh, well, now's not the time for chintz lessons," said Justine. "At least, that's not what I thought you had in mind when you asked me to your West Side aerie."

"No, no, it wasn't," said Bernie.

"Drinks, wasn't it?"

"It wasn't drinks either." By this time Bernie had had enough repartee. He took off his overcoat and dropped it on a chair, untied his black tie, and unbuttoned the top button of his dinner shirt. When he kissed her the first time, he put his hand under her short evening dress and between her legs.

"Oh, the finesse of it all," she whispered. Justine, unused to passion in her few refined forays into physical love, thrilled to his blunt approach. In less than a minute, his trousers and undershorts were off and flung far afield, and he was guiding her hands to his hairy regions. "That's awfully nice, what you're doing," she whispered.

"That feels pretty good, what you're doing, too," said Bernie.

"I feel quite content."

"This is only the pregame warmup, Miss Altemus," said Bernie, taking his tongue out of her mouth only long enough to answer.

"Do you prefer to be called Bernie or Bernard?" she asked, between kisses.

"Whatever turns you on, honey," he answered, unzipping her dress and helping her step out of it. The consummation of their lust was swift and violent. It was only in repetition that the beauty of the act of love became apparent to Justine. She liked looking at his body, every inch of it, and she allowed him to look at hers, every inch of it. With Toby Walters, who later married her friend Marie Harcourt, it was over each time almost before it started. With Jean-Claude St. Cloud, that summer in France, it was romantic but unsatisfying, each too aware of the perfection of the match. With Bernard Slatkin, it was passion and carnality.

"I never heard a man talk so dirty," she said afterward.

"Too low for you?"

"Quite the contrary," she astonished herself by saying.

"I knew we were going to hit it off," he said, smoothing her forehead with his hand. "Why the worried brow?"

"I was thinking of my mother's chauffeur downstairs," replied Justine

Bernie chuckled and shook his head in disbelief. "How old are you, Justine?" he asked.

She blushed. Her age was for her a sensitive subject, as it was one her mother never let her forget.

"Thirty?" he asked when he saw her hesitate.

"Thirty," she conceded.

Bernie got up, making no attempt to cover his nakedness, and walked over to the intercom by the front door and buzzed. "Jose, it's Mr. Slatkin in Twenty-two C. Miss Altemus's chauffeur is in a dark blue Buick station wagon outside. His name is Joe. Would you tell him that Miss Altemus said for him to go home?"

"What am I going to say to my mother tomorrow?" she asked.

"Take this in your mouth while you're thinking about it," he answered, pushing her head down on him. Justine Altemus was not offended. She had fallen madly in love with Bernard Slatkin.

3

INVITATIONS to dinners, dances, screenings of new films, and publication parties to launch new books crowded the chipped gilt frame of a nineteenth-century reproduction of an eighteenth-century mirror. Gus Bailey, bathed, shaved, but not yet dressed, was wearing a white terrycloth robe he had once stolen from the Ritz Hotel in Paris. As he brushed his hair with two brushes, a blizzard raged outside his window, and for an instant he regretted his decision to make the bus trip into New England that he had promised to make.

The doorbell rang, as it always rang, at ten minutes past seven each morning. Gus opened the door. It was, as he knew it would be, Innocento, the delivery boy from the coffee shop on the corner, bringing him his standing order of three dark coffees with artificial sweetener in cardboard containers. Innocento always handed Gus his morning papers, which had already been dropped outside the door by the elevator man, always gave him a weather report, and always received a dollar tip.

"Cold as a nun's cunt out there," reported Innocento.

"Cold as a witch's tit has a better ring to it at this hour of the morning, Innocento," said Gus.

"Hey, I like that, Mr. Bailey."

The interstate bus carrying Gus Bailey traveled between the Port Authority Terminal in New York and Brattleboro, Vermont, with stops along the way. Gus tried to read and could not. He tried to sleep and could not. He wished the man in the next seat would stop smoking, but an attitude of unfriendliness on that person's part made Gus disinclined to make such a request, and there were no empty seats to move to. He wondered again why he had agreed to make the trip that he was making.

People said about Gus Bailey, on occasion, "Isn't it marvelous the way he got over it so well and put the whole terrible thing behind him?" Because he never mentioned it, or rarely, and seemed to have progressed on to a full productive life. He was seen about, asked places, and considered an addition. But none of them could know that his last thought before sleep and his first thought on awakening dealt with his torment. Nor did they notice those moments, sometimes even in the midst of frivolity, when his mind blanked to the topic at hand and dwelled in private thoughts.

He looked out the window of the bus. Near here, somewhere, there was an aunt in a nursing home, an aunt who had brought him up. Tante, they called her in the family. It had started as a joke, calling her Tante. His sister Eliza, dead now, cancer, claimed it was she who had given Aunt Mary the name Tante, but Gus knew it was he. He could even remember exactly when, on the day in French class he had first learned the phrase *la plume de ma tante*. It became the name the whole family called her. Unmarried, by choice, she had always been called Aunt Mary until then, and there were stories that she had once wanted to be a nun but her father had discouraged her from that calling. Even she grew to enjoy the name and signed postcards to them from her endless travels, "Love, Tante." Old now, ninety, she no longer knew him when he visited her, and each day he expected the call that would tell him she was dead.

THREE and a half hours out of New York the bus pulled to the side of the road near the Connecticut-Massachusetts border, and Gus descended onto the icy highway. A car, described to him in advance as a six-year-old Oldsmobile, was parked near the sheltered bus stop. From behind the wheel he saw the driver make a gesture toward him, and he stepped toward and entered the car.

"Mrs. Haber?" he asked.

"Mr. Bailey," she replied.

She was Chinese. It had not occurred to him that she would be Chinese. Her handwriting, in the letter she had written to him, asking him to come, reminded him of Peach's handwriting, suggesting good schools and thrifty wealth. Her voice, when he had responded to her letter by telephone, was unaccented and American, and her name, Faith Haber, certainly gave no indication of an Oriental background. In the car, driving to where they were going, for the reason he had come, he was able to postpone the subject at hand by eliciting from her that she was from a Chinese banking family in Honolulu, had gone to a school there where Peach had gone during the year her parents almost divorced but didn't, and then to college in New England where she had married the brother of her roommate and later divorced him. Gus liked vital statistics and had an ability to draw them out without direct questioning.

"That was a terrible story you told me on the phone about your daughter's death, Mrs. Haber," said Gus, when the car pulled into the parking lot.

"That was a terrible story you wrote about your daughter's death, Mr. Bailey," said Faith Haber.

"Listen, call me Gus."

"Call me Faith."

"Did they catch the guy?"

"No." For an instant their eyes met in the darkened car. Gus reached over and touched Faith's hand, which still gripped the steering wheel.

"He stabbed her twenty-six times," said Faith Haber. "I have never been able to walk into her room again."

Inside the hired room of a church hall where Faith Haber led him, he met the other parents who had suffered the same grievous assault on their lives that he and Peach had suffered. Folding chairs had been arranged in a circle, and the room smelled of the coffee brewing in a small urn plugged into the wall. He wondered, as he always wondered, what he could do to help them, what it was these groups expected from him when they asked him to come, ever since he had written about Lefty Flint, who killed his daughter, Becky.

Faith Haber sat next to him and told about her daughter's murder, and the parents next to her told about their son's, and the single father next to them about his son, and the couple next to him about their daughter. On the other side of Gus sat a woman too numb with grief to tell her story, so recently had it happened, and Faith Haber told the tale for her as the woman sobbed uncontrollably. Gus held her hand.

"No one really understands," said Gus. "All our friends are helpful and loving during the time of the tragedy, but then they withdraw into their own lives, which is only natural, and soon you can see a glaze in their eyes when you bring it up because they don't want to talk about it anymore, and it is the only thing that's on your mind. That's why these groups are so helpful. No one really knows what you are going through like someone else who has been through it."

There were murmurs of assent in the room.

"The thing that makes me most angry is when people say to me, 'At least you have another child,'" said Faith Haber. "What do you say to these people?"

"I have no answers. I know of no secrets to assuage your pain. I can only tell you that you go on. You carry on somehow. You live your life. You work hard. In time you'll go to films and parties again. You'll see your friends and start to talk about other things than this. You'll even learn to laugh again, as strange as that may seem now, if you allow it to happen. My wife and I—"

He stopped. He never said "my ex-wife and I." "Don't call me your ex-wife," Peach had once said to him. It was too complicated to explain about himself and Peach, what it was like between them. Only he and Peach understood that, and, anyway, that was not what he was here to talk about. Dealing with loss. That was the theme tonight.

"But it is always there, what happened to us. It becomes a part of you. It has become as much a part of me as my left-handedness."

He talked on, but he knew that what he said was not reaching them. They wanted an answer.

"Out there, in Vacaville, California," he said, finally, "there is a man called Lefty Flint. Lefty Flint held his hands around my daughter's neck for five minutes, choking her until she was dead. Lefty Flint read the Bible all during the trial. Lefty Flint was sentenced to only three years in prison. In two years he will be out, having atoned, he thinks, for the murder of our daughter."

Gus stopped, withdrawing into his thoughts. He remembered the trial. He remembered her friend, Wendy, who said, on the stand, "It was when she opened the door and saw Lefty Flint standing there that Becky knew, before he even raised a hand to grab hold of her body, that the end of her life was at hand."

"Objection, your honor," Marv Pink, the defense attorney, had screamed at the judge. "The witness cannot state what was in Miss Bailey's mind."

"Sustained," said the judge.

"What would you do if you ever saw him?"

There was a silence before Gus realized that someone in the group had asked him a question.

"What?" he asked.

"What would you do if you ever saw Lefty Flint, after he gets out?" It was the single father whose sixteen-year-old son had been beaten to death with a baseball bat in a racial encounter.

Gus looked at the man. "The thought haunts me, because I feel almost certain it will happen, as if some higher power is directing such an encounter."

"What would you do?" asked the man again.

"I may appear to be a calm man," answered Gus, "but there is within me a rage that knows no limits."

"What would you do?" persisted the man.

"What I want to do is kill him. Does that shock you? It shocks me. But it is what I feel."

He did not add, "It is what I am going to do."

4

ON THURSDAY Justine Altemus canceled out of a benefit performance of the Manhattan Ballet Company, for which she was on the
committee, to have dinner with Bernard Slatkin at a little restaurant
on Bleecker Street in Greenwich Village. On Friday she backed out
of a family dinner at Uncle Laurance and Aunt Janet Van Degan's to
celebrate their thirtieth wedding anniversary to go to the television
studio and watch Bernie's newscast and have dinner with him afterward at a restaurant on Columbus Avenue frequented by theatrical
people. On Saturday morning she called Ceil Somerset and said she
couldn't possibly go to the country for the weekend because she had
such a terrible cold and spent the entire weekend in bed with Bernie
at his apartment on Central Park West. On Monday she told her
mother she wouldn't be sitting in her box at the opera that night for
the new production of *Tosca*, which the Van Degan Foundation had
partially financed, and took Bernie to Clarence's, where he was curious to go, as it was the hangout, as he called it, for all the people he
read about in Dolly De Longpre's column.

"I'm not crazy about the way they cooked this fish," said Bernie.

"Oh, people don't come to Clarence's for the food. People come to
Clarence's to look at each other. Almost everybody here knows each
other. We call it the club, although it isn't a club at all. Of course,
Mother says she won't come anymore because her sable coat was
stolen when she went to the ladies' room, but she'll be back. Just
wait."

"Point out Clarence to me," said Bernie.

"Oh, there is no Clarence. That's just a name. It's Chick Jacoby
who owns Clarence's, and unless Chick likes you, or knows who you
are, you'll never get a table at Clarence's," said Justine.

Bernie looked around him. "Looks like we have the best table."

"We do," laughed Justine.

"I guess Chick Jacoby likes you."

"He does."

"Tell me about your father," said Bernie. "You never talk about him."

"Oh, Daddy," said Justine. "He's so sweet. Drinks a bit. More than a bit, if you want the truth. He married badly after he divorced my mother, and no one in the family sees him. He lives up in Bedford with his new wife in a house she got in her divorce settlement from one of her previous marriages. Belinda, she's called, and she looks like a Belinda. Mother calls her a strumpet, but Mother would have called anyone a strumpet whom Daddy married. She never got over the fact that Daddy left her."

"She loved him then?"

"It's not that she loved him that much. They used to fight all the time, and my brother and I were glad they got a divorce at the time. Mother thought she was calling the shots in the marriage because she was a Van Degan and had so much money. The Altemuses are what's called good goods. Marvelous family. Goes way back, but no money to speak of, at least no money in the way the Van Degans have money. Look, there's Violet Bastedo over there. Your old girlfriend."

"She's not my old girlfriend," said Bernie.

"You went to bed with her."

"She told you that?"

"Oh, she told me a lot more than that," said Justine, her cheeks turning pink with embarrassment.

"What else did she tell you about me?" asked Bernie, amused that this shy girl was embarrassed.

"Oh, nothing."

"Don't give me 'oh-nothing,'" he persisted.

"She said you had a huge you-know-what." Justine covered her face with her hands.

"At least she's not a liar."

Justine laughed. "No, she's not a liar."

"I didn't know proper young ladies like you and Violet Bastedo talked about the size of men's dicks."

Justine blushed. "She said it in French."

Bernie roared with laughter.

"Were you serious about Violet?"

"It was a one-night stand, for God's sake. I never saw her again."

"I wonder if Maisie Verdurin knows that you are the terror of her parties. She thinks her parties are all about conversation, you know, and all the time it's a launch pad for Bernard Slatkin's assignations."

"We're having a conversation right now. Maisie would be proud of us."

"Violet Bastedo is getting another divorce. That's her new lawyer she's having dinner with."

"I want to talk about Justine Altemus, not Violet Bastedo," said Bernie. He put out his hand across the table and took hers. Whereas Violet Bastedo was flighty and silly, Justine, Bernie could see, was more serious. Although she was no less interested in the parties, travels, comings and goings of the people she knew than Violet was, she was also a great reader, of both books and newspapers, and could converse on issues of the day, which Violet couldn't. Justine not only watched Bernie interview news figures on his daily newscast, but could remember specific details of the interviews, and this delighted Bernie. "I didn't believe Assemblyman Walsh for a single moment when you asked him about kickbacks." Or, "That poor little Missie Everett girl. I wept for her when she told you about her sister. I hope that man gets life."

"Did you ever think of having a career?" Bernie asked her.

Justine looked at him. He thought he detected a defensive look in her face. "I do a great deal of charity work," she answered evenly. "Committees and things, and one day a week I work at the hospital as a nurses' aide. And, of course, there's Adele Harcourt's book club. There's an enormous amount to be read for that. I am, at the moment, deep in Dostoyevski."

At that time Bernie had never heard of Adele Harcourt's book club, but, like all New Yorkers, he knew who Adele Harcourt was, and, in time, he became impressed that Justine was a member of it, and had to have, no matter what, *The Idiot* read in its entirety by the following Monday evening when they would meet to discuss it in Adele Harcourt's apartment.

"I suppose never having to worry about food or rent money must make it less urgent for you to compete," he said.

"You're not going to put me on a guilt trip because I was born into a rich family, are you?" she asked.

"No," he said, smiling at her.

She smiled back at him. "I still have a brother you haven't asked me about."

"Hubie. Right. Mysterious Hubie. I've got my theories about Hubie."

"Oh, poor Hubie. The apple of me mum's eye. Blind to all his faults, she is. He's always getting beaten up by all those hustlers he picks up. I mean, my mother would die if she knew. She thinks all the girls are just mad about Hubie and that Hubie's just mad about all the girls. Half the time he's got a black eye or a broken nose."

"Does he drink too?"

"He has an occasional lapse into insobriety, of course, but nothing compared to the way he used to be," said Justine. "Ever since Juanito came into his life."

"Who's Juanito?"

"Don't ask."

Bernie laughed. "We're real square in my family compared to you," he said.

Across the room at Clarence's, Violet Bastedo told Herkie Saybrook, her lawyer for her second divorce, that she didn't want anything for herself from Pony Bastedo except, as she put it, "Out. Out. Out," of the marriage, but she did want a trust set up for little Violet, as well as all the usual things like Nanny's salary, school fees through college, medical care, and "whatever else you can think of."

"I can't believe my eyes," said Violet.

"What?" asked Herkie.

"There's Justine Altemus over there, with Bernard Slatkin of all people."

"Who's Bernard Slatkin?"

"On TV, that one."

"What's so strange about that?"

"He'd fuck an umbrella," said Violet.

Herkie Saybrook blushed.

"Sorry, Herkie. I should have said it in French."

VOICES became reserved at the mention of Hubie Altemus's name, but his mother, Lil Altemus, doted on him completely and knew, simply knew, that the new art gallery in SoHo that she had financed for him, against the advice of her brother, Laurance Van Degan, who handled her money for her, was exactly the place for Hubie to be. All that Van Degan pressure at the bank, being one of the family and all, was what caused the problems there, she was sure.

"I know there's something wrong, Hubie," said Lil, replacing her cup and saucer on the tea table that her butler had set up in her library. She took a moment, before the unpleasant scene that she knew was at hand, to admire the tangerine-colored border of her Nymphenburg tea set. "I can just tell by the way you're standing there that there's something wrong. I can always tell."

"Let up, will you?" said Hubie. Hubie was not as tall as Justine, his sister, but the aristocratic Altemus forehead and the aquiline Van Degan nose made him unmistakably her brother. There was, however, an unsureness of self about Hubie that showed in his eyes and facial expressions. His Altemus father, and his Van Degan grandfather, uncle, and cousin had all gone to St. Swithin's and Harvard, but Hubie had been asked to leave St. Swithin's, under embarrassing circumstances, and then went to several other schools of lesser stature. He was kicked out of Harvard in his first year for cheating in a Spanish examination and called before his Uncle Laurance, who was the head of the family. "Cheating in *Spanish?* The language of maids," Uncle Laurance had said contemptuously, as if it would have been a lesser offense to have cheated in economics or trigonometry.

"Just tell me one thing, Hubie," said Lil.

"What?"

"Is it murder?"

"Good God, no. How could you ask me that, Mother?"

"Drugs, then?"

"No."

"You haven't embezzled, or stolen, or anything like that?"

"Of course not."

"I just wanted to get rid of all the serious things first. So, you see, whatever it is, it doesn't really matter. You're not overdrawn again, Hubie? Oh, please don't tell me that."

"I'm not overdrawn."

"Don't make me play guessing games, for God's sake, Hubie."

Hubie breathed in deeply. "Lewd conduct," he said.

"What does that mean?"

"What it sounds like."

"Well, explain it to me."

"I was caught—" He stopped, unable to finish his sentence. He turned away from his mother before he finished his confession. "I was caught, doing it, in Central Park, with a man."

For a moment Lil was tempted to say, "Doing what?" for innocence was her trademark in the family, but she knew what he meant, and she knew, too, that her son would answer her question with the sort of words she could not bear to have repeated in her presence. Instead she said, quietly, "I don't want to hear." Her copy of *Vogue* slipped from her lap and fell to the floor. She turned her forlorn face toward the fireplace. Hubie, scarlet now, looked down on his mother as she stared at the fire. Her King Charles spaniels, Bosie and Oscar, awakened by the sound of the magazine hitting the carpet, jumped on the side of Lil's chaise, trying to get her attention. Without looking at them, she reached over to a damask-draped end table and took two cookies from a plate and threw them in the air for the dogs to leap at. Hubie watched for a minute and then turned and moved quickly toward the door of his mother's room. "Isn't this what happened at St. Swithin's?" she asked.

"Yes."

"And in Newport that summer with the lifeguard?"

"Yes."

"You promised me when Uncle Laurance got you into Simsbury that it wouldn't happen again."

"It did. At Simsbury, and at college too." Hubie opened the door.

"Don't go, Hubie," said Lil. "Look, we'll figure this out. Come over here. Sit down. Uncle Laurance will know how to get this fixed without any publicity, or fine, or anything. You'll have to go and see Uncle Laurance, Hubie."

"I can't."

"It will be just as important to Uncle Laurance as it is to you, Hubie, that this thing is handled with dispatch."

"I can't go to see him, Mother. I can't. He hates me. He makes me feel like I'm nothing. He's always comparing me to young Laurance. I can't go to see him. I'd rather go to jail," said Hubie, whose body was twisted in anguish. For a minute Lil was afraid Hubie was going to start to cry.

"Don't cry, Hubie. Please don't cry."

"I'm not crying, Mother."

"I'll go to see him."

"I'm sorry."

"If you knew, simply knew, how I hate to have to go to see your Uncle Laurance."

"I'm really sorry. I don't know what else to say."

"I'll tell you what. After this is all over, you and I will go away for a little vacation together. We could go to Venice, and stay at the Gritti, and swim at the Cipriani, and have lunch at Harry's. It'll be divine. Alessandro will be there, in that heavenly old palace of his, and I tell you, Hubie, you have never seen ceilings like the Tiepolo ceilings in Alessandro's palace. To die. It'll be such fun. You'll see. By the time we get back all this will be over. We can count on Uncle Laurance to straighten all this out."

IN JUSTINE'S mind, marriage was the logical sequel to love.

"Didn't you ever hear of an affair?" asked Bernie, for whom marriage held no allure.

"Isn't that what we're having?" asked Justine.

"I was never one to believe that every romance had to end up in marriage," said Bernie.

"But this isn't just any old romance, my darling. Can't you tell? Can't you feel it? This is incredible, what we have."

Justine was fastidious about herself, not only in her neatness of grooming, but in the care of her body, which always carried the expensive scents of deodorants, and bath oils, and powder, and perfume. After they had made love several times, Bernie asked Justine not to mute her natural woman's scents with sprays and atomizers. He told her a woman's scent was like her fingerprints, hers alone, and it aroused him to know her as she really was.

Bernie rubbed his finger up and down Justine's rib cage. Too thin, she wished her ribs did not protrude so much, but she was proud of her breasts, not too big, not too small, just right, perfectly formed. She watched Bernie lean down to kiss them. She liked to watch the total absorption of his eyes on her nipples, and the look of desire on his face.

"I'm glad your nipples are pink," he said. "I like pink nipples better than beige." As his hand traveled down her body to between her legs, he brushed his face back and forth over her breasts, moaning with pleasure, and then his lips began the slow descent downward to where his moist fingers were preparing for his tongue's reception.

"Oh, Bernie," whispered Justine, her hands now in his hair. She had never known there could be such bliss as Bernie Slatkin had brought into her life. She did not know it was possible to love the way she loved him.

"My Aunt Hester asked me if you were pretty," he said, without lifting his head from his carnal task.

"What did you tell her?" Justine asked.

"I said you were as tall as me."

"That wasn't an answer to her question."

"I said you were refined looking."

Justine, enthralled with her lover's lovemaking, replied, "Did you tell her I'm going to marry her nephew?"

5

YOU COULD pick out Constantine de Rham from a block away when he walked up or down Madison Avenue. His enormous head with its black beard and hooded eyes had a kind of reptilian magnificence. He was taller by far than most people and walked with such great strides that strollers on the avenue stepped aside as he passed and turned to stare after him at his aristocratic swagger. In fall and spring he wore his topcoat over his shoulders like a cape.

He had that day, in what was for him a rare burst of generosity, given a dollar to a beggar on the street, and, then, not ten minutes later, returning the same way, was offended and irritated that the same beggar held up his hand for more, having already forgotten him, rather than rewarding him with a smile of recognition and gratitude that he felt his previous contribution to the fellow's welfare deserved.

Augustus Bailey and Constantine de Rham sighted each other from a block away and passed each other without speaking, each aware of the other and each aware that the other was aware of him. An unpleasant feeling stirred within Gus Bailey, as he turned to peer into the window of the Wilton House Bookshop, pretending to concentrate on the display of copies of Nestor Calder's latest novel, *Judas Was a Redhead*, until Constantine de Rham had passed. Sometimes Gus felt prescient, and he felt in that moment of passage that he was sometime going to have to play a scene, as he used to call it in Hollywood, with Constantine de Rham. Concentrating on Nestor Calder's book, Gus did not see Elias Renthal pass behind him and enter a coffee shop, carrying a briefcase.

Inside the bookshop he could see Matilda Clarke, looking at the latest books with Arthur Harburg, the proprietor. He walked in.

"I'm sick, sick, sick to death of reading about the Mitfords," said Matilda.

"There's *Judas Was a Redhead*," suggested Arthur.

"I've read that. I even went to Nestor Calder's publication party at Clarence's."

"Have you read *Inspired by Iago*?"

"Heavens, no!"

"It's not what you think. It opens in a trailer park."

"Right away you've lost me. A little trailer park goes a long way with me."

"What do you like?" asked Arthur Harburg, patiently. He was used to dealing with his spoiled clients.

"I like a book with short chapters," said Matilda. "I love to be able to say, 'I just want to finish this chapter,' and do it. Such a feeling of accomplishment. What have you got with short chapters, about rich people?"

"There's always Trollope," said Gus, breaking in. "He writes short chapters."

"Gus Bailey," said Matilda, with a laugh. "Trollope indeed. You missed such a good weekend in the country."

"Sorry about that."

"How was your mystery weekend in the other direction?"

"Oh, okay."

"This man leads a mystery life, Arthur."

IN GUS'S bathroom, Matilda went through his medicine chest. It interested her to know what men kept in their medicine chests. To her surprise, behind the boxes of his English soap and talcum powder, she found a package of Ramses, a prelubricated prophylactic, according to the copy on the box. She had not thought of Gus Bailey in terms of sexual pursuits. There was always that wife somewhere in his past whose photographs were in his apartment, and the tragedy people talked about, whatever it was. Opening the package of three, she saw that two were missing and was consumed with curiosity to know the kind of women who came to his apartment. She placed the remaining prophylactic in her evening bag and returned to Gus's living room.

There was classical music on the stereo, and Gus was settled into the chintz-covered chair that was obviously his regular chair, leafing through a copy of *Judas Was a Redhead*. For the first time she noticed him in a different way and wondered what he was like as a lover.

"Did you find everything?" he asked.

"Yes," she replied, not taking her eyes off him. With both hands she patted the back of her hair. Nearing fifty, she still wore her hair in the same pageboy style that she had worn as a debutante of eighteen.

"Find your style and stick with it," she was often quoted as saying, when the fashion pages of the papers were still quoting her, before Sweetzer died.

"Drink?" Gus asked, sensing a change in the atmosphere. He rose.

"I'll have a whiskey, with a splash of water," she said. She looked around the sitting room. "Well, how nice this is, your little apartment. It's so chic."

"Hardly chic," said Gus.

"Well, cozy. I meant this run-down look you have. It's so English-second-son sort of thing."

Gus laughed. In the kitchen he made her a scotch with a splash of water. Gus was precise in all things. He refilled the ice tray, put it back in the freezer, and sponged the wet off the kitchen counter before returning to his sitting room.

"It's my first drink since New Year's Eve," she said, taking it from him. "Spirits, that is. Only wine since then, but I don't count wine. What are you having?"

"Oh, bottled water, I suppose. I keep a variety to choose from."

"Bottled water? That's all?"

"Yes."

"You don't drink?"

"No."

"Ever?"

"No."

"Did you ever?"

"Yes, but I stopped."

"Why?"

"I just did."

"By yourself, or with help?"

"With help."

"Oh, so you're a drunk!" she chortled, feeling better about herself.

"No more. Cured in Minnesota," said Gus, smiling. He returned to his chair. "There are several options for the evening," he said. "I called Chick Jacoby, and we can get a table at Clarence's. Or we can go around the corner and see the new Woody Allen movie. Or we can go to the Marty Leskys' who are having a party with a lot of movie stars."

"A veritable olio," she replied.

"Do you have a preference?"

"Yes."

"What?"

"Let me see how you look with this on," she said, opening her bag and tossing the rubber across the room to him.

"YOU ARE surprising, Gus," she said thirty minutes later.

"How so?"

"I mean, you look like and act like you have no interest in this sort of thing whatsoever, and, actually, you're terribly good at it."

"Well, so are you."

"But everybody knows about me, so I'm no surprise. Do you always wait for the lady to make the first move?"

"I suppose."

"Are you, as they say, involved at the moment?"

"I'm more for the quick encounter than for romance," said Gus. "I have been a failure at romance."

"Is that a nice way of telling me no repeats?"

"No, no. It just means, let's wait until we bump into each other at the bookshop again."

She lay back against the pillows, opened her bag, took out a gold mirror, and examined herself. "Look, my color's marvelous. I always feel so much better after a good fuck."

He laughed.

"You should laugh more, Gus," said Matilda. "You sound nice laughing. Sometimes I think that beneath that very calm veneer of yours, you are exploding with thoughts that none of us know anything about."

Dressed, they moved from the bedroom back into the living room. Matilda looked at the photographs on one of Gus's tables.

"May I suggest something to you?" she asked.

"Of course."

"Why don't you remove those pictures of your dead child from your apartment? It's just a constant reminder."

There was a silence before he replied. "May I suggest something to you?" he asked.

"Of course," she answered, unaware of the steel in his voice.

"Mind your own fucking business."

Matilda, scarlet, replied, "But I just meant—"

"I understand what you meant." He breathed deeply. "Now, about tonight. What will it be?"

"You're livid with me," she said.

"I'll get over it."

"I think I should just go back to the country."

"No, you shouldn't just go back to the country. We have had a misunderstanding. There is a part of my life I do not share, that's all, just as I'm sure there is a part of your life that you do not share. We are people of a certain age. We should be able to deal with a crisis. Right?"

"I suppose."

"Now, about tonight, what will it be?"

"You're not just being polite because we had a sort of date?"

"Of course not."

"Let's go to Marty Lesky's movie-star party. I'm so glad you know all those Hollywood people, Gus. I read in Mavis Jones's column that Faye Converse is going to be there."

"Perfect."

"You know Faye Converse, don't you?"

"Yes."

"I read the story you wrote about her."

"I like her."

"You're strange, Gus."

"How?"

"You listen to all of us talk, but you never say anything about yourself."

Gus looked at Matilda but did not reply.

"I better keep my mouth shut and quit when I'm ahead," she said, and they both laughed.

6

VERY FEW people would have guessed that Loelia Manchester was one of the unhappiest women in New York. For twenty years the dazzling blond society figure was known as the girl who never missed a party, no matter where. She had once been reported, in the same fortnight, to have danced at balls at a maharanee's palace in Jaipur, and a German prince's castle in Regensburg, and an industrialist's villa in Palm Beach, and it was true. She flew to Paris thrice a year for her clothes, and was so often photographed in the fashion and society press, for no other reason than her social perfection and perfect taste, that her face had become as familiar in New York as a film star's.

Loelia was the youngest of Fernanda Somerset's four children, the only daughter after three sons, and the child the Somersets called their reconciliation gift to each other following an estrangement that had mercifully not ended in divorce. Arthur Somerset adored his beautiful child and, when he was killed in a plane crash in the Bahamas, left her a fortune equal to the fortunes he left to the three Somerset sons who had preceded her.

When, at twenty-two, Loelia told her mother that Edward Potter Manchester had asked her to be his wife, Fernanda Somerset was beside herself with joy. Ned Manchester was known to have no inclination for social life. He detested dinner parties and charity balls, often refusing even to go. So it was a surprise to one and all when he fell in love with the excessively social Loelia.

The Somerset fortune dwarfed the Manchester fortune, but the Manchester family superseded the Somersets in social standing, going back in American history to Gerald Manchester, who signed the Declaration of Independence, and in American society to Honoria Manchester, whose gold-and-white paneled ballroom in her Fifth Avenue house, now demolished, had been brought over from Castleberry House in London when that great pile of gray stones had been pulled down early in the century.

On each side the families were delighted with the match, from both a family and financial point of view, and the Manchesters felt certain that Loelia would grow to enjoy country life and sport while the

Somersets felt that Loelia would be able to persuade Ned to take more of an interest in social life. Thereafter Loelia, following a brilliant wedding, moved into a world of New York society where she was asked everywhere, even by people who disliked her, and Ned, for years, trailed dutifully behind.

So it was that the rumored divorce of the Edward Potter Manchesters, after twenty-two years of marriage and two children, would put every other dinner-table conversation into oblivion for at least three months that season, or, at least, put every other dinner-table conversation into oblivion in the fashionable world in which Loelia and Ned Manchester moved. Whenever Dolly De Longpre wrote about the Edward Potter Manchesters in her column, which was often—for the Manchesters, particularly Loelia, were not only involved in charitable fundraising at the highest level but entertained privately in a manner that very few social aspirants could hope to emulate—she always used all three of the Manchester names and then added, in case the point was not already made, "of the New York *Social Register*." Furthermore, to add to their cachet, there was, as the saying goes in society, money on both sides.

Cora Mandell, who had decorated the Manchesters' Fifth Avenue apartment, as well as their house on Long Island, and their house in Bermuda, and all the houses of Loelia's mother, Fernanda Somerset, was rarely at a loss for words, but when Ezzie Fenwick, who knew all the news ahead of everyone else, told her about what he called "the Manchester splituation" when they were having lunch at Clarence's, she was so overwhelmed that she was speechless. Cora Mandell always wore black, no matter what the season, always wore three strands of perfect pearls, always wore her white hair parted in the middle, and worked harder than most people half her age. Ezzie often said about Cora that if she'd only let Bobo touch up her hair a bit and give her a more up-to-date coiffure, you'd think she was sixty rather than seventy-eight.

"But it can't be true," cried Cora, putting down her iced-tea glass on the table with such force that Lil Altemus and her daughter, Justine, sitting at the next table, interrupted their argument to turn and stare. "I'm making new summer slipcovers for the dining-room chairs in Locust Valley. Loelia would hardly be ordering new slipcovers if she were getting a divorce. I mean, would she?"

"Take my word for it, honey," said Ezzie, full of himself as he always was when he was the first one with the latest news. "Have I ever been wrong?"

"Who told you?" asked Cora, who knew that Ezzie, even if he was an old gossip, usually had his facts straight.

Ezzie drew himself up archly and announced, "I'm not telling."

"But why? After twenty-one years?"

"Twenty-two years," Ezzie corrected her.

"Twenty-two," Cora conceded. "Don't you think couples should just put up with each other after all that time?"

Ezzie Fenwick, whose restless eyes roamed everywhere, even during the most intimate conversation, followed with undisguised interest the entrance into the restaurant of Constantine de Rham and Yvonne Lupescu and then barely acknowledged de Rham's courtly bow and looked right through Mrs. Lupescu as the couple passed his table on the way to their own. At times, with lesser mortals or upstarts, a favorite word of his, Ezzie's face assumed attitudes of aristocratic hauteur, although they were attitudes studied and memorized but not inherited. Cora liked Ezzie. His snobbery amused her. She could remember many years ago when Ezzie had been considered an upstart himself in New York and people claimed that his father, who bought up all the foreign-car franchises that Ezzie's considerable income was derived from, had anglicized his more exotic name to the Episcopal-sounding Fenwick.

"The things I could tell you about that one," said Ezzie to Cora about Mrs. Lupescu, but Cora had no interest whatever in either Constantine de Rham or Yvonne Lupescu, or any of the other "trash Europeans," as she called them, who were overcrowding New York and driving up the price of real estate.

"Pretty cuff links," she replied, tapping a long red fingernail against one of the tiny green enamel frogs with ruby eyes that Ezzie wore on each wrist.

"Blanche Abdy gave me these when Hector died," said Ezzie, glancing down to admire how perfectly they went with his green-and-white striped shirt and green paisley tie.

Ezzie Fenwick had never had to make a living, and never had, nor had he ever gone in for any of the artistic pursuits of rich men with time on their hands, like founding magazines, or producing plays, or running art galleries or antique shops, offering, as credentials, their perfect taste, as well as their bankrolls. Ezzie was always considered close, meaning, as Laurance Van Degan often put it, that he was tight with a buck, although he was known to be extremely generous, in gifts of flowers and restaurant dinners, to certain hostesses and fashionable ladies of the city whom he particularly admired.

Early on he was known as a good seat, meaning that he was amusing to sit next to at dinner, and ladies vied for his attention, although he was quite capable of wounding any one of those same ladies who were kindest to him if he didn't care for her choice of dress for the evening ("That color yellow is *all wrong* for you!" he once said to Loelia Manchester), or if he thought she had seated a table badly ("Imagine, wasting *me* next to Maude Hoare!" he had complained to Lil Altemus), or if he felt she had redecorated her library incorrectly ("Never, ever, quilt chintz! So tacky!" he once said to Baba Timson).

Although Ezzie was now a stalwart figure in the most fashionable groups in society, it had not always been so. Cora Mandell could remember forty years ago when Ezzie was often asked to leave parties he hadn't been invited to, not only because he was a crasher, but because he dared to criticize the flower arrangements as puny, as he had at Sibila Monroe's coming-out dance, or complain that the chicken hash was all cream and no chicken, as he had at Blanche Abdy's supper party. But that was all long ago and no one else remembered.

"Back to the Manchesters," Cora redirected Ezzie, with a rap on the tabletop to get his attention away from Mrs. Lupescu.

"There's someone else involved," said Ezzie.

"There can't be," replied Cora, with disbelief in her voice.

"There has to be," said Ezzie, knowingly. "Why get a divorce after all that time unless there is someone else in the picture?"

"But Ned doesn't seem like a player-arounder," mused Cora.

"How do you know it's Ned? It might be Loelia," answered Ezzie.

"Never," said Cora affirmatively. "Loelia loves all the parties, and dresses, but she's not the type to have affairs. I mean, I've known Loelia all her life. I decorated all her mother's houses, and I've watched her grow up."

"We'll see," replied Ezzie, raising his eyebrows mysteriously, to let her know he knew something he was not telling her. "Let's have some of that grapefruit sorbet. It's delish and practically no calories. Old big ears Lil Altemus at the next table has been trying to listen to every word we've said. Now, why do you suppose Justine never married, with all that money?"

"Young people are marrying later these days," replied Cora.

"That's not Justine's problem. Justine's problem is that no one has asked her."

WHEN LOELIA MANCHESTER'S private line rang, on the telephone number that not a living soul had, except Lil Altemus, and Matilda Clarke, and her mother, and Bobo, her hairdresser, and, of course, Dimitri Minardos, she was surprised that her caller, when she answered the ring, was Dolly De Longpre. For an instant, her heart sank.

"Listen, Loelia," said Dolly. "The story's all over town that you and Ned are separating."

"There's not a word of truth to it, Dolly," replied Loelia. There was panic in her voice. She had still not told her children, which did not frighten her, and she had still not told her mother, which did frighten her.

"Come on, Loelia, it's me, Dolly. We've known each other twenty-five years," said Dolly. Dolly De Longpre was not to be brushed off.

"I can't think how these stories get started, Dolly," said Loelia.

"Loelia," said Dolly, with great patience in her voice, pronouncing the name Loelia in three syllables rather than two, for greater emphasis.

"Yes?"

"If I don't print it, someone else will," said Dolly, in her direct and plain-spoken manner. There were at this time many social chroniclers in the city, reporting on the comings and goings of the rich and super rich, but everyone agreed, in the opulent and much-photographed circle in which Loelia Manchester moved, that no one approached Dolly De Longpre's supremacy in the field. It was to her column that they all turned first thing each day, after the headlines and before the obituaries, to read about themselves, where they had been the night before, and what they wore, ate, and said.

"Oh, my word," said Loelia, understanding at once that the "someone" Dolly was referring to was Florian Gray, who was young and just starting out in Dolly's line of work, but would never, ever, she and her friends all believed, be able to understand people like them the way Dolly did.

"My word," Loelia repeated, thinking hard.

Dear, darling Dolly De Longpre, she would know how to handle it, thought Loelia. Dolly always knew how to do things just right when unpleasantness of this nature had to be dealt with. It was almost as if she were one of them, she had been writing about them all for so long, and dining with them, and staying with them in the country, and attending their weddings and christenings and memorial services. Even if Dolly didn't have her column, everyone would still invite her, they always said. Yes, Dolly De Longpre would know how to handle the divorce announcement and counteract all the perfectly awful things people were saying about Loelia and Dimitri Minardos.

"Listen, Dolly, why don't you come up and have a cup of tea with me, and that way we can talk, really talk," said Loelia.

AND DOLLY handled it beautifully, just as Loelia had known Dolly would, with a discreet announcement that the Edward Potter Manchesters, of the New York *Social Register*, had agreed to disagree, much to the dismay of their family and friends. But it was young Florian Gray, just making a name for himself as a commentator in the world of high society, who called a great deal of attention to the hitherto undisclosed romance of Mrs. Manchester and the shoe designer Dimitri Minardos, known as Mickie, as well as a great deal of attention to himself.

Hidden in Paris, incognito, on an outing of love, Loelia and Mickie instructed the telephone operator at the Ritz Hotel to take messages from everyone who called from America, and then decided between them which calls to return. Loelia found it irresistible that Dom Belcanto, the Hollywood ballad singer, who had promised to entertain at her benefit for the stroke center, called to wish her well, leaving a call-back number in New York.

"So sweet of Dom to call, Mickie," said Loelia, lying back in her chaise. "People say the worst sort of things about him, that he's Mafia, or mob, or whatever you call people like that, but I don't believe a word of it. When there's good work to be done, like my benefit, Dom Belcanto is there every time."

When she returned the call, the voice that answered the telephone turned out to be that of Florian Gray, who was stealing a bit of Dolly De Longpre's thunder in the New York press.

"I just wanted to know, Mrs. Manchester, if you and Mr. Minardos are planning to marry after your divorce," said Florian quickly, in the event that Loelia might hang up on him. All that he wanted was a single quote from her that would titillate his readers. Loelia, who had still not been able to bring herself to tell her children there was a new man in her life, turned ashen and mouthed to Mickie that it was Florian Gray and not Dom Belcanto on the telephone.

"What a cheap trick this is, you little piece of shit," screamed Mickie, who always became volatile in anger, into the receiver that he had pulled out of Loelia's hand. His voice, beneath the glossy patina of its New York society sound, reverted to the accent of the Greek province where he was born.

The dressing down that Mickie gave the upstart columnist was thought by both Loelia and Mickie to have been brilliant, as if their outrage would quell any thoughts Florian Gray might have had in printing their story before they could get a chance to tell Loelia's family and a few close friends of their intentions.

How wrong they were.

HEIRESS LOELIA SOMERSET MANCHESTER ELOPES TO PARIS WITH HER COBBLER, read the headline in Florian Gray's column the next morning. Florian Gray could have had no way of knowing how wounding to Mickie Minardos that headline was going to be.

7

"WHO'S THAT handsome young man I keep seeing with your daughter?" asked Baba Timson, during bridge.

"A handsome young man with Justine?" replied Lil Altemus, surprised, but delighted. "You don't mean Herkie Saybrook, do you?"

"Oh, no, not Herkie," said Baba. "Everyone knows Herkie."

"Not Thayer Good, I hope?" said Lil.

"Heavens, no. Handsome, I said. Thayer Good looks like a premature baby at thirty-five."

"I don't know," said Lil, who intended to find out. "It's your bid, Loelia."

LATE AT night, after Bernie took Justine home, or early in the morning, when they both woke up, Justine telephoned Bernie, or Bernie telephoned Justine. They seemed never to run out of things to talk about.

"I haven't the vaguest idea how much money I'm going to inherit," said Justine. "I come from the kind of family that never fills the women in on things like that. My brother and I each have a trust, rather ample, and we live on that until Grandfather Van Degan dies, when we'll come into something, and then the rest, I suppose, when Mother dies."

"You don't have to tell me all this, you know, Justine. I can pay the bills. I intend to pay the bills," said Bernie.

"Music to my ears," said Justine. She laughed at her joke. "I've heard since I was five years old to beware of everyone, even the girls I went to school with, because they were only interested in the money. It's an awful way to grow up, you know, distrusting everyone."

"I'm never really gonna understand people like you," said Bernie.

"You know something, Bernie? You're my least suitable suitor, in terms of family and that kind of thing, but you're also the only suitor I've ever had who really didn't give a damn about the money. The things I could tell you about Jean-Claude St. Cloud, for instance, whom my mother had all picked out for me."

"I guess I'm just filled with middle-class values," said Bernie.

"More music to my ears," answered Justine.

"A couple of things I want to talk about, speaking of middle-class values," said Bernie.

"Yes?"

"I don't want to live in the same building your mother lives in, and, I have to tell you right now, I hate cabbage-rose chintz."

Justine laughed again. "Okay," she said. "Good-bye to Fifth Avenue, and good-bye to Cora Mandell and cabbage-rose chintz. But I don't want to live in your building either, and I don't want the minimal look."

"A deal," said Bernie.

"One other thing, so everything's out in the open."

"What's that?"

"I'm a spoiled girl, Bernie," Justine said. "I adore you, worship you, in fact, can't get enough of you, love to look at you, every part of you, but I'm not going to get up every morning to fry your eggs, over easy, when I have a perfectly good cook who can do that sort of thing far better than I can."

"Good. I hate to talk when I'm reading the *Times*."

"We're going to get along great, Bernie."

"Here's to us, kid."

"Want me to come over?" she asked.

"It's two o'clock in the morning."

"I know."

"I'm not shaved, and I stink," he said.

"All the better," she answered.

"I NEED a fourth for bridge," said Lil Altemus, over the telephone. "I've got Matilda, and Nonie, but Loelia has backed out on me. Loelia's always backing out on me these days, and that boring Baba Timson has an appointment with her daughter's analyst that she won't break. Be here at two, will you, or earlier if you want lunch. Matilda's coming for lunch."

"I can't, Mother," said Justine.

"Why?"

"Just because I can't."

"What am I going to do?"

"I hear Rochelle Prud'homme has taken up bridge with a vengeance."

"That's what Matilda said, but I don't think Rochelle Prud'homme is quite right for our little group. You can't talk freely in front of people like that."

"I thought you liked Rochelle Prud'homme."

"She does do wonderful things for charity, but this is just old friends playing bridge."

"It's Matilda who got Rochelle to learn bridge."

"And why would Matilda do that, for heaven's sake?"

"Because Rochelle Prud'homme wants to play bridge with Lil Altemus and Loelia Manchester."

Lil listened, but as a matter of principle, she refused to show undue interest in anything Justine related, preferring to receive her information from other sources. "And why can't you play?" she asked.

"Because I am otherwise engaged."

"People are talking about you and that television announcer."

"I think we should talk about it, Mother."

"This is not at all right, you know, Justine. I'm sure he's very nice and all that, but, darling, listen to your old mother, these things have a way of just not working."

"Oh, please, Mother. Don't say listen-to-your-old-mother to me. You don't know how hilarious that sounds coming from you."

"You're just asking for trouble, Justine, with people like that."

"Have lunch with me tomorrow at Clarence's, and we'll talk."

"CHRIST, I hate sex with condoms," said Bernie Slatkin, removing his and flushing it down the toilet.

"Oh, God, another intellectual conversation," said Brenda Primrose, as she pulled on her pantyhose.

"It just never feels as good," said Bernie.

"The way you cat around, Bernie, it's that or nothing with me," said Brenda. They had been on-and-off lovers for several years, with never a thought of love. Brenda Primrose did the research for Bernie's newscasts. She was smart. She was flip. She was sexy. They both understood their relationship perfectly.

"I don't cat around anymore," said Bernie, defensively. "I've reformed." It was a sensitive point with him. He had been warned by a senior executive at the network, who admired his work, that a promiscuous reputation was not the best one for a successful newscaster with political ambitions.

"Since when?" asked Brenda. "Three minutes ago?"

Bernie paused. It was the reason he had asked her over, to tell her about Justine, but then, sex happened, as it always seemed to happen when they were alone, in his office, in his apartment, wherever, even in an elevator once, always quick, always lustful, never romantic. Then they went back to work, as if nothing had happened, and in her off hours, she had dates with other men, and he had dates with other women, with no need for explanation on either side.

"Since I, uh, became, uh, engaged to be married," he said. The words *engaged to be married* came out as one word, *engagedtobemarried*. He quickly turned to look in a mirror to button his shirt and tie his tie so that he could face away from her for that moment.

"Since you *what?*" she asked.

"Became engaged to be married."

"Who did you become engaged to?"

"She's called Justine Altemus."

"Laurance Van Degan's niece?"

"Yes."

Brenda walked over to the mirror, took hold of Bernie's arm, and pulled him around to face her. For an instant, they looked at each other. He smiled at her his little-boy smile, as if expecting her congratulations. Then she slapped his face, very hard. "You bastard, Bernie," she said.

"Hey, that hurt," he said, surprised, putting his hand up to the spot where she slapped him.

"That was the point of the slap, Bernie," said Brenda, angrily. "To hurt. So like you." Bernie had never seen her angry before, or at least angry with him before.

"What the hell are you talking about, Brenda?"

"You had to wait until after you came *twice* before you told me you were going to get married?"

Bernie, embarrassed, winced. Then he walked to the bar. "Want a drink?" he asked her.

"Sure," she said. She finished dressing and went over to the same mirror he had just used and readjusted her lipstick and started brushing her hair. Watching Brenda from behind, Bernie was struck, as always, by how perfect her legs were. She was the first of all the girls he knew to start wearing the new short short skirts, even before the fashion leaders let the world know it was the right look for the right girl with the right legs.

"Here," Bernie said, handing her a glass of wine.

Brenda took a sip. "You're going to have to get better wine than this, Bernie, if you're going to marry the Van Degan heiress."

"I didn't even know who she was when I met her," he said.

"You don't read Dolly De Longpre's column."

"I didn't then. I do now."

"Where'd you meet her?"

"In an elevator."

"That sounds familiar."

"No, no, no, not like that. We were both leaving a party at Maisie Verdurin's, and she gave me a ride home."

Brenda nodded. "I'm not hurt, Bernie, but I do feel a bit used. I realize I'm just the office fuck, but us office fucks have feelings too."

"Office fuck, indeed," said Bernie. He hugged her.

"Congratulations," she said, finally.

"Thanks, Brenda. I'm really going to make this marriage work."

Brenda didn't believe him, but she nodded. She knew he was an alley cat. She knew that six months after his marriage he would be on the prowl again.

"Have you told Sol and Hester yet?" she asked. Brenda Primrose had once met Bernie Slatkin's aunt and uncle, who brought him up, when they came to the studio to watch him broadcast, and she always called them Sol and Hester when she mentioned them to Bernie.

"Not yet."

"I don't think they're going to be thrilled with a *shiksa* for a niece-in-law, do you?"

"When they meet Justine, they'll like her," said Bernie.

"Sure, Bernie. Probably about as much as Mrs. Altemus and Laurance Van Degan are going to like you."

LIL ALTEMUS looked up and watched her daughter enter the restaurant. Lil resented Justine's height and often blamed her single status, although she was only thirty, on the fact that she had towered

over most of the boys in Mrs. Godfrey's dancing classes at the Colony
Club when her age group was growing up in New York. Mostly, however, Lil Altemus resented Justine's height because she felt it would
have far better suited her son. Still stubbornly mistaken about Hubie,
Lil insisted that he would eventually find a woman, even encouraging
him to pursue this one or that one, and she once gave him her discarded engagement ring, a rather large diamond from her own failed
marriage, when she thought, incorrectly, that he might have found his
life choice in the unlikely person of Violet Bastedo.

Lil watched as Justine, on her way to the table, stopped to speak to
a trio of young married women whom she had come out with who were
lunching together. Justine had never, like the Millingtons' daughter,
taken to dope. Nor had she ever, like Emerald de Grey's daughter,
become radical and slept with NYU associate professors with
ponytails. And, thank God, she hadn't become a dyke, like poor
Baba Timson's Nan, whom Baba never spoke about anymore. Lil
could find nothing to fault in Justine's perfect appearance, but, used
to faulting her, she stared and then squinted at her daughter's hair in
such a way that Justine's hands went immediately to her coiffure, as if
the wind outside had mussed it, although there had been no wind
outside.

"Who's that great fat man with the foot-long cigar?" asked Lil, after
her daughter was seated. Lil Altemus often pretended she didn't
know things she knew very well, and she knew perfectly well who the
great fat man with the cigar was.

"He's called Elias Renthal," answered Justine, who knew that her
mother knew.

"The one who bought Matilda's apartment? Looks horrid. Brown
shoes with a blue suit. His wife is the pushiest woman ever. Ruby,
she's called. She asked me to have lunch. I mean, I know her about
as well as I know this waiter." She waved her hand in the direction of
the waiter who was placing a glass of white wine in front of her. "First
she served a cheese soufflé, and then a chocolate soufflé for dessert.
Can you imagine? Even her Rigaud candles were the wrong color. Get
Matilda going on the Renthals sometime." She sipped her wine.

"Why did you go if you feel like that?" asked Justine.

"I was raising money for the new stroke center for the hospital, and
all my friends said they simply couldn't give another cent, and Mrs.
Renthal couldn't get her checkbook out fast enough so, of course, I

had to go. It's what's called a once-only. Chick Jacoby really shouldn't allow him to smoke cigars in here." Lil waved her napkin back and forth in the air, as if to clear it of the offending cigar smoke.

"Chick Jacoby wouldn't have the nerve to tell Elias Renthal to put it out," said Justine.

"I wonder how he got such a good table," said Lil.

"Rich, rich, rich, Mother. Or, Big Bucks, as Bernard Slatkin would say. Richer even than the Van Degans, I hear."

Lil Altemus had a horror of what she referred to as the New People, and her own immense fortune had always protected her from having to fraternize socially with any of them, except when she asked them for money for one of her charities. Recently, however, with the publication of Mr. Forbes's annual list of the four hundred richest people in America, she was aware that her still immense fortune was less immense than the fortunes of such New People as Elias Renthal "and his ilk," meaning the Bulbenkians, and the Zobel brothers, and the Jorsts. The feeling was unsettling.

"Imagine anyone wearing a pale blue gabardine suit," said Lil, still staring over at Elias Renthal. Then she added, "Who's Bernard Slatkin?"

"He's the man I'm going to marry," answered Justine.

"Goodness," said Lil.

Justine expected a great furor of protestations from her mother, and possibly a scene. Bernard Slatkin possessed none of the requisites that Lil Altemus, who never let anyone forget that she was born a Van Degan, adhered to in past suitors for her daughter's hand. Surprisingly, Lil was, if not exactly enthusiastic, at least not defiant in her opposition to Justine's choice. Justine was, after all, thirty, or, to be precise, practically thirty-one. The kind of boys she had grown up with, gone to dancing school with, spent weekends with at Yale or Princeton, and who now worked downtown, in banks or brokerage houses, almost never married girls as rich as Justine Altemus was going to be. As one after another of them had drifted into solid if less spectacular marriages, Lil's greatest fear was that Justine would fall into the clutches of one of the fortune-hunting foreigners who preyed on American heiresses. Every time she thought of her childhood friend, Consuelo Harcourt de Rham, she shuddered at her sad fate. The sight of Consuelo's widower, Constantine de Rham, several tables away, spending Consuelo's money on a blond strumpet half his age, wearing far too many jewels for daytime, may have softened Lil's opposition to Bernard Slatkin.

"Slatkin," said Lil. "I don't know that name."

"It's not in the *Social Register,* Mother," answered Justine.

"That's not what I meant, and you know it."

"He earns a great deal of money, Mother."

"A television announcer, someone told me."

"No, he is a broadcaster. On the evening news."

"Not the little Chinese?"

"No, Mother, that's the weatherman, and he's Korean, not Chinese. Bernie is one of the anchormen."

"Oh, yes, of course. Is he the one with the dimple or the one with the toupee?"

"The dimple. He's very handsome, Mother."

"Of course he is, darling. Where in the world did you meet such a person?"

"At Maisie Verdurin's."

"Mrs. Verdurin has all those celebrities to dinner, doesn't she? I'm forever reading about her in Dolly's column. What were you doing at Mrs. Verdurin's?"

"We're here to talk about the man I'm going to marry, not about Maisie Verdurin."

"What do you suppose old Cora Mandell and Ezzie Fenwick are being so intense about at the next table?" asked Lil.

"Mother!"

"I'm listening, Justine," said her mother, sharply. "Forgive me if I can't absorb it all in a flash. This is quite important news, and, after all, we don't know anything about Mr. Bernard Slatkin, now, do we?"

Justine knew, before her mother even said it, that she was going to say, "Who is he?" She also knew that her mother meant, "Who is his family? What are his schools?"

"Who is he?" asked her mother.

"His parents are dead. He was raised by an aunt and uncle, Sol and Hester Slatkin. Sol is in the printing business. They live in New Jersey. Weehawken."

"Hmm," said Lil.

"Bernie went to Rutgers on a scholarship," said Justine. She loved saying, "He went to Rutgers on a scholarship," as if it added to the worth of him, a romantic asset to his history. In all her life she had never known anyone who had gone to school on a scholarship, and she found the idea glamorous. Even the names Sol and Hester evoked images in her mind of Ellis Island, and the Statue of Liberty, and huddled masses, although Sol and Hester Slatkin were several generations removed from Ellis Island and lived comfortable lives in comfortable circumstances. "He waited on tables in a fraternity house," Justine continued, her voice filled with excitement. "And then he went to law school for a year, I forget where, but he dropped out, because he was mad-keen to be in television news. First he was an on-the-air reporter covering City Hall, and then he filled in for a week as anchorman when Charlie Walsh broke his leg, and there was such a favorable reaction to him, I mean, people wrote in about him, he's so good-looking, wait till you see him, and then they made him a coanchorman full time after Charlie went to Los Angeles."

"Hmm," said Lil.

"He's not after my money, if that's what you're worried about, because he earns a fortune, an absolute fortune."

"They all earn a lot of money, those announcers, don't they?"

"He's an anchorman, Mother, not an announcer, and he writes all his own copy. He's very successful."

"I meant an anchorman," said Lil.

"I want a big wedding, Mother, with bridesmaids, and a reception at the Colony Club, and, you know, the works," said Justine.

"This is so nice, Justine," said Lil. She shaped her lips into an obligatory smile, but Lil's lips were very little involved in her smiles. Instead she raised her eyebrows and blinked her eyes shut several times in rapid succession in a manner that suggested, somehow, mirth. "You know, of course, there will be things to discuss with Uncle Laurance down at the bank."

"Yes."

"When will I meet Mr. Slatkin?"

"As soon as you say. You won't be difficult, will you, Mother, if Daddy gives me away?"

"Of course not, darling, as long as that tramp he's married to doesn't come within my sight lines and is seated somewhere at the back of the church," said Lil.

"Oh, Mother, I'm so thrilled. And you're going to love Bernie. He knows everything about Libya and nuclear disarmament and all those things. He's fascinating."

"Justine."

"Yes, Mother?"

"Mr. Slatkin, uh—"

"Please call him Bernie."

"Yes, of course, Bernie."

"What about him?"

"He doesn't wear one of those little beanie hats, does he?"

8

PEOPLE who worked for Elias Renthal accused him, behind his back, of course, as having a vile nature, as he had no patience whatever for people who were not as consumed with the desire to make money as he was. The accusation would not have offended him if he had been confronted with it. Elias looked on his unpopularity as a natural consequence of wealth and power. Maxwell Luby, Elias's head trader, was a second-echelon executive, knew it, accepted it, and aspired only to be the best second-echelon executive, an indispensable acolyte to Elias Renthal. Only Max Luby, who had known Elias from the beginning, in Cleveland, did not fear his wrath, which could be extreme, and dared to sometime caution him on the enormity of his wealth, although he refrained from voicing disapproval of the manner of Elias's rapid acquisition of his fortune.

"You're like a heroin addict, Elias," he said, "only about money."

"What the hell are you talking about?" asked Elias impatiently. Introspection was not a thing that Elias had any time for, especially during business hours, when he liked to devote his full attention to the fifty computers in his office, beaming fiscal information.

"I remember when you used to think everything would be all right with your life if you had a million dollars. And then I remember when you set ten million as your goal, and then fifty, and then a hundred. You thought the world was going to be your oyster with a hundred million, do you remember?"

"C'mon, c'mon, we got work to do. What is this? Psych One at Cleveland University?"

"But it still wasn't enough," Max went on, unperturbed by Elias's impatience. "Then it was five hundred million. And then you had a billion, even though Mr. Malcolm Forbes said you only had eight hundred million. And now you got three billion. Where does it stop, Elias? How much more do you need?"

Elias looked at Max. "I can't stop, Max. It's just too fucking easy. You know what it's like? It's like placing red meat in front of a lion."

Even Max Luby, who knew everything about Elias Renthal, did not know about his several secret bank accounts in Swiss banks with branch offices in Nassau in the Bahamas. He thought that when Elias went to Nassau, it was in connection with a new vacation house he was building in Lyford Key. He didn't know that one of the accounts was in his name, Max Luby, or that another was in Ruby's maiden name, R. Nolte. He didn't know that when Elias got a tip, from a variety of young lawyers in firms that dealt with mergers, or young stockbrokers with access to information not available to everyone, he made collect calls to his Swiss banks in Nassau, who did his buying for him, with no one the wiser.

LORD BIEDERMEIER surveyed the lunch crowd from his favorite table at Clarence's with a proprietary air. It was he, he was fond of telling all his friends and acquaintances, who had come up with the name for the popular restaurant, when Chick Jacoby was searching for a name that would have an English flavor. "Call it Clarence House," Lord Biedermeier had proposed, with the speed that he was able to give authors better titles for their books than they had been able to think up themselves. Lord Biedermeier was a great admirer of the Queen Mother, to whom he owed the knighthood that had preceded his title, and had been in the past a frequent visitor at her London residence known as Clarence House. Like all things concerned with Lord Biedermeier, snobbery played a great part. When Clarence House became fondly referred to as Clarence's, by the people who were regularly seated there by the very fussy Chick Jacoby, Lord Biedermeier, who lunched there most days when he was in New York, was delighted.

He waved his hand in greeting to Charlie Dashwood as Charlie passed his table to join Teddy Vermont and wondered what it was the two men were meeting about. Curiosity, both business and social, always consumed Lord Biedermeier, even about people he scarcely knew. Staring, he removed his pince-nez and, with his thumb and forefinger, massaged the reddened bridge of his nose before returning to a photocopy of an article from the front page of that morning's *New York Times* business section about the imminent collapse of Oswald Slingerland's hotel empire.

He pushed back the cuffs of his custom-made dark gray pin-stripe suit and custom-made Turnbull and Asser shirt and looked at the time on his Cartier watch. It was usually he who kept his guests

waiting, but he did not want to risk arriving after Elias Renthal, who
did not feel comfortable at Clarence's, and came ten minutes before
the appointed time. As Rochelle Prud'homme passed his table he
rose and kissed her hand.

"Such a nice party that was, Rochelle," he said to her.

"Your flowers were lovely, Lucien," said Rochelle.

"Who are you joining?" asked Lord Biedermeier.

"My sales staff. I'm bringing out a new line of liquid vitamins,
made from the live cells of sheep embryos," she said.

"My word," said Lord Biedermeier.

"Longer life, Lucien," said Rochelle.

"I'm serious about doing your autobiography," said Lord Biedermeier. "Ah, here is Mr. Renthal." He eyed Elias Renthal's pale blue
gabardine suit critically. "Do you know each other? Rochelle
Prud'homme. Elias Renthal."

"Hello, Eli," said Rochelle.

"Hello, Roxy," said Elias.

"Rochelle," she corrected him, meeting his eye, about her name.

"Elias," he corrected her, about his.

"Ta, Lucien," said Rochelle, moving off to her table. The un-
friendly exchange between Rochelle Prud'homme and Elias Renthal
was not lost on Lord Biedermeier.

"Old friends, I take it," he said, commenting on the scene he had
just witnessed.

"Old acquaintances would be a better description," said Elias.

"Business fallout?" asked Lord Biedermeier.

"A corporate raid on Prud'homme Hairdryers. One of my few fail-
ures," said Elias, smiling. "A tough cookie, Roxy Persky, for such a
tiny little lady."

"It's all this sort of thing, your takeovers, that I think the public
will find so fascinating, Elias. Rags to riches is irresistible stuff for
your American audiences. What you have done is the American
dream," said Lucien Biedermeier. He halted the conversation while
he ordered the wine and the main course, asking Elias to defer to his
culinary decisions because the chef, a Hungarian he had known in
Budapest who later worked at the Ritz Hotel in London, knew how
best to make a dish that was prepared especially for him every time
he called ahead.

"Have you ever written?" Lord Biedermeier asked.

"Just checks for Ruby," replied Elias, laughing, as if he had made a *bon mot*.

Lord Biedermeier smiled appreciatively and then said, "No, seriously."

"I don't have time to do all the things I'm doing," said Elias. "How the hell am I ever to get the time to write my autobiography, Lord Biedermeier?"

"It's Lucien, Elias," said Biedermeier. "You won't have to write a word of your autobiography. I'll make all the arrangements. All that you'll have to do is give two hours a week to the writer I'll hire for you. You just tell him or her your stories, and all the writing will be done for you. It's that simple."

"As soon as I get back from London, I'll meet the writer," said Elias. He was beginning to warm to the idea of an autobiography.

"How long will you be gone?"

"Just a few days. We'll be staying at the Claridge's Hotel."

"No, no, no," said Lord Biedermeier. "Simply say Claridge's. Not *the* Claridge's. Nor Claridge's Hotel either. Oh, dear me, no. Just say Claridge's."

"What difference does it make?" asked Elias.

"These are the little signals by which people like us recognize each other," said Lord Biedermeier.

"Do you think I'll ever learn all these ins and outs?"

"Oh, certainly, Elias. Certainly."

"I had this idea, Lucien," said Elias, taking out a comb from his pocket and combing his hair as he talked.

"No, no, no, you mustn't do that, Elias," said Lucien.

"Do what?"

"Comb your hair at Clarence's, I mean, it's just not done."

"God, you sound like Ruby. She's always telling me I don't do things the right way. Except make money, of course. That's what I wanted to talk to you about. The profits from this book. There will be profits, I assume," said Elias.

"That is always the hope in publishing, Elias, and there is a great interest in tycoon biographies at the moment, especially self-made tycoons. We have every reason at Biedermeier and Lothian to think that there will be a major audience for the story of Elias Renthal, especially since your recent marriage. All that running around you did after your last divorce might not have gone over in middle America, especially for a man your age, but now, with Ruby, you will start to build a place for yourself here in New York. How is the divine Ruby?"

With all his heart Elias Renthal wished he hadn't once told Lord Biedermeier, in a moment of fraternal camaraderie aboard the Concorde from London to New York, that Ruby could take, as he put it at the time, both his nuts in her mouth at the same time. And with all his heart he wished he hadn't added, "And I got big nuts," when he shared that confidence with Lord Biedermeier. He hadn't known at that point that he was going to marry Ruby Nolte. He knew it was what was on Lord Biedermeier's mind every time Lord Biedermeier saw Ruby. He wondered if Lord Biedermeier had told other people what he had said, because he knew he would have told if Lord Biedermeier had said the same thing to him about some girl he was involved with.

"What Ruby and I thought was that I would donate the profits from the book and the paperback sale to the homeless of New York, or to the families of victims of violent crime, or something we think up, as a sort of public-relations pitch."

"What a good idea, Elias. There's that young police officer who was paralyzed by the drug dealer. You could give him something. The public eats up that sort of thing."

"Oh, shit," said Elias.

"What?" asked Lord Biedermeier.

"I dropped some of this goulash you ordered on my new suit."

"Quite dashing haberdashery you are wearing," said Lord Biedermeier.

"Don't you like my new suit?" asked Elias.

"Pale blue gabardine was never one of my favorites."

"Oh."

"But I prefer it by far to the rust-colored gabardine you had on at the office yesterday."

"I'm all wrong. Is that what you're trying to tell me?"

"I think with your growing position in the city, you should give more thought to your clothes. Dark grays. Dark blues. And the subtlest pin stripes. You must let me take you to my tailor," said Lord Biedermeier. "While we're on the subject, what manicurist do you use?"

"Blanchette, at my office," said Elias.

"You must tell Blanchette at your office to buff your nails. That glossy polish is frightfully common."

Elias, bewildered, stared at his fingers. He wondered if he would ever learn all that he was supposed to learn.

"I don't get it," said Elias, looking over at the entrance of the restaurant, where Chick Jacoby was turning away some customers whose look did not appeal to him.

"What don't you get, Elias?" asked Lord Biedermeier.

"This place. Clarence's. Why do people fight to come here?"

"It's cheap. That is Chick Jacoby's secret."

"That's what I don't get."

"My dear Elias. It's something you will learn. There is nothing the rich enjoy more than a bargain, especially a bargain that is reserved exclusively for them."

"Why can't Ruby learn that? She only likes it if it costs the most."

"Oh, look who's coming in," said Lord Biedermeier, whose eyes were riveted on the door where Chick Jacoby was welcoming some arriving guests, with flourishes, to signal their importance.

"The man with Jamesey Crocus is Dimitri Minardos. Some people call him Mickie Minardos."

"Who the hell is Dimitri Minardos, for Christ's sake? Ruby knows who all these people are, but I never do," said Elias, buttering a roll.

"He designs shoes."

"Shoes? That's a big deal? Shoes?" asked Elias, unimpressed.

"Dimitri Minardos is the name on every lip this week," said Lord Biedermeier.

"What did Dimitri Minardos do?"

"The fascinating Loelia Manchester has fallen madly in love with him, and be assured that Ruby knows who Loelia Manchester is."

"Damn, I wish Ruby was here," said Elias.

RUBY AT that time was occupied with Cora Mandell on the re-decoration of the vast apartment that she and Elias had recently purchased from Matilda Clarke, who, even before the death of Sweetzer Clarke, had not been able to afford to live there any longer.

"Those drapes must have been pretty in their day," said Ruby, "but I bet they haven't been changed since the nineteen fifties."

"Those curtains were hung in nineteen fifty-eight," said Cora Mandell.

"How do you know?" asked Ruby.

"I did this room in nineteen fifty-eight for Sweetzer Clarke's mother, before Sweetzer and Matilda were married."

"I'm glad I said the drapes were pretty," said Ruby.

"I had those curtains made up from some antique damask that Sweetzer's mother found in the Fortuny factory in Venice," said Cora.

Each time Ruby said the word *drapes*, Cora Mandell repeated the word *curtains* in the following sentence, as a way of letting her know that *drapes* was a word that was simply not used, an offense even to her ear, without actually correcting the newly rich woman who wanted so much for Cora Mandell to decorate her apartment. By the third time, the point had been made, and Ruby Renthal never used the word *drapes* again.

"The price, of course, is quite different for a window treatment today than it was in nineteen fifty-eight," said Cora.

Ruby Renthal seemed indifferent to cost, but Cora Mandell pursued the topic nonetheless, so that there would be no misunderstandings later.

"You have to figure on not less than seven thousand dollars a window for curtains. That, of course, includes the fringe," said Cora.

Ruby did not react adversely.

"It's how long it takes, not how much it costs, that I am interested in," answered Ruby.

"How many windows are there?"

"Ninety, perhaps, on the three floors, but I shouldn't think the curtains in the servants' rooms need be anything more than something pretty on a rod," said Ruby.

"Exactly," said Cora.

"We have a new painting, a Monet, with water lilies, and I was thinking that the walls of this room should be the same color pink as the inside of the water lilies in the painting," said Ruby. "Pink happens to be my favorite color."

"Persimmon, I think, would be a prettier color than pink. In lacquer, nineteen or twenty coats of lacquer," said Cora.

"Sounds nice," said Ruby.

"Is there furniture you would like me to see, Mrs. Renthal?" asked Cora.

"We have to get everything new," answered Ruby.

"For all three floors? My word," said Cora. "Do you mean there is nothing to recover?"

"We're starting from scratch," said Ruby, "but I want everything first rate."

"I see. There is an auction coming up in London in a few weeks."

"I love auctions," said Ruby.

"The Orromeo family has come on hard times and are selling their priceless collection of furniture."

"My word," said Ruby, using the phrase Cora Mandell had just used.

"There is a pair of eighteenth-century console tables, with inlaid rams' heads, which are too beautiful for words. They would be marvelous right there, on either side of the fireplace, with the Monet over the fireplace," said Cora. It wasn't often, even with the opulence of the decade, and the abundance of the new rich, that she was given carte blanche to start from scratch in an apartment of forty-one rooms. She realized she would have, finally, enough of a nest egg to retire.

"We can fly over in my husband's jet," said Ruby.

"My word, how grand," said Cora.

"We're going to get along great, Mrs. Mandell," said Ruby.

"Yes, Mrs. Renthal," said Cora.

LIL ALTEMUS sat in the back of her car next to her daughter and stared out at Central Park, while she organized her plans for the day in her head. "Tap on the glass, will you, Justine, and tell Joe to take me straight down to the Van Degan Building first."

"Yes, Mother," said Justine. She removed her glove and tapped on the glass with her ring. "Joe, Mother wants you to stop first at the Van Degan Building."

"Okay, Miss Justine," said Joe, closing the glass between them again.

"Is that your engagement ring?" asked Lil.

"Isn't it perfect?" Justine replied, defensively.

"Let me see it," said Lil.

Justine held out her hand to her mother.

Lil picked up Justine's hand and peered at her daughter's engagement ring without comment. She opened her bag, took out her reading spectacles, put them on, and picked up Justine's hand again. "That's not even a ruby," said Lil. "I thought you said he was going to give you a ruby. That's a garnet, for God's sake. He gave you a garnet with a lot of poky little diamonds around it. Now, don't pretend to me you think that's a big deal, because it's not. One thing I can't stand, it's a cheapskate. Either you tell Mr. Slatkin, or I tell him, that this just won't do. A man who earns four hundred thousand dollars a year can do better than a garnet."

"How do you know how much Bernie earns?" asked Justine. "I don't even know how much he earns."

"Uncle Laurance checked him out."

"Mother, I can't tell Bernie that. The ring belonged to his mother."

"Yes, I'm sure it did." Lil turned to look out the window again. "Look, my God, there's Loelia Manchester holding hands on Fifth Avenue with Mickie Minardos. I can't believe my eyes. Look! He's kissing her, right there on the street!"

"And Loelia's kissing him right back. Don't leave out that part of the story, Mother," said Justine.

"I don't know what the world's coming to," said Lil. She sat back in her seat and stared straight ahead. "I'll get out here, Joe," she called to the chauffeur when he pulled up in front of the Van Degan Building. She turned to Justine. "I have to see Uncle Laurance, Justine. There's no need for you to come in. Why don't you take my hair appointment at Bobo's? Then if you'd pick up my shoes at Delman's and then go to Tiffany's and see if the invitations are in for the engagement party. Nevel wants you to look at some preliminary sketches for the wedding dress, but you can always do that tomorrow. I'm meeting Matilda Clarke for lunch at Clarence's, and I'm sure Matilda would love to see you, so join us, but, for God's sake, don't show Matilda that ring."

"JESUS CHRIST, Lil," said Laurance Van Degan. He stood and walked to the window of his office, shaking his head slowly in disgust as he gazed down on the street forty stories below, while Lil told him, in the roundabout fashion she always used when speaking to her brother of Hubie, the son she adored, about Hubie's latest transgression. "I always thought people like that shot themselves."

"Laurance, how could you say such a dreadful thing about Hubie?" screamed Lil, like a tigress protecting her young. Lil, of course, didn't want Hubie to shoot himself, because she loved him in a way that she had never been able to love Justine, but she had always thought, when she and Laurance were growing up, that there was something noble when "people like that" did commit suicide, like Warkie Taylor, who hanged himself at Yale, and poor sweet Mungo Fitz Alyn, Dodo Fitz Alyn's uncle, who quietly slipped over the side of the *Queen Elizabeth* one midnight somewhere between New York and Southampton and wasn't missed for two days, after that terrible situation on board with the sailor who lied so at the inquiry.

"Now, calm down, Lil," said Laurance.

"Once the right girl comes along, Hubie will settle down and be just fine, Laurance. I guarantee it. Look how marvelously he's doing with his art gallery."

"Okay, Lil," said Laurance. "I'll make a couple of calls. Tell Hubie he's got to come in and see me."

"He won't, Laurance."

"If he wants to keep his name out of the newspapers, you tell him to come in."

"Yes, Laurance. Thank you, Laurance."

"Oh, and one thing, Lil. I want a little something in return."

"Of course, darling, anything," said Lil, gathering her bag and gloves and holding up her mink coat for her brother to help her put on.

"When the invitations go out for Justine's wedding, I want you to invite Mr. and Mrs. Elias Renthal. They live in Matilda's old apartment."

"You can't be serious, Laurance."

"I am serious, Lil."

"You mean that fat man with the powder-blue gabardine suits, and the big smelly cigars, and the wife who's trying to push herself onto every committee in New York? Not on your life. Justine's wedding is just for family and friends."

"Family, friends, and the Elias Renthals, Lil."

"But why?"

"Because I asked you to."

9

IT WAS AT the opening night of *Carmen* at the Metropolitan Opera, the new *Carmen*, straight from Paris, that everyone said was to be "too divine for words" and "full of surprises," that Loelia Manchester and Mickie Minardos made their first public appearance together since the word of their romance began to titillate New York society. Even then, observing propriety, they were not together as a couple, merely seated in the same box as members of an extremely fashionable group. Loelia arrived with Ezzie Fenwick, the society wit, who had often in the past few years served as her approved escort when Ned Manchester, tired after squash at the Racquet Club, began to beg off going out every night of the week with the artistic people that Loelia found so fascinating and Ned found so boring.

"Mickie Minardos?" gasped Lil Altemus, in her box, keeping her eyes averted from Loelia's box. "I don't believe it. It can't be true. I mean, Mickie's divine. Such a sense of fantasy. So amusing. And *such* a good dancer. Have you ever tangoed with Mickie, Matilda? To die. And the best possible fun on a weekend, or on someone's boat. But marriage? Loelia can't be thinking of marrying him. I mean, she just can't."

All eyes were riveted on Mickie's box. They called it Mickie's box, and Mickie played host, but they knew, those in the know, that it was Loelia who paid.

"Do stop staring up at their box, and, for God's sake, don't stare with your opera glasses," whispered Ruby Renthal to her husband Elias from their orchestra seats, although her fascination with the romance of Loelia Manchester and Mickie Minardos, if anything, exceeded her husband's.

"She's standing with her back to the audience, so she can't see me," said Elias.

"You sure?" asked Ruby.

"Unless she's got eyes in the back of her head," answered Elias.

"What's she wearing?"

"Pink."

"Long sleeves? High neck?"

"Yeah."

"That's a Nevel. I almost ordered that dress," said Ruby, wishing she had, imagining the furor it would cause if she and Loelia Manchester, whom everybody considered to be the best-dressed woman in New York society, turned up at the opera in the same Nevel dress.

"Who's that fat man staring up at us with his opera glasses?" asked Mickie Minardos, looking down from his box. Mickie Minardos had found fame and fortune as a designer of women's shoes, although his artistic talents, he and his acolytes believed, and none more fervently than Loelia Manchester, were scarcely tapped by his occupation. He could have been, they said about him, a stage designer, or a ballet designer, or, even, an opera designer, and his comments on the opera designs of that evening had been scathing, but amusing.

"He's called Elias Renthal," replied Ezzie Fenwick. "Worth a billion, I understand, at last count, and made it all in the last eight or nine years."

"Oh, and his wife is so pushy," said Loelia, not turning around to look. "Ruby she's called. They bought Matilda Clarke's apartment, and Cora Mandell's doing it up for them, and you should hear Cora's stories about them. Too funny."

"What's he like?" asked Mickie.

"He calls a dinner jacket a monkey suit," replied Ezzie.

"Oh, dear," said Loelia.

"But everything he touches turns to gold. He can't seem to get enough money. And they learn very quickly, those people," said Ezzie, who knew all there was to know about everybody.

"He's supposed to be a great art collector, courtesy of Maisie Verdurin, who guides his every move, and they're doing the apartment around the pictures, according to Cora," said Loelia.

"Elias Renthal has a great collection, but I most certainly don't think of him as a great collector," said Jamesey Crocus from his corner of the box, and they all turned to listen because Jamesey Crocus knew more about fine French furniture and art collecting than any man in New York. Although Jamesey was originally from Seattle, he spoke with an upper class British accent acquired during a year's training course at an auction house in London, and he claimed to have studied as the last pupil of Bernard Berenson at I Tatti in Florence. "He has probably thirty true masterpieces, and many fine lesser pictures, but you have to realize that he acquired the entire collection in a couple of years, and only buys pictures for specific locations in his apartment. A great collector never stops buying. And, besides, you can't take anyone seriously as a collector, no matter what masterpieces he has, if he also collects all those Steuben animals Elias has."

"How do you make so much money in such a short time?" asked Mickie Minardos.

"Airplane wheels first, somewhere out in Ohio. Then a hamburger franchise. The real money came from the takeover of Miranda Industries, where he is supposed to have cleared three billion in under two years," said Ezzie.

"Heavens!" said Loelia, and they all gasped at the amount of money. "But can that possibly be legal?"

"Anyone who acquires that much money in that short a time can't have done it legally. It's simply not possible, but that, whether we approve or not, is not our concern," said Jamesey Crocus, who was involved with fundraising. "Look what he's doing for the museum. What I like about Elias is that you can call him up and ask for six hundred thousand or seven hundred and fifty thousand dollars, or whatever it is you need, for an exhibit, or a purchase, and he simply gives it to you, or he doesn't. There's no board of directors that has to vote on it. He makes all his own decisions, and, of course, he's very generous. But, there's only X number of times you can do that with someone like Elias Renthal before he expects something in return."

"The problem with people like that is before long they want to come to dinner," said Loelia.

"And more," said Jamesey.

"Like what?"

"Like a position on our board at the museum."

"Oh, no. No, no, no," said Loelia. "That would never do. Too rough around the edges."

"Exactly," agreed Jamesey Crocus, nodding his head gravely.

"I play a certain amount of men's doubles," said Laurance Van Degan, from the back of the box, "but I've never played with anyone like Elias Renthal. The way that man plays tennis. To kill. I never saw anything like it."

"I'm told that's the way he conducts his business as well," said Jamesey.

"I'm dying to turn around and look at Mr. Renthal," said Loelia.

"Give me your opera glasses, Mickie. His wife stares at me at the hairdresser, and Bobo says however I wear my hair she wants the same thing."

"She looks pretty," said Mickie.

"She might be if only her nose were her own," said Loelia, staring back through her glasses at the Renthals. "Dr. Apted."

"Who?"

"Dr. Apted does those little turned-up noses where you can see right up the nostrils."

When the photographers from the social and fashion press began to descend on the closed doors of Dimitri Minardos's box during the intermission between the first and second acts, hoping to get a picture of Loelia Manchester and Mickie together, Loelia, always cooperative with the press because of her numerous charitable activities, came out and posed in animated conversation with Ezzie Fenwick, who loved to be photographed, but who was not the one they wanted to photograph, while Mickie remained inaccessible in his box.

Ezzie Fenwick was critical of everything. With so much free time on his hands, he was always the first to see the new films, new plays, new art shows, new musical events, new fashion collections, both in Paris and New York, and he could amuse at lunch and dinner parties with his witty critiques, because, quite frankly, he enjoyed watching failure.

"Simply ghastly!" he said, rolling his eyes in mock horror, about the *Carmen* that was being sung in front of them, and declared out loud that the role of Carmen was beyond, simply beyond, the vocal capabilities of the soprano at hand. During the second act, after the photographers had returned to the bar until the next intermission, Ezzie rallied the inhabitants of Loelia's box to sneak out, giggling, on tiptoe, to a marvelous party he knew about at the Rhinelander.

AFTER the opera, Ruby Renthal, disconsolate, sat at her tenthousand-dollar table on the promenade of the opera house and surveyed the empty table next to hers. With a promise to Janet Van Degan of a large donation by her husband to the Opera Guild, Ruby had secured a table strategically placed next to the table that was supposed to be occupied by Loelia Manchester and Dimitri Minardos and their friends, but they, alas, had fled.

"Elias, you're not supposed to wipe the plate clean with your dinner roll," whispered Ruby, irritably. "You're supposed to waste some of the food."

"I get hungry, Ruby," said Elias.

"I tell you what we're going to do. I'm going to have the cook feed you before we go out to these functions, and then you can pick at your food, like all these people do, when we sit down to dinner."

"I'll buy that," said Elias, reaching out to hold his wife's hand. Elias's bow tie was black on one side and red on the reverse, and, in the tying, the left half was black and the right half red. He seemed inordinately proud of it, as if he were dictating a new fashion.

"Honey, that bow tie has got to go," said Ruby.

"I just bought this tie," said Elias. "What's wrong with it?"

"It's the only two-tone bow tie here; that's what's wrong with it," she said.

"It's the latest thing, the guy in the shop told me," insisted Elias.

"The latest thing somewhere else, not here."

"But—"

"The invitation said black tie. It did not say half black, half red tie. If there's going to be a new fashion, we aren't in any position to be the ones setting it."

"Yet," said Elias.

"Yet," agreed Ruby, smiling at him. She looked back at the empty table next to her. "I wonder what happened to Mickie and Loelia."

10

"I THOUGHT I might get a little drunk if you don't mind. Or even if you do mind," said Hubie Altemus. "All this terribly good champagne just sitting here."

"Why did I think you weren't drinking?" asked Lil, looking at her son through the mirror of her dressing table. He looked back at her as he picked up a bottle of champagne from a silver tray and poured himself a glass. Lil bent her head and concentrated on fastening the clasp of a diamond and sapphire bracelet on her wrist.

"I really don't know why you thought that, Mother," answered Hubie.

"What's he called, that friend of yours from the gallery, with the Spanish name?"

"Juanito?"

"Yes, Juanito. I thought Juanito got you to stop drinking."

"He did. I'm on what's called a slip in some circles, in honor of the bride- and groom-to-be."

"You will behave in front of the family, won't you, Hubie?"

Hubie poured another glass of champagne, all the time looking at his mother.

"I really wish you'd worn a suit, Hubie. Not those damn jeans. And you're going to have to borrow a tie. With the whole family here, you simply can't dress like that. You know how Uncle Laurance gets."

Hubie laughed.

"What did Uncle Laurance say, Hubie?" asked Lil. "You did see Uncle Laurance today, didn't you?"

"He said I was a disgrace to the family. He said I had no consideration for you whatsoever. Stuff like that. He said that he always thought people like me shot themselves."

"He didn't say that!" said Lil.

"He said it was the last time, the very last, that he was going to get me out of trouble. He said from here on in he didn't give a flying fuck what I did."

"Really, Hubie. You know I can't bear that kind of talk."

"He's your brother, Mother. You asked me what he said, and I told you."

"You won't get in trouble again, will you, Hubie?" Lil looked up at her son. For an instant their eyes met, and then they both looked away. "Look, darling, let's just get through this damn party, and then we'll sit down and have a real talk."

"I'm not staying for the party, Mother," said Hubie.

"Of course you're staying for the party. We'll find you a tie. It's your own sister's engagement party. And your old mother needs all the moral support she can get."

"I can't stay."

"Fulco made this bracelet for me years ago with the stones from Granny B.B.'s tiara, but I never, not in thirty years, have been able to work this goddamn clasp. Fix it, will you, Hubie?" She held out her wrist to her son. "Why can't you stay? Don't you like Bernie Slatkin?"

"I like Bernie Slatkin fine. I just wish he was as gung-ho on this wedding as Justine is," said Hubie.

"What are you *talking* about?" asked Lil, waving her wrist in the air, waiting for Hubie to take it.

"Just what I said."

"Oh, don't be silly. He's *mad* about Justine."

"No, Justine's mad about him. It ain't the same thing."

"Push that bell for Lourdes, will you, Hubie? She'll find you a tie. There must be some in your old room. Or in the present drawer."

"Mother, I said I'm not staying for the party."

"But why?"

"I can't face all those fucking Van Degans," said Hubie. He picked up his mother's wrist and fastened the clasp for her.

"Even your grandfather is coming."

"That's what I mean. Grandfather Van Degan. Uncle Laurance. Aunt Janet. Young shitface Laurance and his dreary wife with her homemade dresses. I can't stand any of them. Except poor Dodo."

"There's the doorbell. People are beginning to arrive. Answer it, will you, Hubie?"

"That's what you keep a butler for, Mother. I'm going out the back way."

"Justine will be so disappointed."

"If anybody will understand, Justine will understand."

"You look tired, Hubie."

"I'm not sleeping well."

"You stay out too late. That's your problem."

"Not anymore."

"Don't you think you're getting too thin, Hubie?"

"Yeah, I do," he answered.

"We all love to be thin. 'You can't be too rich or too thin,' as the Duchess used to say to Mother, but there's a limit."

"Good-bye, Mother."

"YOU SHOULD understand something, Bernie," said Justine.

"What's that?" asked Bernie. They were standing in Lil's drawing room waiting for the guests to arrive, while Hubie was in with his mother.

"Sometimes my mother can be dreadful. Polite and charming, you know, but dreadful."

Bernie laughed. "I read my Edith Wharton. I know all about people like your mother."

Justine kissed Bernie on the cheek. It fascinated her that he was not intimidated by her family or her life. Bernie, with Lil or the other Van Degans, was always polite and charming, but he never backed down when disagreeable subjects, like politics and religion, came into the conversation. Once he even mocked the President and First Lady, fully aware that Lil and her friends revered and sometimes even entertained them, and, after the silence that followed, did not disagree when Uncle Laurance explained to the family that people in the media more often than not held liberal views.

"IT'S JUST one of my boring old migraines," said Lil Altemus to her father, Ormonde Van Degan, who, after his eightieth birthday almost four years ago, rarely ventured forth to any social event, much less a cocktail party. Lil lounged elegantly on a deep tufted red damask sofa at the far end of her massive drawing room overlooking Fifth Avenue during the whole of her cocktail party to announce Justine's engagement to Bernard Slatkin.

Once Ormonde Van Degan had commanded as much respect in banking, political, and social circles as his son Laurance presently commanded, but age had diminished his capabilities, and pity among Lil's and Laurance's friends and suppressed smiles among the next generation had taken the place of the awe he inspired in earlier times. As he shuffled through his daughter's drawing room, forgetful now, only Dodo Fitz Alyn seemed able to communicate with him. Dodo Fitz Alyn, a Van Degan poor relation and the object of family jokes, had the job of leading Ormonde Van Degan around the room in his walker to greet all the family members. Poor Dodo, as she was referred to behind her back, had long since abandoned hopes of marriage and ceased to care about weight or appearance. Her wispy hair was parted in the middle and pulled together behind her ears with a rubber band, or, on party occasions, like today, with a black ribbon.

"Dodo, dear, take Father around the room, will you?" said Lil, with effusive cordiality, as if she was speaking to a beloved nanny who had long served the family well, instead of a relation.

"I have taken him around the room, Lil," said Dodo.

"Tell him Matilda's coming," said Lil to Dodo, in front of her father, as if he were deaf and blind, rather than merely old. "He's always been so fond of Matilda, and he adored Sweetzer." With that instruction taken care of, Lil went back to her guests. It was not lost on any of them that it was Lil and not Justine who was the center of attention at Justine's engagement party. She held a glass of champagne, which was constantly replenished by her maid Lourdes, and lifted her cheek to be kissed by her old friends like Matilda Clarke and Mary Finch and Cora Mandell, and practically the whole of the Van Degan family.

"Dodo Fitz Alyn always leaves the chair seats warm when she gets up. Have you noticed?" asked Cora Mandell, when she lowered herself into a black Regency chair next to Lil's sofa that Dodo had just vacated.

"Poor Dodo," said Lil, rolling her eyes.

"Bernie's *so* attractive," said Mary Finch to Lil. "Lucky, lucky Justine. I was always *mad* about men with dimples in their chin. Who was that movie star who had the dimple? You know the one, in the picture about Africa, that one."

Bernard Slatkin watched the spectacle of the Van Degan family and their friends with an amused and remote smile. He stood near the piano, on the other side of the long room from Lil, talking and joking with Justine, often with his arm around her waist, and fulfilling his social obligations by chatting charmingly with each person that Justine introduced him to.

Loelia Manchester entered the party in a whirl of raspberry satin, on her way to another party. Mickie Minardos was not with her, as Lil Altemus's drawing room was practically home ground for Loelia and her estranged husband Ned. As always, people turned to look at Loelia, because of her clothes and because of her scandal. Thin beyond thin, fashionable beyond fashion, Loelia had taken to wearing her now very blond hair pulled back into a tiny knot, a style favored, people said, by Mickie Minardos, but a style deplored by the popular hairdressers of the city who feared, because of Loelia's influence in matters of taste and style, that it might become a rage. Loelia's eyes moved rapidly around the room, even as she was kissing relations and old friends on first one check and then the other, or greeting Justine, or being introduced to Bernie, not wanting, if possible, to have to come into contact with Ned Manchester, who would certainly be there.

"When you set the date, Justine, let me know immediately, and Mickie and I will give a little dinner for you and Bernie at the Rhinelander," said Loelia. "I'm so pleased to meet you, Bernie. I always watch you, and Mickie thinks you're the best, absolutely the best, of all the anchormen."

Every time Bernie received a compliment, on his work as an anchorman, or on his good looks, or both, Justine beamed with pride and moved even closer to her fiancé.

"Thank you, Mrs. Manchester," said Bernie, who seemed to be enjoying all the attention he was getting. "I'd like you to meet some of the gang from the news staff," and he pulled over his coanchorman and his weatherman to meet the glamorous Mrs. Manchester, whom they had all read about in the newspapers and magazines.

"Who's the little Chinese eating all the cheese puffs and talking to Dodo Fitz Alyn?" asked Cora Mandell, surveying the scene.

"Oh, Charlie *quelque chose*," answered Lil, rearranging the pillows behind her. "And don't say 'Chinese.' They get so upset. He's Korean, or Vietnamese, one of those. He's the weatherman on Bernie's show, and the other one, with the salt-and-pepper toupee and the drink in each hand, is Bernie's cohost, or coanchor, or whatever they call them."

"I've never seen poor Dodo so animated," said Cora.

Lil screened her lips with her left hand and said to Cora Mandell, "Whisper to Loelia that I told Ned not to come until after eight, so she can relax for an hour. Ned was thrilled to come late because it won't interfere with his squash game."

"Do you think it's true that Ned won't agree to give Loelia a divorce? It was in Dolly's column," said Cora.

"I know it's true," answered Lil, "but Ned is my cousin on the Altemus side, and I'm godmother to Charlotte, and I just can't take sides. I mean, what's happening to everyone these days? I suppose it'll be poor Dodo and the weatherman next."

"Lil, how sad you're not feeling well," said Loelia Manchester.

"Hello, Loelia. Kiss kiss."

"How exciting this must be for you, Lil," said Loelia. "Mickie thinks Bernie is just about the best of all the newscasters. When's the wedding going to be?"

"Too soon for this old mother to make all the proper arrangements," said Lil. "You look different, Loelia."

"How do you like my new face?" asked Loelia.

"I liked your old face, and I'm sure I'll get to like your new one," answered Lil. Loelia looked at Lil Altemus and decided to let the jibe pass.

"I want to say hello to Uncle Ormonde," she said, indicating with a little half wave to Lil that she would slip out without saying good-bye, like an experienced leavetaker who had another party to attend.

"I don't think she liked what you said," said Cora.

"Well, you know, since Mickie Minardos came into her life, Loelia's seeing all the New People in New York. She's moved on from us."

THE ELEVATOR door opened. "Big hug," said Loelia to Matilda Clarke in farewell and turned to get on the elevator. Getting out of it at the same time as Loelia was about to get on were Ned Manchester with Charlotte and Bozzie, Ned and Loelia's children. Ned and Loelia stared at each other. As always Ned's hair was wet, as if he had just showered after his afternoon game of squash. Loelia noticed that hardness had come into Ned's face and that his look showed cold dislike for her.

"Oh, hello, Ned," she said to her husband.

Ned, who had loved her so much for so long, nodded, shifted his eyes, and replied, "Hello." Loelia remembered once when his mother, Honoria, long dead, had replied to someone she disliked who had greeted her in a public place. "Hello," she replied. Nothing more. It was exactly the way her husband had greeted her.

Loelia turned away quickly, aware that her color was rising, as Ned passed by her into the entrance of Lil's apartment.

"You look lovely, Charlotte," she said to her daughter. She had forgotten her children would be invited to this family party. Charlotte passed her mother without speaking and hurried after her father.

"Bozzie," said Loelia.

"Hello, Mother," said Bozzie.

"How grown up you look," said Loelia. "And handsome, too." They looked at each other and smiled.

"Thank you for my birthday present, Mother," said Bozzie.

"I thought it would be perfect for Bermuda."

"It is."

"I hope the size was right."

"It was."

"I'm sorry I couldn't get to your party, but, you know, I was on the committee for the Opera Guild benefit that night, and—"

"It's all right."

"Charlotte didn't speak to me."

"Charlotte was afraid you might be here with Mr. Minardos, and she didn't want to see you with him," said Bozzie.

Loelia blushed.

Charlotte reappeared in the entry. "Bozzie, Daddy wants you to meet Uncle Ormonde Van Degan."

"Good-bye, Mother."

"Good-bye, Bozzie. Good-bye, Charlotte." Loelia stepped into the elevator and turned to look back to face her children.

"You look beautiful, Mother," said Bozzie. As the elevator door was closing, Loelia looked at Charlotte, who stared back at her mother without replying. Alone in the elevator, Loelia sank back against the mahogany-paneled wall and closed her eyes. Then she opened her eyes and turned around to face the elevator mirror, but there was no mirror.

"If I lived in this building, I would insist that there be a mirror in the elevator instead of all these wood walls," said Loelia to the elevator man.

"Yes, ma'am," said the elevator man.

Loelia opened her gold minaudier and took out a mirror and looked at herself. She wiped away a tear at the corner of her eye and pinched some color into her cheeks.

"Shall I ring for a taxi, ma'am?" asked the elevator man.

"What?"

"A taxi. Do you want me to ring for a taxi?"

"No, thank you. I have a car."

When the elevator door opened, Loelia pulled her raspberry satin coat with the sable collar and cuffs around her and walked through the lobby to the door. The doorman opened the door for her and she walked out under the canopy onto Fifth Avenue. A limousine that had been double parked pulled up to the entrance of the building. Before the driver could get out, the back door was opened by someone inside, and Loelia stepped quickly into the car. Mickie Minardos, in evening clothes, was seated there.

"Are you all right?" asked Mickie.

"Why do you ask that?" Loelia replied.

"I saw Ned and the children get out of a taxi and go in."

"Did they see you?"

"I don't know. I ducked down in the seat."

"It was awful. Ned didn't speak to me. Neither did Charlotte. Only Bozzie. It was awful."

"Do you want to skip the party and go back to the hotel?"

"No. I want to be occupied. I don't want to have to think. I'm desperate to get a bit inebriated."

"Are you sorry?"

"Sorry?"

"Sorry this has happened, between you and me?"

"No, I'm not sorry. I'm madly in love with you, Mickie Minardos."

"Even if you can't include me in your family gatherings?"

"Even if I can't include you in my family gatherings."

THE NEXT morning Bernie Slatkin read of his engagement to Justine Altemus in the *New York Times*. It said that the Van Degan family had been prominent in the affairs of the city—socially, politically, and in business—since the beginning of the century. It was the first time he knew that Justine was descended, not just from the Van Degans, but from the Rhinelanders and the Republican branch of the Whitbecks as well. He thought he'd better call his Aunt Hester and Uncle Sol Slatkin, in Weehawken, New Jersey, to tell them of his engagement before someone else told them first.

11

"MAISIE, will you explain to me why this horror I am looking at is a work of art?" asked Ruby Renthal, perplexed, as she stared up at the huge canvas. She had asked Maisie Verdurin to take her on a tour of the SoHo galleries on a Saturday afternoon.

"A horror! How can you say it's a horror?" asked Maisie Verdurin, aghast.

"All those broken cups and saucers stuck into that canvas. I don't understand why that is great art. I'm perfectly willing to learn, but you must explain it to me."

It interested Maisie that Ruby never pretended to like something that she didn't like, even if it was enjoying a great success. "I think perhaps Julian Schnabel is not your cup of tea," answered Maisie.

"Tell me what is then."

"Elias has developed a great fondness for Rubens and El Greco," said Maisie.

"I can't bear all those martyrs with blood coming out of their wounds hanging on my living room walls," said Ruby.

"I think the Impressionists, or the Post-Impressionists will be more to your liking," said Maisie. She was used to dealing with wives of rich men who needed pictures to hang on their walls. "You liked the Monet, remember."

"I liked the pink in the Monet. I'd rather put the money into jewelry myself," said Ruby.

"But people don't come to your house for dinner to see your jewelry. They see your jewelry when you go out. People come to your house for dinner to see your pictures, though," said Maisie. It was an argument she often used to explain to the wives of great financiers the social advantages of collecting art.

"Ah ha," answered Ruby, understanding immediately. More than anything, Elias wanted to be made a member of the board of directors of the museum and was anxious to develop a great collection as soon as possible. "No wonder everyone says you're the best at what you do, Maisie. Let's give some more thought to the Impressionists, or the Post-Impressionists."

12

CORA MANDELL, the fashionable decorator, knew everything about everyone in society and gossiped on to Ruby Renthal, who never got sick of hearing her stories, especially her stories about Loelia Manchester, whom Ruby admired more than any other woman, and whose friend she yearned to be. Ruby now knew, from Cora, that Loelia Manchester's brothers and their wives had sided with Ned Manchester and not Loelia in the approaching divorce, and that Fernanda Somerset, Loelia's mother, did not speak to Matilda Clarke, and had not for years, although Ruby did not yet know the reason. She felt a connection to the last bit of news, as Ruby was herself now the owner of Matilda Clarke's apartment, although she wished fervently that people would stop referring to it as the old Sweetzer Clarke apartment and begin to refer to it as the Elias Renthal apartment.

Ruby and Cora were seated facing each other in Elias Renthal's company jet. Between them the stewardess had set up a table for them to go over the revised floor plans for the new apartment. In tote bags on the floor beside Ruby were four Fabergé eggs that she had just bought at an estate sale in New Orleans, and a gold tea service that had once been given to the Empress Josephine as a wedding gift by the island of Martinique. Cora had said it was much too expensive when they saw it at an antiques shop on Bourbon Street, but Ruby had insisted it would be a perfect wedding present for Justine Altemus.

"Oh, are you going to the Altemus wedding?" asked Cora, hoping that the surprise she felt did not show in her voice.

"Yes," said Ruby.

"I didn't know you knew Lil Altemus."

"I don't."

"Justine, then."

"Not even Justine. I sat next to Bernie Slatkin at my first New York party, at Maisie Verdurin's."

"Oh, I see," said Cora, as if the problem was solved. "You're a friend of Bernie Slatkin's." That made more sense to Cora, who knew that Lil Altemus abhorred all the New People, and the Renthals could not be classified as anything other than New People.

"No, I'm not," answered Ruby. "I never saw him again after that night."

"Oh," said Cora, dying of curiosity, but she couldn't bring herself to ask Ruby how she had received an invitation.

"Elias and Laurance Van Degan do a great deal of business together," said Ruby, understanding what Cora was thinking.

"I see," said Cora. She did not say that Laurance Van Degan did business with a lot of people who would certainly not be getting an invitation.

"Go on with your story, Cora," said Ruby.

"Where was I?" asked Cora.

"Bitsy and Brassy," prompted Ruby.

"Oh, yes. Bitsy inherited all the money," said Cora. "She's gone off somewhere, I don't remember where. Antibes, I think. Someplace like that. The other sister is called Brassy. Actually she's a half-sister. She married Harry Kingswood, but they were divorced years ago. Her son by Harry died of a heroin overdose. Did I tell you that story? Awful. Brassy didn't marry again. They say she's a lesbian with one of the English duchesses, but I don't believe it. They both love horses. That's all. People are so quick these days to say that women are lesbians when they're just great friends."

Bitsy, Brassy, Harry, dykes. Ruby closed her eyes to store all this information. She always wanted to take notes when Cora told her stories, so she could repeat them all to Elias, who was as interested as she was, although he sometimes missed the point, the way he did when she told him about the marriage of Justine Altemus's aunt, Grace Gardiner, who had had, according to Cora, *a mariage blanc, and a very happy mariage blanc,*" until the death of Winkie Gardiner.

"What the hell is a *mariage blanc?*" Elias had asked Ruby, giving the words the exaggerated pronunciation he always gave to foreign words, which embarrassed him to speak.

"A marriage of companionship, friendship, that sort of thing," Ruby had answered, in her explaining voice, giving Elias the same explanation Cora had given her when she asked the same question.

"You mean, no fucking? Is that what you're trying to say?" Elias had said.

"Oh, Elias," Ruby had replied in an exasperated voice.

All this time Ruby had been perusing the revised floor plans of her apartment on the table between them. She knew that if her apartment ever got finished, it would be the most discussed apartment in New York, but it drove her mad that everything took so long to complete, especially when she was willing to spend any amount of money to speed things along. She could never say to Cora, who had just told her that a fringe she had ordered from Paris for the window hangings in her persimmon drawing room would not arrive for another six weeks, that she felt her New York life could not begin until she was in her grand apartment, receiving all the people she was only hearing about and reading about and watching from afar.

"Where's my bidet in this bathroom?" asked Ruby Renthal, changing the subject, as something caught her eye on the floor plans.

"Oh, there's not going to be a bidet in that bathroom," answered Cora Mandell.

"Who said there's not going to be a bidet in that bathroom?" asked Ruby.

"Elias said he only wanted to spend thirty thousand doing over that bathroom, and it would cost an additional ten to remove the tiles to put the bidet in, so we decided to dispense with the bidet," said Cora.

"Let me get this straight," said Ruby, slowly and carefully, drumming her long red fingernails on the floor plan. "You made the decision that I wasn't going to have a bidet. Is that correct?"

"No, Ruby, I didn't make the decision," replied Cora evenly. "It was Elias who said he didn't want to spend—"

"Never mind about Elias," snapped Ruby, who was really annoyed about the six-week delay of the French fringe. "The bottom line is that you made the decision that I wasn't to have a bidet. Is that it?"

Cora Mandell began to finger her three strands of pearls as she stared back at the beautiful young woman with the beautiful jewelry who was behaving in a manner Cora would have described as ungracious. "It was not a decision I made by myself, Mrs. Renthal," Cora said, aware that her shift from first name to formal address was not lost on Ruby. "It was after I showed the plans to your husband at his office that the decision was arrived at."

"Fine," said Ruby. She began folding the floor plans and then pushed them away from her to Cora for Cora to fold. "I don't care how much it costs to remove the tiles, Mrs. Mandell. I want a bidet in that bathroom. I'm going to have a bidet in that bathroom, and don't bring up the matter to me again."

If Ruby Renthal could have read the thoughts of the distinguished older woman, who had decorated all the Van Degan, Manchester, and Altemus houses, she would have read, "I've seen these people come, and I've seen these people go," but she could not read Cora Mandell's thoughts, and Cora Mandell was not the type to make known such thoughts.

"Of course, Mrs. Renthal," said Cora, folding the plans and putting them in the bag where she carried her needlework.

"One other thing," said Ruby.

"No, there's no one-other-thing, Mrs. Renthal," said Cora, rising from her place and moving toward another seat in the back of the empty plane.

"And what is that supposed to mean?" asked Ruby. Looking after the retreating figure, she was instantly aware that she had offended her one precarious link to the world of Loelia Manchester and Lil Altemus.

"Your next decorator can deal with whatever your one-other-thing is," said Cora, seating herself. She reached into her bag and brought forth a copy of Nestor Calder's book, *Judas Was a Redhead,* and proceeded to read.

"I don't want another decorator, Cora. I want you. After all these months, we can't stop now. Think of the delays, just trying to get to know someone else. And there's the Orromeo auction coming up in Paris. You promised you'd go with me. Besides, you're the best. The very best. Everyone says so. Forgive me if I appeared rude. I have the curse, you know, and every time I get my period, I don't behave well. Just ask Elias. He'll tell you. Please don't go, Cora. Please. There's the big party that Elias and I are giving, and we have to have the apartment finished by the party. Please."

"YOU KNOW, poor Ruby hates me to smoke cigars," said Elias. "So she's fixing up this room for me to smoke in to my heart's content. I think it's called a fumary, or some goddamn fancy name like that."

Ruby had made a rule that no one would get in to see the new apartment until Cora Mandell had finished all the decorating, but

Elias took advantage of Ruby's being out of town on a shopping trip with Cora to bring a young man called Byron Macumber from the law firm of Weldon & Stinchfield up to the new place and give him a tour. It was, he thought, a safer place for a first meeting than a restaurant, or even a coffee shop, where he might run into someone he knew.

Byron Macumber, thirty-four, was dressed in a bankers' gray suit, with a blue shirt and dark red tie. Looking around at the unfinished rooms, he was dazzled by the magnificence of the Renthal apartment.

"I'd love to bring my wife here sometime, after you all get moved in," he said, showing the trace of a Georgia accent.

"I'm sure in time that could be arranged, Byron," said Elias.

"She would drop dead seeing a place like this."

"Do you have children?"

"Two little girls. Kimberly, three, and Sharon, one."

"Where do you live, Byron?"

"We have a condominium in Bronxville, but one day, if I ever strike it rich, I'd like to build a house on the water in Fairfield, or Darien, or someplace like this," said Byron.

"And have a tennis court and a swimming pool. Right?"

"Something like that," said Byron, laughing.

"For the arrangement I have in mind, Byron, there would be nothing risky. All that you would have to do is identify certain companies that retain Weldon and Stinchfield for protection from the predators, not to mention guys like me."

Byron Macumber, nervous at being in such an intimate conversation with a man of Elias Renthal's wealth, took out a handkerchief from his pocket and wiped his forehead, at the same time nodding an acknowledgment that he understood Elias's request.

"Timing is everything, you see," continued Elias, as if he were giving a lecture in finance. "I want to get into situations so early that my activities couldn't possibly attract attention from," he paused, and shrugged, and then finished his sentence, "whomever."

In the room that would be Elias's smoking room when the apartment was finished was an antique pool table that had recently arrived from England. Byron Macumber rubbed his hand across the mahogany of the table and the faded green felt.

"This is beautiful," he said.

"Used to belong to Edward the Seventh," said Elias. "That's the original felt."

"Beautiful," repeated Byron.

"It'll happen to you too," said Elias, meaning possessions. "Whatever profit I make on a tip you give me, I will pay you five percent. Five percent, paid in cash, on, say, eighty thousand shares of Tennessee Natural Gas, is a very handsome amount of money. Enough to have a nanny for your kids and pay her for a year, and to take your wife on a nice vacation to Mustique, and maybe even buy her a mink coat for Christmas. And that's only one tip."

"Holy smoke," said Byron Macumber.

13

AS THE wedding day approached, with the heightened activity that surrounded the coming event, Lil Altemus's enthusiasm for Justine's marriage increased, or, to be more exact, her enthusiasm for the wedding increased, while her enthusiasm for the marriage remained tepid, as she was of the school that firmly believed in what her own mother used to call marrying your own kind.

The nuptials were frequently mentioned in the social columns of Dolly De Longpre and Florian Gray, when friends of Justine's gave dinners and cocktail parties, most of which, but not all, Lil attended. She chose to have a headache on the night of Violet Bastedo's dinner, and did have a "nasty cold" on the night Bernie's Aunt Hester and Uncle Sol entertained a small group of Bernie's relations and friends from the television station in a favorite steak house of Bernie's. She attended all the Van Degan family celebrations and most of the parties given by her friends, like Loelia Manchester's dinner at the Rhinelander, and the old friends of Justine from school and debutante days.

She took a particular interest in the wedding gifts as they began to pour in, judging each one accordingly. Grandfather Van Degan sent gold candlesticks, and Uncle Laurance and Aunt Janet Van Degan personally dropped off a tiny Renoir, "marvelously framed," as Lil was the first to point out, from their own collection. Pearls came from Aunt Minnie Willoughby, who said she saw no point in waiting until she died to leave them to Justine, and Lil's great friends the Todescos, with whom she always stayed in Rome, sent a Chinese export vase that Lil explained to Bernie was of museum quality. Pieces of silver in vast quantity, old and new, large and small, ornate and plain, came from cousins and friends, as well as from business associates of Bernie's. From Justine's father, whom Lil never saw again after her divorce and his unfortunate second marriage, came a vermeil clock that Lil recognized as having belonged to his mother. Hubie sent something frightfully modern, as Lil described it, from his art gallery in SoHo, which Lil asked Justine to pretend to like, and Lil herself, after much deliberation, decided to give Justine an

Aubusson carpet that had been in storage since she gave up the house in Newport, after Hubie's unfortunate incident with the lifeguard at Bailey's Beach, as well as the diamond-and-sapphire bracelet with the clasp that never worked that Fulco de Verdura had made for her from her Granny B.B.'s old tiara.

Bridesmaids were something of a problem for a girl of Justine's age. The friends of her school and debutante years were all long married and having their second and even third child by this time. The thought of all married bridesmaids only pointed out the lateness of Justine's journey to the altar, and the notion of pregnant bridesmaids was abhorrent to Lil. On one thing both mother and daughter, who rarely agreed, agreed totally. No matter what pressure was brought by the family, Dodo Fitz Alyn, poor Dodo, the poor relation, would not, absolutely would not, waddle up the aisle in the bridal party. Of all people, Lourdes, Lil's maid Lourdes, came up with the idea of having only children as attendants, and the idea thrilled Lil. There were several Van Degan nieces, she pointed out to Justine, and little Nina Willoughby, and Violet Bastedo's daughter, and the Trefusis twins. "It will be divine, and so chic, little taffeta dresses, like shepherdesses," said Lil. "They could even carry crooks, and Lorenza could do something marvelous with trailing ivy and rosebuds." Lil, who loved to organize, was in heaven.

"Justine," she said, in a voice that Justine recognized as a prelude to a request.

"Yes, Mother," replied Justine, who seemed to lose all the wedding decisions.

"I think Herkie Saybrook should be an usher," said Lil.

"Herkie Saybrook, Mother? Bernie doesn't even know Herkie Saybrook. A groom can't have an usher he doesn't even know."

"There has to be someone from our side who knows who all our friends are. You can't expect that Chinese weatherman, excuse me, Korean, to know where to seat Aunt Minnie Willoughby and the Todescos."

"Hubie knows who all the family are, Mother," said Justine.

"Hubie is not an usher. Hubie is going to take me down the aisle and sit with me. I am most certainly not going to sit with your father."

"Hubie can take you down the aisle, sit with you, and still be an usher, Mother."

"Will you please just talk to Bernie about Herkie? For me? For your mother, Justine?" asked Lil.

The tension between mother and daughter was broken when Lourdes walked into the room carrying another wedding present.

"Oh, heaven," cried Lil, clapping her hands, which she did each time a new present arrived.

"Look how beautifully wrapped this box is, Mrs. Altemus," said Lourdes. "Save me the paper and ribbons."

"Who's it from?" asked Lil, still in bed with a breakfast tray.

"Young Laurance and Laura Van Degan," said Justine, reading the card.

"Good wrapping, cheap gift, wait and see," said Lil, sipping her hot water and lemon juice.

"Oh, Mother," said Justine, tearing apart the white satin ribbons and gold and white paper.

"They're so tight. They sent Baba Timson a lucite paperweight, after Baba had lent them her house in Barbados for their honeymoon. Save all those ribbons and wrappings for Lourdes. God knows what she does with them. Where's it from?"

"Scully and Scully," said Justine.

"Don't tell me, let me guess," said Lil, holding her hand over her eyes. "A wastebasket with a horse print by Stubbs."

"Wrong," said Justine.

"A white bamboo breakfast tray with a place for the *New York Times*."

"Wrong again," said Justine.

"Five dinner plates from your Morning Glory pattern."

"A cut-glass vase," said Justine, holding it up.

"I knew it. I knew they wouldn't spend over sixty dollars," said Lil. "The Van Degans are all the same. Let me see it."

Justine handed the vase to her mother.

"Not bad," said Lil, handing it to Lourdes.

"It'll be marvelous for anemones," said Justine.

14

GUS BAILEY, working at his computer, heard the telephone ring several times before he remembered he had forgotten to put on his message machine.

"Hello?"

"Is that Gus Bailey?"

"Yes."

"It's Ceil Somerset. Do you remember me?"

"Yes," he answered, but he didn't actually remember. She had the fashionable voice of someone he had probably been introduced to at a fashionable party, and he knew before the conversation began that she was going to invite him to another fashionable party, probably as a last minute fill-in.

"We met at Justine Altemus's engagement party," said Ceil Somerset.

"Oh, yes," replied Gus. He still didn't remember, but it didn't matter. If he was free, he would go. It interested him to see how the various groups of New York overlapped.

"I was the one who loved your article about the movie star who gave up booze."

"Oh, yes." Gus was fifty by the time people started to recognize him by name, and even face, and it never ceased to amaze him.

"Are you still writing about that ghastly gigolo who took all that old lady's money?"

"Yes, I am. I thought this call might be he. He hasn't shown up for the last two appointments I had with him."

"You can't trust people like that, Gus. You should know that by now."

Gus laughed. "What can I do for you?"

"I'm Loelia Manchester's sister-in-law. My husband's her brother."

"Yes."

"You're not by any chance free for dinner tonight, are you? I know this is terribly last minute, but, you see, someone's dropped out, and I'm having a dinner before Mary Finch's dance for Justine Altemus and Bernie Slatkin, and Justine said you were coming to the dance, so I wondered if maybe you'd like to come to dinner." She talked very fast, as if she thought he would be offended at being asked so late.

"Sure," said Gus.

"You would?" She sounded amazed that he had accepted. "Oh, you are divine. Eight o'clock. Our apartment's too small, so we're giving it at my mother-in-law's. Do you know where she lives?"

"No."

"The same building as Lil Altemus."

"YOU'RE over here, Gus, next to me," called out Lil Altemus, patting the needlepoint seat of a Chippendale chair, when she saw Gus make a late entrance into the dining room, after being shown through the apartment by Ceil Somerset's mother-in-law, Fernanda Somerset. Gus was overwhelmed by the art on the walls, and Fernanda Somerset, who was also the mother of Loelia Manchester, was always keen on showing off to an interested guest the masterpieces that her late husband, who had a taste for art and a lust for the gentlemanly sport of collecting, had amassed and that her own children and their friends simply took for granted. Fernanda Somerset was known to be dismayed and distressed over her daughter's liaison with Dimitri Minardos, the shoe designer, whom she considered totally inappropriate for her daughter, but she kept her opinions on the matter to herself. When Gus excused himself to go into dinner, Fernanda retired to her room, as she was not a member of the party going on that evening.

"I hear you've been getting the grand tour from Fernanda," said Lil, when Gus was seated.

"And grand is the right word," said Gus, sitting down, after giving Lil a kiss on the cheek. "That's what's called a collection."

"All going to the museum when Fernanda dies," said Lil.

"She told me that."

"Did she tell you about Mr. Renthal's offer?" asked Lil.

"Elias Renthal? No."

"He offered to buy the entire collection, can you imagine? 'Name your price,' he said. Or had Mrs. Verdurin say for him. To furnish his new apartment," said Lil.

She gave a sharp little laugh, her Lil laugh, her children called it, a sort of intake of breath that sounded a bit like a cultured snort, although, according to Janet Van Degan, it would have been better named her Van Degan laugh, for both Lil's mother and her grandmother had had the same laugh when they were amused by the pretensions of the New People. "Too funny, really," she finished by saying. Lil looked around her at the dining room and the people in it. This was her kind of life. These were her kind of people.

"I didn't see Justine and Bernie."

"Bernie had to work at the last minute, and Justine wouldn't come without him. We'll meet up with them later at Mary's dance."

"Congratulations on Justine's engagement."

No words of disapproval for her daughter's choice of partner passed Lil Altemus's lips, but her wry smile, her weary shrug, and her look of forebearance conveyed her feelings more than any expressed thoughts ever would.

"He's charming," said Lil cautiously. "Not one of us, of course, but charming."

Gus laughed. It amused him when she said *not one of us* to him, as if he were. "Neither am I," he said.

"Neither are you what?"

"One of you."

"But you're not going to marry my daughter," she replied.

"I know Bernie," said Gus. "I like him."

"On TV, you mean?"

"On TV, yes, but in life too. I see him at Maisie Verdurin's parties."

"Awfully good looking. I'll say that for him," conceded Lil.

"Far more than good looking, Lil," said Gus. "He's a very successful young man. He earns a fortune. He's working. That's more than most of the guys do whom Justine could have married. People say he'll get the top spot one of these days."

"You sound just like Justine. That's what she keeps saying." Lil gave a little dismissive laugh. Earned money, no matter how abundant, never impressed Lil Altemus the way inherited money did. Then, not unexpectedly, she mouthed but did not speak the word *Jewish*.

In the several years Gus Bailey had known Lil Altemus, he had seen her, in other circumstances, about other people, mouth but not speak other words in explanation of their identities: *Cancer*, she once mouthed about Honoria Manchester. Or, *Adopted*, about Dodo Fitz Alyn. Or, *Alcoholic*, about Sweetzer Clarke. Or, *Lesbian*, about Nan Timson.

A young man on the other side of Lil cleared his throat to get Lil's attention, in order to resume a story he had been telling her when Gus came to the table.

"Laurance has been telling us the most fascinating story," said Lil. "Do you know my nephew, Laurance Van Degan? Gus Bailey. And Maude, you know, don't you? Maude Hoare?"

Sure of himself, bespectacled, balding too early, Laurance Van Degan, whom everyone in the family called young Laurance, acknowledged Lil's introduction of Gus without absorbing his name, eager to continue with his story. Lil often wished that her son Hubie was more like her nephew, who fit in, who continued on in the things that had made the family famous, or even that her son and her nephew were friends, which they never had been. "There's a man called Elias Renthal," said Laurance Van Degan, in explanation to Gus about the subject of his story, as if Gus would have no idea who Elias Renthal was. Young Van Degan, like a lot of the group at Ceil Somerset's who thought of themselves, without actually putting it into words, as old New York, had strong feelings about Elias Renthal and his manner of conducting business.

"You see the Renthals everywhere these days," he continued. "They were at the opera the other night, with Constantine de Rham, and that woman he is always seen with, Mrs. Lupescu, who was wearing white fur and far too many diamonds."

"She's ghastly, that woman," said Lil.

"Renthal is apparently an old friend of Constantine de Rham," continued Van Degan.

"Doesn't that tell you a lot?" said Lil, who still had not been able to bring herself to tell anyone that the Renthals were coming to her daughter's wedding.

"Hear me out, Aunt Lil," said her nephew, who didn't like to be interrupted. "Mrs. Renthal, however, who's on the make, as everyone knows, didn't enjoy being seen in public with de Rham and his girlfriend, and she and Elias had a few words during the first act, and the people around them kept shushing them up."

A waiter from the catering service brought in to supplement the

Somerset staff nodded a greeting to Gus over Lil Altemus's head while she took asparagus from a silver platter he held for her.

"Oh, hi," said Gus in return to the waiter.

"But that was nothing," continued Laurance Van Degan with his story. "You won't believe what happened. During the second act, when Montserrat Caballe was singing her *Vissi d'Arte*, more beautifully than I've ever heard it sung, incidentally, one of Mrs. Lupescu's diamond earrings fell with a great clunk to the floor of the Metropolitan."

"No," cried Lil.

"Oh, yes, and both she and de Rham got right down on the floor to look for it, first things first, right in the middle of the aria, and even lit a match to aid their search."

"Extraordinary," said Lil.

"Laura and I were there with Mother. You can imagine Mother's reaction, Aunt Lil. She insisted they halt their search until the end of the act when the house lights came on."

"Good for Janet," said Lil.

"Mrs. Renthal is trying to get on Mother's opera committee, and she was so embarrassed that Mother saw her with de Rham and Mrs. Lupescu that she took off, and, of course, Elias had to follow her. He's a bad apple, de Rham."

"Consuelo was one of my best friends," said Lil, shaking her head.

"Bad apple, how?" asked Gus, entering the conversation for the first time.

"Owes money everywhere. Rents out that house he inherited from Consuelo for all sorts of purposes, they say. Herkie Saybrook says if he ever wanted to have someone taken care of, he'd go to Constantine de Rham."

"No," said Lil, in disbelief.

"I don't mean to imply he'd do anything himself, but he would know exactly the person to go to to have it done."

"What exactly do you mean?" persisted Gus.

"Just what I said," replied young Laurance Van Degan, who then turned to speak to Maude Hoare on his other side.

On the other side of Gus sat a young woman who did not seem to know anyone at the party but acted perfectly content to watch it without participating. When Gus turned to speak to her, he found that she was staring at him. He picked up her place card and saw that her name was Inez Peretti.

"Are you a friend of Justine's?" asked Gus, trying to find an opening for conversation.

"I've never met Justine," replied Inez Peretti.

"Bernie then. Are you a friend of Bernie's from the television station?" asked Gus again.

"I've never met Bernie either. I don't even know his last name, just that he's going to marry Justine Altemus," said Inez.

Gus, curious, framed his next question.

"I'm Ceil Somerset's psychic," she said in explanation to Gus, who had been about to ask her what her connection was to all these people, and Gus laughed that she had anticipated his question.

"Ah, a psychic. How interesting."

"Have you ever been to one?"

"In California. Not here. Do you make house calls?" asked Gus, making conversation.

"I prefer not to."

"Where do you live?"

"Sullivan Street. Do you know where that is?"

"Off Houston. Right?"

"Right. Most of these friends of Ceil's think it's in Tasmania, or someplace equally remote. That Mrs. Lupescu, Mr. Van Degan was just talking about. She got my name from someone and called for an appointment, but when she heard where I lived, she canceled, saying she never went below Fiftieth Street. She said Saks Fifth Avenue was her downtown limit."

Gus laughed. "That sounds like the sort of thing Mrs. Lupescu would say, from what I gather about Mrs. Lupescu," he said.

"You're going somewhere tonight, aren't you?" asked Inez Peretti.

Gus looked at her. "Mary Finch's dance for Justine and Bernie," replied Gus, cautiously.

Inez Peretti ignored his evasive answer. "Before that, I mean."

Gus continued to stare at her.

"Whatever it is you're planning on doing, don't," she said. Their eyes met for an instant. Gus picked up Inez's place card again.

"Next you're going to ask me for my telephone number," said Inez, smiling.

"Right," replied Gus, and he wrote it down on the place card when she gave it to him, then put the card in the pocket of his dinner jacket.

Laura Van Degan appeared behind young Laurance and put her hand on his shoulder. He looked up at Laura and smiled. She wore no makeup, a plain evening dress, and her uncoiffured hair, straight with bangs, hung like a schoolgirl's to her shoulders. Ruby Renthal would have said, had she been present to make the comment, that you had to be as rich and as entrenched as the Van Degans to appear at a party dressed like that. Laurance, however, seemed delighted with her. "Time?" he asked.

"Yes, darling," she replied.

"Laura's still breastfeeding the new baby," explained Laurance to Lil. "We're going on home, and we'll meet up with you later at Mary's."

"Little Janet is so excited about being a bridesmaid for Justine, Lil. You just can't imagine," said Laura.

"You're missing all this delicious coconut ice cream," said Lil, spooning out some from the silver bowl the waiter held.

"My favorite thing," said Gus, when the waiter held the bowl for him to take some.

"There's rum in the coconut ice cream, Gus," whispered the same waiter who had spoken to Gus earlier. Gus looked longingly at his favorite dessert and declined with a shake of his head.

"Who's your friend the waiter?" asked Lil.

"Someone I know from A.A.," said Gus.

"That reminds me, Evangeline Simpson's drinking again," said Lil.

"Do you suppose Constantine de Rham will be at Mary Finch's dance tonight?" asked Gus.

"Not likely," answered Lil.

"But they're the couple of the season, it seems," said Gus.

"Maybe at Maisie Verdurin's, and at Clarence's, and all those places you frequent, Gus, but not in this crowd," answered Lil, waving her hand to indicate the thirty-two guests in the Somerset dining room. "I think everyone's moving on to Mary's. Do you want a ride? My car's downstairs."

"No, thank you, Lil. I'll meet you there. I have to make another stop first."

"That's what Matilda always says about you."

"What does Matilda always say about me?"

"That you're always going somewhere mysterious."

IF CONSTANTINE DE RHAM thought it strange that he should be receiving a call at ten o'clock at night from a man who had refused to speak to him at Maisie Verdurin's parties, he gave no such indication. Gus Bailey was surprised that he answered his own door, although a butler of advanced age hovered disagreeably in the background, as if his duties of door opener had been usurped. Later, Gus remembered that de Rham wore velvet slippers with the initials *C de R* elaborately intertwined in gold and a smoking jacket of dark green velvet, but at that moment, standing outside in the rain on Sutton Place, looking into what had once been Consuelo Harcourt de Rham's house, he was aware only of the marble stairway behind Constantine, down which Consuelo had fallen two years earlier, and the black-and-white marble floor on which she had landed.

"My name is Augustus Bailey," began Gus.

"Yes, I know who you are," answered Constantine. "You refused to shake my hand at Maisie Verdurin's party."

Gus, having come as a supplicant, blushed.

"I remember slights. Even averted eyes are recorded in my computer up here," Constantine said, pointing to his head. He stared at Gus, cold and wet, standing in the street under an umbrella, as if he enjoyed the feeling of power he possessed by not immediately giving him entrance. "My inclination is to slam the door in your face, but curiosity overrides that desire. Come in."

Gus passed him and walked into the house.

"Give your wet things to Ramon," he said, as Gus took off his coat. The butler gathered up Gus's umbrella and coat, soaking the front of his white jacket in the process.

"The Filipinos, they say, are an intelligent race, but my butler is an exception to the rule," said de Rham, in front of the butler. "Don't put those wet things on the upholstered bench, Ramon. Take them into the kitchen."

Gus turned to a mirror and readjusted his black tie, which had become crushed under his coat.

"You are either coming from or on your way to Mary Finch's dance for Justine Altemus and Mr. Slatkin," said de Rham, observing Gus's dinner jacket and black patent-leather pumps.

"On my way to," replied Gus.

"Wouldn't you love to have been a fly on the wall when Justine told Lil she was going to marry Mr. Slatkin? Or perhaps you were, Mr. Bailey. A fly on the wall, that is."

"No, I wasn't, Mr. de Rham."

"With one of your magazine articles?"

"No."

"I'm sure Mr. Slatkin wasn't quite what Lil had in mind for Justine. I rather think her hopes were higher."

It had not occurred to Gus, in his anticipatory thoughts about his night visit, that Constantine de Rham would gossip with him about an approaching society wedding. From another room, the sounds of a television drama could be heard.

"Yvonne is watching *Dynasty*," explained Constantine, with a tolerant smile. He pronounced *dynasty* "dinasty" in the British manner and indicated with a head gesture that Gus should follow him. They walked down a hallway into Constantine's den, and Constantine closed the door behind them.

On one dark red wall, over a deep tufted sofa piled high with damask and tapestry pillows, was a large painting of a stag being torn apart by hounds. On another Gus's eye was drawn to a bookcase full of tall slender volumes, bound in red Moroccan leather with gold lettering, that appeared to be privately printed: aristocratic biographies of aristocratic de Rhams: Casimir, Stanislaus, Edouard, and Thierry, the revered ancestors that Constantine claimed as his own. "The guillotine played havoc with my family during the Terror," de Rham said, watching Gus look at the books, "but enough members survived to perpetuate the name and reclaim the estates."

Gus turned from the books and looked up into the eyes of the tall man whose gaze was boring into him, daring him to disbelieve his ancestral claims. In the close quarters of the den a scent of not-quite-fresh perspiration clouded the air. It occurred to Gus that perhaps Constantine de Rham was not an everyday bather. Inwardly Gus asked himself why he was in this man's house, on this rainy night, and for an instant he considered flight. Instead, needing him, he fought his distaste and admired the elegant French desk behind which de Rham seated himself. The desk was, de Rham explained, signed by Boulle. He passed his long fingers lovingly over its highly polished ormolu-encrusted surface.

"But surely you have not delayed going to Mary Finch's dance to come crosstown on a rainy night to discuss a Boulle desk," said de Rham.

"No."

De Rham rose and pulled the velvet curtains closed on the two windows behind his desk. When he turned around, he made a show of surprise, by raising his eyebrows, that Gus had already seated himself, as if he had expected him to remain standing until he had been invited to sit.

"No, not there. Sit in the Regency chair," Constantine said, pointing to a black lacquer chair with a cane seat that looked considerably less comfortable than the club chair that Gus had chosen. "I can see you better there."

Gus complied, understanding that Constantine needed to be in charge.

"Now, how can I help you, Mr. Bailey?" asked de Rham.

"There is a man who will be coming up for release from prison," began Gus, cautiously.

Constantine de Rham again raised his eyebrows, in an exaggerated grimace of amazement. "Yes?"

"I would like to have this man followed."

"I find it utterly extraordinary that you should come to see me on such a matter."

"I was told that you knew people who could lead one to other people who performed such services."

"Am I supposed to feel flattered by such a reputation?"

"Please let me finish."

De Rham shrugged, as if the matter were of complete indifference to him.

"I want this man followed," Gus repeated.

"You've already said that."

Gus, sweating a bit, wished he had not come.

"Starting when?" asked Constantine, surprisingly.

"From the day of his release."

"Where is the prison?"

"California."

"Where in California?"

"Vacaville."

"How long will you want him followed?"

"Indefinitely."

"That sort of thing can prove very expensive."

"I don't care."

"Have you thought of the police?"

"I don't want the police."

"Perhaps a private detective would be more what you wanted."

"I don't want a private detective either."

"Is it possible you have something more in mind than merely following him?"

"Perhaps."

"That sort of thing can be arranged from within."

"I don't want it to be arranged from within," said Gus.

"What is the name of this man who haunts you, Mr. Bailey?"

"I didn't say he haunted me, Mr. de Rham."

"You didn't have to, Mr. Bailey. I know an obsession when I see one."

Gus laughed. "Hardly an obsession."

"Hmm." Constantine de Rham folded his arms and waited for Gus to answer.

"Flint. Francis Flint. He is called Lefty Flint," said Gus, quietly, but a movement of his shoulders belied the sound of his voice.

"Even the sound of Mr. Flint's name seems to upset you, Mr. Bailey."

Gus looked at Constantine for a moment.

"What has this man done to you?"

Gus shook his head and waved his hands to indicate that he did not wish to discuss the matter.

Constantine watched him and then rose and walked toward the window. He pushed back the red velvet curtain he had just closed and looked out at the rain coming down on Sutton Place.

"I think I know someone who might be able to lead you to someone, as you put it."

Constantine de Rham unlocked a drawer of the Boulle desk and withdrew a worn leather address book that he carried to the sofa, settling himself. As he slowly looked through the pages, he seemed interested only in a piece of skin on his thumb, which he tried first to twist off and then to bite off.

Yvonne Lupescu opened the door and entered without knocking. Her satin-and-lace negligee revealed the cleavage between her breasts.

"Finally Alexis Carrington has gotten her come-uppance!" she said, referring to the television series she had been watching. Both men turned to look at her, and she turned from Constantine to Gus, as if she had been unaware of his presence. "But, Constantine, I didn't know you had a guest," she cried, crossing her hands modestly over her breasts.

Gus rose to his feet. It was the first time that he had seen Yvonne Lupescu with her blond hair hanging loosely about her shoulders. They looked at each other.

"An unexpected visit, my dear, at this late hour. Mr. Bailey. Baroness Lupescu," he said, making an introduction. "You remember, Yvonne. Mr. Bailey was not friendly toward us at Maisie's parties."

"Yes, yes, I remember. He and Matilda Clarke were speculating about me across the table," said Yvonne.

Again Gus blushed.

"Ah, look at him, Constantine. He blushes. How smart you look, Mr. Bailey. Now let me guess: you're going on to Mary Finch's dance," said Yvonne playfully.

"Correct."

"Of course, we weren't invited."

"I've explained that to Mr. Bailey."

"I don't know Mr. Bailey's first name, Constantine."

"It's Augustus," said Gus.

"And, of course, they call you Gus. Or is it Gussy?"

"Gus."

"That's what I'm going to call you. Now, Gus, before you go off to Mrs. Finch's, come into the library and drink a glass of champagne with Constantine and me."

"No, no, thank you. I don't drink, and I must be off, Mrs. Lupescu."

"Leave your address," said Constantine.

Gus leaned over and wrote it on a pad on the desk.

"I'll see Mr. Bailey to the door, Constantine," said Yvonne.

Mrs. Lupescu preceded Gus down the corridor.

"Tigers' whiskers," she said.

"Tigers' whiskers?" repeated Gus, not understanding.

"Chopped very fine and mixed with food. The victim dies a few days later, and nobody can detect the cause." She turned to him and smiled.

Gus realized she had listened to the conversation.

"Ah, but where does one find tigers' whiskers?" he asked, as if they were sharing a joke.

"That, of course, is the problem," said Yvonne Lupescu. "Once, in Albania, my grandmother, who was the mistress of King Zog—"

Gus's coat and umbrella, dried, had been left in the hallway. He again turned to the mirror and straightened the bow of his black tie.

"That's not the way to tie a black tie," said Yvonne, interrupting her story.

"What's the matter with it?" asked Gus, fingering it on both sides.

"It's entirely too lopsided. See? Too much tie on the left. Not enough on the right. Here, let me do it for you," Yvonne said, untying his tie and standing close to him while she held each end, looking him squarely in the eye. "You start this way, with both sides even, and then you make a half bow on the right side, like this, and then you wrap the left side around the half bow, like this, and then you pull it through this hole, like this. *Voilà*."

She moved even closer to him. Her breasts had become more exposed in the tying of his tie. Gus, embarrassed, blushed again.

"Do you want me to take care of that hard-on for you?" she whispered, smiling at him.

"No," whispered Gus, looking back toward the door of Constantine's den.

"Danger's half the fun, Gus," she said.

"I'm late."

"What I have in mind won't take a minute and a half."

"That's incredibly kind of you, but no, thank you," said Gus, heading for the door.

"What do you want, Mr. Bailey?"

"I'd like to hear about King Zog and your grandmother some time," said Gus. He opened the front door and left.

15

IT WAS the same conversation that was going on everywhere for the few weeks that people were discussing the breakup of the Edward Potter Manchester marriage and the romance of Loelia Manchester and Mickie Minardos. It did not rivet Gus Bailey the way it riveted those who knew the principals better than Gus knew them, but by now Gus understood that these people were more interested in talking about themselves than any other topic.

"You see, it was all so well disguised, Gus. No one suspected a thing," said Lil Altemus, settling back into her chair at Clarence's. "*I* certainly didn't and I, after all, am one of Loelia's very best friends."

Michael, the waiter with the ponytail, who was everyone's favorite waiter at Clarence's, came up to them and told them the specials. Lil never spoke directly to a waiter if she was dining with a man. "Tell him I'll have the chicken paillard with some sort of green vegetable. Nothing first, and perhaps some of that marvelous Chilean wine, whatever-it's-called, that they have here. Tell him to ask Chick Jacoby the name. Look, there's Ezzie Fenwick.

"Anyway, Mickie Minardos made Loelia laugh. Mickie was a marvelous dancer, all that sort of thing, and we all know how Loelia loves to dance, and Ned, Ned always had two left feet when it came to dancing. But no one suspected for an *instant* that a romance was involved. Least of all poor Ned. Did you know that Ned was a cousin of mine on the Altemus side?

"But then, in Egypt, in Luxor, where they went to hear *Aida* sung at the pyramids, with people from everywhere who knew them, it was obvious to anyone with half a brain that they had progressed from giggling best friends to romantic lovers. It was my friend Gertie Todesco, poor Gertie, never could keep a secret, who spread the word, and what Loelia did, to make matters worse, was call Ned from Cairo, with a bad connection, and ask him for a divorce, after twenty-two years. Can you imagine? Is it any wonder that Ned is put out?"

ALTHOUGH Loelia Manchester was a rich woman in her own right, the bulk of the Somerset fortune, which was considerable, was controlled with an iron hand by Fernanda Somerset, Loelia's mother, and Fernanda Somerset was fond of saying about herself that she understood money management like a man.

Loelia and Fernanda had always enjoyed the closest of mother-daughter relationships, and it was no secret that Fernanda took great pride in Loelia's social accomplishments. She was, furthermore, greatly attached to her son-in-law, Edward Potter Manchester. Even though she found his constant talk of sport dull at times, she admired his country ways, especially as she spent more and more of her own time in the country, so she could be near Ned and Loelia's children, on whom she doted, especially Bozzie, their teenage son.

Fernanda and her daughter lunched that day at a table set up in a corner of the room Fernanda called her garden room, with its antique bamboo furniture, orchid plants, and blue-and-white porcelain garden benches. A René Bouché portrait of Fernanda arranging flowers, wearing trousers and a straw hat, that had been painted thirty years before in this same room, dominated the wall behind her, reminding Loelia of how beautiful her mother had been. The topic that was the purpose of this country lunch had not been broached, although Loelia knew when she was summoned from the Rhinelander, where she now lived, by a note from her mother delivered by her chauffeur that the conversation she dreaded was at hand.

"Have you had another facelift?" Fernanda asked her daughter.

"Don't you think it's a good one?" Loelia replied.

"You didn't need it."

"Oh, but I did. It's a new way Dr. James does it. He cuts up here on the scalp and then pulls it all back, and your hair covers all the scars. Too marvelous."

"Your eyes look like they're popping out of your head."

"They do not!"

"They do. And your hair is much too blond."

Loelia's hands went to her hair, defensively. "Mickie likes it this color," she said.

"I'm sure," said Fernanda. "Stop taking food off my plate."

"I'm not taking food off your plate."

"You've taken two shrimp, half my roll, and now you've scooped up a spoonful of my cheese soufflé."

Loelia, nervous, pushed back her bamboo chair from the table, and it made an unpleasant screeching sound on the terrazzo floor of the garden room. "Mother, why are you being so cranky with me?" she asked. For an instant she thought she was going to cry.

"Let's get down to brass tacks, Loelia. What is going on in your life?" asked Fernanda.

"I'm going to marry Mickie Minardos," said Loelia.

"What a grotesque announcement," said her mother.

"I didn't think I'd hear that from you, Mother!"

"Yes, you did. You knew perfectly well that was what you were going to hear from me. Isn't this man younger than you?"

"Yes."

"How many years?"

"Ten."

"He's a gigolo."

"He is the most successful shoe designer in the world."

Fernanda shook her head impatiently. A shoe designer was not a person who was going to impress Fernanda Somerset, no matter how successful he was.

"Someday he is going to design for the theater and the ballet," insisted Loelia.

"A lady can take her chauffeur to bed, but she can't take him out to dinner, Loelia," said Fernanda. "I'm surprised you of all people don't understand that."

"How incredibly unkind that is, Mother."

"You're going to be kicked out of the *Social Register* if you marry this man."

"You know that means nothing to me."

Fernanda looked at her daughter, whose greatest achievement had been as a figure in society, and disbelieved her.

"What do you know about his family?"

"His father is a banker," said Loelia proudly, playing her trump card, to prove that her fiancé was not a fortune hunter.

The flowered uniform on the maid who came in carrying demitasse cups matched the flowered tablecloth and the flowered napkins of the luncheon table. "Just leave the coffee there, Adoración, and don't bother to clear," said Fernanda to the maid, waving her off.

"You know, Loelia. There are Greeks and Greeks, and none of the Greeks we know, like Stavros and Christina and Alecco, have ever heard of the family of Mickie Minardos."

"I don't care," said Loelia quietly.

"I do," replied her mother, just as quietly.

Fernanda Somerset was not an impractical woman. She understood the callings of sexual desire and recognized it as that in her daughter's attachment to Mickie Minardos. She had herself briefly enjoyed a discreet indiscretion during the time her husband had engaged in his affair with Matilda Clarke. When the affair ended, after Sweetzer came out of the alcoholic institution in Minnesota where he had lingered for six months, both marriages resumed into the companionship that all successful marriages become, with neither the children having to suffer the trauma of divorce, nor the Somerset fortune having been dissipated as it would have been by divorce.

"Take a trip with your Greek," said Fernanda. "And when it's over, as it will be over, come back to your husband and children. Ned will wait for you. He loves you."

"I'm going to marry Mickie Minardos."

"You have crushed your family."

"Help me, Mother."

"No, I won't help you, Loelia. And there is something else I have to remind you of, though I had hoped that I would not have to."

"Money, I suppose," said Loelia, picking up her things, as an indication of leaving.

"Yes, money. What you have is all you're ever going to have, if you go through with this, Loelia."

LOELIA MANCHESTER was horrified when she learned from her lawyer a week later that Ned had asked for half her fortune before he would agree to the divorce she wanted so much, so that she could be free to marry Dimitri Minardos. Ned Manchester was already rich, although not as rich as Loelia, and it was uncharacteristic of him to ask for money from a woman. In the years of their marriage, he had never shown any sign of avarice. Loelia knew immediately that her mother had joined forces with Ned to block the divorce, as neither he nor her mother wanted Loelia to leave him.

Loelia had countered with an offer of half as much as he had asked, but Ned, again through the lawyers, had turned down her offer and declared that he was sticking to his guns. All her friends told Loelia that Ned was acting the way he was because he was so hurt and didn't want a divorce at all and certainly didn't want her money, but none of that information was of any comfort to Loelia. She had given herself up to a passion she had never experienced before and wanted to marry Dimitri Minardos more than anything else in the world. Of course her children had to be considered and proprieties to be observed. She had moved out of the beautiful Manchester apartment, leaving behind everything but her clothes, and moved into a large suite in the Rhinelander Hotel, where everyone they knew who was getting a divorce moved. Her friends consoled her with lovely baskets of flowers, and needlepoint pillows, and scented candles, and pieces of china to use for ashtrays to make the suite more home-like, and Lil Altemus, who didn't even approve of the romance with Mickie, lent her pictures to hang on her walls after she confessed to Lil that she found the hotel pictures too dreary for words.

One afternoon Loelia was on her way to meet her realtor, Helene Whitbeck, to look at an apartment on Fifth Avenue that had just come on the market. Helene said it might be the ideal place for Loelia and Mickie to live after they were married. When she stepped into the Rhinelander elevator, Elias Renthal was standing there. She was impressed that he took off his hat when he spoke to her.

"I'm Elias Renthal, Mrs. Manchester," he said, making a slight but courtly bow.

"Yes, of course," Loelia replied. "Howareyou?"

Elias could see right away that Loelia was unhappy and, when the elevator came to the lobby, he asked her if she wanted to have a drink in the bar, which was always quiet at that time of the afternoon. Loelia was amazed to hear herself say that she wouldn't have a drink but she would have a cup of tea. She hoped that Elias didn't know that it was she who had blackballed him from being elected to the board of directors of the New York Art Museum, even though he had been a generous contributor. Since then, she had heard from Jamesey Crocus and others that he had become very polished in the interim. "That wife of his, Ruby, is sandpapering the edges," Jamesey had said.

In no time at all Loelia and Elias were talking as if they were old friends, and Loelia poured out her heart to the famous financier about her troubles with Ned and the divorce. Loelia became so engrossed in her conversation that she forgot all about her appointment with Helene Whitbeck, who was waiting for her in the lobby of the Fifth Avenue apartment building.

"I can't believe he'd hold me up for money," Loelia confided to Elias about her husband. "Ned really never had any interest in possessions. I told him he can have the house in the country, and the house in Bermuda, and he wants them, but he also wants I-don't-know-how-many million on top of that. Imagine Ned acting like that after all these years. It's not as if Ned doesn't have any money of his own."

"His pride's hurt, and he's being vindictive," said Elias.

"I'm deeply sick of hearing about Ned's pride being hurt," replied Loelia. "After all, we are not the first couple in the world to get a divorce."

"Why not call his bluff? Why not offer him more than he's asking? It's not how much you pay them," Elias said, "it's how you pay it out to them."

"I don't understand what that means, Mr. Renthal," said Loelia.

"Let's say, for instance, you offer Ned twenty million in alimony," Elias began.

"Twenty million!" exclaimed Loelia. "Please, Mr. Renthal!"

"A ballpark figure. Now hear this through," said Elias patiently, taking a cigar from a case. Elias enjoyed talking about money. It was the one area of conversation in which he bowed to no man in his opinions. He opened the button of his gray pin-striped suit and made himself comfortable. Loelia noticed, while he was lighting his cigar, how much better dressed Elias had become than when she first met him. His suit was beautifully cut, and his pale pink shirt with white collar and cuffs and discreet rose monogram on his chest, and his enamel-and-gold cuff links could all have been things Mickie Minardos might have worn.

"However much money it is, you have no choice in the matter if that's the only way Ned's going to divorce you so that you can marry Mickie. You don't give him the five million or the ten million bucks all at once. You spread it out. You work it out so you pay him a million a year for ten years, or even half a million a year for twenty years, but you can afford a million a year with your kind of money."

She wondered how he knew how much money she had, but she felt sure that he did know. In time she would discover about Elias Renthal that he knew exactly how much money everyone had.

"Understand?"

She did understand. She could afford a million a year. Suddenly it was all beginning to fall into place. She wondered why her expensive lawyers had not come up with so simple a solution as Elias Renthal had come up with in ten minutes.

"And then," Elias continued.

"Yes," said Loelia.

"In a year or so, Ned will meet someone and probably remarry, and then, when he's happy again, he won't hold you to this agreement. After all, everyone says Ned's a gent."

"Yes, of course," said Loelia. It had not occurred to her until that moment that Ned would fall in love again and even marry again. She had only imagined him alone, or with the children. "Do you live here in the Rhinelander, Mr. Renthal?" Loelia asked when she was gathering up her gloves and bag.

"No, no, Ruby and I are just camping out here while Cora Mandell is doing over the new apartment we bought from Matilda Clarke. We thought we'd be in in time for Easter, but you know what a perfectionist Cora is. She's got nineteen coats of persimmon lacquer on the living-room walls, and the rugs are being woven in Portugal, and things like that take time. Not to mention all the faux marble," Elias added with a grin that charmed Loelia. "She's got some guy she brought over from Rome just to paint all the faux marble. The truth of the matter is, Loelia, I never heard of any of these absolutely essential refinements like persimmon lacquer and faux marble six years ago, and now they're dictating our lives."

Loelia laughed. "And Mrs. Renthal? How is she?"

"Her name is Ruby. And I'm Elias, Loelia."

"Yes, of course, Elias."

"Ruby's over in London bidding on a pair of eighteenth-century console tables at the Orromeo auction."

"Oh, yes, I heard about those tables from Jamesey Crocus. Inlaid, aren't they, with ram's heads on the legs?"

"I dunno."

"Sad about the Orromeos, isn't it?"

"I dunno."

"They've lost everything."

Elias shuddered. There were very few things in life that could make Elias Renthal shudder, but the thought of losing his fortune, as the Orromeos, whoever the Orromeos were, had lost theirs, was one of the things that could make him shudder.

"How?" he asked.

"How what?"

"How did the Orromeos lose all their money?"

"The usual thing that happens several generations down the line," replied Loelia.

"Spoiled brats that don't work? Like that?" asked Elias.

"I suppose. Too many divorces. Nothing depletes a fortune like divorce these days."

"As we were just saying," agreed Elias.

"When is Mrs. Renthal, I mean Ruby, coming back?" asked Loelia.

"She'll be back in time for Justine Altemus's wedding. Ruby wouldn't miss that event for all the tea in China," said Elias, stubbing out his cigar.

"Oh, I didn't know Ruby was a friend of Justine's," said Loelia, trying to keep the surprise out of her voice.

"She's not. Never met her."

"Oh, Bernard, then, of course. You're friends of Bernard Slatkin's."

"No, don't know Bernie Slatkin either, except on TV, of course."

"You're not a friend of Lil's, are you? I've never seen you at Lil's, have I?"

Elias laughed. "We're not planning on crashing, Loelia, if that's what you're thinking."

"Of course that's not what I'm thinking, Elias!"

"I'm involved in a couple of business deals with Laurance Van Degan, and he arranged for Ruby and me to get invited."

"Oh," said Loelia, again keeping the surprise out of her voice. "I'm staying here at the Rhinelander too, at least until I find a new apartment. Perhaps when Ruby gets back from London, the four of us can have dinner here in the hotel one night."

"That would be just swell, Loelia," said Elias. "Give my best to Mickie." Elias couldn't wait to get to the telephone so that he could call Ruby in London to tell her to get her ass home so that they could have dinner right out in public with Loelia Manchester and Mickie Minardos.

"YOU PAID *how much* for those fucking tables?" shouted Elias Renthal over the telephone to his wife in London.

"You can't lose money on eighteenth-century French furniture, Elias. I swear to God," shouted Ruby back over the telephone.

"How much?"

"You heard what I said the first time."

"I couldn't have heard right."

"You'll love them, Elias. I swear to God. On either side of the fireplace, with the Monet with the water lilies overhead. Wait till you see them."

"Inlaid, aren't they, with ram's heads on the legs?"

"What do you know about ram's heads?" asked Ruby, surprised.

"Only what Loelia Manchester told me when I had tea with her this afternoon," replied Elias.

"What? You had tea with Loelia Manchester? Tell me everything."

"I'll tell you all about it when you get home."

"Are you sending the plane for me, or am I taking the Concorde?"

"Whichever's fastest."

"Elias. Is it okay about the consoles?"

"I don't even know what the fuck a console table is, Ruby."

"Is it okay?"

"Yeah, it's okay."

"You know what I'm going to do to you, Elias, when I get home, don't you?"

"I know, but I want to hear you say it."

"Your favorite. Both of them in my mouth. At the same time. Just the way you like it."

MICKIE MINARDOS was in a quiet rage. He threw down the newspaper and leaped to his feet, pulling the belt of his green silk polkadot dressing gown tighter around his slender waist. Loelia, seated at her dressing table, watched him in the mirror and noticed that his face was pink and his lips were pursed tightly together.

Since Florian Gray, in revenge for Mickie's verbal attack on him, had referred to Mickie in his column as a cobbler rather than a shoe designer, the word *cobbler* had caught on. He was told from time to time, always causing him great pain, that many of Loelia's friends, including her husband, now referred to him, behind his back, as the cobbler.

What Florian Gray had no way of knowing was that Mickie Minardos's father, back in his provincial town in Greece, was the village cobbler for all of Mickie's youth. Then Demetreus Minardos, who knew nothing of society and the grand life, achieved a certain local fame by designing a sandal popular with the working classes that utilized the rubber from discarded tires as soles and sold for less than the equivalent of a dollar. With the windfall, or what seemed like a windfall to old Demetreus Minardos, he was able to send his son, named Dimitri, but called Mickie, to a better school in Athens than any that existed in the place where they lived, and later, to Paris to study. Mickie's aim was to "do something" in the theater, but the something was undefined.

In Paris, attractive Greeks had always enjoyed a popularity, because, as Bijou McCord Thomopolous, the great hostess, who had married several Greeks, said, "They are such wonderful dancers, and they know how to treat their women." Mickie Minardos, who was a wonderful dancer, and an admirer of beautiful feet, began his career as a shoe designer, until the time came when he could "do something" in the theater. Before New York and Loelia Manchester, he had enjoyed the companionship of several fashionable ladies, among them Bijou McCord Thomopolous.

It was a curious aspect of Mickie's makeup that, although he felt shame about his father's profession, he had achieved great success in a more glamorous version of it. When interviewed by the fashion press, Mickie Minardos always described his father as a banker, which he did become, in a small branch of a small bank in the provincial town where his sandal factory was, giving the impression to the interviewer that banking, rather than the unmentioned cobbler business, was the source of the family fortune. A misprint in the fashion pages of the *Times* called his father a baker rather than a banker, and the mistake sent him into paroxysms of grief, as a baker was to him even lower on the social scale than a cobbler. He demanded a retraction from the *Times* and got one.

"What's the matter, darling?" asked Loelia finally, knowing that her beloved was upset.

"Nothing," Mickie replied. Already, in the months they had been living together, she had discovered that Mickie was inclined to sulk when he became angry and tended to deny anger when questioned about it.

"Darling, I can see that you're upset over something. What is it?"

"Florian Gray."

"Him again," said Loelia. "Now what has he said?"

"Don't read it."

"Of course, I'll read it. What difference does it make what people like that say? The only one of those people who matters is Dolly, and Dolly has been lovely to everyone."

"He calls me a cobbler again and says my father was a baker, instead of a banker, when he had to have seen the retraction in the *Times*."

"So what?" said Loelia. It always amazed Mickie that Loelia was unaffected by criticism of him.

"He says your friends don't accept me."

"Oh, puleeze, Mickie. It's too ridiculous."

"He says your mother is saying she will disinherit you if you marry me."

"I assure you, Mickie, that if my mother were ever to make such a statement, which she would not, it would never be to a gossip columnist from a tabloid newspaper. So calm down. It's simply not true."

"It is true that your friends won't accept me."

"But it was you who said that my friends were very dull. Narrow-in-their-outlook is what you said. You said people like Lil Altemus and Matilda Clarke and all the Van Degan clan were the most boring people in the world."

Mickie Minardos turned away from Loelia. He had said what Loelia said he said about her friends and relations, but he hadn't meant it. He had also said that the New People were more interesting by far than the old families, but he hadn't meant that either. In his heart, the world of Loelia Manchester was the part of New York that he most wanted to enter.

"One of these days they'll see how talented I am, and they'll be fighting to have me," he said.

Loelia heard the petulance in his voice. She looked at Mickie intently in the way a woman looks at a man she loves, but in whom she discovers an unpleasant trait that she had not known he possessed.

"Darling, you are considered to be the most successful man in your field in New York. Tell me how many shoe designers there are who have your sense of style."

"I'm going to break his face, that little pipsqueak Florian Gray, the next time I run into him."

"I adore you when you act tough, Mickie." She stood up and turned to him. "How do I look?"

"Turn around," he said.

Loelia assumed a model's pose and whirled around. Mickie eyed her critically, as if she were his creation, and she watched his face for his approval.

"Almost perfect," he said. "Sit down a minute. Here, let me do your eyes again. You need a little more green shadow to go with the color of your shoes."

16

WHEN JORGIE SANCHEZ-JULIA failed to show up for two scheduled interviews with Gus Bailey, Gus decided to abandon the story he was planning to write, which dealt with the growing trend of rich and elderly widows and widowers to leave their entire fortunes to late-life mates. Or, at least, he decided to abandon that part of the story that dealt with Jorgie Sanchez-Julia, a thirty-year-old Spanish gigolo who had married a crippled Washington millionairess almost fifty years his senior and then inherited her entire fortune, down to family heirlooms, much to the consternation of her children.

"Tell Jorgie to shove it," Gus told the young lady who answered the telephone in Jorgie's suite at the Rhinelander, when he called to complain that he had been kept waiting over an hour for the second day in a row.

The next morning a large bouquet of roses from Lorenza's shop arrived at Gus's apartment in Turtle Bay, together with a contrite and charming note from Jorgie Sanchez-Julia, saying that he had been unexpectedly called to Washington the day before. Gus didn't believe that Jorgie had been called to Washington, but he did believe that Jorgie, who loved publicity, did not want to pass up the opportunity to be interviewed, so a third appointment was set.

It surprised Gus that Jorgie wanted to meet at Clarence's rather than in the privacy of Gus's apartment, or in his suite at the Rhinelander, or in a less conspicuous restaurant than Clarence's, as Jorgie Sanchez-Julia was involved in a court battle over the money that he had inherited. Gus, his back to the room, flicked through the pages of his looseleaf notebook and read some previously written notes, while Jorgie Sanchez-Julia watched with inner excitement but a sullen expression the passing parade that lunch at Clarence's always was. Gus noted that Jorgie had a spoiled, full-lipped, pouting mouth, sallow skin, curly blond hair, and wore a Spanish suit that showed to full advantage his slender hips, waist, and rump.

"Help me out here, Jorgie," said Gus. "How old were you when you married Mrs. Acton?"

"Countess Sanchez-Julia," corrected Jorgie. A cigarette hung from the corner of his mouth.

"But certainly she was Mrs. Acton when you married her?"

"I was twenty-six."

"And the countess was how old?"

"Oh, seventy something or other. Geraldine, you know, never talked about age. She was so young in heart," answered Jorgie, his eye on the door of the restaurant where fashionable people kept coming in.

"And the title of Countess came from where?"

"Papal," replied Jorgie. "Geraldine was rewarded by His Holiness for her philanthropic endeavors."

"Ah, yes, papal. Tell me about the Countess's limp," said Gus. "Did she always have a limp?"

"She was born with a clubfoot," answered Jorgie. "Look, there's Yvonne Lupescu coming in. Do you know her? Used to be one of Madam Myra's girls. Carried her whips in a custom-made Vuitton bag. Such a dominatrix she is. Oh, my dear, the things I could tell you about that one."

Gus, working now, looked up from his notes to register what Jorgie had just said.

"I didn't know Mrs. Lupescu was one of Madam Myra's girls," he said.

"Used to be," Jorgie corrected himself. "You know of Madam Myra then?"

"Yes," replied Gus. "Ms. Myra she's known as in New York."

"How very amusing," said Jorgie. "I must remember that."

Gus tapped his pencil on the tabletop to get the subject back to the point of the lunch. "But your wife, the Countess, the late Countess, danced so well for a woman with a clubfoot."

"I taught her how to dance," said Jorgie. "Geraldine loved to dance. You see, I brought joy into her life. Those twins of hers, those playboys, paid no attention to their mother at all. Wait for her to die, that's all they thought, so they could get the money. If I hadn't come along and swept her off her foot, they would have put her in an old ladies' home. I gave her a wonderful life. Now they say about me that I exerted undue influence on her to leave me all her money. It was Geraldine's choice. I was as surprised as everyone else when the will was read."

"Yes, yes, of course," said Gus, writing down Jorgie's words.

"She was a wonderful woman," said Jorgie.

"Is it true that the pair of Renoir paintings were copies and you sold off the originals during her last illness?" asked Gus.

"Heavens, no!" replied Jorgie, laughing merrily at the absurdity of Gus's questions. "How do these terrible stories start?"

"There's something I'd like to ask you. Rather personal."

"You ask me, Mr. Bailey."

"Gus."

"You ask me, Gus."

"Did you, uh, have to make love to the Countess?"

"Oh, yes, on a regular basis. Geraldine was very attracted to me."

"I see." Gus sipped his water, as if it were a drink. "Tell me, Jorgie. Isn't it difficult to make love to a septuagenarian lady with a limp?"

Jorgie Sanchez-Julia smiled and shook his head. "I have never met the person, woman or man, I couldn't get it up for, Gus," he said. He thought for a moment, and then added, with a slight wink, "if the price was right."

"This is on the record, I assume," said Gus.

"On the record means what?" asked Jorgie.

"Hello, Jorgie," said Yvonne Lupescu, coming up to the table. "I didn't know you were in New York."

"Hello, Yvonne," Jorgie said unenthusiastically, holding out his hand to her without rising.

"Up," said Yvonne, with a thumbs-up gesture for him to rise. "That's no way to greet a lady."

"I just arrived on the Concorde yesterday," said Jorgie, rising lazily and winking at Gus to cover his lie. He kissed Yvonne in a lackluster manner on both cheeks, at the same time looking around the restaurant. They were both young and attractive, but indifferent to each other physically. "And you?"

"I live here now," said Yvonne.

"Oh, yes, I heard something about that. Constantine de Rham, isn't it?"

"I read that Geraldine died," said Yvonne.

"I miss her dreadfully," replied Jorgie.

"I'm sure."

"Do you know Mr. Augustus Bailey? Baroness Lupescu," said Jorgie, introducing.

"Yes, we know each other," said Gus.

"Jorgie, Fritzi von Stauffenberg is in the other room and would like you to say hello," said Yvonne.

"Fritzi is here? How marvelous. This is why I wanted to come to Clarence's, Mr. Bailey. Everyone who is in New York comes here. Would you excuse me for a minute?"

When Jorgie Sanchez-Julia moved away from the table, Gus, not wanting to get into a conversation with Yvonne, went back to studying his notes.

"May I sit down, Gus?" asked Yvonne.

"Of course."

"Such a naughty boy, Jorgie Sanchez-Julia," she said. "The things I could tell you about that one. But he was so sweet to his poor sister, the nun. He inherited everything, I heard."

Gus put away his notebook.

"That makes him the most successful male hooker in the world, I suppose," said Yvonne.

"Did the old lady know, do you suppose?"

"Geraldine? She couldn't have cared less. Jorgie showered her with roses, dozens at a time, which, of course, her accountants would get the bills for eventually, but she loved the attention."

"Good God," said Gus.

"Better than a nursing home," answered Yvonne, with a shrug of practicality.

"Depends," said Gus.

"I was wondering about something, Gus," said Yvonne.

"What?"

"How about doing one of your articles on me? I could stand a little exposure in New York."

"You'd have to shoot someone first, Mrs. Lupescu. Or inherit someone's money. Those are the kind of people I write about."

"I'm too dull, is that it?" asked Yvonne, smiling at him. "I'm twenty-eight years old. I've never been divorced. I've never even been married!"

Gus smiled, wanting to, but refraining from, asking her about Ms. Myra. "How's Constantine?"

"Oh, the same as ever."

"What is the-same-as-ever with Constantine de Rham?"

"He is dismayed that he is no longer received in New York," said

Yvonne. "It haunts him. After all, for him, what else is there to life but lunching out and dining out?"

"Mrs. Verdurin invites him," said Gus.

"That's only once a month. There are twenty-nine more nights with no place to go. He came here for dinner the other night, and Chick Jacoby made him wait an hour for a table. He blames me. He thinks he is not invited because I am an encumbrance. The time is coming, I know, I can feel it, when I am going to have to leave him."

"Then what happens to you? Where will you go?"

"I know, if I left him, he would be in despair," said Yvonne, as if Gus had not spoken. "In fact, just between us, Gus, I rather enjoy Constantine's despair. It's so utterly abject. I like it when he begs me not to leave him. All his grandiosity leaves him completely. It makes me feel, oh, what is the right word for the feeling? Imperious, I suppose. I feel filled with power that a man could love me so passionately."

"Like a dominatrix, you mean?" asked Gus.

Yvonne smiled. "Jorgie's been gossiping about me, has he?"

Gus, paying his check, looked at Yvonne.

"You look so disapproving, Gus. So proper. So aboveboard."

"I don't know. Am I so different from any of the rest of you?"

"THIS IS my stepson," said Fritzi von Stauffenberg, introducing Jorgie Sanchez-Julia to his luncheon companion.

"Yes, I know Jorgie," answered Jamesey Crocus. "He used to be my stepson."

GUS HAD no instinct for the chase. He had no desire for love. He did not want an involvement that would complicate his life and deflect him from what he knew he was going to do when Lefty Flint was released from prison. It was his friend George Eardley who introduced him to Myra Wealth. In Europe, they called her Madam Myra. In New York, they called her Miss Wealth. She preferred to be called Ms. Myra, a name that amused her, once she favored you. Ms. Myra ran an establishment of utter discretion from her apartment in the once-grand Murray Hill section of New York, catering to what she herself described as some of the most successful men in the city, although, she was quick to point out, none of the political crowd—since they lowered the standards of a place and, invariably, brought down an establishment as their political opponents and enemies sought to undo them.

"On the turn," was the way she described herself. Closer to forty than thirty, perhaps even beyond, she was in a voluptuous period of life and felt not remotely threatened by the younger girls of her establishment who were in greater demand than she was. She could spot in an instant the sort of men who were attracted to her ripe charms. Ms. Myra, in time, grew fond of Gus, whom she liked to call Augustus, and their business arrangement settled into a weekly visit, at his apartment, on Saturday nights, when most people he knew were in the country. No whips. No chains. No aberrations. No cocaine. His sexual tastes were plebeian, rarely varying from the missionary position. She stayed for an hour and a half, but one hour of the time was always taken up with conversation, when she told him tales of more exotic behavior of the clients of her house, always careful never to name names.

"There is a man on Wall Street, very important, you would know his name in a minute, lives on Park Avenue, has a house in Southampton, and his wife is always written up in Dolly De Longpre's column. He likes to cross dress." Or, "There is a Hollywood producer. Very important. You must have known him from your time there, when he was at Colossus. Old now. He only wants me to sleep by his side. Nothing more. Nothing ever happens. So sweet." Or, "I've stopped seeing the rich Arabs entirely. Two of my girls have disappeared." In turn, she would ask him about people he had written about. "I read your article about Faye Converse. She was always my favorite movie star, when I was growing up in Paris. Some people say I look like her. Do you think so?"

Leaving, Gus never handed her her money outright. In advance he placed the several hundred dollars in an envelope and left it on the hall table. It was only after he helped Ms. Myra into her black mink coat that he discreetly placed the envelope into her pocket.

"So sweet," she said to him, touching his face. She reapplied her lipstick, using his chipped gilt mirror. Then she put on the evening hat she always wore and arranged a black veil over her face.

"Ravishing," said Gus, smiling at her.

"So sweet," she said again.

"Saturday," he said.

"Saturday," she repeated, acknowledging the date.

He opened the front door of the apartment to ring for the elevator.

"When does that man get out of prison?" she asked.

"Much too soon," Gus answered. He never minded when she asked him questions that he would have minded from someone else.

"Does it worry you?"

"Yes."

From below, he could hear the elevator.

"Did you ever hear of someone called Yvonne Lupescu?" he asked her.

She looked at him, and their eyes met. Then she lifted her hand to her face and assumed a pensive expression, as if she were searching her memory. "No," she answered.

The elevator came. She got in and turned back to him as the door closed in front of her. They smiled at each other.

17

WHEN EZZIE FENWICK looked in the mirror, he turned his head sideways so that he would not have to confront his peculiar eye, the one that looked off in a different direction entirely. If Ezzie could have had a say in his own physical formation, he would not only have given himself eyes that matched, but a pencil-slim silhouette as well, and higher eyebrows, and more height, but, alas, weight problems also plagued his life, and, in retaliation, he long ago discovered that solace for what God had denied him was to be found in clothes, for which he had a limitless passion. Each day, dressing, Ezzie Fenwick gave as much thought to combinations and compatible colors as Elias Renthal gave to making money and Nestor Calder gave to plots and characters.

On the day of Justine Altemus's wedding, Ezzie Fenwick was fit to be tied. The lavender shirt with the violet monogram and the white collar and cuffs had not arrived from London as his shirtmaker there had promised it would, along with the eleven other shirts he had ordered weeks earlier, but the eleven other shirts didn't matter, only the lavender shirt with the violet monogram and the white collar and cuffs, because Ezzie had expressly explained to his shirtmaker that he must have it finished and delivered in time to wear with his new pearl gray flannel suit, with the gray-and-white striped silk lining, to Justine Altemus's wedding to the television announcer.

CONSTANTINE DE RHAM tapped his boiled egg with a knife and then, with a clean thrust, like a beheading, cut off the top of it, and proceeded to eat the egg from the shell in silence. Yvonne Lupescu, watching from her end of the table, knew when not to talk to Constantine and returned her eyes to Dolly De Longpre's column, about the excitement in society over Justine Altemus's wedding that day. She knew that Constantine's anger was because he no longer was invited to the sort of rarefied social events, like Justine Altemus's wedding, that he had been invited to during the years of his marriage to Consuelo.

When he left the breakfast table, carrying the *Times*, there was a look of hostility on his face that prevented her from telling him that there was egg on his chin. He walked very slowly past her to the door of the dining room, but he always moved slowly on the mornings after she had whipped him. She was aware that he never responded to her on those days, although it was he, never she, who instigated the arrangement and begged to be whipped. At the door, before walking out, he said his first words of the day to her, without turning to look at her. "I would like you to pack your bags and get out."

"I NEVER saw you in an outfit like that before," said Juanito, lying on the bed as he watched Hubie dress for Justine's wedding. Juanito was in one of his sullen moods, which always happened when Hubie had family obligations from which he was excluded.

"I don't often wear striped trousers, a cutaway, spats, and a top hat," said Hubie. "That's why you never saw me dressed like this before."

"I want to go to the wedding," said Juanito. It was not the first time that day or that week that Juanito had said, "I want to go to the wedding."

"You can't," said Hubie, patiently. It was not the first time that day or that week that Hubie had said, "You can't."

"Why?"

"You know why, Juanito. We've been through all this a hundred times."

"Tio Laurance, I suppose," said Juanito, doing a facial gesture of Uncle Laurance's Van Degan grandeur that always made Hubie laugh.

"Yeah, that's it. Tio Laurance. Not to mention Madre Lil. And Padre Hubert. And Hermana Justine. And *todos los* Van Degans."

"I thought you said your sister liked me," said Juanito, in his sulking voice.

"Well, she does, in her own way, but this is a situation she doesn't want to have to deal with on her wedding day at St. James's church. She's already walking on eggs with her TV announcer."

"You and your sister both go for the lower classes, it looks like."

"Bernie's not lower class. Just different from us."

"But I'm lower class, right?"

"Come on, Juanito. I'll make it up to you. I promise." He opened his wallet and took out some bills and handed them to Juanito. "Go buy yourself that leather jacket you said you liked."

"Don't blow my low," said Juanito.

"Sometimes you're a real pain in the ass, Juanito," said Hubie.

They both laughed. "You look classy, Hubie."

"Thanks, Juanito. How does this look?" he asked, patting his chin. He had applied a flesh-colored makeup base where the skin of his chin was blemished.

"You could never tell."

"Can you tell there's makeup on over it?"

"No. I told you, you look great."

"Listen."

"What?"

"A church is a public place, even St. James's. I can't keep you out of the church if you want to stand in the back and look."

"You mean it?"

"They let the homeless stand in the back and look."

"Oh, thanks."

"But no Colony Club." Hubie looked out the window of his loft. "My mother's car is here." He opened the window and called down, "I'll be right down, Joe."

"Joseph," corrected Juanito. "You're supposed to call your chauffeur Joseph, not Joe, for God's sake."

"Oh, is this something you know a lot about?" asked Hubie, amused.

"Sure, my family always had chauffeurs down in Puerto Rico."

Hubie put on his top hat.

"Let me see you in your top hat," said Juanito.

Hubie, shy, turned around.

"Give it a little angle," said Juanito.

Hubie gave his hat a little angle.

"You look just like a swell."

Hubie shrugged. "I *am* a swell."

"Will you give me a ride uptown?" asked Juanito. "I never rode in a limo."

"Let's go."

Juanito opened the door and, with a flourish, waved Hubie out the door.

"After you," said Hubie.

"No, after you. AIDS before beauty."

Hubie shook his head. "You're a class act, Juanito."

"I DO WISH you wouldn't pee in my new bidet, Elias," said Ruby. "It's disgusting. The new maid is going to think we don't know anything."

"Let's worry a lot what Candelaria with the harelip who can't speak a word of English thinks about us," said Elias.

"I'm not wearing too much jewelry, am I?" asked Ruby.

"You look great, Ruby. New dress?"

"Of course it's new. Pretty soon they're going to say about Ruby Renthal that she never wears the same dress twice. Do you think mink or sable?"

"Honey, I don't know."

"This is the first time we've been to one of these affairs where we haven't had to buy tickets to get in."

"Nervous?"

"Yeah."

"Me too."

"Don't leave my side the whole time, Elias."

"I won't."

"Elias, I just love my new ring."

"I HEAR YOU had the about-to-be bride and groom out to the country for the weekend, Matilda," said Maisie Verdurin, walking down Madison Avenue to St. James's church after Violet Bastedo's lunch at Clarence's.

"Just a little dinner for the Bedford crowd," said Matilda.

"Bernie and Justine met at one of my parties. Did you know that?" asked Maisie, pleased with her matchmaker role.

"I'm not sure the Van Degans are going to send you a thank-you note for that, Maisie," said Matilda.

"Don't you like Bernie?"

Matilda Clarke, who thought Bernard Slatkin was very attractive, hesitated for a moment before answering. "Tall, dark, handsome, clever. Too clever. Won all the word games as if his life depended on it. And he might, just might, have a bit of a roving eye. My God, look at the crowds outside the church."

YVONNE LUPESCU pushed open the door of Constantine de Rham's den, entered, and closed the door behind her. The room was, in the absence of its occupant, dark, but she dared not pull back the red velvet curtains to let in light or turn on the wall lights. She knew exactly how much time she had. Constantine was in the lavatory off the entrance hall. She stood for several moments until her eyes became accustomed to the dark. Then she crossed and seated herself behind Constantine's ormolu-encrusted Boulle desk. She opened the long center drawer and felt around inside, under papers and leather address books. She closed the drawer quietly and opened the top drawer of the two drawers on the left and immediately she felt what she was looking for. At that instant the door opened and the lights went on.

"What are you doing here?" asked Constantine.

Yvonne Lupescu, frightened, rose.

"There is no money in that desk if that is what you are looking for, Yvonne," said Constantine.

"My passport, Constantine," she replied. One of her hands was behind her back. "I cannot leave without my passport."

"Your passport, Yvonne, is in your traveling case where you always keep it. What are you looking for in my desk?"

"Where's Ramon?" asked Yvonne.

"It is Ramon's day off."

Yvonne smiled.

"I asked what you were looking for in my desk," he repeated.

Constantine walked over to the desk where Yvonne was standing. Calmly she brought her hand around from behind her back and pointed a pistol at him.

"Oh, Yvonne, don't be ridiculous," said Constantine, dismissively, as he moved around the desk toward her.

"You can't think, Constantine, that I am going to walk out of here without any, shall we say, compensation," said Yvonne, thrilled by the excitement of such a scene, as she backed away from him.

"For the past six months I have given you a home such as you have never lived in," said Constantine.

"Am I supposed to consider that a generous act?"

"There are some who would think so."

"Without what I do to you, Constantine, you can't get erect, and you know it, and that's worth a lot more than a free bed with some of your dead wife's Porthault sheets on it."

"I will have the accountant send you a check for your services," said Constantine.

"You're in a vile mood because you weren't invited to Justine Altemus's wedding, and in an ugly mood because there are welts on your ass that you begged me to put there. Don't hold either of those things against me."

Constantine moved forward and held out his hand for Yvonne to give him the gun. She, defiant, continued to hold it on him. In an instant, Constantine leaned forward and grabbed Yvonne's wrist.

"What in the world do you want with that gun, you foolish girl?" he asked.

Instead of releasing the gun, Yvonne pulled it back toward her. Laughing at her, Constantine pulled it up toward him, as a shot rang out in the room. For an instant they held each other's eye, disbelief on his face, excitement on hers. She watched as the color drained from his face and he crumpled in front of her and fell to the floor.

"Oh, my God, Constantine," she said. She moved to his body, knelt by him, and listened to his heart. Sitting up, she leaned into his face. His eyes, glazed, stared back at hers.

"You pulled that trigger, you son of a bitch. I didn't pull that trigger," she hissed at his face.

Then she carefully erased her fingerprints from the trigger and handle of the gun with a handkerchief she took from Constantine's jacket and placed the gun in his hand, arranging his finger on the trigger. Slowly she rose from the floor, closed the drawers of the desk, and walked to the door of the room. In the hallway she listened for a minute to the silence of the mansion. Closing the door of the room behind her, she raced for the marble stairs and ran up them. In her bathroom, she turned on the taps of her shower to full blast, rushed to her closet, and began pulling out dresses, rejecting one after the other, until she found the yellow one that looked so right for the occasion at hand.

ON THE third ring, the message machine in Gus Bailey's apartment answered. "Hello, this is Augustus Bailey. I'm not able to come to the telephone right now. Leave your name and number and the time you called, and I will get back to you as soon as possible. Wait for the beep."

"Call me, Mr. Bailey. I have some information for you." The voice was Detective Johnston and Detective Johnston never called Gus unless there was a very good reason.

THERE were so many more people on the bride's side of the church than on the groom's side that the ushers ceased to ask the guests on which side they wanted to be and seated the later arrivals on the groom's side to correct the imbalance. Only the Elias Renthals, not wishing to be thought of as friends of the groom, insisted to the usher, whom they mistook for Chinese, that they be seated on the Altemus side rather than the Slatkin side, although they had barely met Lil Altemus and only knew Justine from seeing her across the rooms at Maisie Verdurin's parties or nodding to her at Clarence's. However, their credentials, coming as they had from Laurance Van Degan, were the best, and they were seated impressively toward the front of the church, only two rows behind Loelia Manchester and Matilda Clarke, who were practically family, and one row behind Ezzie Fenwick, the social arbiter, beneath the famous rose window given to the church by the late Alice Grenville in memory of her son.

Ezzie Fenwick knelt, head bowed in a devotional attitude for a minute, and then sat back in the pew and looked around to see who was there. He waved to the Todescos across the aisle and blew a kiss to old Aunt Minnie Willoughby and Cora Mandell. Ruby Renthal nudged Elias to watch Ezzie. Then both Elias and Ruby knelt, heads bowed in devotional attitudes for a minute, and then sat back in their pew and looked around to see who was there. Ruby waved and blew a kiss to Cora Mandell who was the only person present she knew well enough to wave and blow a kiss to.

Everyone was enchanted with the string quartet on the altar that Jamesey Crocus, who knew more about Bach fugues than anyone, had found for Justine, who wanted Bach, and Bach alone. The flowers, fully opened peach and coral roses in great abundance, all arranged by Lorenza, were admired by everyone. There were nods of approval for old Ormonde Van Degan, as he inched his way up the aisle on his walker, helped along by a smiling and considerate Dodo Fitz Alyn.

"I think Ormonde must have had a stroke," said Aunt Minnie Willoughby to Cora Mandell. "Something about his mouth doesn't work very well. Droops a bit."

"Drips a bit too," said Cora.

Aunt Minnie Willoughby mouthed but did not speak the word *incontinent*.

"Poor Dodo. She looks happy though. Lil says she's been an angel to Ormonde," replied Cora.

"Nevel did Justine's dress and all the bridesmaid's dresses and Lil Altemus's too," whispered Ruby to Elias.

"Who's Nevel?" asked Elias.

"Leven spelled backwards," whispered Ruby.

AFTER forty minutes, the guests became restless and began to wonder if the wedding was about to be canceled. Then, led by Ezzie Fenwick, who loved social drama, they began to speculate, pew by pew, to great guffaws, that the holdup was because Bernie Slatkin was refusing to sign the prenuptial agreement that Lil Altemus, as a last-minute precaution against fortune hunting, had insisted upon. It was not so. Bernie Slatkin, whose broadcasting income was far more impressive than any of Justine's Wall Street suitors' incomes had ever been, had willingly signed a prenuptial agreement several weeks earlier, but, waiting in the groom's room for the bride to show up, he told his best man, Fielder Black, the coanchor on the evening news, that he bet the people in the church were making jokes about his not wanting to sign a prenuptial agreement. He worried about his aunt and uncle, whom he could see sitting in the front row, and hoped they would not think that Justine was not going to show up.

Sol Slatkin, seated in the front row on the groom's side, patted his wife's hand. Hester, staring straight ahead, nodded her head in acknowledgment of Sol's pat.

"I hate to think what these flowers must have cost," said Hester.

"They can afford it," said Sol.

"Where do you suppose she is?"

"Aren't brides always late?" asked Sol.

"I wasn't," said Hester.

Sol smiled at his wife. "There's Bernie. Do you see Bernie? Peeking out the door of the groom's room."

"It's not Bernie I'm worried about, Sol. I know Bernie's here. It's Bernie's intended I'm worried about. Do you dare turn around?"

"Why?"

"Pretend you're looking for the Perelmans and see if there's any activity at the back of the church. You don't think she wouldn't show up, do you, Sol?"

Sol Slatkin turned discreetly in his place. He waved a half wave to the Perelmans and then turned back. "Something's happening back there," he reported.

Lil Altemus, helped out of her car by her driver Joe, smiled at the photographers who took her picture. She was wearing a gray chiffon afternoon dress under her sable coat. Lest it be considered too somber in coloring, Nevel, who designed it, had added shades of coral and peach into the gray chiffon hat that he also designed. Lil wore, as always on great occasions, her famous pearls, inherited from her mother, and a sunburst of diamonds on her shoulder. Hubie Altemus, very thin, but sober, took his mother by the arm and led her up the steps into the church, but his presence was so overwhelmed by his mother's magnificence that the makeup he wore to cover the lesion on his face went unnoticed.

In the backseat of the Van Degan limousine on the way from Lil Altemus's apartment to St. James's church, a distance of only a few blocks, but a journey made slow by one-way streets and late afternoon traffic, Justine Altemus, her face veiled, sat next to her father.

"Are you happy with this guy, Justine?" he asked.

"Daddy, what a time to ask me such a question. You've had weeks to ask me that."

"But I never see you alone," he said, turning to look at her through her veil.

Justine smiled fondly at her father. She remembered the smell of his kisses when he used to stop by to kiss her good-night on his way to whatever dinner or party he was always going to: a romantic mélange of Floris shaving lotion, Camel cigarettes, and scotch from the scotch mist he always drank while he was dressing.

"I'm sorry about Belinda, Daddy, that Mother wouldn't let her sit up with the family."

"We're all used to your mother by now," said Hubert. From a small silver flask, he hastily swallowed a gulp of scotch whiskey.

"Here we are at the church," said Justine nervously. "Oh, look, an awning. I'd forgotten there was to be an awning. I adore awnings at weddings."

"This is where your mother and I were married," said Hubert Altemus.

"That's a very somber thought," said Justine. They both laughed. "Yes, Daddy, I am very happy with this guy."

"Good," he said and patted her hand. "An awful lot of photographers out there."

"That's not for the Van Degans, you know, or the Altemuses. That's for Bernie Slatkin. My guy's a star, Daddy."

"Good God."

In the vestibule, the small bridesmaids, nervous and tittering in the final moments before the processional, greeted the radiant bride on her arrival with her father. Lil Altemus and her former husband looked at each other.

"Hello, Lil," said Hubert.

"Hubert," replied Lil, in a return greeting.

"You're looking well, Lil," said her former husband.

Lil Altemus, who had never been able to deal with the fact that Hubert Altemus had left her, bent down, in a rare motherly gesture, to straighten out the cream satin folds of Justine's train.

"Your bouquet is lovely, Justine," said Lil, rising, eyes away from Hubert. "There's no one like Lorenza for flowers."

"Do I look all right, Mother?" asked Justine.

"Perfect. Nevel at his best."

"I meant me," said Justine.

"You look beautiful, Justine," said her father.

"I guess it's time for you to take me up, Hubie," said Lil to her son, who had been watching the family exchange from a corner of the small room.

"Good luck, Justine," said Hubie.

"Oh, Hubie," said Justine, leaning down to kiss her shorter brother on the cheek. She saw the makeup that covered the lesion on his chin. "What is that?" she whispered.

"Nothing," answered Hubie. "An astringent in my aftershave lotion caused an irritation."

Their eyes met, in a moment of silent understanding, like when they were children long ago.

"Come along, Hubie," said Lil.

When the strains of *Lohengrin* were finally heard, to everyone's relief, Justine Altemus, billowing in cream-colored satin and rose-point lace, carrying cream-colored roses, fully opened, nearly ran up the aisle to her groom, restrained only by the careful walk of her slightly inebriated father. Preceded by ten little girls dressed as shep-herdesses carrying crooks, Justine's eyes searched longingly ahead for the husband who was waiting for her. Not a person present, except possibly her mother, did not think that the match, although unusual, was not romantic.

THE BRADLEYS' cook jumped out the window, "splash, splash, all over the corner of Park Avenue and Sixty-second Street," as Ezzie Fenwick was to report it later, just as the wedding party was entering the Colony Club for the reception, but, inside, it was a thing not to be mentioned, as no one wanted to cast a pall on the happy occasion of Justine Altemus's marriage to Bernard Slatkin. The Bradleys, whose cook had just jumped, stayed, for propriety's sake, only long enough to go through the line and greet the handsome couple.

"So marvelous, Lil. All the old families," said Mame Bradley. "None of those New People." Just then Elias and Ruby Renthal came into her line of vision. "Except, of course, the Renthals."

Lil Altemus mouthed but did not speak the word *business*, so there could be no misunderstanding as to the reason for the presence of the Elias Renthals at her daughter's wedding.

Justine, standing in the receiving line between Bernie and her mother, shielded her mouth with her bouquet and whispered into Lil Altemus's ear, "Mother, *please*, speak to Mrs. Slatkin. She's just standing there with no one to talk to."

"Come stand here by me, Hester," said Lil. "Have you met my great friend, Cora Mandell?"

"Hellohowareyou?" said Cora to Hester.

"Isn't this all lovely?" replied Hester, trying to make conversation with the septuagenarian decorator, whose work she read about in house magazines.

"So pretty, yes. I'm looking everywhere for Ezzie," said Cora, turning to Lil. "He's in such a snit about his shirtmaker. Really too funny."

"He's over there talking to Madge Tree's son," replied Lil.

"Excuse me, Mrs. Slatkin. I must see this friend of mine," said Cora Mandell, hurrying off. Hester, aware but unfazed, knew that she was the aunt of the handsomest young man in the room.

"Now, Hester," said Lil, "who don't you know?"

"HELLO, Uncle Ormonde," said Matilda Clarke. Old Ormonde Van Degan, afflicted now with sporadic senility and an unreliable memory, smiled blankly at Matilda without recognizing her. Dodo Fitz Alyn opened her handbag, took out a handkerchief, and wiped the saliva off his chin.

"What is he becoming, Dodo? Blind or deaf?" asked Matilda. "I mean, should I talk louder or move closer?"

"It's Matilda Clarke, Ormonde," said Dodo in a loud voice directly into Ormonde's ear. "Sweetzer's widow, Matilda."

"Good God, he knows that, Dodo," said Matilda.

"I miss Sweetzer," said Ormonde Van Degan, finally placing Matilda. His voice was as frail as his body was fragile. "He was a keen sportsman. Marvelous fisherman. Good shot, too. I miss Sweetzer."

"Thank you, Uncle Ormonde," said Matilda, rushing on.

"THAT WAS your great aunt Grace Gardiner," said Laurance Van Degan, looking at a white marble bust on a stand in the entrance to the ballroom. "The New York Gardiners used the *i* in their name, but the Boston Gardners spelled it without the *i*. Your great aunt Grace was one of the founders of this club, and, from all reports, was a very interesting woman."

But Hubie Altemus didn't want to hear what made old great aunt Grace Gardiner, spelled with an *i*, a very interesting woman. For years he had heard his uncle expound on the various branches of the family, but it was a topic that never interested Hubie in the least.

What interested Hubie was Juanito Perez. "Excuse me, Uncle Laurance, I have to make a call."

In the men's room, standing at the urinal, was Hubie's cousin, young Laurance Van Degan, who was everything in the family that Hubie was not. As Hubie approached the second urinal, Laurance, spotting his first cousin, turned his body away in a protective gesture.

"If you think I have any curiosity about your pecker, old man, give it another thought," said Hubie.

"You're disgusting, Hubie," said young Laurance Van Degan, his face acquiring the haughty Van Degan expression that Juanito could mimic so well.

Hubie, seeing it, laughed. "Asparagus for lunch, huh?" he asked.

"Have you become psychic in addition to your other worldly successes?" asked Laurance.

"No. Your piss stinks," said Hubie.

"You're disgusting, Hubie."

"You put those three inches of yours away so fast, Laurance, you forgot to shake it off, and now you've got a big wet urine stain all over your grays."

Laurance, red-faced, headed for the door.

"You better hurry back to Laura, Laurance. It must be time to breastfeed the baby again."

"I CAN REMEMBER the Depression only too well," said Cora Mandell. "We had to sell half the land in Bar Harbor. I couldn't go to school in Switzerland, and Uncle Joe Leyland had to pay for my debut dress."

"It's a terrible thing to have a great name and not enough money," said Ezzie Fenwick. Then he turned to Dodo Fitz Alyn and asked, "Don't you think so?"

Dodo, poor always, blushed.

"A perfect world for me would be where everyone I know and cared for had about forty million dollars," said Ezzie. "With forty million you can do everything you want to do and go everywhere you want to go, but you're not up there with Rochelle Prud'homme and Elias Renthal, thank the good lord. How do you suppose the Renthals got here? They made a big fuss about sitting on the bride's side, did you notice?"

"Mrs. Renthal fired me, then begged me to come back," said Cora, looking over at Elias and Ruby.

Ezzie Fenwick often used the word *frightfully* in conversation. "Frightfully funny," he'd say about an amusing story. "Frightfully nice," he'd say about some people. "Frightfully grand," about others. Or, "frightfully common." He said frightfully common more often than he said frightfully funny or frightfully nice or frightfully grand.

"Frightfully common," said Ezzie Fenwick.

"Who?" asked Cora Mandell.

"Mrs. Renthal, that's who. Look at the size of the ring on her finger. If that rock is fake, it's silly, and if it's real, it's ridiculous."

"It's real, all right," said Cora. "I can assure you of that."

"Bernie and Justine are dancing, Cora. Do you want to come and look?" asked Tucky Bainbridge.

"I'm perfectly content to sit right here and listen to Ezzie criticize everyone's clothes," said Cora.

"TALK TO ME, Elias. We can't stand here like we don't know anyone," said Ruby.

"Why do mice have such small balls?" asked Elias.

"So-few-of-them-dance-well. You already told me that one, Elias."

"I'm just trying to make it look like we're having a conversation, Ruby. Don't bite my head off because you already heard the fucking joke."

"My God, Elias, here comes Loelia Manchester to speak to us. Don't tell her any of your jokes, and don't say *fuck*."

"I get along with Loelia Manchester just fine, Ruby," replied Elias.

Loelia, approaching them, was struck anew by the change in the appearance of Elias Renthal, a change far more profound than could be brought about by expensive tailoring and barbering. What she saw in the florid face that she had once considered vulgar was the unmistakable look of power, and she was drawn to it.

Whatever reservations most of the guests of Lil Altemus and the Van Degan family might have about people like Elias Renthal and his third wife, there was the beginning of a noticeable change in the whispered information about them whenever someone asked, "Who in the world is that?" or "How do you suppose they got here?" Elias Renthal, it was now said, was a wizard in business, and his com-

ments about "interesting situations" in the stock market, with which
he was selectively generous, were to be acted upon by all means if
one was so favored. Indeed, it was said that Laurance Van Degan
himself, that most conservative of bankers and investors, had made a
killing on a stock tip from Elias Renthal. Then, of course, there was
the much discussed Renthal apartment, as yet unseen, but tales of its
splendors were constantly circulated. "The furniture, my dear, is
priceless," said no less an authority than Jamesey Crocus. Dolly De
Longpre had spread the word in her column that Elias Renthal had
also purchased Merry Hill, the magnificent estate and horse-breeding
farm that, years ago, had belonged to a family called Grenville, and
already dozens of masons and carpenters were at work to enlarge and
refront the mansion from Tudor to Georgian as a fitting residence for
his beloved Ruby. There was also, one heard, a house in the tropics,
and apartments in London and Paris, where Elias's business interests
took him frequently, always on his own plane with its own computers
and telephones and other equipment so that his work day need never
be interrupted. Certainly there was money, seemingly limitless
money, and no disinclination on the part of either Mr. or Mrs. Renthal
to spend it. Mrs. Renthal wore the largest gems in New York and
traveled to and from her hairdresser and to and from her other appointments in a pale blue limousine of foreign make that was the only
one of its kind in New York. Her wedding gift to Justine Altemus and
Bernie Slatkin was of such extravagance that Lil Altemus insisted it
be returned, and only the intervention of Laurance, her brother, who
suggested that it would be "unseemly" to return the gift, a gold tea
service that had once belonged to the Empress Josephine, prevented
Lil from carrying out her threat.

"Hello, Elias," said Loelia, and Ruby was thrilled with the proximity of her, as well as the vocal tones that announced her utter
perfection of birth and breeding. Loelia Manchester's attire was simplicity itself, as Dolly De Longpre said the next day in her column,
but she was by far the best-dressed woman in the room.

"Loelia, this is Ruby," said Elias.

"Your husband was so charming to me, Ruby, when you were away.
I've looked forward to meeting you."

"Same here," said Ruby. "Love your outfit."

"Love your ring," said Loelia, and the two ladies laughed.

"We were wondering, Mickie and I, if you and Elias would dine with us on Monday and go on to the opera."

"Monday?" asked Ruby. She looked at Elias. Monday was the night of the birthday of Elias's daughter by his first marriage. Their eyes met. He nodded that it would be all right.

"We'd be delighted, Loelia," said Ruby in her smartest voice.

"Jaime's coming," said Loelia.

"Hymie?" answered Ruby.

"You'll adore Jaime."

"Hymie who?"

"The Honduran ambassador."

"HAVE SOME champagne, Gus," said Lil Altemus. "There's going to be toasts."

"I have my old faithful here," said Gus, clutching a glass of fizzy water. Gus always held his water glass as if it were a cocktail.

"Oh, I always forget," said Lil. "One glass can't hurt, surely?"

"I'm fine, thanks."

"Do me a favor, will you, Gus?" asked Lil. "Will you talk to those Renthals. They don't know anyone here, and Laurance is determined that they have a good time, God knows why."

"Loelia Manchester is dancing with Elias Renthal," said Gus.

"Loelia? Really? That's a new one. Be a love and go dance with what's-her-name, his wife," said Lil.

"Ruby," said Gus.

"Yes, of course, Ruby," said Lil, who had known her name was Ruby all along.

Ruby was thrilled to dance with Gus. Her conversation with Loelia Manchester had made her feel for the first time that she was going to be able to make it in New York.

"I'm just an old fox-trotter," said Gus. "I'm not up on all the new steps."

"You and Elias," said Ruby.

"You're looking great, Ruby. I read about you in the papers all the time."

Ruby laughed. "How's everything with you?" she asked.

"Okay."

"You feel tense to me."

"Our mutual friend, Lefty Flint, is up for a parole hearing on the thirteenth of next month," said Gus.

"I can't believe it," she said. The color drained from her face.

"It's true."

"Are you going out for the hearing?"

"No."

"Why?"

"He's got an automatic release. A perfect jail record. Everybody's little darling."

"You know he's going to do it again, don't you?" she said.

"I do."

"Where's the hearing?"

"The Men's Correctional Institute. Vacaville, California."

Ruby looked at Gus, as if she were going to say something.

"My husband's about to cut in on you," she said.

WHEN THE drummer from Peter Duchin's orchestra rolled the drums for silence, Lil Altemus went to the microphone with a glass of champagne in her hand and made a charming speech, even if she didn't believe what she was saying, which she didn't, saying how much she liked Bernie Slatkin and how perfect she thought he was for Justine, and how glad she was to have Bernie's aunt and uncle, Hester and Sol Slatkin, in the family. When Bernie got up to deliver his speech, he said he thought he was the luckiest man on earth to be married to Justine Altemus, and his dimple was admired by all of Justine's friends as he raised his glass to toast his beautiful new wife.

"You should be off, Justine," said Lil.

"After I throw the bouquet, Mother," replied Justine.

"Throw it to poor Dodo," said Lil.

"Isn't it sweet the way she takes care of Grandfather, wiping all the drool off his mouth all the time," said Justine.

"Where's Bernard?"

"Dancing with his aunt."

Lil Altemus and her daughter both looked toward the dance floor. Bernie, dancing with Hester, gave Justine a wink. At that moment a late arriving guest entered the ballroom. Wearing a turban, she had an exotic look about her. She appeared to be looking for someone.

"My God, there's that horrible woman," said Lil. "What's she doing here?"

"What horrible woman?"

"In the yellow dress, and the turban. Mrs. Lupescu. Did you invite her?"

"I certainly didn't invite her, Mother."

"She's surely not one of Uncle Laurence's business acquaintances, like Elias Renthal."

"Do you suppose Constantine de Rham is here too?"

"He'd better not be. Consuelo was one of my best friends. That woman crashed. I never heard of anyone crashing a wedding reception before. That's the tackiest thing I ever heard. Throw your bouquet, Justine. I want to wind up this party."

"OH, HELLO, Gus. I'm sorry I'm so late," said Yvonne Lupescu.

"Late?" asked Gus, surprised to see her.

"I was so thrilled when you asked me to come. Poor Constantine wasn't feeling well. He's been so depressed, and he thought it would be marvelous for me to get out. So sweet of you, Gus," said Yvonne.

Gus looked at Yvonne. She smiled at him and linked her arm in his and looked at the dance floor. "Shall we dance?" she asked.

"No," said Gus. "I don't like to dance."

"I bet you're a marvelous dancer."

"I'm not."

"Oh, look, Gus, Justine's going to throw her bouquet. Let's go watch." She took Gus by the arm and led him into the room.

Justine, with Bernie by her side, stood on the stairway of the club, her train wrapped around her arm, and looked down at her friends. People pushed Dodo Fitz Alyn and Violet Bastedo to the front. There was a drumroll from Peter Duchin's band, and Justine raised her hand and threw the bouquet. Dodo, crimson with embarrassment, reached her hands up in the air. Violet, already twice-married, squealed with excitement as she held up her arms. In an instant, Yvonne Lupescu stepped in front of both ladies and grabbed the bouquet just as it was about to land in Dodo Fitz Alyn's hands.

"Oh, how marvelous," said Yvonne. "Wait till Constantine hears. Gus, isn't it exciting?"

Gus, speechless, stared at Yvonne Lupescu.

MEANWHILE, Constantine de Rham's body, as yet undiscovered, lay in a pool of blood on the floor of the den in his house on Sutton Place.

18

THE NEXT morning, Gus was rushing for the airport to go to Los Angeles, in response to a message Detective Johnston had left on his answering machine. At the same time Innocento was arriving in the lobby of his building with Gus's standing order of three containers of coffee and the morning papers. "I'll be gone for a few days, Innocento," said Gus, grabbing the papers and the coffee and heading for the car that he had ordered to take him to the airport. "I'll call you when I get back to start up the papers again."

"Have a good trip," called out Innocento, but by that time Gus was telling the driver not to put his bag in the trunk of the sedan but to keep it on the seat next to him, as he was late, so that he could just make a run for it when he got to JFK. The driver, who looked Hispanic, nodded as if he understood Gus's instructions, but he didn't understand Gus's instructions and put the bag in the trunk of the sedan anyway.

"Innocento," Gus called out. "Tell this guy I'm in a hurry. I've got an eight ten to catch."

If the plane hadn't been late, Gus would have missed it, but planes were always late these days, and he arrived at the airport in plenty of time, although not on speaking terms with his driver.

"When was the last time you were on a plane that wasn't late starting?" asked the pretty middle-aged advertising executive who was sitting next to Gus in the business section, looking up from some copy she was revising with a pink Hi-Liter. She was wearing a tailored suit and gold jewelry, and her nails were perfectly manicured. And she was ready for some cross-country conversation.

Gus smiled politely and said, "I can't remember." Then he picked up the newspapers that Innocento had brought him and buried his face in them, starting with the tabloids, saving the *Times*, because he didn't want to get into a conversation about late planes and the reason for their lateness, and because he knew, from instinct and experience, that by the time the plane had flown over the border of the state of New York, the woman would have told him about her impending divorce, her husband's girlfriend who used to be her best friend, her daughter's abortion, and her ideas for the new advertising campaign of a cigarette company her agency had just taken on.

It was then, aloft, that Gus read about the suicide attempt of Constantine de Rham. De Rham, dying, had been discovered by his Filipino butler, who had returned early to the house on Sutton Place from his day off, because he was feeling unwell. The butler, Ramon Enrile, 62, found de Rham when he began turning on lights in the darkened house, lying in a pool of blood on the floor of his den, beneath a painting of a stag being torn apart by hounds. In his left hand was a revolver. A single shot had been fired into his stomach. At first the butler thought he was dead. He went to look for Mrs. Yvonne Lupescu, Mr. de Rham's companion, who was a visitor in the house, but she was not there. He then called the police. De Rham was in the intensive care unit of New York Hospital under police watch. No note had been found near the body nor was any reason given as to why the 50-year-old de Rham should wish to take his life. When Mrs. Lupescu returned to the house, she was informed by police of the suicide attempt and became hysterical. She blamed herself, she said, because she had decided to leave him. It was later ascertained by police that at the time of the suicide attempt Mrs. Lupescu had been attending the society wedding reception of the Van Degan heiress, Justine Altemus, to the television anchorman Bernard Slatkin at the Colony Club.

Gus, stunned, put down the tabloid and stared out the window of the airplane. In his pocket, on a sheet of expensive but plain white paper, typewritten, was the name, address, and telephone number of a man in Los Angeles called Anthony Feliciano. It had arrived in the mail the day before in an unmarked envelope, with no accompanying letter, several hours before Detective Johnston's message had been left on his answering machine telling him the date Lefty Flint was to be released from prison. Gus knew that the sender was Constantine de Rham.

GUS APPROACHED Los Angeles with dread. He always approached Los Angeles with dread. Once he had lived there. Once he had worked there. Once he had raised a family there. Once he had been happy there. But that was long ago and far away.

There were several places Gus could have stayed. Peach, possibly,

would have him. Peach no longer lived in the house where they had
lived when they were married. Several years earlier she had moved to
a smaller house in the part of Beverly Hills known as the flats. She
did not enjoy guests, but the house had a guest room, which she
called a spare room, to discourage guests, as well as a small apartment in the pool house that she let out to students from U.C.L.A. so
that there would always be someone on the property, and Gus happened to know that the apartment was empty at the moment. But Gus
didn't want Peach to know he was in town until after he had done
what he had come to do.

He thought about staying at Cecilia Lesky's house in Bel-Air, but
Cecilia, who was the daughter of the film mogul Marty Lesky, as well
as an old friend of Gus's, was always giving parties, or going to parties, or having people drop in from noon until two in the morning.
There were times when he enjoyed Cecilia Lesky's kind of pandemonium, but this was not one of them.

Then there were his friends Nestor and Edwina Calder, who had
rented a house in Malibu while Nestor was writing the screenplay for
the mini-series of *Judas Was a Redhead,* but being with Nestor and
Edwina would have meant having to answer questions about his trip
to Los Angeles, and he did not wish to either lie to them or be questioned by them.

In the end Gus decided to stay at a hotel on the Sunset Strip where
it was unlikely he would run into anyone he knew, as he most certainly would have if he had stayed in any of the well-known hotels in
Beverly Hills or Bel-Air, where even the waitresses in the coffee
shops all called him by name. Checking in at the Sunset Marquis, he
was pleased to find out it was within walking distance of the address
that Constantine de Rham had given him for Anthony Feliciano.

"How did you get my name?" asked Anthony Feliciano.

"In New York, where I live," said Gus.

"New York, huh?" Anthony Feliciano seemed pleased that he had
been discussed in New York. "Who told you about me in New York?"

"A man called Constantine de Rham."

"That's a name from the past. How is Constantine de Rham?"

"Almost dead, apparently, according to this morning's New York
papers."

"How almost dead?"

"Shot in the stomach, by his own hand."

"He never struck me as a suicide type," said Feliciano.

"Nor me," replied Gus.

"Did you know him long?"

"No, and not well at that."

Anthony Feliciano sat behind a desk of fake mahogany in a small office in a second-class building on a street that looked down on the Sunset Strip. Behind him on a credenza that matched the desk was a huge fake orchid plant in full purple bloom. Next to it were several color photographs of the same woman, excessively blond and pretty, one of her in a bathing suit, arm in arm with Feliciano, stripped to the waist, on what appeared to be a Hawaiian beach.

"That's Wanda," said Feliciano, seeing Gus look at the photographs. "My wife Wanda."

"Very pretty," replied Gus.

"What is it you wanted to see me about?"

"There is someone I would like to have followed."

"And you went to Constantine de Rham?"

"I felt he would know."

"He did. Who is this person you want to have followed?"

"His name is Francis Flint. He is called Lefty Flint."

Anthony Feliciano jotted the name on a pad in front of him with a desk pen. "What is it you want to know about this man?"

"I want to know where he lives. I want to know what he does with his time."

"When will you want me to start?"

"October thirteenth. That is the day he is to be released from prison."

"Where is the prison?"

"Vacaville."

"What is he?"

"A strangler," replied Gus.

"A strangler?" repeated Feliciano, surprised.

"A strangler is someone who puts his hands around another person's neck and chokes the life out of that person," said Gus.

"I am aware of the definition of a strangler, Mr. Bailey. What I meant was, what is this man's profession."

"Oh," said Gus, shaking his head. "Jack of all trades."

"Like what?"

"A guitarist sometimes. Or a singer. Then again a sculptor."

"A nothing, you mean," said Feliciano.

"No, that's not what I mean. A charmer would be a better word to describe him. The ladies always liked him."

"What is this man's connection to you?"

"He has caused grievous harm to me and my wife."

"Grievous harm of a strangulation nature, I take it?" asked Feliciano.

Gus did not reply directly to the question. "He was also a jury pleaser, especially to the ladies on the jury. They all wanted to be his mother. He carried a Bible. He used to be an altar boy, his lawyer said. He wore preppy clothes. No, no, he could never be what they said he was, he convinced them. It was a one-time thing, a crime of passion, a boy who simply loved too much. That's what he made them think. Or, rather, that's what his lawyer made them think about Lefty Flint."

Feliciano nodded but did not press for a more specific answer. "That shouldn't come as a surprise to you, Mr. Bailey. Any smart defense lawyer's going to do that. He's only interested in one thing— getting his client off, guilty or not guilty. It don't matter to him."

"And slander the victim? That's okay too?"

"I didn't say it's okay. I said it was legal."

Gus shook his head.

"How long will you want him followed?" asked Feliciano.

"Indefinitely."

"You have credentials?"

"Constantine de Rham, if he lives, will back me up."

"What is it you have in mind, Mr. Bailey?"

"I've told you, Mr. Feliciano."

"You've only kind of told me. Do you want this guy thrown out a window?"

"No. I don't want anything like that."

"It will look like an accident. No one will ever know. You won't meet the person who is going to do it, and he will never have heard your name. Very easily arranged. Not cheap, but safe."

"No, that's not what I want," said Gus, shaking his head.

"I sense there's more that you want than what you're telling me."

Gus looked out the dirty window at the flat sunlight of the California afternoon beating down on the Sunset Strip. "How do you think I feel, knowing that Lefty Flint is going to be out there, living a free life, having dinner in restaurants, going to movies, moving in a world of people who probably don't know that he has killed someone, and served a joke sentence, and that he feels he has atoned and has a right to a normal life?"

Gus made no effort to raise his voice for Anthony Feliciano to hear him, as if he were voicing to himself for the first time what he felt and what he wanted to do. "I used to think how great it would be if he was murdered in prison. Or raped, by gangs of prisoners. He was an arrogant son of a bitch, and I prayed for something like that to happen to him, but, alas, he has proved to be a model prisoner."

"You don't go around expressing these thoughts to people, do you, Mr. Bailey?"

"No."

"Don't confide that sort of thing to anyone. It can all be used against you."

"Strangling, you know, requires a great deal of strength. It's not every killer's choice," said Gus.

"What is it you have in mind, Mr. Bailey?" asked Feliciano. He wondered for a moment if Gus was mad.

"I want his hands put in a giant vise and crushed," said Gus, calmly, without turning to face Anthony Feliciano.

Feliciano remained silent for a moment, staring at Gus. Then he chuckled. "He won't be able to strum a guitar anymore," he said.

"He won't be able to strangle anyone either," said Gus.

"*LA SEÑORA*," said Immaculata, the housekeeper, "is in the garden."

Gus walked toward the French doors at the back of the small house. To the right was the dining room. To the left was the living room. The furniture was furniture he had once lived with, in different arrangements and different coverings. On the piano were silver-framed photographs of a family that once was and now was no longer, a family demolished by divorce and disease, estrangement and murder. Gus did not stop to look, other than to notice that Immaculata had been sparing of late with the silver polish, a housekeeping shortcoming that would go unnoticed by Peach, who had long since ceased looking at the photographs, or who looked at them without seeing them. He went out the door and across the lawn to the white stucco wall that ran from the house to the pool house. He pushed open the wrought-iron gate that led into Peach's small garden. For a moment the wisteria bushes on each side of the gate, dripping in heavy lavender bloom, partially obscured his view of the rose bushes that were Peach's pride and joy.

"I'm over here," called Peach, when she heard the wrought-iron gate slam. She was sitting in her wheelchair next to a wooden bench. Gus walked toward her on a grass path between two rose beds with blossoms of every color mixed together, without thought of symmetry or balance. Symmetry was of no concern to Peach. Symmetry, when they were married, had been Gus's concern, which Peach resisted. Without Gus, it became inconsequential. Her garden flourished with a sort of wildness and lack of design.

Gus knew, even before he reached the place where Peach was sitting, that gardening was not what was occupying her thoughts. Her clippers, her gloves, her wicker basket filled with roses lay on the wooden bench. She was wearing, as always, a caftan, to cover her useless legs, and she had sheltered her skin from the sun with a wide-brimmed straw hat. Next to her, sleeping, was one of the several black cats that were always with her. Gus had not seen her for five months. The disease that ravaged her beauty and incapacitated her legs had taken five months' toll.

"Oh, hi," she said when she saw who it was. She never said more than, "Oh, hi," to Gus when he came to visit her on his infrequent trips to Los Angeles. She did not register surprise, or delight, or displeasure.

"Hi," Gus answered, in the same manner. He looked at her for a minute. He used to think there was a natural conclusion to love. He had, after all, been in love before Peach, and after her he had been involved several times, but it was always to Peach that his thoughts and longings returned.

"What kind of a name is Peach?" he asked her the first time they met.

"It's what I'm called," she answered simply.

"Gus and Peach. How do you think that sounds?" he asked her.

"It doesn't really get me," she replied.

"Maybe Peach and Gus sounds better," he said.

Actually her name was Rebecca, but if there was ever anyone who was not a Rebecca type, it was she. Her father, whom she loved, called her Peach, and Peach became what she was called.

When Gus asked Peach Prindeville to marry him, he didn't really expect her to say yes. He thought that she had seen the deficiencies in him, recognized them inwardly, the way women were supposed to. The surprise was when, after thinking about it, she said yes, she would like to marry him. She said it by letter. He was thrilled. He was also terrified. He was in awe of her. Always was. Still was. Awe, of course, was never what Peach wanted.

If a day went by when he did not telephone her, on some pretext, often invented, he missed her. But she rarely telephoned him, and then only for an important reason. Peach would never call Gus to say, "You won't believe who's getting married," or divorced, or who's inherited a great deal of money, or gone broke. But he would call her with that kind of news, and he felt sure that although she often sounded indifferent, she enjoyed his calls. Since Peach, he had distanced himself from the possibility of love.

"I'm just in town for overnight," said Gus.

"Did you tell me you were coming?" she asked. Her question acknowledged that she sometimes forgot things.

"No."

"Is anything the matter?"

They were people who had known extreme grief and had become able, among themselves, to ask and answer questions pertaining to disaster in an impersonal way.

"I wanted to tell you that I have hired a private detective."

"Why did you do that?"

"Lefty Flint is getting out of prison."

"I know," said Peach.

"You know? Detective Johnston just called me in New York last night. He wanted me to be the one to tell you."

From a pocket in her caftan, Peach pulled out a cheap white envelope and handed it to Gus. The stamp, imperfectly cornered, said LOVE.

"It's from him," said Peach.

Gus blanched and felt the sick feeling he always felt when Lefty Flint's presence was sensed. He moved Peach's gardening equipment from the bench and sat down next to her. He looked at the envelope but didn't open it.

"What's he want?" he asked.

"He wants to come and see me."

"Jesus Christ."

"When he's out, that is."

Nearly three years earlier Gus and Peach Bailey, separated in marriage but brought together by adversity, had sat side by side in a courtroom for seven weeks, a kind-of couple again. She needed him then, as much as he needed her, and they became, in a way neither had tried to explain to the other, closer than they had been when they were close. Less than ten feet from them sat Lefty Flint, the killer of their child, holding a Bible in his hands and with a look of piety on his face, dressed with the black-and-white simplicity of a sacristan in a seminary, although he was previously known to be a mocker of God. Peach had shuddered, seeing through it all, the sham of justice they were witnessing, knowing how it was going to end, that poor sweet Becky was going to be forgotten and Lefty Flint was only going to get his wrist slapped, in the name of love.

"Do you have any statement to make?" a television reporter had asked Gus at the conclusion of the trial.

"I sometimes wonder why the prosecution does not have the same relentless passion to convict the guilty that the defense attorneys have to free them," Gus had answered.

"Get me a gun, will you, Gus?" said Peach, simply.

"Would you kill him if he came here?" asked Gus.

"Of course," she answered.

"You can't do that, Peach," said Gus.

"You don't think they'd send a crip like me to prison, do you?"

Gus hated it when Peach called herself a crip, but it wasn't the moment to get into that.

"He can't come to see you. It's in violation of his parole if he contacts us. Detective Johnston told me that. He can't go to visit her grave either," said Gus. "Let me take this letter and turn it over to the police."

"Who's the private detective you've hired?"

"Let me put it this way, 'private detective' is kind of a classy description of him."

"Dicey, huh?" she asked.

"Dicey, yeah," he replied.

"Where did you hear about him?"

"Constantine de Rham."

"Speaking of dicey," said Peach, shaking her head dismissively at the mention of Constantine de Rham's name. "You do know the swellest people, Gus."

"Lefty Flint's going to be followed. If he comes anywhere near this house, they're going to throw him right back in the can."

"Does Detective Johnston know you've hired this private detective?"

"No."

"Are you going to tell him?"

"No."

Peach nodded. "Wheel me inside, will you, Gus. I have to get back into bed."

GUS LOOKED at his watch. It was time to leave for the plane to fly back to New York. Peach was lying in bed looking at a soap opera on television.

"Turn off the sound, will you?" said Gus.

Without replying, Peach felt around on her large bed between slumbering cats, mail, magazines, books, packages of cigarettes, and an assortment of Cricket lighters until she found the remote control for the television. Three times a day Immaculata came in to straighten out the jumble that the bed became. Peach adjusted the remote control but continued to stare at the set after the sound stopped.

"Time to go," he said.

"You just arrived."

"I'm going to Paris the day after tomorrow."

"What's in Paris?"

"I'm interviewing someone for my gigolo story."

"Is Paris safe? There're a lot of bombings in Paris these days."

"Just my luck to get killed on my way to interview the new ladyfriend of a bisexual gigolo who married an old lady millionairess and inherited all her money."

"Where do you dig up these awful people you always write about?" asked Peach.

"The gigolo told me he never met the person yet he couldn't get it up for, if the price was right."

"Those people might fascinate you, Gus, but they don't fascinate me," said Peach.

"Don't knock it, Peach," said Gus evenly. "It keeps my mind occupied. It keeps me from going nuts. It keeps me from dwelling on things I can't do anything about."

"I know, Gus. I'm not criticizing you. I might even envy you, now that I come to think of it."

"I have to go."

Peach continued to stare at the television set. People were yelling at each other, but the sound was still off. In bed, she was barricaded from him. What had once been a coffee table, now piled high with the accoutrements of an invalid's life, ran the length of her bed. Her wheelchair blocked the opening between the end of the table and her bed. Gus moved her wheelchair aside and bent down and kissed her on the cheek.

"I'm sorry I made you unhappy, Peach," he said.

Peach knew what he meant without his having to spell it out for her. She knew he was talking about back then, when they were married, not now.

"I'm not much for looking back, Gus," she said, staring at the set.

"I just wanted to tell you I'm sorry."

"Okay. You told me."

"Aren't you ever going to let up on me?"

"Oh, Gussie, come on. That was a long time ago."

He took hold of her foot and squeezed it. "So long, Peach," he said.

She understood there was affection in the gesture. "Good-bye, Gus," she answered.

EVERY time Gus drove out Wilshire Boulevard past the cemetery where Becky was buried, he beeped twice on his car horn in greeting to her, wherever she was.

19

"THAT'S WHERE the butler found poor Constantine," said Yvonne Lupescu, pointing to the dark spot on the Portuguese carpet.

In the week following Constantine de Rham's suicide attempt, Yvonne Lupescu knew happiness. "Yvonne," the tabloid papers called her, simply Yvonne, with no last name, signifying her new-found prominence as the "companion," which the papers always used with quotation marks, to the mysterious Constantine de Rham, who had, apparently, shot himself after he thought the Baroness Lupescu was going to leave him.

"No, no, I would never leave my darling Constantine," Yvonne was quoted as saying to Mavis Jones, the Broadway columnist, to whom she gave an exclusive interview, sitting in the very room where Constantine de Rham had been found bleeding. "It was all a terrible misunderstanding. We love each other."

"WE LOVE EACH OTHER," SAYS YVONNE, ran the headline in Mavis Jones's column.

"Where are you from, Baroness?" asked Mavis, trying to place Yvonne's accent.

"Paris," replied Yvonne.

For six days Yvonne gave daily bulletins from the hospital steps on Constantine's condition, dressed always in new suits that might have been from Chanel, but weren't, but she kept her pithy quotes for Mavis Jones, who was, after all, syndicated in sixty newspapers throughout the country. "He squeezed my hand," she said. Or, "To-day he begged me not to leave him."

Yvonne wanted her prominence to last forever, but, alas, Faye Converse, the film star, was robbed of all her jewels by a masked gunman in the elevator of the Rhinelander Hotel, and Yvonne could only get Mavis's assistant, Claire, on the telephone, as Mavis was having an exclusive interview with Faye Converse. The story was moved to the back pages and then disappeared entirely, and Yvonne complained bitterly to Ramon, the butler, that the city had no heart.

During the weeks of Constantine's recuperation at New York Hospital, Yvonne could often be seen dining alone at Clarence's. Sometimes she brought a book to read, but mostly she sat quietly, exotically turbaned, and watched the ebb and flow of the restaurant, as if she were looking at a film. Occasionally she made notes in a notebook that she always had with her.

Sometimes Chick Jacoby would sit at her table for a few minutes, perched on the edge of a chair to indicate that his visit was merely transitory, and get the latest reports on Constantine's condition, which he would then pass on to anyone who happened to evince interest in the subject of Constantine de Rham's gunshot wound. If it hadn't been for Chick Jacoby, no one would have spoken to Mrs. Lupescu, but she gave no indication that that was a matter of concern to her.

20

FOR LIL ALTEMUS and her friends, there were only ten buildings in Manhattan where people like themselves could live, four on Fifth Avenue, three on Park Avenue, one on Gracie Square, one on Sutton Place, and, of course, River Place, but even River Place had begun to let in what Lil called "a certain element."

After their marriage, Justine and Bernie Slatkin moved to a new apartment in a new building on Park Avenue that Lil Altemus described as "one of those buildings on Park Avenue where no one we know lives," although that was a statement she made to her daughter, but not to her son-in-law. Bernie Slatkin, she soon found out, did not capitulate to her every wish, as Justine once did, nor was Justine available anymore to make up a fourth for bridge at the last minute or fill in at the opera if someone dropped out of her box.

"Poor Cora Mandell is very hurt that you didn't use her to decorate your new apartment," said Lil Altemus to her daughter. "After all, she's done every one of the Altemus houses."

"Bernie didn't like cabbage-rose chintz," replied Justine. "In fact, Bernie hates cabbage-rose chintz. And, lest you forget, Mother, I'm no longer an Altemus. I'm Mrs. Slatkin now."

"No, I haven't forgotten that, Justine," said Lil.

"Come and see how the living room looks. It's marvelous, really. A whole new look for me."

LIL ALTEMUS, on her first visit to the new apartment, walked silently through Justine's just completed living room. Occasionally she nodded at things she recognized from before. "Sweet," she said finally in judgment, in a qualified tone. And then she repeated the word again. "Sweet."

"Sweet?" replied Justine.

Lil continued looking, without further comment.

"Sweet wasn't the effect I was striving for, Mother," said Justine.

"But it was meant as a compliment, Justine," said Lil.

"I find the word inadequate," said Justine.

"My dear, isn't marriage making us independent," said Lil. She sat down in a bergère chair and took off her gloves. "These lamp shades aren't quite first rate. They should be lined in pink."

"'Lined in pink,'" repeated Justine, as if she were making a list. "It so happens that my husband doesn't like lamp shades lined in pink."

"It makes women look so much prettier, tell him," said Lil, giving a gracious smile to her daughter. "You have far too many hyacinths in here, darling." She fanned herself with her gloves and pretended to reel from the heavy scent.

"Make the best of it," said Justine, impatiently.

Lil, who had expected Justine to remove the hyacinths, said, "Well, pardon me."

"I wouldn't, if I were you, Mother, make any of these comments in front of my husband," said Justine. "Hubie and I, we're used to you. We put up with you. But Bernie will let you have it."

"Ho, ho, ho. I'd like to see Bernie Slatkin let me have it," said Lil, chortling at the thought.

"Just be warned."

"Hmmm," said Lil. She continued to look around the room. "What do you call this color?"

"Green, mother."

"Well, of course, it's green. I know it's green. What I meant was, does the green have a name?"

"Oh, I don't know, Mother. Forest, I think it's called. Or evergreen. I can't remember. Do you like it, and, please, don't say it's sweet."

"Where's my Aubusson rug?" Lil cried, as she suddenly remembered that her wedding gift was not under her feet.

"Bernie didn't like it."

"Bernie Slatkin didn't like my Aubusson rug! That's the laugh of the week. If you don't like it, I'll take it back then, thank you very much," said Lil, indignant.

"We sold it," said Justine.

"You what?"

"Ruby Renthal bought it for her swell new apartment."

"That rug belonged to Grandmother Van Degan, from the house in Newport."

"That's why Ruby liked it so much. 'It has history,' she said."

"Really, Justine. That awful Mrs. Renthal."

"Bernie calls Ruby Renthal the talk of the town," said Justine. "Here, there, and everywhere, as Dolly says."

"I'm going to ask Cora to get it back from Mrs. Renthal," said Lil.

"Look, you gave it to us, Mother. You didn't say there were strings attached," said Justine.

Lil nodded, then rose, putting her gloves back on. "Well, I'm off."

"I thought you came for tea," said Justine. "Bonita's making tea."

"No, I must go. What's all that ladder equipment in the dining room?" asked Lil.

"I'm having the wall behind the buffet painted in *trompe l'oeil* to look like a coromandel screen. Don't you think that's a good idea?"

"Donina did that in her dining room," said Lil.

"You're a hard lady to get a compliment out of," said Justine. "I'm using the same painter that Donina used."

"He better paint quick, from what I hear."

"Why?"

"What's that disease they all have, those boys, where they're dropping like flies?" asked Lil. Justine turned quickly to look at her mother. "Bobo says there won't be a man left in New York to hang a curtain or hem a dress." Bobo was her hairdresser.

Justine continued to look at her mother.

"How's Hubie?" she asked.

"Hubie? Fine. Why?"

"Just asking," said Justine.

21

"DO YOU MIND if I light a cigar?" asked Elias Renthal.

"No, not at all," replied Ruby Nolte, who loathed cigars, especially in confined areas.

"Some women do," said Elias.

"Surely you can't think I am one of those women who would interfere with a man's pleasures, Mr. Renthal," said Ruby, smiling at him.

"It's Elias, please," replied Elias, smiling back at her.

"Elias," repeated Ruby, as if she were savoring the word. "Here, let me light it for you."

Ruby Nolte took Elias's gold lighter out of his hand and leaned forward toward him, holding the lighter in both hands. Elias, as if to steady her hands, took them both in his as he put his cigar into the flame.

"How come you took off your wedding ring?" asked Ruby.

"Well, you know." Elias, embarrassed, shrugged.

"Put it back on."

"Why?"

"What's the point of adultery if you pretend it's something else? Right? Besides, it adds to the charge."

Elias, only just satisfied minutes earlier, was ready to go again. They stared into each others' eyes for the several moments of the lighting process. Only then, her head surrounded by clouds of pearl-gray smoke, did Ruby allow her imagination to revel in the possibilities that the future held for her with this immensely rich man: the clothes, the jewels, the furs, the houses, and that which meant more to her than anything else, money of her own, in her own name.

All of this had happened four years ago. Or five. In Cleveland. It was not the first time Elias Renthal had removed his wedding ring for the purpose of extracurricular love, but, as things turned out, it was the last. Gladyce Renthal, the wife from that marriage, Elias's second, had been taken care of quite handsomely in the divorce settlement. She continued to live in her large suburban house in Shaker Heights, the smart part of Cleveland, and, until she began to read in the press of the splendors of the life-style of Elias and his new wife in New York, she had been reasonably contented. People from Cleveland, when they ran into Elias, told him that Gladyce had started to drink and, when drunk, talked badly about Elias, saying he had treated her shabbily. They didn't tell him that Gladyce called Ruby a whore, if she was feeling kind, or a cunt, if she wasn't.

Ruby Renthal's picture was everywhere. Photographers waited for her on the opening nights at the opera and ballet, at the library and the museum. She became known as a patroness of the arts but, in truth, she only attended the opera and the ballet on the nights of the gala performances when there were supper dances on the promenade afterward. Pieces on the life-style of the Renthals had begun to appear in all the fashionable magazines. The name Renthal was, in short order, becoming as well known in social circles as it already was in business circles. If Ruby Renthal's name was on the committee of a charity, followers of such matters knew that that was the event to be at that night.

Matilda Clarke said to Lil Altemus about Ruby Renthal, "She has someone," and Lil Altemus nodded in agreement. They didn't mean a lover. They meant a publicist, someone quietly behind the scenes orchestrating Ruby's rise to social prominence.

"They come, they go, these people," said Lil Altemus. "Last year everyone was talking about Constantine de Rham. Now you never hear his name, or you hear it and people shudder. This year Mr. Renthal's is the name on every lip, and his wife is here, there, and everywhere, and it seems like only yesterday that no one had ever heard of them."

"Loelia Manchester claims that Ruby Renthal is here to stay," said Matilda.

"We'll see," said Lil.

"THAT'S Lorenza, isn't it?" asked Ruby, looking at an antique coffee pot crammed full with dozens of multicolored roses in various stages of rose life, from buds to swollen blossoms, the trademark of Lorenza, the most expensive florist in the city, that was only one of several on the tables in Loelia Manchester's temporary suite in the Rhinelander Hotel.

"What?" asked Loelia.

"The flowers? Aren't they Lorenza?"

"Lorenza, oh, yes. She comes here every Monday and Thursday to do the flowers."

Ruby was thrilled with this information. Imagine, she thought, having Lorenza herself come to your house to arrange your flowers twice a week, even when there were no parties planned. It seemed to her yet another level of refinement what these people, who had begun to take her into their midst, understood and took for granted as normal living.

Loelia Manchester snuggled back against the pale yellow damask of a bergère chair, one arm resting on the gilt frame over her head. What an elegant pose, thought Ruby. I must practice that. Loelia dazzled Ruby with her glamour. Ruby was spellbound and, at first, tongue-tied in her presence. She had not imagined that such a thing as conversation could be so exhilarating, and she was always asking Loelia to speak louder so as not to miss anything she said in her husky, fashionable voice. Loelia, in turn, was flattered by Ruby's adoration, especially as her own friends, like Lil Altemus and Matilda Clarke, were being cool to her since she had abandoned Ned for Mickie, whom they all liked to dance with at charity balls but found totally inappropriate as a suitor for her. Loelia also found Ruby lacking in artifice and was herself spellbound by the truth of her tales.

"Go on," said Loelia to her new friend, prodding her to continue with her story.

"I began having my period when I was eight," confided Ruby.

"Eight?" cried Loelia, aghast.

"I was advanced for my age," explained Ruby.

"An understatement!" exclaimed Loelia.

"By the time I was ten, I was like a woman, full breasts, the works. By the time I was twelve, I was having sex. By the time I was fourteen, I was having affairs. By the time I was sixteen, I was married for the first time. By the time I was twenty-two, I was married three times."

"Heavens!" said Loelia, fascinated with such a story.

"I was twenty-eight when I met Elias and ready to settle down. By that time I'd seen a thing or three. I knew about people like you and how you live. I wanted to be one of you. And when I met Elias, I knew I could be, with his bucks and my brains."

"Riveting," was the only thing that Loelia could think to say about Ruby's life.

"Let me tell you one thing, Loelia. You see me do anything wrong, ever, you correct me. I guarantee you I won't take offense."

"Of course, Ruby," replied Loelia. "Tell me something."

"Shoot."

"Were you the cause of the breakup of Elias's marriage?" Loelia asked.

Ruby shrugged her shoulders. "They'd been together for fourteen years. That was long enough."

Loelia stared at Ruby. The directness of Ruby's answers to questions about herself always fascinated Loelia.

Ruby, mistaking Loelia's stare for disapproval, continued. "Look, Loelia, I wasn't the first little chickadee Elias Renthal had dallied with, believe me. If it hadn't been me, it would have been someone else. But I was the one who told him it was one thing to be the biggest fish in Cleveland, Ohio, where they wouldn't even let him in the country club, and quite another thing to be the biggest fish in New York City."

"Is it true you were a stewardess?"

"Among other callings."

"You met him on a flight?"

"'Coffee, tea, or me,' I said. He picked me."

Loelia laughed.

"I was also a hostess at Howard Johnson's, but, for God's sake, don't tell anyone that." said Ruby.

"Do you love Elias?"

"Sure, I love him, and of all the wives he's had, I'm the best one for him. It's a package deal when a young girl marries an older man. He has this talent for making money. I have this talent for spending it. We needed each other."

"And if he weren't so rich?"

"Would I still have fallen in love with him? Is that what you want to know?"

Loelia, embarrassed, blushed.

"Probably not," Ruby answered. "But he is so rich, and I love him very much. How's that for an answer?"

"Honest," said Loelia, smiling at her.

"Tell me something about Mickie, Loelia," said Ruby.

Loelia knew what Ruby was going to ask her about Mickie, but she was not prepared to be as forthright about her private life as Ruby was about hers. Ruby, studying Loelia, noticed the slight stiffening of her body and understood the reluctance it implied.

"Don't misunderstand me, Loelia," she said, as a new idea suggested itself to her. "What I meant was about Mickie's career at the moment. You see, Elias and I are planning to give a ball, to show off the new place, whenever Cora Mandell finishes it, for about four hundred guests. *Tout* New York, as Dolly De Longpre would say, and we were wondering if Mickie would be interested in designing it for us. I mean, you're always saying how Mickie really should have been a stage designer instead of a shoe designer. We want it to be something they write about for years to come. The Renthal ball. I've been thinking of butterflies for a theme. Do you think that would appeal to Mickie?"

"Oh, Ruby, darling Ruby, I can't think of anything more marvelous," exclaimed Loelia, hugging her new friend. "Wait till Mickie hears! He will be beside himself. Fantasy, Ruby. Mickie has such a sense of fantasy. And butterflies! If you knew how Mickie adores butterflies! It will be magical, whatever he does. I can guarantee you of that. And everyone will come. I can guarantee you of that too."

Ruby pushed back the sleeve of her perfect red suit and looked at her perfect gold watch, oval shaped with Roman numerals, that once belonged to the Duchess of Windsor. Ruby's watch, although beautiful and historic as a piece of jewelry, was often inaccurate as a timepiece, falling behind twenty minutes every twenty-four hours, with the result that she always arrived late to her hairdresser, or for her lingerie fittings, or her French lessons, to the consternation of those poor souls who serviced her, but she was so abject with apology for the inconveniences that she had caused, that she was instantly forgiven, and her tips and her gifts at Christmas were such as no other client in the city gave. "Holy cow, I gotta get my ass in gear," she said to Loelia. "I have a French lesson with Count Motulsky at two. I'm going to Jamesey Crocus's lecture on Sèvres china at the museum at four. I have to be at Madame Orromeo's cocktail party at six thirty, and we're going to the opera with Laurance and Janet Van Degan at eight."

THE FOLLOWING morning Ruby flew on her husband's plane to Vacaville, California. She told Elias she wanted to use the plane to attend an auction at a California ranch. She said some horse sculptures by Frederick Remington were being offered, and she thought she might add one or two to the collection that Elias had begun for their house in the country. Ruby promised Elias she would be back in New York in time for Loelia Manchester's dinner.

A car and driver waited for her at the small airport in Vacaville. A decorator friend of Cora Mandell's had purchased two Remington horse sculptures from a San Francisco collector and placed them in the car for Ruby to take back to New York. She told the pilot of the plane that she was attending an auction but would not be long. In the car was a lawyer from San Francisco.

"Hi, Mrs. Renthal, I'm Morrie Sable."

"Hello," she replied.

"All the arrangements have been made. The hearing is scheduled for eleven. It's about a fifteen-minute drive."

"Let's go," said Ruby.

As the car drove over the dusty roads to the prison, Morrie Sable several times tried to make conversation with Ruby, but she was preoccupied with her own thoughts.

"Shall I send the bill to your husband's office in New York, Mrs. Renthal?" he asked.

"Heavens, no," she replied. "I've brought a check with me."

"But I won't know how much the tally is until I've figured out the hours involved," he said.

"It's blank, and it's signed. You fill it in, Mr. Sable."

"Okay."

"Under no circumstances do I want my husband to know about this."

"Mind if I ask you why you're doing this?" he asked.

"Four years ago I sat in a car outside a church in Beverly Hills during Becky Bailey's funeral, feeling too guilty to go in, because I knew that if I had stepped forward when I should have stepped forward, what happened to that poor young girl might not have happened. This is my way of seeing that it doesn't happen again," she answered.

Morrie Sable looked at her.

In the hearing room, the session was already in progress. Lefty

Flint sat at a table, with his lawyer, Marv Pink, at his side. He held a ballpoint pen in his hand and wrote notes on a yellow lined scratch pad. At another table sat the prison warden and two parole officers. Several guards from the prison sat in the spectators' section, as did Marguerite Hanrahan, Lefty's fiancée, who was waiting to testify on Lefty's behalf.

When the doors of the room opened, everyone turned to look at the beautiful and elegantly dressed woman who entered. She carried an alligator bag with a gold chain. Lefty Flint, seeing Ruby, blanched.

Ruby walked past the table where Lefty was seated without looking at him and took a chair that had been placed for her next to the presiding parole officer. After introductions had been made, the warden called on Mrs. Renthal to speak.

"My name is Ruby Nolte Renthal," she began. "I have come here today from my home in New York to plead with you not to grant Francis Flint an early release from his prison sentence."

"Warden, I object," said Marv Pink, rising from his seat.

"This is a hearing, not a trial, Mr. Pink. There are no objections recognized. Mrs. Renthal's lawyer called me and asked that his client be allowed to come here to speak," said the warden. "Go on, Mrs. Renthal."

"I had a two-year relationship with Francis Flint that ended several years before the murder of Becky Bailey. On four separate occasions Mr. Flint beat me. Once when I tried to escape from him, he threw me down a stairway. On two separate occasions I was hospitalized as a result of his beatings. The latter time, Mr. Flint, whom I called Lefty, broke my nose and teeth, blacked my eyes, and fractured my jaw."

"Did you press charges at the time?" asked the warden.

"No," replied Ruby. She opened her bag and took out a handkerchief.

"May I ask why, Mrs. Renthal?"

Ruby looked at Marv Pink and answered, "I was warned not to."

"By whom?"

"It doesn't matter now," she replied, wiping a tear away. "The jury at his trial for the murder of Becky Bailey was allowed to think that her strangulation was a single isolated incident on the part of Lefty Flint in an otherwise impeccable life. This is not true. Mr. Flint is a classic abuser of women, and his weapon is his hands."

The room was in silence.

"Are you finished, Mrs. Renthal?" asked the warden.

"Yes, sir, I am, except to say that I feel this man is a danger to women. I have seen him froth at the mouth in anger. I know how little it takes for him to lose control."

Lefty Flint, breathing heavily, pushed back his chair from the table. The ballpoint pen that he had been holding snapped in two in his hand. Marv Pink placed his hand on Lefty's arm in a cautionary gesture.

"Sit down, Lefty," whispered Marguerite from behind him.

"Thank you, Mrs. Renthal," said the warden.

"Am I excused?" she asked.

"Yes."

Ruby rose. Morrie Sable rose. As Ruby walked past Lefty Flint on her way to the door, their eyes met for an instant.

22

ROMANTIC longevity was never Bernie Slatkin's long suit. He was used to the adoration of five or six women at the same time, in the compartmentalized way he had always lived his life, with no part encroaching upon another. Women who watched him on television wrote him letters, or waited for him outside the studio in the hopes of meeting him. Even women he met at society parties looked at him across dinnertables in an inviting manner, sometimes even slipping their place cards into his pocket with their telephone numbers hastily scribbled on them. He liked the chase. He liked seduction. He liked the madness of ecstasy that came with new partners. He liked not having to answer to anyone for his time and affections. His affairs, when he had had them before his marriage, were brief, mostly culminating after week-long love-soaked sojourns to tropical islands, when the sameness began to pall.

Bernie could not deny that Justine's love had begun to bore him. He preferred the flippancy of Brenda Primrose, in the news room, with whom he had had an affair and with whom, from time to time, for old times' sake, if they had both been working late, he still sought quick satisfaction. He knew that during their affair she had been seeing two other men at the same time, and he liked her for it because it showed that she played the game the way he did, for sex, not love.

At the bal masquè following the opening of the ballet, Bernie and Justine Slatkin were the guests of Elias and Ruby Renthal. Ruby, the best dancer on the small dance floor, could feel Bernie Slatkin's erection boring into her. Looking up, she could see that his eyes had the look of a man in the throes of deep desire. "Uh, uh," she said, shaking her head in refusal, at the same time backing her pelvis away from him without missing a beat of the dance. "It feels good, Bernie, and I hear you're great in bed, but I already got myself a fella. And you've already got yourself a lady, and I do mean a lady, in case it slipped your mind." The music stopped. "Thanks for the dance, Bernie. I love to samba. Now I'm off to find my husband."

THAT YEAR Justine gave Bernie many gifts: gold cuff links from Tiffany for day, sapphire-and-gold cuff links from Cartier for evening, silk pajamas with his monogram over the pocket, a maroon polka-dot dressing gown, and writing paper with his name engraved in all sizes and shapes. For a while Bernie loved her gifts and was amused by her extravagances. In return, on Justine's occasions, Bernie was never ungenerous, but often unimaginative, settling at the last minute for flowers, or a gold bracelet, when their apartment was already full of flowers arranged by Lorenza and Justine had more gold bracelets than she could ever wear. But Justine, madly in love, raved over his gifts as if they were precious and special, conceived only for her.

Bernie enjoyed Justine's kind of social life, up to a point, although it dismayed him that they went out almost every night. He also enjoyed the kind of sporting life that Justine's friends led on the weekends in the country: tennis, golf, shooting. He enjoyed the kind of powerful people he met through his marriage into the Van Degan family, like the Elias Renthals. He enjoyed the admiration he felt he received from Uncle Laurance Van Degan because of the kind of money he earned, and the recognition factor he possessed in public. He was quick to act on any tips in the stock market that Uncle Laurance offered him. If he were to go into politics sometime in the future, which people told him he could, with his sincerity and his dimple, the kind of people he was meeting and being accepted by were the kind of people to guide and finance him in his political schemes.

He could have been happy. But he couldn't be faithful.

23

LAURANCE VAN DEGAN accepted the astonishing news without astonishment. It was not for him to register shock, or surprise, or fear, in front of a servant, although, strictly speaking, Miss Mae Toomey could not exactly be classified as a servant. Laurance Van Degan's consciousness of his superiority did not desert him during the fifteen-minute encounter with his father's nurse. However, when Laurance Van Degan imparted that same news to his sister later in the day, in his office, it was almost more than Lil could bear. Their father, Ormonde Van Degan, the head of the family—although stroked, incontinent, and possibly senile—had made it known to Miss Toomey that he intended to elope with Dodo Fitz Alyn.

Lil, weeping, said, "But, surely, Laurance, there can be nothing *intimate* in their relationship."

"Don't be too sure of that, Lil," said Laurance.

"What do you mean? The man is eighty-four."

"She runs dirty videos for him."

"Oh, Laurance, for God's sake. It's too ridiculous."

"It's also true."

"How do you know that?"

"Miss Toomey."

"Who's Miss Toomey?"

"The nurse."

"Oh, yes, of course, Miss Toomey. I always called her Mae."

"And then she jerks him off."

"Miss Toomey jerks Father off?"

"No, Lil, for God's sake. Don't be so dense. Dodo jerks off Father when he looks at the dirty videos."

Lil shuddered. "After all we've done for Dodo Fitz Alyn, Laurance. No one wanted her. Reared among all those peculiar people. Her father went to prison for tax evasion. Her mother ran off with one of those awful Orromeo brothers. Her uncle jumped off the *Queen Elizabeth* after doing whatever unspeakable act he did with that Cockney sailor. And we, poor fools, took her in and gave her a home and paid for her education."

"I know her history, Lil."

"Next thing I suppose she'll expect to figure in Father's will?"

"More than that."

Lil stiffened. In matters of inheritance and heirlooms, Lil Altemus always became alert. "What do you mean?"

"Up front. Dodo wants money up front as well."

"How much money?"

"Twelve million."

She laughed at the absurdity. "I can't believe any of this, Laurance."

"Plus," he added.

"What do you mean *plus?*"

"She wants the house in Southampton to be put in her name."

"Mother's house?" asked Lil, aghast.

"And she wants the Romney picture of Lady Rushington to be hers. And the Fabergé eggs to be put in her name as well."

"But those were Mother's things, Laurance," said Lil.

"Now they're going to be Dodo's," answered Laurance.

"But Mother always said they were to be mine. You know that. You heard her say it a thousand times, Laurance."

"She didn't put it in writing, though. She just assumed Father would leave them to you in his will."

"All this time we thought 'poor Dodo' was pushing around his wheelchair, she's been taking inventory?"

"So it appears."

"And you're going to allow this, Laurance? You of all people? The strength of the family. You're going to let this fat orphan dictate those terms to us? Stand up to that sneaky bitch. Show her who's boss. What's she going to do if you tell her no, absolutely no?"

"She's going to stop jerking off Father. That's what she's going to do. And, apparently, Father likes to be jerked off."

Lil, crestfallen, began to gather up her things. "I always thought—" she said and then stopped midsentence.

"Thought what, Lil?" asked her brother.

"I always thought Dodo was a dyke."

Laurance looked at her. "What's a dyke?" he asked.

"A Daughter of Bilitis," said Lil, in explanation.

"I don't know what the hell you're talking about, Lil," said her brother.

"Like Aunt Grace Gardiner."

"Oh," said Laurance, understanding at last. "A lezzie, you mean. Do you know something, Lil? I always thought Dodo was a lezzie too."

They looked at each other and started to laugh. Within seconds they became helpless with laughter. Laurance rested his forehead against the cool glass of the window looking down on the street below, and shook with uncontrollable laughter. Lil fell backward onto the sofa and stared upward, shrieking with laughter. Images of their octogenarian father being jerked off by fat Dodo Fitz Alyn brought fresh torrents of laughter.

Only the appearance of Miss Wentworth, Laurance's secretary, entering without knocking, quelled their near hysteria. Lil reached again for a handkerchief in her handbag and blew her nose and wiped her eyes. In charge of herself once more, she wondered why Miss Wentworth dyed her hair so very black. She considered offering Miss Wentworth a free appointment with Bobo, to have her hair colored and frosted correctly, and then abandoned the idea.

"Yes, Irene," said Laurance, collecting himself.

"I'm sorry, Mr. Van Degan, but I rang and you didn't hear me."

"What is it, Irene?"

"Elias Renthal is on the telephone. He says it's important."

"Oh, yes, thank you, Irene." Laurance Van Degan was back to business again, his momentary lapse into mirth already forgotten. He picked up the telephone. "Hello, Elias," he said, with the sort of cordiality he usually reserved for cabinet ministers. It was only later that Lil remembered that note of affability in her brother's voice as he spoke to a man she still considered the most vulgar man in New York.

24

"'I'M THINKING of writing a book," said Yvonne Lupescu.

"These days everyone's thinking of writing a book," replied Gus Bailey.

"Very few people know anything about Albania, as it was, before communism, of course, but it has a fascinating history. My grandmother was the mistress of King Zog."

Gus stared at her. "You once told me that, as I remember," he said.

"I wondered if you'd help me with it," she said. They were sitting at Clarence's, having lunch.

"Is that the urgent thing you wanted to discuss over lunch at Clarence's? Court life in Albania?" asked Gus.

"Yes."

"It is not a topic that enthralls me," said Gus.

"But it's fascinating. You know what Constantine always says, don't you?" she asked, smiling in advance at the quotation she was about to give.

"No, I don't know what Constantine always says," he replied.

"He always says, 'Life at court is rotten to the core, but it spoils you for everything else.'" She laughed. "Don't you think that's marvelous?"

"It was even more marvelous when Congreve wrote it," replied Gus.

Undeterred, she proceeded. "I'd tell you everything, and you would write it."

"I'm planning on writing my own book."

"You're not turning me down?"

"Yes."

"You turn me down a lot, Gus."

"You've noticed."

She stared at him.

"Why did you aim so badly?" asked Gus.

"What is that supposed to mean?"

"People say you shot Constantine," said Gus.

Yvonne smiled wearily and shook her head slowly, as if what Gus had said was a falsehood that she had grown accustomed to hearing. "It's not true," she said calmly. "Constantine shot himself. What is true is that I was going to leave him. My bags were packed. The police will tell you that. He couldn't bear it when I told him I was going to leave, and, poor darling, he tried to do away with himself."

"Where were you?"

"When?"

"When he shot himself."

"I was at Justine Altemus's wedding reception. You saw me."

"So did half New York."

"I hear Bernie Slatkin's playing around already," said Yvonne, her eyes sparkling with the latest gossip.

"I don't know anything about that," said Gus quickly, determined not to let her change the subject.

"Someone I know saw him at an out-of-the-way restaurant on the West Side with a young lady. Very beautiful," she said.

Gus ignored her. "You weren't invited to Justine's wedding, and you came."

"But I was meeting you."

"But I didn't ask you to meet me."

"Gus," she said, in a tone a mother would use to a favorite forgetful child.

"Yvonne, it's me," said Gus, pointing to himself. "Don't bullshit with me. You crashed the wedding. You pretended you were meeting me. You caught the bride's bouquet just to make sure everyone saw that you were there. The wedding reception was your alibi."

"You should take up fiction, Gus."

"Aren't you afraid Constantine will blow the whistle on you?"

"No."

"Why not?"

"Because Constantine needs me in a way you know nothing about," replied Yvonne, smiling mysteriously.

"He likes it when you whip him, is that it?"

"Wherever did you hear such a story?"

"One of your cohorts."

"That awful Jorgie Sanchez-Julia, I bet."

Gus did not reply.

"It was never an every-night sort of thing," said Yvonne, dismissively. "Nor remotely dangerous. Quite mild, in fact. I just whip him on his buttocks and sometimes on his back. A few welts, that's all, enough to feel pain, but nothing serious. I call him a failure, a flop, a nothing, while I whip him. It's his deepest fear, you see, under all that pomposity of his, that that is what people think of him. Curiously, it excites him. Otherwise he can't become erect."

Gus stared at her. He never knew if she was lying or not.

"The boredom, of course, is that he becomes so bad tempered on the mornings afterward, after begging me to do it," said Yvonne.

"Where did you first connect with Constantine de Rham?"

"I was in Paris on my way to Brazil to meet the grandmother of a man I was at the time engaged to marry," said Yvonne. Yvonne enjoyed telling Gus tales of her adventures. She saw herself as the basis for a character in a novel and could even imagine herself saying at some future dinner party, "Oh, that Gus Bailey. That awful man. He based that character on me, but he got it all wrong. I should sue. Really, I should," but all the time basking in the importance that the notoriety gave her.

"Rudi Guevara, he was called," she said, going on with her story. "Did you hear of him? His brother was the polo player, Carlos Guevara?"

"No," answered Gus. "I don't know any of those people."

"His grandmother had all the money, and Rudi insisted I meet her before we married so that we could be in her good graces. At the last minute the grandmother got sick, and the trip was canceled. At least I got canceled. Rudi went on to Brazil. I was all alone in Paris and didn't know many people there. There was a big party that night for an American financier, and they needed an extra girl, someone pretty, and a friend of a friend suggested that I go."

"Was the friend of the friend Madam Myra, by any chance?"

Yvonne looked at Gus and ignored his interruption. "I suppose I was meant to provide amusement for the rich American. I was asked to come in late, after dinner, something I wouldn't do now, come in after dinner—it's an insult to be asked to come in after dinner—but I was lonely and had nothing better to do. Are you listening?"

"Yes, I'm listening," said Gus.

"I was looking great that night. I even remember what I was wearing, a little number from Dior that Rudi bought me to knock them dead in Brazil, and I put his engagement ring on the other hand and went to the party. When I walked into the party, there was the financier sitting on a chair with his teenage daughter on his lap. When he saw me, he stood up, and the daughter went toppling over on the floor. The financier didn't ever notice her. He came right over to me and introduced himself. He had a big fat stomach, and he was drunk, but he was said to be one of the richest men in America, and everyone overlooked his drawbacks. He followed me around all night and kept whispering to me that he was going to marry me."

"How does Constantine de Rham fit into this story?"

"Constantine rescued me from the rich, fat, drunk American. He was so charming."

"I see. And it went on from there?"

"It went on from there," answered Yvonne.

"What about the Brazilian?"

"Oh, Rudi. He got lost along the way."

For a while they sat, saying nothing.

"I thought you were a good reporter, Gus?"

Gus shrugged.

"You didn't ask me who the rich, fat, drunk American was."

"You're right. I didn't."

"Elias Renthal."

Gus did not react to what she had said. He had long ago learned to look as if nothing startled him.

"That was just before he met the present Mrs. Renthal, of course, Ruby, and she classed him up," said Yvonne.

"You mean, if you'd played your cards right that night in Paris, you might be the immensely rich Mrs. Elias Renthal these days, instead of the companion, with quotation marks, as Mavis Jones refers to you in her column, to Constantine de Rham."

"Something like that," replied Yvonne, shaking her head, to indicate she had made a wrong choice.

"My feeling is that Constantine is not generous with you. Am I correct?" asked Gus.

"It's a myth that Constantine is so rich," answered Yvonne. "He's not. A few million, that's all, that he can't even touch the principal on."

"That's not rich, a few million?"

"Rich to him, perhaps," she answered, pointing her fork at the waiter, Michael, with the ponytail, who was removing the dishes from the table, as if he were blind and deaf. "But not rich like people are rich nowadays, like Elias Renthal is rich, for instance. Now that's rich."

"What's going to happen to you? Where are you going to live now?"

"In the house on Sutton Place. Where else? It's a divine house. You saw it. Whatever one thought about Consuelo, she had perfect taste. The house couldn't be more comfortable."

"But surely you can't continue to stay there when Constantine gets home from the hospital?"

"Of course. He'll need me then."

"How will he feel having you there after what happened?"

"Safe," said Yvonne simply. She smiled.

Gus shook his head and laughed. "What was really the purpose of this lunch?" he asked.

"Chick Jacoby has taken to seating me in the back room," she said. "And I wanted a better table."

Gus signaled for a check. When he was helping Yvonne into her coat, he said to her, from behind, "That's your book, Yvonne. The story you just told me. Big bucks in a book like that, and you like big bucks. *Ms. Myra's Girl*, you could call it. Forget about your grandmother giving head to King Zog of Albania."

25

BEHIND Ruby Renthal's back, there was no snickering. Those who took it upon themselves to instruct her in fashion, in decoration, in French, in literature, and in life, their kind of life, became her champions. They were entertained by her wit. They were charmed by her honesty. They were struck by her determination to learn, and to learn fast.

Jamesey Crocus, who had been handed over to Ruby Renthal by Loelia Manchester, for assistance in her furniture-buying spree, gave a practiced eye to Ruby's console tables, finally arrived, from the Orromeo auction in London. When people spoke of Jamesey Crocus, they usually added "who knows his antiques." He was a connoisseur of objects of art who liked nothing better than to give advice, with an air of expert knowledge, on furniture, porcelain, carpets, and paintings.

"Marvelous, Ruby," he said, moving one of Lorenza's multicolored rose bouquets aside to touch the marble top and rub his hand over an inlaid ram's head. "Simply marvelous."

Ruby modestly preened a great collector's kind of preening, as if Jamesey's words were a compliment to her increasingly expert eye for French eighteenth-century furniture.

"Klaus van Rijn himself made these," Jamesey Crocus went on. "I recognize his work every time. A genius, van Rijn. Wasn't even French, you know. Lived in Antwerp, and he made these simply brilliant reproductions of eighteenth-century French furniture. I went to see him once, when I was studying with Bernard Berenson at I Tatti, but he was so old and doddering by then that he wasn't making sense."

Ruby's face went white. "Reproductions? Surely, Jamesey, you can't think my console tables are reproductions?" She almost, but did not, tell him that she had paid one million dollars for them.

"About nineteen thirty-six, I would think. The late thirties were his peak years. He didn't make much furniture during the war. I, for one, never believed those stories that he was a collaborator. It was simply that he was besotted with a German soldier, and all those stories started that ruined him. Mr. Berenson believed—"

But Ruby was not listening to the saga of Klaus van Rijn. "You must be wrong, Jamesey," she said, remembering not to lose her new cultured speaking voice that she had copied from Loelia Manchester, even in an urgent moment. "These console tables were from the Orromeos' house in Paris."

"Old Bolivio Orromeo had a lot of van Rijn pieces. He really foxed the auctioneers, you know, when he went broke and sold everything. The auctioneers were *furious* when they found out. But these are very good, Ruby. You could realize forty or fifty thousand for them any day. I guarantee you."

"Nineteen thirty-six?" she asked.

"Thereabouts."

"A lousy fifty years old? That's all?"

"More or less."

"Get rid of them," said Ruby.

"What? You can't be serious, Ruby."

"Get rid of them. I only want the best in this house. No repros. But, for God's sake, don't tell Elias they're fakes."

"Heavens, no," said Jamesey.

"He'd kill me."

"Nonsense," laughed Jamesey. "They say there are only two things in the world Elias Renthal loves: making money and Ruby Renthal."

"He'd still kill me. I haven't told you how much I paid for those lousy fakes."

Jamesey Crocus snapped his fingers as an idea came to his mind. "You know, Ruby, I have the most marvelous idea for these console tables," said Jamesey.

26

OTHER than Loelia Manchester, Jamesey Crocus, and Cora Mandell, Gus Bailey was the only person allowed to see the new residence of Elias and Ruby Renthal prior to the splendid ball that was being planned to launch it. His visit, which was professional, had been arranged for by Loelia Manchester and Jamesey Crocus, who felt that a Sunday piece in the *Times Magazine* would be an important way for the rich newcomers to talk about their many charitable interests, especially since Florian Gray had started referring to Ruby in his column as the Billionaire's Wife.

The fabulous Renthal Impressionist and Post-Impressionist art collection, ever growing, rested against the drawing-room walls, ready to be hung after the final of the nineteen coats of persimmon lacquer had been applied to the huge room. Ancestral portraits of other people's ancestors, grand ladies and patrician gentlemen, some in coronation robes, by Sargent and Boldini and Oswald Birley, leaned against the hall and dining-room walls.

"That's King Boris of Bulgaria, in hunting attire," explained Elias to Gus, in his role of art collector.

Drop cloths covered pieces of antique furniture, which Jamesey Crocus told Gus over and over again were of museum quality, ready to be arranged. Upholstered pieces, the trademark of Cora Mandell's look of cozy grandeur, were wrapped tight in brown paper and tied with ropes. All work was at a momentary standstill, waiting for the nineteenth coat of persimmon lacquer to dry before the twentieth and final coat could be applied.

"Elias adores collecting. He thinks nothing of getting on our plane and flying anywhere when Maisie Verdurin or our curator, Jamesey Crocus, tell him about any artwork that is coming on the market," said Ruby. She had become conversant in matters of art and furniture and porcelain and decoration and knew the history of each addition to her new collections.

Gus Bailey marveled at the transformation of Ruby Renthal since their first meeting at one of Maisie Verdurin's dinners, when she had been dressed in bright blue sequins and shared with Gus a deep secret of her life that bound the two of them together. Since then, almost no reference to that moment had ever been repeated on the several occasions they had met in New York, but there was an unspoken understanding between them. Dressed now in simple but stylish elegance in a black-and-white hounds-tooth skirt and black cashmere sweater that perfectly showed her splendid breasts that people said had been reduced to their present perfection by cosmetic surgery in Brazil, she lounged gracefully on the edge of a packing case. Her only jewelry was the massive diamond she wore on her engagement finger. She had removed the hounds-tooth jacket that matched her skirt, and it lay next to her, the label Nevel, Leven spelled backwards, visible on its satin lining. Her smart Minardos pump dangled elegantly on the tip of her toe as she described their life.

"As you can see, we're camping out, Mr. Bailey," she said, and they all chuckled, as if Mrs. Renthal had made a witticism. "But if we don't, you see, the work will never get finished."

"How many houses do you have, Mrs. Renthal?" asked Gus.

"Does that include apartments?" she asked. "We have apartments, you know, in both London and Paris."

"Yes, of course," said Gus, adjusting his notes. "Homes, I should have said, not houses."

Ruby, puzzled, turned to her husband. "Is it eight or nine, darling?" she asked.

"We sold Palm Beach," replied Elias, nervously.

"But bought in Nassau," answered Ruby, as if to remind him of something he had forgot. She thought she detected a signal to halt from her husband.

"Nine, Mr. Bailey," said Elias, answering the question put to Ruby by Gus. "But, you know, that don't sound so good in the papers and the magazines, if you see what I mean."

Ruby mouthed but did not speak the word *doesn't* to Elias, correcting his grammar, in the way she had watched Lil Altemus mouth but not speak words.

"What?" asked Elias.

"Nothing," said Ruby.

There had also been a transformation in Elias Renthal, Gus noticed, a kind of sureness of self that comes with the accumulation of great wealth and the public respect that wealth engenders. There were neighbors Elias encountered in the elevator of his own exclusive building who still did not speak to him and continued to refer to his apartment as Matilda Clarke's apartment, but the doormen and the elevator men in the building, who were recipients of his large tips, gave him precedence over all the old swells who had dwelled there for decades. That, coupled with his change of tailor, gave the stout financier an impressive and even friendly presence.

"I'll keep it at eight, if you think that will sound better," replied Gus. "Is that complicated? Eight houses?"

"Oh, puleeze," replied Ruby, in the same way that she had heard Loelia say *puleeze*. "Just to remember the names of the staff in each house is complicated. And I always find that the shoes I need for the dress I'm going to wear that night are in the apartment in Paris when I need them in London and then the plane has to go and pick them up. This is all off the record, Mr. Bailey. This is what Loelia calls the problems of the very, very rich."

Gus shrugged. "This is good stuff you're telling me I can't write."

"Do you see, Elias, how nice Mr. Bailey is? My husband is convinced, simply convinced, that the press is out to get us."

"I meant the financial press, Ruby," said Elias.

"And he thinks my picture is in the paper too much, too, Mr. Bailey," said Ruby.

"It is," said Elias.

"'The Billionaire's Wife,'" said Gus. "How could it be otherwise?"

"I wish I could get my hands on whoever gave me that name," said Ruby. "It makes me sound like a lady who lunches, and I'm not, except occasionally. I want to do something meaningful. The problem is that there are so many causes after us, and I haven't sorted out yet what it is that we are going to concentrate on. I mean, of course, after the museum and the ballet."

"Do you always have bodyguards, Mr. Renthal?" he asked.

"Oh, yes, twenty-four hours a day. They work in shifts," said Elias, beginning to relax. "When I drive to and from our house in the country, or to and from my office, I don't like them in the car with me, not even up front with the chauffeur, because I do a great deal of work in my car, mostly on the telephone, and I don't like other people listening to me, so the guards always follow in a second car."

"I see," said Gus, making a note. "Have you ever been threatened or harmed?"

"No. But, you know, there are so many mad people out there who read about people like us."

"My husband is security mad, Mr. Bailey," said Ruby. "He built a ten-foot-high brick wall all around our place in the country, with electrified wire on top of the wall. And guards everywhere you look."

"Ruby," said Elias, in mock exasperation, as if to control her.

"It's true," she went on. "And even this. He wants me to carry a gun. Look at this little pearl-handled number he gave me as a stocking present last Christmas. It used to belong to Queen Marie of Rumania. Elias bought it at auction in London and had Purdy's put it in working order."

"Ruby," repeated Elias.

"Fits right into my bag, it's so small. I wouldn't dream of using it, no matter what, but it makes Elias happy for me to carry it."

"How about if I take you on a tour of the apartment, Mr. Bailey," said Elias, standing up to terminate the interview.

LATER, dressing for a party, Ruby said to Elias, "Who's Byron Macumber?"

Elias, who was putting studs in his evening shirt, paused, startled. "Why?" he asked.

"Why?" repeated Ruby. "What kind of an answer is why to your own wife?"

"Oh, he's just some kid who works for Weldon and Stinchfield," replied Elias.

"He's a lawyer then?"

"Yeah, a junior lawyer. Why this big interest in Byron what's-his-name?"

"Charming on the telephone. He called you when you were taking Gus Bailey for the tour of the apartment. He wants you to call him. He said you knew the number."

"He called *here?*" There was surprise in Elias's tone.

"Yes, Elias, Byron Macumber called here, and your wife answered the telephone, and he asked that you call him as soon as you were free. Where are you going?"

"I'm going downstairs. I left my briefcase down there."

"WHAT THE fuck are you calling me at my house for, you ass-hole?" said Elias, in whispered fury into the telephone.

"I'm sorry, Mr. Renthal, but you'd left your office, and I knew by morning that the word would be out, and I thought that you'd want to know."

"What word?"

"Omaha Natural Gas has hired Weldon and Stinchfield as adviser in connection with a proposal by Tri-World, Inc., to acquire ONG," said Byron Macumber.

"Holy shit," said Elias.

"I'm sorry I bothered you at home, Mr. Renthal."

"No, no, Byron. I'm sorry I blew my stack. You did the right thing. Now, listen, it's not a good idea to call me here at home, but if you have to, here's a different number, five-five-five, four-one-two-eight, my own private line. I'll put a message machine on it by tomorrow, and just leave a message, and I'll get back to you, and, listen, Byron, use a different name. You're Mr. Brown. Okay?"

WHEN ELIAS hung up, he looked at his watch while lighting up a cigar. He picked up the telephone again and dialed some numbers. "Operator, this is a collect call to Mr. Rufus Courtauld, in Nassau, from Mr. Nolte."

Elias drummed his fingers on the table while waiting for the long-distance call to go through.

"Nolte here," said Elias, when Rufus Courtauld picked up the receiver on the other end. "Fine, fine," he went on impatiently, getting over with the pleasantries that his Swiss connection invariably engaged in at the beginning of every conversation. "Buy a hundred and eighty thousand shares of Omaha Natural Gas the instant the market opens in the morning." With that he hung up the telephone.

The door to the little room opened, and Ruby entered. She was dressed in evening clothes. "I can hardly see you through all this cigar smoke, Elias," she said.

"That's why you gave me this smoking room, Ruby, so that I could cloud up the air here and not in the swell rooms up front."

"I'm not complaining. I'm just commenting."

"You look beautiful, Ruby," answered Elias. "New dress?"

"Of course, it's new," she said, tweaking his chin. "You wanted a wife on the best-dressed list and you're going to get a wife on the best-dressed list. I need some help with this necklace, Elias. Can you do the clasp?"

"With pleasure," he said, standing behind her. When he finished, he leaned down and kissed Ruby's bare shoulder. "Did I ever tell you I was crazy about your shoulders?"

"Yeah, but it's not something I get sick of hearing," said Ruby, rubbing her shoulder against his lips.

"Where are we going tonight?" he asked.

"Adele Harcourt's, and we can't be late."

"Oh, Adele Harcourt?" he said, impressed. "Fancy-schmancy." He pulled himself out of further amatory pursuit.

"Don't say fancy-schmancy."

"Why?"

"It's tacky. We're past that."

27

AFTER Sweetzer Clarke died, Matilda felt very lucky to be able to finally sell the great Fifth Avenue apartment Sweetzer had grown up in and later inherited after his mother's death. The building had been constructed on the site of what had once been the Clarke townhouse, and the apartment, forty-one rooms on the top three floors, had been built to the extravagant specifications of Sweetzer's father in the late 1920s as part of the transaction for selling the land and tearing down the Clarke house to make way for the building. Matilda and Sweetzer and their children lived there for nineteen years, first closing up rooms and then whole floors as the cost of maintaining the vast establishment drained their steadily diminishing resources.

When the lawyers handling Sweetzer's estate told Matilda that she would have to give up either the apartment in town or the place in the country, she said, without a second thought, that she would give up the apartment, as life without Malvern, the Clarkes' place in Bedford, would have been absolutely unthinkable for Matilda, who raised Norwich terriers and rode horses every day of her life. Her two sons had married early and advantageously and retreated to other parts of the country, away from the sight of their mother in decline.

At the time of Sweetzer's death, forty-one-room apartments were not in great demand, and the apartment stood empty for several years. Finally, in desperation, Matilda sold it for a negligible sum to someone whose name she pretended she could never remember. The problem had been getting the purchaser, Elias Renthal, approved by the board of directors of the building, and it was only the purchaser's guarantee, in writing, that he would not break up the apartment into smaller apartments that finally assured his acceptance into a building that otherwise was deeply selective about what Matilda called "the sort of people" who lived there.

The first time Lil Altemus visited Matilda's new small flat, which she had taken for the few nights a week she spent in the city, she pronounced it charming, calling it Matilda's *pied à terre*, as if Matilda had done something "frightfully clever," in abandoning such an enor-

193

mous establishment for something so very manageable. But Matilda brushed aside all compliments on its charm, or coziness, a word she despised, referring to it always as "my little hovel," because it was, at least in her eyes, a little hovel compared to the grandeur of her former home that was now being done up by the Renthals. She was often heard to exclaim, "The things they've done to it!" about the new owners, rolling her eyes and shaking her head, although she had not seen it, did not know anyone who had, and knew, from personal experience, that Cora Mandell was not only the best decorator in New York but had been her own decorator when she still had money.

"Sweetzer left me high and dry," said Matilda. "And I was a very good wife to Sweetzer, except for that one time. I had to auction off all the French furniture and sell the apartment. I wasn't doing all that because I chose to live a simpler life, as Dolly De Longpre, dear sweet Dolly, told her readers. I sold everything to survive."

"But, darling Matilda," cried Lil. "We've been friends all our lives. You could have come to me, and I would have seen that Laurance took care of you."

"Oh, no. That sort of thing never works out," said Matilda. "I'm not a charity case. And, besides, along came Rochelle Prud'homme, and she put me on the board of directors of Prud'homme Products, and pays me a salary. Now, I know you don't give Rochelle the right time, Lil, and won't have her to your house, but she happens to be a damn nice woman, and a damn rich woman, and a damn successful woman in the hairdryer business. They call her the Petite Dynamo. All she wanted was to become a queen in society, and she couldn't get to first base. She needed me to open some doors, and I needed her, and everybody's happy. What Ezzie Fenwick calls tit for tit."

"But what in the world do you do on the board of directors?" asked Lil. "You've never worked a day in your life."

"I don't do anything," answered Matilda. "I just go to meetings several times a year and sit there, and Rochelle nods to me which way to vote."

"Then why does Mrs. Prud'homme want you on her board of directors?" asked Lil.

"Oh, Lil," answered Matilda, as if the answer were so apparent the question needn't have been asked.

"Why?" insisted Lil.

"For the same reason Elias Renthal has your brother and Loelia Manchester and Lord Biedermeier on the board of Miranda Industries. We add class."

"Heavens!" said Lil, clapping her hands, and the two old friends roared with laughter.

28

AMONG THE New People, with whom Loelia now felt more comfortable, everyone that season called Mickie Minardos and Loelia Manchester the lovebirds. "We've just had lunch with Mickie and Loelia," people said, and it immediately identified them as intimates of the most in-love couple in the city. If, at dinners, they weren't seated together, which they preferred to be, they wrote notes to each other during the meal and passed them behind the backs of the intervening people, read them, and then shrieked with private laughter together, or simply met each other's eyes and stared deeply. Everyone in this group said, leaving them, "They're madly in love."

THE ALTOGETHER splendid invitation to the Elias Renthals' ball in honor of the Earl and Countess of Castoria was the talk of every table at Clarence's that day. Ezzie Fenwick, who usually waited until the very last minute to reply to invitations, in case a better one to a grander party should come along, accepted his invitation on the same day it arrived, because he knew, absolutely knew, that on that night, June 21, there would be no better place to be in the whole world.

The ladies who gave parties never invited Matilda Clarke and Fernanda Somerset to the same parties, because Matilda had once had an affair with Fernanda's husband, and Fernanda never spoke to Matilda again, but Ruby Renthal invited both of them, and everyone was curious to see how the two ladies in question would handle the problem. At the large charity dinners, when it was inevitable that both would attend, the ladies who seated the tables knew that they had to seat Fernanda and Matilda as far from each other as possible, in separate rooms even, if there were more than one, with Fernanda Somerset always getting the better seat in the better room because she was a benefactress, which Matilda Clarke, for economic reasons, could no longer be.

"You're not going to the Renthals', are you?" asked Lil Altemus.

"Of course, I'm going," said Matilda to Lil.

"I'm not," said Lil.

"You have to play along with these New People," said Matilda.

"Why do I have to play along with these New People?" asked Lil.

"People like us, WASPS in the *Social Register*, we're practically an extinct race. These New People are the ones who are taking charge."

"My brother Laurance is still in charge. The Van Degan bank is his. The Van Degan Foundation is his. The Van Degan Building is his," stated Lil. "You can't get more in charge than that."

"But Laurance is the exception to the rule. Most of the kind of people who were the heads of Wall Street and the banks when Laurance took over from his father have been sent out to pasture. All these New People are the people with the money nowadays. The kind of money we thought was money is nothing to the kind of money these New People have."

"I have no intention of playing along with them," said Lil emphatically.

"You're going to have to," said Matilda quietly.

"Have to what?"

"Go to the Renthals' ball."

"Why am I going to have to?"

"Because Laurance is going to insist you go."

Lil looked at Matilda. It was impossible for her to understand her brother's affinity for a lout like Elias Renthal, but she would never discuss her brother with anyone, even someone she had known all her life, like Matilda Clarke.

29

LIL ALTEMUS had Easter that year. It alternated each year between Laurance and Janet Van Degan's apartment and Lil's, and it was Lil's turn, although she felt a bit put upon by so much family so soon after Justine's wedding. Justine and Bernie were there, of course, although their roles as newlyweds had been superseded by Ormonde and Dodo Van Degan, recently returned from their Hobe Sound honeymoon. Hubie came, without Juanito, of course, who always caused a scene whenever Hubie was summoned to one of the family rites. Christmas he could understand, he said. Easter he couldn't, even after Hubie told him they had been having Easter lunch, at either Uncle Laurance's or his mother's, ever since he could remember, and the practice had been started long before that, at Grandfather Van Degan's when he and Grandmother, dead for years, still lived in the old Van Degan house on 79th Street. "If it's any consolation to you, Juanito, I hate going," said Hubie, leaving.

"I really wish you wouldn't dress like that, Hubie, especially with the whole family here," said Lil to her son, when he greeted her on his arrival.

"What's wrong with the way I dress?" asked Hubie.

"You know perfectly well what's wrong," said his mother. Although Hubie dressed in blue jeans and cowboy boots, he did not remotely resemble a denizen of Greenwich Village, which his mother insinuated, as his shirts, with their button-down collars, were so unmistakably from Brooks Brothers, and his tweed jackets, with their double vents, were made to order for him by Mr. Sills. Even during the period when he exasperated his mother even more by wearing his hair too long for her taste, and certainly too long for the taste of Uncle Laurance, he had it trimmed every two weeks by the barber at the Butterfield, his father's club, so that he ended up by being an outsider in the world he was born into as well as the world he aspired to be a part of.

Ned Manchester, Lil's cousin on the Altemus side, who, since the romance of Loelia Manchester and Mickie Minardos, had to be taken care of on family occasions, was present that Easter, as he had the two children who refused even to meet Mickie. "What a wonderful father Ned is," everybody always said. The lunch party was filled out by old friends like Matilda Clarke, whose sons lived in Santa Barbara and Santa Fe, and who always came. And then there were what Lil always called her strays, like Gus Bailey, who had no family that she knew of and no place to go. Ezzie Fenwick, who usually came, backed out at the last minute when he was asked to spend the weekend in the country with Elias and Ruby Renthal at Merry Hill, their new weekend retreat.

"Tell me about this marvelous picture," said Gus Bailey, admiring a large family painting over a sofa in the drawing room.

"That's the whole Van Degan family painted by Mr. Sargent in nineteen ten," said Lil, who loved to describe the picture to newcomers. "That was the drawing room in the original Van Degan house on lower Fifth Avenue, where the New York Public Library is now. You see, there's the Commodore, and his wife Annie. She was one of the Houghton sisters, meant to be ugly beyond belief, but look how beautiful Mr. Sargent made her look. And that little boy there, in the pale blue satin suit, playing with the collie, is my father, Ormonde, age six."

"My dear, look at your dogwood! Too beautiful!" cried Janet Van Degan, entering her sister-in-law's drawing room. "Lorenza's been here, I see."

"Only just left minutes ago. It's getting harder and harder to get Lorenza these days," said Lil. "Of course, her success pleases me, but, after all, it was *I* who discovered her." She spoke in the possessive way that she claimed also to have discovered Bobo, her hairdresser, and Nevel, her dress designer, meaning that she had been the first of the ladies in her group who had her flowers arranged each week by Lorenza. "Mrs. Renthal seems to be monopolizing all her time."

"Mrs. Renthal, Mrs. Renthal, that's all I ever hear these days," said Janet, throwing her hands up in the air in mock horror.

"And that damn ball. I can't believe the things Lorenza's been telling me about it," said Lil.

"Unbelievable," agreed Janet Van Degan.

"Imagine brand-new people like the Renthals giving this kind of party," continued Lil. "And inviting all of us. Two years ago no one ever heard of them. I wouldn't *dream* of going."

Laurance, overhearing, said to his sister, "We should talk about that, Lil."

Their conversation was interrupted by the arrival of the young Van Degans, Laurance and Laura, with little Janet, and the baby, Laurance III, whom everyone called Third. Little Janet, whom everyone said was a handful, made a dash for her grandmother.

"Who is this who is coming to see me? Who is it? Who?" cried Janet Van Degan, as her granddaughter ran to throw herself into her arms. Amid great screams of laughter, Janet picked up the child. "The preciousness of her! Look at this adorable creature, Lil. Edible, that's what she is. Edible."

Lil watched her sister-in-law and envied her her joy. If she had a grandchild, which she did not have and which she might never have, she suspected, she wondered if she would, and doubted if she would at the same time, feel the kind of joy that Janet felt every time she saw her granddaughter.

"I suppose I should ask Bernie to carve the lamb," Lil said to her daughter. "Does Bernie know anything about carving, Justine? Hubie is so hopeless at it, and you know how cross Uncle Laurance gets if the roast isn't carved right."

"You ask Bernie, Mother," replied Justine.

Bernie, as it turned out, carved very well. Bernie played games very well. Bernie danced very well. Bernie knew how to decant wine. Bernie knew how to give charming toasts. Lil always wished that Hubie took as naturally to these things that she thought so important in a man, or gentleman, as Bernie, whom she did not think of as a gentleman, did.

"No more peanuts, children. You won't believe the goodies Gertie has in store for us," said Lil to the Manchester children. "Laurance, help me with the seating. Where shall I put our new stepmother?" she asked, pointing ironically toward Dodo. "She's so used to sitting at the wrong end of the table, but I suppose I have to move her up this year."

When Lil's butler, Parker, told her that luncheon was served, he handed her a silver bell, and she rang it and rang it from room to room, to announce to her family and friends to move into the dining room. It was one of Lil's characteristic things to do at all her parties, and it was thought to increase the merriment of the occasion.

There were two tables at lunch, the long table with the Chippendale chairs, called the grownups' table on family occasions, and, in the window, the smaller round table, called the children's table. Looking down, Lil admired the vermilion-colored border of her fish plates. She loved her dozens of sets of dishes and took as much pleasure in their selection for each course as she did in the exquisite food that her cook prepared to go on them. Glancing down from her place at the head of the grownups' table, Lil was glad to see that Matilda Clarke, dear Matilda, her oldest friend, was making Ned Manchester laugh, the first time anyone had seen Ned laugh since Loelia ran off with Mickie. Across from Matilda, she looked at her new stepmother, Dodo Fitz Alyn Van Degan, poor Dodo, no longer poor Dodo, rich Dodo, who would always remain poor Dodo to Lil. Dodo's appearance in the brief weeks of her marriage had improved, and Lil wondered if she were dieting strenuously or better corseted, and if her suit was a real Chanel. A curious alliance in the family was the friendship of Dodo and Hubie. Dodo, it developed, had bought several of Juanito's paintings at Hubie's gallery in SoHo and hung them in the hallway of Ormonde Van Degan's apartment on Fifth Avenue, a few buildings up from Lil's, that was now hers to do with as she saw fit. "I think they're charming," she said, about Juanito's work, the first time she saw them, and she did. She sent several other people to Hubie's gallery to buy Juanito's pictures too. In return, Juanito got her the dirty movies that she was too embarrassed to rent herself to show old Ormonde night after night.

"You will be sure, won't you, Parker, to tell Gertie how much we enjoyed the fish mousse," said Lil to her butler, as he cleared away the first course. Gertie was her cook, and Lil always interrupted her own conversation to send her compliments via her butler. "You used to be able to drive through Southampton and know who everyone was. Or, if you didn't actually know them, you knew who they were. Now you see all these new names on those same houses, and you don't know who any of them are, except they've all got about fifty million dollars. Who, pray tell, are the Reza Bulbenkians who just bought Evangeline's house?"

Lil, who had cases of champagne left over from the wedding, decided to dispense with red and white wines that day and serve only champagne throughout the meal, making the occasion more festive. She raised her glass and welcomed the new members of the family, meaning Bernie Slatkin and Dodo Fitz Alyn, although Dodo could not strictly be considered a new member of the family, having been a part of it, at a secondary level, since she was taken in by them as a teenager. Dodo, blushing, thanked Lil and raised her glass to Ormonde, who wore his napkin like a bib, whom she said had changed her life. Lil and Laurance exchanged glances, as if to say, "I should say so," but only applauded both Dodo and their father. Bernie sprang to his feet and made everyone laugh telling what it felt like for a person like him to suddenly find himself a member of a family like the Van Degans. Justine hopped to her feet and kissed Bernie, whom she had started to call dear heart when she addressed him, although it was a name that Bernie could not bear to be called. It was not lost on Matilda Clarke that Bernie Slatkin found Justine's excessive affection irritating. Old Ormonde, seated next to Matilda, told her three times how much he missed Sweetzer and what a keen sportsman he had been. The toasts ended with Uncle Laurance asking everyone to rise to thank Lil for the wonderful day she had provided for them.

The late spring afternoon had turned rainy and chilly, and Parker lit a fire as the group reentered the drawing room to settle in Lil's dark red damask sofas and chairs for coffee. Hubie and Justine stood together in front of one of the tall windows and looked out at the park, talking quietly. Laura Van Degan minded little Janet, who needed changing. Dodo minded Ormonde, who needed changing. Bernie Slatkin settled into a spirited game of backgammon with Matilda Clarke, who considered herself a champion, and was mildly put out that Bernie kept winning. Ned Manchester talked with Uncle Laurance and young Laurance about the state of the stock market and expressed concern about what he, too, called the New People, like Elias Renthal and Reza Bulbenkian, who seemed to be running the financial world, but Uncle Laurance assured Ned that Elias Renthal was the most fascinating man in the financial community in years, and necessary to it. Gus Bailey, quiet that day, as he always was on holidays, talked with Lil Altemus, who had placed him next to her at lunch, about Trollope, who was her favorite writer, as she fed cookies to her King Charles spaniels. Bozzie Manchester excused himself to go to the men's room but used the escape to telephone his mother, Loelia, at the Rhinelander Hotel to wish her a happy Easter; there was no answer and he did not leave a message.

Inevitably, during Van Degan gatherings, photograph albums were brought out and several people at a time pored over the pictures and captions. "Do you remember that time, Laurance, at Evangeline Simpson's wedding? Look how pretty Evangeline was way back then. Poor Evangeline. She was so drunk the other night at the Dashwoods'," said Lil.

"Look at Sonny Thomas. My God, Lil. Whatever happened to old Sonny?" asked Laurance.

"He married that woman with one leg, what'shername, with the son on heroin. Betsy Babcock. He married Betsy."

A sense of melancholy filled the air of Lil's large room, as if they all knew that this would be their last Van Degan Easter.

"Where's Juanito today?" asked Justine. She and Hubie were staring out the window at a bag lady establishing a beachhead for herself on a park bench across the street. Behind her a magnolia tree was in its first day of full blossom.

"Oh, lordie, I haven't a clue," replied Hubie, as if Juanito were no more than a casual acquaintance. It was not a truthful answer, but he did not wish to appear, even to his own sister, from whom he had no secrets, or very few, to be in the thrall of his Puerto Rican lover, even though he knew that she knew that he was. Juanito Perez had the power to make him miserably unhappy with his rampant promiscuity, as well as ecstatically happy on the occasions he focused his amatory attentions on Hubie.

"Hubie, when are you going to tell me?" asked Justine suddenly.

"Spring is bustin' out all over," replied Hubie, pointing to the magnolia tree.

"Hubie?" insisted Justine.

"Tell you what?"

"Hubie, it's me, remember, your sister."

"What's to tell? You already know. I knew you knew."

"How?"

"At your wedding. Just before you were going up the aisle. When you kissed me. I saw in your eyes then that you knew."

Her eyes filled with tears. "What's going to happen, Hubie?"

"I'm going to cool, I suppose."

"Don't be flippant about this, Hubie."

"I'm not being flippant, Justine. Believe me. I just haven't arrived at my attitude yet. I don't know how to play this scene."

"Are you afraid?"

"Yes."

"Do you think it was Juanito who gave it to you?" asked Justine.

Hubie smiled. "Could have been. He tested positive. On the other hand, it could have been about six hundred other guys too. I was never what you would call inactive. Does that shock you, Justine?"

"I'm trying not to be shocked, Hubie."

"Given my proclivities, there was a time not too long ago I even would have put the make on that hot number you got yourself married to."

"Bernie?" They both laughed. "He would have broken your nose."

"Wouldn't have been the first time somebody broke my nose."

"Oh, Hubie," said Justine, putting her hand on her brother's shoulder.

"Don't cry, Justine. Just don't cry. Not here. Not with all this family around."

"I won't, Hubie. What about Mother? When are you going to tell her?"

"After everyone leaves today."

"Do you want me to be with you?"

"I think this is something I have to do alone. But, thanks, Justine."

IT RAINED the whole Easter weekend at Merry Hill, and the men of the house party, except for Ezzie Fenwick, were put out that the inclement weather thwarted their sporting plans.

The Renthals had bought a house where, years past, a shooting had taken place. It had belonged to a family called Grenville, a name long faded from day-to-day usage, but, still, a name that recalled past glories. "This was once the Grenvilles' house," people would say about it, traipsing through the woods to look at the structure, boarded up, unwanted for several decades, since the scandal that rendered it unlivable. "He was going to leave her, and she shot him. Something like that," they would say.

For the Renthals, however, who didn't know the Grenvilles, had never even heard of them, other than a faint recollection of grandeur associated with the name, there was not a moment's hesitation about buying the property when the only daughter of that sad family decided to sell. They liked owning things that had once belonged to

grand people. At a Rothschild auction in Europe, Elias bought every
bit of glass, china, silverware, and household linen with the letter *R*
engraved or embroidered on it, more than enough to accommodate
vast groups at both his enormous apartment in town and his new
estate in the country.

Ruby was awakened early by the sounds of her maids arguing below with Lorenza, about vases. Temperamental and demanding
Lorenza, in her miniskirt, had arrived early from the city to arrange
the peonies and delphinium, and the forsythia and lilac branches in
the downstairs rooms, and she always argued with the maids about
vases. Far from being cross, Ruby stretched luxuriously and nestled
into her linen sheets, enjoying hearing the bustle of a life below that
was preparing for her day. She never took her new status for granted
and always, in moments like these, when she stopped to notice, she
said, to whomever it was one thanked, a short and shy prayer of
gratitude. Then, glancing at her gold vermeil traveling clock, which
had once belonged to the Empress Elizabeth of Austria, she knew, in
her perfectly run life, that in nine minutes Candelaria would knock
on her door with her tray, her mail, and her morning papers.

It had taken but one weekend at Castle Castor, the Wiltshire seat of
the Earl and Countess of Castoria, for Ruby to learn most of the
amenities of grand country life: bags unpacked by the butler, clothes
pressed by the maid, biscuits and fruit and bottles of Malvern water
on the bed tables, breakfast on trays for the ladies, breakfast in the
small dining room for the gentlemen, and separate newspapers for
all.

ELIAS RENTHAL, his eggs finished, lit the first cigar of the day as
he read the business section of the *Times*. He and the male members
of the weekend party had gathered for breakfast in the smaller of the
two dining rooms in the house, while the ladies took breakfast in their
rooms. Elias relished the thought that important men, in dressing
gowns, reading newspapers, were his weekend guests, at his country
estate, while their wives and lady friends breakfasted above in their
rooms. It was not until his marriage to Ruby, whose desire for social
life was insatiable, that Elias began to understand the pleasures of
popularity. It was Ruby who made Elias understand the advantages of

social life for his business career, knowing the players at dinner, as she put it, instead of only at lunch. He found to his astonishment that people found him amusing, and he decided that he quite liked being liked. He even began to enjoy dinnertable conversation, as it was a way of spreading the word on his ever increasing art collection. "You must let me show you my new Caravaggio," he liked to say, or, "Personally, I prefer Picasso's blue period." His most fervent secret hope was that, in time, a place would be found for him on the board of directors of the museum.

"Journalism is not an exact science," Elias stated impatiently, hurling the newspaper to the floor, a gesture that caused the others to look up from their papers.

"Is something wrong?" asked Lord Biedermeier.

"I gave this fella from the *Times* an interview, and he misquotes me all the way through the article," said Elias.

"About what?" asked Mickie Minardos.

"My takeover of Miranda Industries. He says, in effect, that I took away the personality of the company. What he don't realize is I gave the company its identity. In the first place, I'm the one who renamed it Miranda. It had nine names and no corporate identity at all until I bought the company. These are things I understand. This article makes me sound like a predator, for Christ's sake, moving in for the kill. What I learned a long time ago is to sell a company, or a hotel, or a business as soon as I start to love it."

"I don't understand that," said Mickie Minardos.

"What's to understand?" asked Elias.

"If you love a company, why do you sell it?"

Elias looked at Mickie. "That's why you're not rich," he said.

Mickie, who thought of himself as rich, assumed a look of one whose worth has been underestimated.

Elias understood his look. "I mean really rich," he said. "What I am is a man who understands timing, the exact moment to make a move. That's my instinct. That's something I was born with. You either got it, or you don't. I deal with hundreds of millions of dollars a day in my business. I didn't fire more than five hundred people, and I brought in a whole new board of directors, responsible people like Laurance Van Degan, Loelia Manchester, Lord Biedermeier here, and my English friend the Earl of Castoria, high-profile people like that. Now we have a working operation. By the end of this year, I expect we'll do something like a billion two, a billion five, around there."

Elias's guests listened avidly. Elias Renthal talked a great deal about himself: his takeovers, his boards of directors, his profits, his acquisitions. And his guests listened, mesmerized, as if they, too, would get rich by sitting at the table of such a rich man.

"All right now," said Elias, clapping his hands, changing the subject. "Let's see what you've got, Winston."

Winston Bergerac, half French, half English, was famed for his paintings of horses. A modern Stubbs, they called him in the Sackville's catalogue. He had painted the horses of the Queen of England and had only just completed a painting of Elias Renthal's prize stud, Flash, which Elias had acquired from the Saratoga sales.

Winston Bergerac left the small dining room and returned in an instant with an easel, which he set up at the head of the table by the seat of Elias Renthal. He left the room again and returned in another instant with a painting under his arm, faced away from his audience, which he then turned around and placed on the easel. Murmurs of pleasure at the beauty of the elegant animal went around the table. Elias puffed at his cigar and stared at his latest commission, like a great collector collecting. He rose from his seat and went closer, bending in to look, stepping back to look, bending in to look again.

"I don't like it," he said finally, and a low gasp went around the table.

"But why?" asked the astonished Winston Bergerac.

"The prick's too big," said Elias. "I can't hang that in my dining room like that, with that big dork hanging down there. Ruby wouldn't approve."

"But, surely, Mr. Renthal," remonstrated Winston Bergerac, "that is the nature of the animal."

Elias scowled at what he sensed to be a superior tone in the voice of the painter. Lord Biedermeier, who knew that Elias could be formidable in displeasure, stepped in to make the suggestion that perhaps that part of the beautiful animal's anatomy could be repainted.

"All right. All right. Make the prick smaller, and I'll reconsider," said Elias, magnanimously. He gathered up the rest of his newspaper and walked out of the room to spend an hour on the telephone on business calls and to give some attention to the book on corporate takeovers that he was writing for Lord Biedermeier.

ON A FIREPLACE bench in the library lay newspapers and magazines from all over the world, rarely read, changed weekly by the butler, and available for any guest to take along to his room. Ezzie Fenwick, who disliked sport of any kind, excepting country walks, was the only member of the house party who enjoyed the bad weather. Long afternoons of bridge, or reading in front of the fire, or gossiping over drinks about parties and fashion and the upcoming Renthal ball, were to him infinitely preferable to swimming pools, or tennis courts, or golf links, or horseback riding, or, horrors, skeet shooting.

"Elias Renthal has taken to the grand life as if he's afraid it's not going to last," Ezzie said to Loelia Manchester.

"Shh," cautioned Loelia.

"These New People spend more for their houses than rich people in my day used to inherit," went on Ezzie.

"Shh," said Loelia.

"There's a Toulouse-Lautrec in the gentleman's loo. I've never seen that before," Ezzie continued, undaunted.

"Shh," said Loelia.

Like trophies, invitations to the best parties in town were lined up one next to the other on Ruby's elegant mantelpiece. Ezzie nosed through them. Mrs. Sims Lord's dinner. Mrs. Van Degan Altemus's dinner. Mrs. Laurance Van Degan's dinner. Mrs. Charles Bradley's dinner. Miss Maude Hoare's dinner. Mrs. Violet Bastedo's cocktail party. Mrs. Loelia Somerset Manchester's opera supper.

The door of the library opened, and Ruby Renthal entered, carrying her copy of the *The Memoirs of Madame de la Tour du Pin*, which Jamesey Crocus told her she simply must read if she wanted to understand about life at Versailles under Marie Antoinette in the final days before the Revolution.

"The flowers are beautiful, Ruby," said Ezzie Fenwick quickly, moving away from the invitations, as he nodded approvingly at the masses of blue delphinium and pink peonies that Lorenza had arranged on the console tables while they were all still at breakfast.

"Thank you, Ezzie," said Ruby, beaming. The ladies of the group always craved Ezzie's approval of their clothes, houses, flowers, and the seating of their tables. The men were less enthusiastic about Ezzie.

"I don't understand why you kowtow to that guy, Ruby," Elias had said to Ruby the evening before, in a loud whisper in the hallway, after Ezzie said that only waiters and bandleaders wore black tie on Sunday nights, when Ruby suggested they dress for dinner.

"Ezzie Fenwick's an arbiter," replied Ruby.

"Ezzie Fenwick's an asshole," answered Elias.

Ezzie pretended not to have heard. It was a way he had learned of ignoring the cruel taunts of his youth. Instead he went on chatting nonstop, over bridge, at which he excelled, about the terrible state of Aline Royceton's teeth, and why didn't she do something about them; about Evangeline Simpson throwing up in the powder room at Adele Harcourt's during one of her book-club meetings, and why didn't someone simply take poor Evangeline by the hand out to Minnesota where they do all those marvelous things about drunks; and about the vicious rumor that the Duchess of Windsor was really a man, and how can those terrible stories like that get started, when the truth of the matter was that not a soul in the room had heard the story before that moment.

Ruby took Mickie Minardos away with her, and they locked themselves behind closed doors to go over plans for the ball, which we_ being kept secret from even the closest of friends, except L__ , of course, but Loelia wasn't telling. After she left, everyo_ _marked on the beauty of Ruby Renthal. She had recently re___ _d from a trip to Brazil with a changed chin and smaller b___ _s. Her marvelous clothes, even in the country, her fabulous jewels, even for day, her newfound ability to enter a room so that everyone turned to look at her, and the allure of vast wealth that had become a part of her drew people into her orbit. Near, they were not disappointed. Her voice, changed too, so like the voice of Loelia Manchester, her greatest friend, enhanced the wit and charm that had been hers to begin with. Had she met people from the earlier parts of her life, before her prominence, she need not have worried, and didn't, for, most likely, they would not have recognized her. Ruby Renthal had become a great lady.

Lord Biedermeier removed his pince-nez and, with his thumb and forefinger, massaged the reddened bridge of his nose, all the time staring at the tropical fish in the aquarium that Elias Renthal had recently installed in the morning room of his new house.

"Are you shaking your head at those tropical fish, Lucien?" asked Loelia Manchester, looking up from her needlepoint.

"My first wife was Venezuelan. Do you remember her, Loelia?" Lord Biedermeier asked.

"Mother knew her," answered Loelia.

"Concepción de la Madrid she was called," continued Lord Biedermeier.

"Marvelous skin, I remember," said Loelia.

"Yes, she had beautiful skin, and her flesh was not quite firm. Just the way I like it."

"Really, Lucien! That's a conversation for the men's breakfast. Not here."

"The Latins, you know, are superstitious. Concepción always said that fish in bowls were bad luck."

"Oh, dear," said Loelia, staring at the fish tank. "I never heard that."

"Oh, yes, true," agreed Ezzie Fenwick, from his deep chair, laying aside a *Vogue*. "Fish in bowls are meant to be bad luck."

"Almost as bad luck as peacocks," chimed in Winston Bergerac, from his easel, where he was repainting Flash's prick.

Later, after tea, the sun came out. Ruby came into the room. "Outside, everyone. There's a rainbow."

For Ruby the beauty of the locale was secondary to the beauty that she created for the locale. The rainbow was less beautiful to her than the Edwardian gazebo she had built where she took her guests to watch the rainbow.

Lord Biedermeier, who was stout, said, "To the pool, finally. You really must not miss the opportunity to see me in a bathing suit." Everyone laughed.

"And you must see the new peacocks that Elias has bought for the place," said Ruby. "Too beautiful for words."

ENTERING the room that had been set aside as his weekend office, Elias closed the door behind him. At the console where his computers were placed, in a modified version of the switchboard with a hundred direct telephone lines to brokers and traders that he had in his Fifth Avenue offices, sat Maxwell Luby, dressed in lime-green country clothes of a different variety from the country clothes of the houseguests sitting in the smaller of the two dining rooms.

"Oh, Max, sorry if I have ruined your Sunday by asking you out here," said Elias. "There's a favor I'd like you to do me in the morning. I'm not going to be able to get back to town until after noon tomorrow. There's a new horse I have to see in the morning, and this simply has to be done at ten fifteen, no earlier, no later."

"What is it, Elias?" asked Max, used now to strange requests.

"Do you know the coffee shop called the Magnolia on Madison Avenue and Sixty-second Street?"

"No."

"Well, it's there. Just in from the corner. East side of the street. You've walked by it a hundred times without noticing."

"What about it?"

"I'd like you to go in there at exactly ten fifteen tomorrow morning. There will be a young man sitting at the counter on the second stool from the end. About thirty-two years old. Ivy League look. Dark hair, crew cut, just the beginning of going bald. He'll be wearing a gray flannel suit, blue shirt, dark red tie."

Max, used to such assignments, nodded.

"He will be reading the *Times*. On the empty stool next to him will be an old copy of *Forbes*, the one with the picture of me on the cover. You say to him, 'Do you mind if I move your *Forbes?*' That's all. No more. When he says, 'Excuse me, I'll move it,' you sit down next to him and order a cup of coffee."

"That's it?" asked Max, with a question in his voice to indicate there was an element missing.

"That's it," answered Elias. "Oh, yes, one more thing. You'll be carrying this briefcase. All you have to do when you sit down is leave the briefcase next to his leg. When he gets up, he'll take it with him. Okay?"

"Okay, Elias," said Max, lifting the briefcase and testing it for weight. "Why ten fifteen exact?"

"After the breakfast crowd. Before the lunch crowd. There'll be an empty stool."

"This is not Guy Howard again, is it?"

"No, no, not Guy," said Elias, shaking his head with displeasure at the name of Guy Howard. "He's called Byron Macumber, but no names are necessary." He looked for a moment at Max Luby's lime-green country clothes in the manner that Lord Biedermeier had once looked at Elias's clothes, although Elias had now forgotten that he had ever worn similar lime-green country clothes. "I'd ask you to stay, Max, but Ruby's got a house party going."

Max knew he didn't fit. "No problem, Elias. I've gotta get back to Pelham Manor anyway."

Later, in his car, when he stopped for gas, Max opened the briefcase. Beneath the newspapers on the top, there were, as he knew there were going to be, packets and packets of hundred-dollar bills for Byron Macumber.

"ISN'T THIS nice, Hubie? Dinner on trays, just the two of us, in front of the fire? Oh, the deliciousness of an evening at home," said Lil Altemus, clapping her hands. "I get so tired of going out, out, out, all the time. You can't imagine how thrilled I was when you said you wanted to spend an evening alone together."

"There's something I wanted to tell you, Mother," said Hubie.

"I bet you didn't know your old mother could rustle up such a good meal, did you? I couldn't ask Gertie and Parker to stay on, after all those people all day long. And Lourdes is hopeless on days like Easter. Has been hopeless the whole of Holy Week! Church, church, church, she can't get enough church. On her knees every minute."

"Mother."

"Look at the doggies, Hubie? Aren't they precious? Worn out. Simply worn out. Those children ran them ragged all afternoon. Do you know that Bosie's going to be twelve?"

"Mother."

"The baby's adorable, isn't she? Hubie?"

"What?"

"The baby. Little Janet. Don't you think she's adorable?"

"Cute. Farts a lot. But cute."

"Hubie, you know how I hate words like that. What did you think of the newlyweds?"

"Which set?"

"Dodo and your grandfather."

"Good for Dodo is what I say," said Hubie.

"Oh, Hubie, you always say exactly the opposite of what you

should say. Dodo's turned out to be just a little gold digger, and after all this family has done for her."

"You didn't want to change Grandfather's diapers, Mother."

"That's not the point. That's what nurses are for."

"Better he marries Dodo than Miss Toomey, Mother."

"Oh, Hubie, you are the limit. She's getting everything, you know. Laurance has seen Father's new will. All the paintings, all the furniture, all the bibelots on the tables even, all Mother's silver and china. Everything." There was such sadness in Lil's voice that Hubie turned to look at her.

"Mother, it would be hard in court for anyone to feel sorry for you, you know," said Hubie.

"What do you mean? Some of those things aren't even Van Degan things. Some are from Aunt Grace Gardiner's side of the family," insisted Lil.

"Mother," said Hubie, holding out his hands in exasperation. "There's not a spare inch in this huge apartment that is not crammed with valuable objects. What more do you need?"

"It's the principle of the thing," Lil said, rising and going over to the television set.

"Now, listen, Mother, we have to talk," said Hubie.

"Do you want to watch 'Sixty Minutes' or just talk? Diane Sawyer is interviewing the First Lady."

"Just talk."

"Good. Try some of this fig mousse. It's Gertie's specialty. I don't know how she manages to make it so light. Something about the egg whites, I think. I watched her once."

"You can see that I'm not well, can't you, Mother?" Hubie raised the level of his voice.

"The figs have to be very ripe," Lil continued. "And white figs only. That's very important."

"I have AIDS, Mother."

"It's just your color, darling. Your color's not good. And you need to fatten up a bit. You eat like a sparrow, you know. What you need is some good food and some good mountain air." Lil broke two cookies and threw them up in the air for Bosie and Oscar to catch. "There you are, you naughty doggies. I knew what you were waiting for. Yes, I did. Look at them, Hubie."

"I've got lymphoma, Mother. That means three or four months, the doctor said. Maybe no months," said Hubie, so quietly that he thought perhaps she had not heard him.

"I thought you and I might take a little trip to the mountains. They say Saint Moritz out of season is too beautiful for words, and so healthy. But when? That is the problem. There's that damn ball of the Renthals' that Laurance insists I not miss, and the Todesco wedding, and the final gala for the ballet where I'm the chairperson. After that, we'll go."

"By September I might very well have been dead for several weeks," said Hubie.

Lil had started to breathe heavily. "Oh, please, Hubie. This sort of talk is so morbid. I don't know how you could do this to your family."

"Thank you for your support, Mother."

"Does anyone know?" asked Lil.

"Juanito knows."

"Oh, I don't care about *Juanito*, for God's sake. I mean, does anyone we know or anyone in the family know?"

"Justine, only."

"Before me, you told Justine?"

"She guessed."

Lil put her hand to her heart and held it there, as if she were attempting to calm herself from considering the consequences of what her son had just told her.

"Paris!" she screamed.

"What?"

"Paris. That's where you should go. The Duchess, Wallis, Windsor, you know, my mother's great friend, she and the Duke used to stay with Mother and Father in Palm Beach every winter."

"I'm telling you I'm going to die, and you're talking to me about the fucking Duchess of Windsor?"

"No, no, there is a point to all this. She left all her money to the Pasteur Institute, and they do all those marvelous things for that particular disease. I'll send you to Paris."

"Do you want to get rid of me, is that it, Mother? So your friends don't have to know that your son is gay and has AIDS. That's why you want to send me to Paris, isn't it? Well, I'm not going to go to Paris." He got up from his chair, kicked the tray table with his foot, and the tray went flying to the floor. Bosie and Oscar began barking and tearing at the uneaten food on the plates. Hubie watched the manic scene for a moment and then started for the door.

"Please, please, Hubie, don't go," cried Lil. "Please don't leave me now. *Please*. I've heard all about that disease from Bobo, you know, my hairdresser Bobo. His salon has been decimated. Alfonso, Peregrine, Jose, they're all gone, and all those dancers in the musicals, and in the ballet, and, oh, my dear, in fashion, you wouldn't believe the numbers. Nevel told me. But I didn't think people like us got it, Hubie. I didn't. I didn't."

Even through her sobs, Lil could hear the door close and knew Hubie had gone. For a long time she sat in her chair without moving. When the telephone rang, she did not answer it. Then, slowly, she rose and carried her tray out to the butler's pantry and left it on the counter. Then she returned to the library and picked up Hubie's tray off the floor where he had kicked it, replaced the plates and glass on it and carried it back to the butler's pantry where she placed it on the counter next to her own. She turned off the lights and started to leave the pantry. Suddenly, she turned on the lights again and went back to the counter.

She picked up her mother's apple-green-bordered Meissen dinner plate that Hubie had used and looked at it, in a porcelain farewell. Then she dropped the plate on the pantry floor and watched it smash into irretrievable disrepair. Then she dropped the wine glass that her son had used and watched it smash. She picked up a fork and spoon off his tray, looked for an instant at the Montmorency pattern with her maiden monogram *L V D* engraved on the handles, and dropped them down the trash chute.

By the telephone on the counter was a pad and pencil where Gertie kept her notes. "Order Malvern water," it said, and under that, "Israeli melons." Under these reminders, Lil wrote:

"Gertie: Please forgive the ghastly mess I've made. I tripped. P.S. The fig mousse was yummy!"

30

LAURANCE VAN DEGAN rarely lunched in the fashionable restaurants of the city. Unlike his sister, Lil Altemus, who lunched out almost every day, and usually at Clarence's, Laurance preferred lunch in the private dining room of his offices in the Van Degan Building, or, on special occasions, at the Butterfield, where he felt almost as at home as he felt in his own home. The Butterfield on Fifth Avenue in the Sixties was the least known and most exclusive of the men's clubs in New York. Unlike the Knickerbocker Club, the Racquet Club, or the Union Club, the Butterfield was never called the Butterfield Club, simply the Butterfield, and membership was by invitation, never by application. Laurance had been invited to join by his father, Ormonde, the year after he graduated from Harvard, and Laurance had invited his son, young Laurance, on his graduation from Harvard.

The entrance to the Butterfield was sedate and identified only by a small brass plaque, so long embedded in the red brick of the building as to be virtually unnoticeable. Within, the austerity gave way to more noble trappings: red carpets, paneled walls, crystal chandeliers, and what many considered to be the most graceful marble stairway in New York, winding elegantly upward for four stories. Large undraped windows looked out on Fifth Avenue and the park opposite, and in two tufted green leather chairs in front of one of these windows sat Laurance Van Degan and his luncheon guest, Elias Renthal.

"Another martini?" asked Laurance.

"No, no, Laurance," said Elias, raising his hand in mild protest. "I make it a point never to have more than one drink at lunch."

"A man after my own heart," said Laurance, who then signaled to old Doddsie, the waiter, who had been at the Butterfield as long as Laurance had been a member, to bring the menus. It had amused Laurance earlier in the day when Elias had suggested lunching at the Butterfield, saying he would like to see the famous staircase that

Ruby had heard about from Jamesey Crocus since he and Ruby were planning to rip out the staircase at Merry Hill and build a new one there.

Old friends of Laurance's like Addison Cheney, Charlie Dashwood, and Sims Lord had nodded greetings when he and Elias had entered the bar shortly before one, but none made any effort to join them, and Laurance understood, as their behavior was consistent with what his own would have been under similar circumstances. Laurance watched Elias survey the scene.

"I think it might be a good idea for you to buy a couple of thousand shares of Sims Lord's company, Laurance," said Elias, as his eyes rested on Sims Lord. "It's a little high now, sixty-eight, and it'll take a dip in a couple of weeks down to about forty-two, but then it will begin to make a climb up, up, up, and go right through the roof. It's good to get in early and ride with the dip so as not to attract any undue attention, if you get what I mean."

"Sims Lord's company?" asked Laurance. He could feel himself beginning to redden. Laurance and Sims Lord had been in the same class at St. Swithin's and at Harvard and had been ushers in each other's weddings. Sims Lord was one of his oldest friends, and for years Ormonde Van Degan had sat on the board of Lord and Co. In the last year Elias Renthal's tips preceding his corporate raids had enriched Laurance Van Degan by millions. It was not that Laurance Van Degan, or any of the Van Degans, needed more money than they already had, but Laurance had found that the Van Degan Foundation, which benefited museums, opera companies, ballet companies, several hospitals, and other causes, equally worthy, was hard pressed to address the problem of the homeless of the city, and he had taken to supplementing the income of the foundation, for philanthropic purposes only.

"We don't talk business here at the Butterfield," cautioned Laurance Van Degan. "House rule."

"Got you," answered Elias. "Have any women members in the club?"

"No, no, goodness, no," answered Laurance. "And we won't have any, I assure you, despite those women's libbers always protesting at the Century. Twice a year we have ladies' nights here, and that's it."

"Nice chairs," said Elias, patting the arms of the green leather club chair. "I like a chair you can sink yourself into. English Regency, these chairs, aren't they?"

"Yes, they are," said Laurance, impressed. "You're becoming quite the authority on furniture."

"I'm spending enough dough on furniture, thanks to the very expensive advice Ruby's curator, Mr. Jamesey Crocus, is giving Ruby, so I figure I should get to know something about it."

"I hear your country house is charming. Loelia Manchester told Janet."

"Ruby and I want you to come out some weekend real soon."

"Delightful."

"It's English looking, like the Butterfield here. I said to Ruby, 'You got all the Louis the Terrible French furniture in New York. Let's have a little comfort in the country.'"

Laurance smiled appreciatively at Elias's little joke. "I know your house well. Billy Grenville was a few classes ahead of me at St. Swithin's."

"The wife shot him, I hear. Is that right?"

"It seemed."

"Where did that take place?"

"In your house."

"Merry Hill?"

"Yes."

"Christ, you'd think the realtor would have brought that up."

"Perhaps she didn't know. It all happened thirty-five years ago. People forget."

"This club all wasps?" asked Elias. Laurance noticed that Elias often shifted themes abruptly, as if his mind were on one thing while he was talking about another.

"Wasps?"

"Protestants, I mean. Are there just Protestants in this club?"

"Oh, goodness, no, Elias. That sort of thing went out years ago. Over there, at that table by the bar, for instance. The man playing backgammon with Herkie Saybrook is Quentin Sullivan, one of the outstanding Catholic laymen of the city, knighted by the Pope, all that sort of thing."

"Mother was a Morgan too. That don't hurt, I suppose."

"Mother was a Morgan. Yes, you're right. She was. I forgot about that."

"I'd like to become a member here, Laurance," said Elias.

Laurance, startled, picked up the menu and started to peruse the specialties of the day. Elias's request was not a thing that Laurance had expected. In the name of business, Laurance Van Degan could insist that his reluctant sister invite the Elias Renthals to the wedding of her daughter, or that his equally reluctant wife include the Elias Renthals as guests in her box on the fashionable nights at the opera, or that his wife, sister, son, and niece change whatever plans they had in order to attend the forthcoming ball of the Elias Renthals, but he did not have the same altruistic feeling about membership in the Butterfield, which his own grandfather had helped to found.

"Well, we must discuss this, Elias," he said, meaning at some time in the future.

"What's to discuss?" asked Elias.

"May I suggest to you either the cold poached salmon, which is marvelous, or the chicken hash, which is the best anywhere in New York."

"I'll try the hash."

"Marvelous choice." Laurance picked up the pad and small pencil that Doddsie had left on the table and wrote the order down. He then tapped on a bell to signal the waiter.

"You write up your own order, huh?"

"No mistakes that way."

"Yes, sir, Mr. Van Degan," said Doddsie, arriving.

"Here you are, Doddsie," Laurance said, tearing off the page and handing it to him.

"Nothing first, sir?"

"I think not. Must watch our waistlines, Doddsie."

"You have nothing to worry about, Mr. Van Degan," said Doddsie, looking down at Laurance Van Degan's slender waist.

"Don't look over at my waistline, Doddsie," said Elias, patting his girth, and the three laughed. "And I will have something first. Like a salad."

"Yes, sir. House dressing?"

"Thousand Island."

"We'll go up to the dining room in a minute, Doddsie," said Laurance.

When the waiter left, there was silence for a moment. Herkie

Saybrook, on his way up to the dining room, passed the table and greeted Laurance Van Degan.

"Playing squash later today with young Laurance, Mr. Van Degan," said Herkie.

Any mention of his son always brought a smile of pleasure to the face of Laurance Van Degan. "Mr. Saybrook, Mr. Renthal," he said, introducing them.

"What a pleasure, Mr. Renthal," said Herkie Saybrook. "May I present Quentin Sullivan. Elias Renthal."

"Pleasure, pleasure," said Elias. "I was just saying to Larry here what a nice club this is."

No one ever called Laurance Van Degan Larry. Even as a boy in school, no diminutive of the name Laurance was applied to him. For an instant Laurance assumed the look on his face of a person who had been called by a wrong name. Then, not wanting to correct Elias in front of other people, he smiled and winked at Herkie Saybrook, as if amused by the presumption of the billionaire.

"We'll see you upstairs," said Laurance.

"Nice fella, Herkie Saybrook," said Elias.

"Lovely," agreed Laurance. "A great friend of my son's."

"What about it?" asked Elias.

"About what?"

"Me joining the club."

"You see, Elias. It's not that easy. There would be opposition."

"What kind of opposition?"

"All the members of the Butterfield have to have been born in New York."

"Quentin Sullivan was born in Pittsburgh."

"There are occasional exceptions, and in the case of Quentin Sullivan, his grandfather on the Morgan side was a member, and his great grandfather as well."

"How would I go about joining?"

"You have to be invited to join by someone who has been a member for at least twenty years."

"That's you."

"You have to have letters of recommendation from six other members."

"That shouldn't be difficult."

"Ah, but it is, you see."

"I've been helpful to a few people I've seen around here today," said Elias.

"We should go upstairs to the dining room," said Laurance.

"I'm starved."

"One other thing, Elias."

"What's that?"

"If the person who has been proposed for membership is turned down, the member who proposed him must resign."

"That's the best news yet."

"How so?"

"Don't tell me anyone is going to ask Laurance Van Degan to resign from the Butterfield. No fucking way. Say, I'm dying to walk up that winding stairway."

THE FOLLOWING Saturday afternoon, on the seventeenth hole of the golf course of the Maidstone Club in East Hampton, Long Island, Laurance Van Degan said to his son, young Laurance, "I would like you to write a letter for Elias Renthal."

"What sort of letter, Dad?" asked young Laurance.

"For membership in the Butterfield."

"You must be joking."

"I'm not joking."

"I can't believe what I'm hearing."

"It would mean a great deal to me, Laurance," said his father.

"Elias Renthal? Herkie Saybrook told me he called you Larry the other day. Herkie said he didn't know which way to look."

"He did, yes, he did call me Larry, but you see, he didn't know."

"There are so many clubs he could join, Dad, if he wants to join a club, but not the Butterfield. You can't mean the Butterfield."

"I do mean the Butterfield."

"But, Dad, only a year ago you blackballed—"

"I hate the world *blackballed*, Laurance," said his father, cutting in on his son's sentence. He leaned down to place his ball on the tee.

Young Laurance began again, rewording his sentence. "You kept

Whelan O'Brian from joining, when Sonny Thomas, your old friend, proposed him. You called him a mick, don't you remember?"

"I would appreciate it if you would ask Herkie Saybrook to write a letter also, Laurance," said Laurance, as if his son had not spoken. "I need six letters."

31

GUS WAS expecting to hear from Peach in California and picked up the telephone on the first ring, but it was not Peach, who had promised to call after she spoke with Mr. Feliciano. Instead it was Matilda Clarke.

"Oh, Gus, good, you're home," said Matilda.

"Yes," answered Gus.

"I'd like to stop by."

"When?"

"Now."

"I'm going out to dinner at eight."

"I'll be there in ten minutes."

"Is there anything wrong?"

"Heavens, no. I just felt like seeing you for a drink."

Gus continued to dress, expecting the telephone to ring at any time. He hoped Peach would call before Matilda arrived. When his black tie was tied and his cummerbund in place, he picked up the telephone and called California. Peach answered on the first ring.

"It's Gus," he said.

"I was going to call you," Peach answered.

"I've been waiting."

"I was waiting until five our time before calling."

"Why?" But, of course, he knew the answer why. He had been married to her for years.

"The rates go down at five."

"For God's sake, Peach," said Gus. It was a bone of contention between them always. Peach was one of the thrifty rich, even in semi-emergency situations. "I would have been gone by then."

"Well, anyway," said Peach. "I talked to your private detective."

"What did he want?"

"He said he's going to get married."

"He's already married. To someone called Wanda. He's got pictures of her all over his office."

"No, Gus, not Mr. Feliciano. He told me Lefty Flint is going to get married, as soon as he's released."

Gus was silent.

Peach continued. "Someone he's been corresponding with the whole time he's been in prison. You know those nuts who write to prisoners and fall in love with them. One of those."

"Who is she?"

"She's called Marguerite Somebody. She owns a bar in Studio City where he's going to work when he gets out."

"Is Marguerite Somebody out of her mind?"

"Perhaps she doesn't have a mind."

"Look. I have to go. There's someone ringing my bell."

"All right."

"Listen, Peach. I may be coming out for a day."

"I won't be going anywhere."

When he put down the telephone, he had the same disquieting feeling he always had when he talked with Peach, as well as the same feeling of anger he always got when anything about Lefty Flint was mentioned to him.

As he went to the front door of his apartment, he put on his dinner jacket. Opening the door, Matilda Clarke was standing there. Behind her was Ned Manchester.

"Don't you look smart, Gus," said Matilda. "Gus is one of the most popular men in New York," she said, turning to Ned. "You know each other, don't you? Ned Manchester. Gus Bailey."

"Easter at Lil Altemus's," said Gus, remembering where they had met.

"Exactly," said Ned. He seemed slightly ill at ease. "Charming, your flat," he said to Gus.

"Isn't it?" agreed Matilda. "Exactly the right amount of shabby."

Gus laughed. "Such compliments. How about if I make you drinks in some chipped glasses?"

"Scotch for me," said Ned.

"Wine for me," said Matilda.

When Gus went into the kitchen, Ned picked up some books on tables to look at the titles. "I wish I had time to read," he said.

"Play a few less hours of squash every day, and you'd have time to read," said Matilda.

"You sound just like someone I used to be married to," said Ned.

Matilda snapped her fingers quietly to get Ned's attention and pointed to the photograph of Gus's daughter on a tabletop and mouthed but did not say the word *dead*.

"I saw Constantine de Rham today at Clarence's," said Matilda, when Gus returned with the drinks.

"Out again, is he?" asked Gus.

"Looks about a hundred," said Matilda.

"Very aging, a gunshot wound in the stomach," 'ered Ned Manchester.

"Did you talk with him?" asked Gus.

"Heavens, no. He was with that young woman with the E   Perón hairstyle," said Matilda.

"Yvonne Lupescu, her name is," said Gus.

"She was playing nursie, leading him to his table."

"A strange pair," said Ned.

"I'm sure she's the one who shot him," said Matilda.

"It's a theory," said Gus.

There was a pause in the conversation. Gus, curious, wondered what the purpose of the visit was.

"What time are you off, Gus?" asked Matilda.

"Almost immediately, in fact," said Gus. "I'm going to Maisie Verdurin's, and you can't be late at Maisie's. In at eight. Out at eleven. Like clockwork."

"Loelia and Mickie are going to Maisie's too," said Matilda to Ned.

"Lucky Maisie," said Ned. There was a note of bitterness in his voice.

"Listen, Gus," said Matilda. "My son's here from Santa Barbara. He's turned my little hovel upside down. Would you mind very much if we stayed on a bit after you left?"

Gus looked up and immediately understood the situation. Ned, turning away, went back to examining the books on Gus's coffee table. Gus smiled at Matilda.

"No problem," said Gus, taking his glass into the kitchen, and Matilda followed him.

"We're having dinner around the corner, at that little French place, whatever it's called, and we thought we could wait here until our reservation at nine," Matilda went on quickly. "I mean, it's so cozy here."

"No problem," repeated Gus.

Matilda turned on the tap in the sink and rinsed out Gus's glass. "Don't you *dare* say loose woman to me, Gus Bailey," she whispered.

"Who said loose woman?" asked Gus.

"You're thinking it."

"No, you are," said Gus, laughing.

"He's so forlorn since Loelia," said Matilda.

"You know where the rubbers are," said Gus.

"You are *awful!*" she said, pretending to pound him with her fists. "I could ask that nice elevator man of yours to lock up after we leave."

"Sure," said Gus.

"Would you like to come out to the country over the weekend?" asked Matilda, in a normal voice, returning to the living room.

"I'll be away," answered Gus.

"Another one of your mysterious trips? This man, Ned, I'm sure he's leading a double life. One of these days we're going to find out he's not a writer at all, but an assassin."

''GUS, I WAS thrilled with the piece you wrote about us for the *Times Magazine*," said Ruby Renthal, at Maisie Verdurin's dinner.

"Thanks," said Gus.

"You were a pal not to repeat some of those damn fool things I said," said Ruby.

"I told you I wouldn't."

"A lot of you guys say you won't and then you do," said Ruby. Gus noticed that people stared at Ruby Renthal the way they stared at film stars.

"If I had, I wouldn't have gotten invited to your ball, and I want to go to your ball," said Gus. They both laughed.

Lest anyone had not picked up on the change in status of Elias and Ruby Renthal, Maisie Verdurin, whose dinners were always a barometer of exactly who was successful in the mercurial world of big business, seated Elias Renthal on her right that night, the place of honor that she usually reserved for cabinet ministers and former presidents. As Ruby Renthal was every bit as important a social star as her husband was a business star, Maisie had been in a quandary all day at exactly how to seat Ruby at no less elevated a place than Elias's, especially as the invitations to their ball were out and they had become even greater objects of curiosity.

Finally Maisie had broken one of her own rules never to seat husbands and wives at the same table and placed Ruby across from her between the chief executive officers of an airline and a petroleum company.

"I have never seen Mrs. Renthal wear the same dress twice," said Rochelle Prud'homme to Maisie. Rochelle, who had resisted the Renthals' rapid rise, had now fallen into line, praising them on every occasion, especially as they were giving the grandest party of the decade. "I hear Ezzie Fenwick tells her what to wear."

"Isn't she beautiful?" Maisie had replied. "I think she's the chicest woman in New York." Maisie did not add that she had never had clients like Elias and Ruby Renthal for buying art, even though she could not bear Jamesey Crocus, who had now become their private curator. As Elias's walls, both in town and country, were now filled with works of art, his collecting spree had abated somewhat, except for the occasional swap, when a finer specimen of a painter's work came on the market. Maisie, ever on the lookout for new walls to fill, had taken an interest in Reza Bulbenkian, another of the New People whose wealth was incalculable, and invited him and his wife Babette to the same party that the Renthals were attending, but she seated them at less exalted tables than her own. The Bulbenkians were also rising in society, although in adjacent groups of lesser smartness than the group that had taken in the Renthals, and they were not often mentioned in social conversation, except in that month each year when Mr. Forbes brought out his list of the four hundred richest people in America, on which Reza Bulbenkian's name kept rising.

"Who in the world is this Reza Bulbenkian?" Loelia had asked Ruby, looking up from the magazine.

"You see him at benefits," answered Ruby. "He always buys several tables, or whole rows of seats, and fills them with people you never saw before."

"With the hair in his ears, that one?" asked Loelia.

"Exactly. And the wife who weighs about three hundred."

With that, the Bulbenkians were dismissed until the following year, except, of course, on Wall Street, where he was discussed almost as much as Elias Renthal.

Maisie placed Reza Bulbenkian at what she considered her third

best table, next to Yvonne Lupescu, and she placed Babette, who
had been married to Reza for thirty years, in the little room in the
back, next to Constantine de Rham, who was responsible for introducing the Bulbenkians to Maisie, just as he had been responsible
for introducing Elias Renthal to Maisie. Maisie knew that the dream
of the Bulbenkians' life was to be asked to the Renthals' ball, but she
had declined to intercede in their behalf, agreeing only to have them
to the same party and let them take it from there.

"Marvelous, your toupee," said Yvonne Lupescu to Reza Bulbenkian, in an effusive tone, as if she were complimenting him on an
exquisite article of clothing, and then continued, pretending not to
notice the look of discomfort on his face, "No one would ever know."

Bulbenkian had heretofore paid no attention to his dinner companion, casting looks instead at the table where the Renthals were
seated, in the hopes of catching Elias Renthal's eye to wave a greeting to him. Now, furious, he turned to Yvonne, picked up her place
card to familiarize himself with her name, and saw that she was a
baroness. Thereafter he gave her his full attention, not only to quiet
her enthusiasm over his toupee, which he thought no one, not even
his wife of thirty years, had ever detected, but because Baroness
Lupescu proved to be an enchanting dinner companion, whose dia-
mond-ringed fingers found their way to the bulge between his legs
beneath Maisie's pristine white tablecloth at the same time that she
was telling him stories of her grandmother in the court of King Zog of
Albania.

At Maisie's table, Ruby Renthal held her dinner companions in
her thrall. "At the White House the other night, the First Lady seated
me next to the Vice President," she said to the table at large. "I said
to him, 'You've got to change your glasses, sir. No one is ever going to
be elected President of the United States who wears rimless
glasses.'"

"You didn't say that to the Vice President?" asked Maisie Verdurin, aghast, as the rest of the table laughed at the audacity of the
beautiful Mrs. Renthal.

"Oh, I did, and he's going to change them. You mark my words,
Maisie. Just keep watching him on the news."

"How was the White House?" asked Maisie, wistfully. She longed
to be invited there.

"So pretty, the whole thing," said Ruby. "The First Lady had rose geranium in the finger bowls, Maisie. We must all try that."

Looking across the table, Elias Renthal caught Ruby's eye and winked at his wife. She smiled back at him. What Elias knew, as surely as he knew that he was the fifth richest man in the United States, was that he had married the perfect wife. When he had been married to Gladyce, and before that, when he had been married to his first wife, Sylvia, his social life in Cleveland was confined to an occasional party for a special event, or dinners in restaurants with business associates and their wives. Being in society, as he now was, was a different thing altogether. He and Ruby were out every night, usually "dressed to the nines," as he put it, and, although he grumbled about never staying home, he liked being invited everywhere almost as much as Ruby did. Ruby, who was born for society, had taken on the airs of someone who had always been rich. She understood the intricacies of the overlapping groups in the two thousand people who went out to dinner every night. With neither Gladyce nor Sylvia could he have risen to the heights that he had risen to with Ruby by his side.

Ruby had not resisted earlier that day when Elias told her he had settled a portion of his fortune on her. That way, he told her, in the unlikely event of adversity, the money that was in her name would be secure.

"We are a team," he said to her.

"A great team," she agreed. At that moment in time, she was the happiest that she had ever been in her life, and no man could have attracted her in the way that her husband did.

Although Ruby claimed not to understand a thing about business, she had taken to reading the financial pages with the same relish with which only last year she had read the society columns. She would have been able to tell anyone, if anyone had thought to ask her, which they didn't, that Sims Lord & Co. had closed at thirty-seven and an eighth the day before the takeover, fallen immediately to twenty-four, and then risen to forty-six, and that Elias, even on that relatively small buyout, had profited by twenty-four million dollars.

Maisie Verdurin, the evening's hostess, had been struck dumb by the grandeur of Ruby Renthal's conversation about the White House. She waited an appropriate length of time while Elias Renthal, on her right, explained to the table the modus operandi of his takeover of Sims Lord & Co., the kind of conversation that usually took place at Maisie Verdurin's tables. When Justine Altemus Slatkin, who had been unusually silent throughout the evening, accidentally knocked over a glass of red wine and the waiters came scurrying to place napkins over the wet tablecloth, Maisie, unconcerned about Justine's accident, said casually to Elias, "I didn't realize Ruby was so friendly with the First Lady."

"Oh, yes," said Elias proudly. "The First Lady is very fond of Ruby, ever since Ruby's gift to the White House."

"Her gift?" asked Maisie.

"She gave her console tables, the ones she bought at the Orromeo auction in London, with the inlaid rams' heads, to the White House for the redecoration of the Green Room."

"My word," said Maisie.

"After the First Lady came to lunch at the apartment, Ruby just gave them to the White House. She said the country had been good to her and she wanted to give something back to the country."

"The First Lady went to Ruby's apartment for lunch?" asked Maisie.

"If I tell you a little secret, Maisie, you won't let on to anyone, will you?"

"Me? Never!" said Maisie.

"Because if this got out—"

"My lips are sealed. Talking to me is like talking to the dead," said Maisie.

"The First Lady might, just might, come to the ball, if she can readjust her schedule so that she can visit an orphanage in Harlem on the same day."

"My word," said Maisie.

Of all the news that went around Maisie Verdurin's tables that night, the death of Baron von Lippe in Brussels from AIDS, the divorce of the Herkie Saybrooks, the death by overdose of the Wagstaffs' daughter, and the rumored merger of the airline and the petroleum company, whose CEOs had graced Maisie's table, none was more repeated the next day than the news that the First Lady might, just might, be coming to the ball of the Elias Renthals.

32

IN THE Ambassadors' Club of the airline, Gus watched as the film star Faye Converse entered, causing excitement and stir, even among the corporate executives waiting for their planes. Faye Converse, a star for as long as most people could remember, still created a glamorous havoc in her wake, although her screen appearances had dwindled to the occasional mini-series on television. Finally, seated, a soft drink brought to her, she engaged in conversation with a young companion, probably a secretary, Gus thought, who nodded assents and occasionally wrote something down on a list.

"Is that you, Gus?" Faye called out, having caught his eye.

"Hello, Faye," said Gus, rising to go over to her.

"Leave it to you not to make a fuss over me," she said.

They both laughed.

"You look great, Faye," he said.

"That's better," she said. "You know how I like compliments. If I hadn't spotted you, I bet you wouldn't have gotten up to speak to me."

"Oh, yes, I would have. I was just waiting for your usual hubbub to quiet down."

"You going to L.A. or Europe?"

"L.A. For a day."

"I liked that piece you wrote about me."

"Thanks."

"Still off the sauce, you see," she said, holding up her soft drink.

"Same here," he said, holding up his.

"This is my secretary. Brucie Hastings. Gus Bailey."

"Oh, I read your piece on Faye," she said.

Gus shook hands with the young woman. Her handshake was gentle.

"Are you working?" asked Gus, turning back to Faye.

"I'm going to be in *Judas Was a Redhead*. Have you read it? Marvelous book."

"Nestor Calder's a friend of mine," said Gus.

"I'm playing Magdalena, the old hooker with the heart of gold," she said.

"Perfect," said Gus.

"How do you like that, Brucie? Did you hear what this son of a bitch said to me? I tell him I'm playing a hooker with a heart of gold, and he says 'perfect,' like in perfect casting."

Brucie laughed. She appeared fragile to Gus.

"Are you in first class, Gus, or are you still riding back in steerage?"

"Steerage."

"Here, give me your ticket. Brucie, take Mr. Bailey's ticket over to that nice lady at the desk, Robin I think her name was, the one I gave the autograph to, and ask her to upgrade Mr. Bailey to first class and seat him next to me, and you sit in his seat in steerage. There are a few things I want to talk to Gus about."

"I DON'T normally sign autographs in planes, but I'll make an exception this time," said Faye to the woman who interrupted her conversation with Gus when the plane was aloft.

"Oh, thank you, Miss Converse," said the woman. "Will you sign it to Darlene?"

"She looked like a Darlene, didn't she?" said Faye, when the woman had gone back to her seat. Gus laughed. "I bet you were an only child, Gus," said Faye. They were drinking Perrier water.

"No, I wasn't."

"You seem like you were an only child. That loner thing about you."

"One of four, as a matter of fact."

"New England, right?"

"Hartbrook. A little town on the Connecticut River that you'd have to be born in to know about."

"Where's the rest of the four of you?"

"Two dead. One suicide. One cancer."

"The other?"

"A brother."

"Where is he?"

"Boston, I think. We don't keep in touch."

"What does he do?" asked Faye.

"Designs condominiums in New England resorts, to the great displeasure of the Old Guard and the environmentalists," said Gus, shifting in his seat. "This isn't why you kicked Brucie out of her first-class seat to sit back in steerage, is it, so you could ask me about my background?"

"No. I was just vamping."

"That's what I thought."

They laughed again.

"You know someone called Elias Renthal, don't you?" she asked.

"I know him, kind of. I interviewed him and his wife."

"I read it," said Faye.

"I see him at parties. The last time I saw him, he said, 'Hi, Bus,' and I said, 'It's Gus, not Bus,' and he said, 'That's what I said.' That's how well I know him. Why?"

"He's rich, isn't he?"

"Oh, yes, he's rich."

"Very rich?"

"We're talking big bucks here."

"Generous?"

"What are you getting at, Faye? I don't think he'd finance a movie, if that's what you're interested in."

Faye shook her head no. She looked out the window of the plane. Then she said, "Brucie, my secretary."

"In steerage."

"She's dying."

"Oh, no."

"She's got the dread disease," said Faye.

"God almighty," said Gus.

"She's married to a dancer on the Larkin show. He has it too. Get the picture?"

"Got it," said Gus.

"I'm trying to raise money for the disease, a lot of money, big money. Do you think Mr. Renthal would help me out?"

"I don't know. He gives to the opera. He gives to the ballet. He gives to the museums. I don't know about disease. I especially don't know about that disease. He's still on the make. So far he only does the social-advancement charities."

"All I want, Gus, is an introduction to Mr. Renthal, and I can handle it from there," said Faye.

"Faye, you're a famous woman. You can get to anyone in the world you want to get to. You don't need me to meet Elias Renthal."

"He didn't return my call."

"I can't believe it."

"He didn't return my two calls."

"What did the secretary say?"

"'Will he know what this is in reference to?' she asked."

Gus shook his head.

"I could do a fund-raiser," said Faye. "But it takes time. And time is not on our side."

"Elias Renthal's wife is the key," said Gus. "He does whatever she tells him to do. Her name is Ruby Renthal."

"I've seen her picture in the magazines. Pretty."

"Very pretty," said Gus. "And nice, too."

"Can you set it up for me to meet her?"

"I think so. She liked the piece I wrote on her. I'll set up a lunch."

"At Clarence's. I've always wanted to go to Clarence's."

"Okay, I hope."

"Thanks, Gus. Will you have time for dinner while you're in L.A.?"

"Probably not."

"You out on an article?"

"Family stuff," said Gus.

"Listen, Gus. I'm sorry about what happened to you and Peach. I mean, about your daughter."

Gus nodded.

"I was doing a picture in Italy at the time, or I would have written," she said.

Gus nodded.

"I don't know how you behaved so well under the circumstances. If that had happened to me, I would have shot the son of a bitch."

Gus nodded. It was the sort of thing that people said to him.

WHEN GUS stepped into the dark bar after the bright sunlight of Studio City, he was temporarily blinded and waited for a minute at the entrance until he got his bearings. It was two o'clock in the afternoon, and the bar was empty except for a young woman sitting on a stool behind the bar adding up receipts at the cash register.

"Help you?" she asked, when Gus settled himself on a stool.

"Perrier," he said.

"Out of Perrier," she said, not moving from her stool.

"Coke?" he asked.

She rose, put her receipts on the cash register, picked up a beer mug, filled it with ice, and from a spigot filled the mug with the soft drink.

"It's Pepsi," she said, putting it in front of him. She was pretty, under thirty, Gus figured, and stared at him as if she knew the purpose of his visit was not to drink a Pepsi Cola at two o'clock in the afternoon. Her blouse was made of a thin material, through which the shoulder straps of her undergarments could be seen.

"Are you Marguerite?" Gus asked.

"What can I do for you?" she asked, without answering his question.

"I wanted to ask you a question."

"About what?"

"Is it true that you are engaged to marry Lefty Flint?"

"Who are you?"

"Is it?"

"What the hell is it to you?"

"The man is a killer. The man has taken a girl's life."

"Who the hell are you?"

"I am the father of the girl he murdered."

"He was drunk when he did that. Now he doesn't drink anymore. That was a one-time thing. He explained all that to me."

"You know then what he did?"

"Yes, I know."

"And you're still going to marry him?"

"You better get out of here, Mr. Bailey."

"Yes, you're right," said Gus. He was drained, white, shaken. For an instant their eyes met.

"Good-bye," he said.

"Good-bye," she answered.

"Look," said Gus.

"What?"

"Here's a telephone number and name. If you ever are in trouble of any sort, ring it."

"Whose number?"

"It's not mine. It's just if you're in trouble. Keep it."

"I'm not going to be in any trouble, Mr. Bailey."

"I hope not, Marguerite. With all my heart, I hope not."

He turned and walked out of the bar.

Marguerite picked up the card that Gus had dropped on the bar and read it. On it was the name and telephone number of Anthony Feliciano.

"MAY I GO down into your storeroom?" asked Gus.

"For what?" asked Peach. Divorced, with her own house, which was not the house of their marriage, Peach sometimes objected to Gus's use of her home.

"I'm looking for something I might have left behind when I moved out," he answered.

"All your things were packed up and sent to New York," said Peach.

"There's something I can't find."

"What?"

"Some letters that my father sent me during the war," he answered.

"All right," she said.

Somewhere, not lost, but long out of sight and reach, in a box, or trunk, or drawer, was a black leatherette box, lined with satin, on which rested a medal and ribbon, commemorating an act of bravery in a war. With it was a Luger, taken off the body of a dead soldier.

IN THE GUN shop, he waited until a customer had finished his business and the shop was empty before he ceased looking at the racks, as if he were planning on making a purchase.

"Help you?" asked the salesman.

"I have a German Luger from World War Two," said Gus. He opened his briefcase and took out the gun, which was still wrapped in a brown paper bag grown soft and greasy through the years.

The salesman watched as Gus unwrapped the paper on the glass counter and picked up the gun.

"A beauty," he said. "Worth a bit of money, you know. They don't make them like this anymore. Is it for sale?"

"No," replied Gus. "I wanted to get it put into working order. Could I get that done here?"

"How much of a hurry are you in?"

"I'm not in a great hurry," said Gus.

"A week? Ten days? It's a busy time here with hunting season underway."

"That's all right. I live in New York, not here, but I'll be back out in a month or so, and I can pick it up then."

"I'll need a deposit."

"How much?"

"Seventy-five."

"Okay." Gus reached in his pocket and brought out some money.

"Is it registered?"

"No."

"Name?"

"Mertens. Gene Mertens."

33

WITH THE invitations to the Renthals' ball in the mail, addressed by Mrs. Renthal's calligrapher, and supervised by Mrs. Renthal's social secretary, it quickly became the most highly anticipated party in New York in years. Ezzie Fenwick, who had taken upon himself the role of champion of Ruby Renthal, told certain people that he would be able to secure invitations for them, implying, not quite honestly, that he advised Ruby on her list. Those who had not been invited, and thought they should have been, planned earlier than usual migrations to their houses in Newport and Southampton, their ranches in Wyoming, their cottages on the coast of Maine, or elsewhere.

There was no one quite so distressed by his exclusion from the Renthals' list as Constantine de Rham, recovered now, nearly, from his gunshot wound, which he continued to insist was self-inflicted. In his own mind he felt the shooting had added a tragic melancholy to his persona, coming as it did so few years after the death of his wife Consuelo. He imagined, walking daily to his lunch table at Clarence's, first on a walker and then on a cane, usually led by Yvonne Lupescu, that people said of him, "Poor man. What a lot he has suffered."

When Elias Renthal was still married to his second wife, Gladyce, Constantine de Rham had made his house on Sutton Place available to Elias as a location for his assignations with Ruby Nolte. Had his affair with the airline stewardess been public knowledge, Elias would have had a more difficult and costly divorce from Gladyce than he already had. Constantine had been handsomely rewarded for his services, but he still felt entitled to an invitation and silently sulked every time he read something in the newspapers about the forthcoming party, even though his somewhat sullied reputation and his affair with Yvonne Lupescu had made further contact with the high-rising Renthals an impossibility.

But for a chance meeting in the fitting rooms of Sills, Lord Biedermeier's tailor, between Elias Renthal, who now ordered suits twenty at a time for each season, and Constantine de Rham, who, because of his extreme weight loss due to the bullet that had briefly lodged itself in his stomach, was having his own summer suits taken in by several inches, the matter might have gone unnoticed, for Constantine would never have shared with anyone, least of all Yvonne Lupescu, his extreme hurt at the social slight by the Renthals.

That day at Sills, only the lateness of Elias, due to a business emergency, caused the overlap of appointments between the one-time friends. Mr. Sills was a stickler for promptness among his fashionable clientele, but he dared not reprimand Elias Renthal for his tardiness, for who else these days, except Arabs, he once pointed out to Lord Biedermeier, ordered suits twenty at a time on a seasonal basis.

As Elias Renthal's time was limited, and Constantine de Rham's time hung heavily on his hands, Mr. Sills silently signaled to Sal, the fitter, to move from Mr. de Rham's mirrored cubicle to Mr. Renthal's, so that the busy tycoon could be dealt with instantly. De Rham, who had taken his snubs from people he once dined with on a nightly basis, was in no mood to take a snub from a fitter with pins in his mouth and moved outside his cubicle in order to complain loudly to Mr. Sills. It was then he saw Elias Renthal in his cubicle, with a large cigar in one hand, remove his trousers and put on the first of the twenty pairs he was to have fitted, beginning with the satin striped trousers that would have to be ready in time for the ball.

"What a handsome pair of legs you have, Elias," said Constantine, joking, with a recurrence of the Continental charm that had once worked magic for him.

"For heaven's sake, Constantine," said Elias, surprised. "What are you doing here?"

"The same thing you're doing here," said Constantine. "On a somewhat lesser scale."

Elias chuckled. He quite enjoyed references to his extravagances. He put his cigar in his mouth and puffed on it, ignoring the NO SMOKING IN THE DRESSING ROOM sign posted on the wall.

Constantine, following suit, took a cigarette from a leather case he removed from his jacket pocket. "Do you have a match?" he asked.

"Leather? In town?" asked Elias, touching Constantine's case, pretending astonishment. "What would Ezzie Fenwick say about that?"

They both chuckled. Elias reached into his suit pocket and handed a dark blue packet of matches to Constantine. It was not lost on Constantine that in discreet green letters were the words *The Butterfield.*

"Swell places you're going to these days, Elias," said Constantine. "Whose guest were you?"

"I'm a member," said Elias. "I want the break lower on those trousers, right above where the pump will be," he said to Sal on the floor, pinning the cuff.

"You're a member of the Butterfield?" asked Constantine.

"Why, yes."

"I thought they didn't take, uh—"

"You thought wrong."

"Consuelo once asked Herkie Saybrook to put me up for the Butterfield."

"What happened?"

"Herkie said you had to be born in New York."

"That's right."

"But you weren't born in New York either."

"I'm going to need this suit, with the tail coat, for next week, Sal," said Elias, cutting Constantine short. "Very important. You better get me Mr. Sills, so there's no misunderstanding about anything. The other stuff I don't care about until I leave for Europe on the sixteenth."

"I was wondering if there's been some mistake, Elias," said Constantine.

"Mistake? About what?"

"You know how social secretaries sometimes get things mixed up."

"Get what mixed up?" asked Elias. Like the deal maker he was, he gave no indication that he knew exactly what Constantine de Rham was hinting at, and he was determined to make de Rham spell out the words before he refused him.

"You don't know what I'm talking about?"

"I haven't a clue."

"Your ball for the Earl and Countess of Castoria."

"What about my ball?"

"I haven't been invited."

"A lot of people haven't been invited. There's just so many people the ballroom can hold. Ezzie Fenwick tells me Mrs. Astor could only have four hundred people to her ball because that's all her ballroom could hold."

"You're having four hundred, I hear," insisted Constantine.

"That's as many as my ballroom can hold, too."

"I see," said Constantine.

"How are we doing here?" asked Mr. Sills, as he walked into the fitting room. The air was blue with cigar and cigarette smoke, and he waved his hand to clear it.

"We're doing fine, but I'm running late," said Elias, wanting to get away from Constantine. "How about if you send Sal here up to the house about six, and we can finish the other ten suits up there."

The small room was now very crowded, with Elias, who was large and stout, and Constantine, who was large and slender, Mr. Sills, and Sal, who was still kneeling on the floor, pinning a cuff. Constantine, insufficiently bathed, as usual, increased the foulness of the air. He leaned against the back wall and caught Elias's eye in the mirror. Elias met his stare.

"Do you remember when you were fucking Miss Ruby Nolte in my house on Sutton Place, Elias?" he asked. "When you had no other place to go because your wife, Gladyce, was suspicious of you?"

Sal, the fitter, coughed in astonishment, and the pins in his mouth were spat out on the floor.

"Such language, gentlemen," said Mr. Sills, attempting to make a joke, but he realized that he had walked in at an inappropriate time. He signaled to Sal, and the two of them left the fitting room.

Elias, who understood when to give in on a business negotiation, merely answered, "I'll see that you get sent a card, de Rham."

"That's very kind, Elias," said Constantine, reverting to his charming self.

"But one thing."

"Yes, Elias."

"This invite is for you solo, not you and Mrs. Lupescu."

"Oh?"

"That's right."

"That will make things quite awkward for me."

"As we used to say in Cleveland, tough shit."

"But Yvonne will be so disappointed."

"No way that Ruby will let Yvonne into this party, after what she did at the Altemus wedding."

"The Altemus wedding?"

"She crashed the Altemus wedding. You must have known that."

Constantine looked at Elias. He had not known that Yvonne had crashed Justine Altemus's wedding.

"Not only crashed it. Caught the bride's bouquet," said Elias, imitating Yvonne with a derisive gesture.

Constantine blushed at his mistress's gall. Elias's derision of Yvonne was hurtful to Constantine, not for the pain that her exclusion from the ball would cause her, but for the aspersion that it cast on him that he should be allied with such a woman, who would crash a society wedding.

"Oh, yes," went on Elias. "Yvonne is not in good stead with Lil Altemus. Or Janet Van Degan. And they're both coming to the ball. So it's you alone, or not at all."

"Perhaps, Elias, rather than mail me an invitation to Sutton Place, you would leave it for me at your office with your secretary. That way no one will see it but me."

"Any way you wish," said Elias. Elias had dressed by now and was back in his business suit and ready to go. "Now let me tell you something, you foreign piece of shit," he said. Gone from his voice was any semblance of charm or bonhomie. "It was your dead wife's house I was using, not your house, and you, pimp that you are, were well paid for the use of your dead wife's house. So don't strong arm me again ever." He put his finger right in Constantine's face. "What I know about you could send you to jail."

Weak still from his wound, Constantine de Rham sank into a chair, his face white from Elias's attack.

"See you at the ball, Constantine," said Elias. "Oh, one more thing. Try to remember to take a bath that night, and use a little spray in those moist armpits of yours."

If Elias hoped, by insulting him, to dissuade Constantine from attending the ball, he was to be disappointed. Constantine, the very next morning, appeared at Elias's office and picked up his invitation, on which Ruby Renthal's calligrapher had written the word *Alone* at the top of the engraved ecru card to indicate, in case the point had not been made sufficiently clear in the fitting room at Mr. Sills's, that Yvonne Lupescu was not included.

IT WAS ON ladies' day at the Butterfield that Ruby Renthal was introduced for the first time to Ned Manchester, the estranged husband of her great friend, Loelia Manchester.

"Mrs. Renthal, may I present Mr. Manchester," said Laurance Van Degan, making the introduction.

Ned Manchester, whom Ruby had heard so much about, from Loelia and others, was not at all the way she had imagined that he would be. As fair-haired as Mickie was dark, as pink-complexioned as Mickie was olive, as lapis-lazuli—eyed as Mickie was black, as tall, as slender, but with the appearance of a life of sport and exercise rather than rigorous dieting, it was hard for her to imagine that Loelia could have fallen in love with two such different men.

"I know your children," said Ruby.

"I've heard," Ned answered, smiling at her. "They enjoyed visiting you in the country."

"That son of yours is the best-looking young man I've ever seen in my life, and Charlotte is to die she's so pretty," said Ruby.

"Thank you," Ned replied, smiling proudly over his children. Ruby Renthal, whom he had heard used to be a stewardess, was not at all how he expected her to be. In some ways she reminded him of Loelia, at least in the way she talked. "You may know my children, Mrs. Renthal, but I know your house. I used to go to Merry Hill when I was a child. The Grenvilles' son was a friend of mine when we were little."

"I think you probably wouldn't recognize the house," Ruby said.

"That's what I hear. Do you still have the indoor tennis court?"

"Oh, yes. Elias plays every day when we're in the country."

"That's where I learned how to play tennis, on that court."

"You must come and see the house."

"I'd like that, sometime."

"And play tennis. Elias is always looking for a fourth."

It was not a thing Ruby would ever mention to a soul, not even to Elias, but she wondered why her great friend Loelia would find Mickie Minardos more attractive than Ned Manchester. She loved all those people she met every night at dinner, like Ezzie Fenwick and Jamesey Crocus. There was no one more amusing in the city to sit next to at dinner. And the way Mickie Minardos could dance! She was forever telling him that he made her feel like Ginger to his Fred, but when it came to marriage, give her men every time, like Elias. And Ned. Even if they did have two left feet when it came to dancing.

34

GUS, LATE, was stopped on the way out his door by the telephone.

"Feliciano here," said the voice on the other end when he answered.

"Oh, yes," said Gus.

"You were out here in L.A., I understand, and you didn't call."

"I was out on personal business," said Gus.

"To see a lady called Marguerite who runs a bar in Studio City," said Feliciano.

Gus paused. "Oh, yes, I did stop in there," said Gus.

"Not smart, Gus," said Feliciano.

"It was to warn her."

"That's not your job, Gus. That's only calling attention to yourself. When whatever happens is going to happen, I don't want you or your name to be involved in any way."

"Yes," replied Gus. He wondered if Mr. Feliciano knew about the gun he had left at the gun shop.

"Marguerite called me. You gave her my card evidently. She thought you were a nut," said Feliciano.

"Listen, I have to go," said Gus.

"It's Sunday morning. Where do you have to go on Sunday morning?"

"Mass," replied Gus.

GUS BAILEY, a long lapsed Catholic, had lately, and quietly, returned to his faith. He himself could not understand his revived attachment to God, but attachment it was, even though he sometimes experienced comfort from imagining Lefty Flint dead.

He was surprised that Sunday to see Loelia Manchester sitting several rows ahead of him. She prayed with the intensity of a non-regular attendant at church, one who was there for solace and answers on a particular matter of distress rather than a commitment to religious ritual. Once, when Gus looked over at her, he saw her raise a handkerchief to her eyes and brush away what must have been a tear.

Only leaving, on the church steps outside, did she look and catch sight of him. Her eyes, which had appeared melancholy, sparkled back to attention, as if they had been caught out in an impropriety, and her face assumed the look he had often seen on her when she arrived at parties or when she smiled at photographers at the opera.

"Hellohoware?" she said.

"Good morning," Gus replied.

"Sweet, wasn't he, that little altar boy with the red hair and the Adidas sneakers under his cassock? Couldn't wait, absolutely couldn't wait, could he, to get to the park to play baseball? So sweet." Piety abandoned, she had reverted to her society-woman character.

"I didn't know you were a Catholic," said Gus.

"I'm not," she said. "I was out walking, and I heard the music, and I wandered in."

"They have good music at St. James's too," said Gus.

"True, but I know everyone there, and I didn't think I'd know anyone here. I only go to church when I have troubles."

"I take it you have troubles," said Gus.

Loelia looked at Gus, as if she wanted to say something and then decided against it. "I can't bear all that peace-be-with-you business and shaking hands with all these strange people you've never seen before," she said instead. "I just kept my head bowed, praying like mad all through that part. Is that awful?"

"I'm sure the Pope won't hear about it," said Gus. They both laughed. She opened her bag and took out a gold cigarette case, from which she removed a cigarette.

"I don't have a match," said Gus.

"I do," she said, lighting her cigarette with a lighter. She inhaled deeply. "My mother used to say that no lady ever smoked a cigarette on the street. So much for early training, Mr. Bailey."

"Gus," he answered.

"Is it true that you had my husband to dinner in your apartment?"

"No, it's not true. I've never had anyone to dinner in my apartment. I don't know how to cook."

"But he came to your apartment."

"He came to my apartment for a drink."

"How did that come about?"

"It was the night I saw you and Mickie at Maisie Verdurin's."

"I know."

"A friend of mine brought him by for a drink."

"Was the friend of yours who brought my husband by for a drink Matilda Clarke?"

"Yes."

"She seems to have a thing for the men in my family. She once had an affair with my father, when her husband was in one of those alcohol places in Minnesota he was always being sent to."

Gus made no reply.

"After you left for Maisie Verdurin's party, did Matilda and my husband stay on in your apartment?"

"This is a conversation I don't think I want to be in," said Gus.

"I'm sorry. Of course you don't."

"Which way are you walking?"

"Up."

"I'm walking down."

"Gus. My friends all seem to know you, but I don't. I don't suppose I could talk you into coming to have tea with me one day this week. I live at the Rhinelander."

"Sure."

"How about tomorrow?"

"Sure."

ENTERING the suite in the Rhinelander Hotel that had been Loelia Manchester's home since she moved out of the apartment she shared with Ned Manchester and their children, Gus was aware of rooms that had been transformed, even for a transitory period, to the specific requirements of a woman long used to beauty and luxury. Loelia was standing, her back to him, as if looking out the window. As Gus walked farther into the room, she, without turning to greet him, raised her hand, which held a cigarette, to halt him. On the stereo Beethoven was playing; the Leonore Overture from *Fidelio*; Loelia remained transfixed until its grand conclusion. Then her back, so straight, collapsed. "Please forgive me, Gus. I cannot resist *Fidelio* when I hear it, especially the Leonore Overture."

"I feel that I have come at a wrong moment," said Gus.

"It's all right, Gus," said Loelia. Sitting, she lit another cigarette.

Loelia Manchester, he saw, was fastidious in everything but her cigarette habits. Her smoking was constant and slightly furtive, as if she had been told over and over again that smoking was bad for her, a filthy habit, and that statistics showed all sorts of dire consequences were in store if she did not stop, but she, powerless, could do nothing but continue, even in the face of constant disapproval. She only half stubbed out the butts into a green Meissen dish that served as an ashtray. A dozen or more butts already lay smoldering and smoking there, but she seemed not to notice. With a table lighter she used with two hands, she lit another cigarette.

"You didn't really want tea, did you?" she asked suddenly.

"No."

"Lil Altemus tells me you don't drink."

"That's right."

"How about a Coke? Will that do?"

"Perfect."

"I'll have one too. I drink about twenty Cokes a day. I seem to have all the noncriminal addictions, cigarettes and caffeine."

She rose and went into a small kitchenette to get the Coca-Colas. He could hear the sounds of a refrigerator door being opened and closed, of ice being removed from an ice tray, of glasses, of bottles being opened, of pouring. Looking around the room he thought, how alike they all are, these women. Bowls of roses, dozens of buds and blossoms, were on every table, all arranged, he knew by now, by Lorenza. Scented candles, needlepoint pillows, baskets for magazines, sofas covered in chintz, photographs in silver frames. Their houses were beautiful, and expensive, and interchangeable. When Loelia came back into the room, she carried a silver tray with the two glasses. She handed him a small linen napkin on which to place his glass, in which a thin slice of lemon had been placed. Her mind, he could see, had remained fixed on the cause of her distress during her bartending duties.

"I'm afraid you might laugh."

"I won't."

"The listener, they call you."

"Who calls me that?"

"Ezzie Fenwick. He says you're going to write about us all."

"Then don't tell me."

"But I have this urge to talk to you."

"Then I'm listening."

"It's not as if I am unaware of the consequences of falling in love with a man like Mickie Minardos. I am aware. I would have criticized any friend of mine who did what I did, but I can't help it. It is like another of my addictions. I cannot give him up. I absolutely adore him."

Gus did not reply.

"When I am not with him, I cannot stop thinking about him," she continued. "There's nothing about him I don't know, and I don't care. He's a snob. I know he's used me to make it socially in New York, but I don't care. He's bad-tempered at times. But when he's a good boy, and he's a good boy more than he's a bad boy, there is no one whom I've ever known I would rather be with. And the presents he gives me, to make up, are perfect, always perfect, exactly right."

Gus looked out the window.

"You see, he is frustrated by his enormous success because he wanted to be a success designing for the ballet and the opera, but he became a millionaire designing these damn shoes that he hates so much, and, in the meantime, all his creative energies are being wasted."

Gus, the confessor again, merely stared at Loelia.

"Mickie fell in love with my feet. Did you know that?"

"How would I know that?" asked Gus.

"He adores feet."

"I see."

"I, of course, had heard of people who admired feet, but I had never met anyone, nor ever expected to for that matter."

"Yes, of course."

"He likes me to wear shoes with very high heels, and black stockings, with seams up the back. Rather tartlike. Imagine! Me! He likes to watch me walk in them, back and forth across a room, his eyes riveted on my feet. He then likes to take off my shoes, very slowly, first one and then the other, the left one always first for some reason, touching, rather featherlike, the back of my legs and the bottom of my feet."

Gus, embarrassed, rose. "Would you mind if I got myself another Coke?" he asked.

Loelia nodded that she didn't mind and continued talking. "My own mother barely nodded to me when I saw her at Flora Spalding's memorial service. My brothers are tolerant but disapproving, and my sisters-in-law are, of course, siding with my mother. My daughter, Charlotte, played Roxanne in *Cyrano de Bergerac* at St. Cyprian's and didn't ask me to any of the three performances. I only found out she was in the play from Violet Bastedo, who has a daughter in the same school. Yesterday, before I saw you in church, my son, Bozzie, told me he wouldn't spend his summer vacation with me if Mickie was about. I know it's a terrible thing for a mother to say that she loves one child more than another, but it's true. It's always been rare and special between Bozzie and me, and now he doesn't want to have anything to do with me because of Mickie. But I can't give up Mickie, Gus. I can't. I just can't."

35

AS THE BALL drew near, Lorenza, the florist, and Mickie Minardos, the designer, fought bitterly for artistic supremacy, and each complained to Ruby Renthal about the other. Mickie called Lorenza a shop girl, and Lorenza called Mickie a prima donna. Lorenza thought her bowers for lilies and tulips and orchids were going to be overwhelmed by the weeping willow trees that Mickie thought were a necessity for the ten thousand live butterflies, in yellow and orange colors, that he planned to release at midnight on the night of the ball itself, and Mickie thought that Lorenza's bowers for lilies and tulips and orchids were no more than a backdrop to the fantasy of flora and fauna into which he was transforming the Renthal ballroom. Finally people had stopped referring to the apartment as Matilda Clarke's old apartment, or the Sweetzer Clarke apartment; it had become, if not forevermore, at least for now, the Elias Renthal apartment, and Matilda Clarke herself, who had lived in it for twenty-two years, could not recognize it as having been her own.

After midnight on the night before the ball, fifty flower arrangers and scene builders arrived at the Renthal triplex to begin the transformation of the first-floor rooms into sit-out rooms and the ballroom into a fairyland of flowers and twinkling lights for the ball. For Elias, who needed his sleep, the sounds of hammering and talking were too much, and he departed for the Rhinelander Hotel around the corner on Madison Avenue to secure his rest.

The weeping willow trees that Mickie Minardos insisted were absolutely essential to the décor of the Renthals' ballroom were too large by far to fit in the freight elevators of the building, and cranes were hired to raise the trees the sixteen floors from the street to the penthouse floor. Windows on that floor had to be removed for the trees to get into the apartment. When the crane stalled between the fifteenth and sixteenth floors, a workman, Julio Martinez, reached out to keep the weeping willow from swinging into the windows of the apartment below and fell to the ground. As if aware of the exclusiveness of the neighborhood he was working in at that hour, his fall to his death was unaccompanied by a scream.

Elias, asleep finally at the Rhinelander, was roused by a call from an hysterical Ruby. "Come back immediately, Elias," she said, crying. "Something terrible has happened."

In case the point was not made a police car arrived at the hotel to bring Elias the half block from the hotel to his apartment.

"This is a terrible thing," said Elias Renthal, and then repeated, "a terrible thing," all the time pacing back and forth on Fifth Avenue in front of his building, a fat cigar in his hand, waiting for the ambulance to arrive and put the mangled body of Julio Martinez in a body bag.

"We won't have to cancel the party, will we, Elias?" asked Ruby, nervously, when the policemen and foreman were out of hearing distance. She had pulled on a sweater over a pair of trousers.

Elias, without an answer for once, just looked at her.

"I know it sounds awful, Elias, but we have to be practical. The First Lady told me this evening when I was talking to the White House that she is ninety percent sure she's going to be here. She's opening a drug center or orphanage or something in Harlem. The Castorias have arrived from England and are staying at the Rhinelander. There are people from all over the world here for the party. We're going to look like fools."

"I don't know how I can keep this out of the papers, Ruby," said Elias.

"Bucks, Elias, bucks," said Ruby. "You once told me that there's nothing that bucks can't do."

"It ain't going to look good: father of four kids falls to his death raising weeping willow trees sixteen floors up to a forty-one-room apartment at two o'clock in the morning so the Elias Renthals can carry out a butterfly theme for their ball for four hundred guests from around the world."

"You sound like you used to work on a newspaper."

"Well, that's what it's going to be. Count on it."

"You can delay it being in the newspapers until after the party, Elias. Or at least have it buried in the back pages."

"How?"

"You're the country's success story, Elias. Figure it out."

"Help me, Ruby."

"What's the poor man's name?"

"Julio Martinez."

"He's got four kids?"

"And a widow."

"As soon as it's light, let's get in a car and go out to the house, in Queens or wherever he lives. Bring some lawyers with us. Set up educational trusts so that each kid's college education is paid for. Pay off the mortgage on their house so it's free and clear. Set up a trust fund for Mrs., uh, what's-her-name again?"

"Martinez," said Elias.

"For Mrs. Martinez, guaranteeing her an income for life that exceeds the yearly salary of her husband."

"That's a good idea, Ruby," said Elias, recovering himself.

"We'll go to the wake. We'll say the rosary. We'll send flowers like they never saw before and provide the limousines for the funeral."

"What about the papers?"

"Workmen are always falling off cranes. Just see that the address isn't given and our names aren't mentioned."

"You're a wonder, Ruby," said Elias.

"Are you carrying one of those big gangster rolls of bills in your pocket, Elias?" asked Ruby.

"Yeah, why?"

"Big tips to all the cops, all the doormen, and bonuses to every guy on the crane crew, after they get the last weeping willow tree up to the sixteenth floor."

LATE IN the afternoon on the same day, Bernard Slatkin telephoned his wife Justine at Bobo's hairdressing salon, where she was having her hair set with ribbons and rubrum lilies to match the new dress Nevel had designed for her to wear to the Renthals' ball that night.

"Just wait till you see me," said Justine to Bernie, looking at herself in the mirror while Bobo continued his work. "Bobo is so clever. He's taken the centers out of the rubrum lilies, the yucky part that gets all over your fingers and makes everything such a mess, and they look so beautiful. Why haven't I ever thought to do that? Now, don't tell me you're going to be late."

Justine's joyful attitude changed to one of dismay when Bernie told her to back out of the Renthals' party because there was something important that he wanted to talk to her about. Concerned with propriety, she wanted to plead that she couldn't, absolutely couldn't, upset Ruby Renthal's seating arrangement at the last minute like this, especially as they were two of only forty people who had been asked to dine first before the swarms of people came in after dinner for the dancing, but there was something in Bernie's voice and manner that forbade her from doing that. He was probably, she thought, calling from the control room at the studio and would hate to have to carry on that kind of conversation, about seating, with his buddies from the newsroom listening. "Justine's Crises," Bernie once told her his friends in the studio said about her kind of problems.

"Everyone will be there," said Justine wistfully, although she knew, even as she said those words, that they would not entice Bernie to change his mind, because, unlike most of the people she knew, missing a party where "everyone" would be was not a matter of great concern to him. What Justine feared more than anything else in the whole world was that Bernie was going to tell her that they were going to be transferred to Los Angeles and that he was going to have his own show as sole anchorman. Justine hated, absolutely hated, Los Angeles.

She didn't want to tell Bobo, after all his work, to take out the flowers and ribbons because she wasn't going to go to the ball at the Renthals' after all, so they were still in her hair when Bernie came home from the newscast. When she called Ruby to back out of the dinner, she was told that Ruby was attending a wake in Queens, which seemed odd to Justine, but that she would be back by seven, an hour before her dinner.

"Who is this speaking?" asked Justine, not recognizing the voice.

"This is Mrs. Renthal's calligrapher."

"Her what?" asked Justine.

"Her place-card writer."

"Oh," said Justine. "Just the right person. Will you tell Mrs. Renthal that an emergency has arisen, and Mr. and Mrs. Bernard Slatkin will have to cancel for this evening."

"Oh, dear," said the calligrapher.

WHEN ELIAS and Ruby made their second call of the day on the family of Julio Martinez in Queens, this time at the Margetta Funeral Home, for the wake, they expected to stay only ten minutes. Neither realized that the arrival of Father Francis X. Mulcahey, from the

Church of Our Lady of Perpetual Sorrow, whom they felt it was politic
to meet before departing, signaled the saying of the rosary.

"It's a great pleasure to meet you," said Father Mulcahey. His gentle voice still bore the traces of his Irish birth. "Poor Teresa has told
me of your generosity to the family during their great loss. Now, if
you'll just sit here behind Teresa and the children, we'll be kneeling
for the rosary. Are you Catholic, Mr. Renthal?"

"No, no, I'm not," said Elias.

"Mrs. Renthal?"

"Uh, no," said Ruby. She had been once, but wasn't anymore, and
didn't want to get into the matter, at least at this time, with forty
guests arriving for dinner in two hours, and four hundred for dancing
thereafter.

"We'll be saying the Sorrowful Mysteries," said Father Mulcahey.

Elias and Ruby looked at each other, dismayed. The massive bouquets of lilies and roses that they had sent were displayed near Julio
Martinez's closed casket, mingled with the carnation and stock
sprays, with lavender ribbons and gold condolence lettering, that had
been sent by family friends and relations, and the air in the un-air-
conditioned room was oversweetened and close.

"I hate the smell of stock," whispered Ruby. She took a perfumed
handkerchief from her bag and held it up to her nose. "How many of
these Sorrowful Mysteries are there?"

"You're asking me?" Elias answered.

"The first Sorrowful Mystery. The Agony in the Garden," said Father Mulcahey. "Our Father, Who art in heaven, hallowed be Thy
name, Thy kingdom come, Thy will be done,—"

"Bobo's coming to do my hair at six," whispered Ruby, pulling
back the sleeve of her dark blue suit to steal a look at her oval-shaped
Cartier watch with the Roman numerals that had once belonged to the
Duchess of Windsor.

"He'll wait," whispered back Elias.

"Hail Mary, full of grace, the Lord is with thee," said Father
Mulcahey, and the other mourners in the room prayed along with
him.

"I still have to put out the place cards," whispered Ruby.

"Just don't seat me anywhere near Rochelle Prud'homme," whispered back Elias.

"The second Sorrowful Mystery," said Father Mulcahey. "The Scourging at the Pillars."

Dorisette, the youngest of Julio Martinez's children, began to cry. "Daddy, Daddy," she wailed, by the side of her father's casket, as Teresa Martinez held on to her, and her older brothers and sisters patted her head.

"Do you think I dare faint?" whispered Ruby.

Elias looked around him in the crowded room of the funeral parlor and considered the logistics of his wife's suggestion. If his chauffeur and his bodyguard had been in the room, he could have signaled them to pick up Ruby after her faint and carry her out, but he had asked them to remain in the limousine, so as not to appear conspicuous during what he had supposed would be a ten-minute call. He arrived at the conclusion that a faint would cause further delays with the upheaval that would certainly occur among the mourners. "No," he whispered.

"Then make a beeline for the door after the last Sorrowful Mystery," whispered Ruby.

THAT AFTERNOON, in the prestigious law firm of Weldon & Stinchfield, a weeping young lawyer named Byron Macumber was arrested and handcuffed and taken out the rear entrance and down the service elevator, so as to attract a minimum of attention. It happened that Gus Bailey, still investigating the financial affairs of the late wife of Jorgie Sanchez-Julia for the article he was writing, was in the law firm at the time and witnessed the hasty exit.

"What happened?" Gus asked.

Beatriz Love, the young lawyer with whom he was meeting, simply shrugged her shoulders in a gesture that indicated she knew nothing of the matter at hand. She pushed her horn-rimmed spectacles up on her nose with her forefinger and returned her attention to the court papers in a manila file folder in front of her.

Gus Bailey knew when not to press, and he went on with his questions about the tangled estate of the crippled septuagenarian millionairess Geraldine Sanchez-Julia, establishing a friendly rapport with Beatriz Love at the same time. It was when he finished his questions and was ready to leave that he said, referring back to Byron Macumber, "Rather a dramatic exit for that poor fellow, wasn't it?"

"Hmm," answered Beatriz.

"Must have a wife and kids, a young man that age," said Gus.

"Two daughters," said Beatriz Love.

"Whatever could he have done?" Gus asked, in a rhetorical fashion, as if he didn't expect an answer. Gus had a way, even with lawyers, of having people tell him more than they planned, so he was not surprised when she added, "Something about an account in a Swiss bank in the Bahamas."

"Ah, the plot thickens," said Gus.

"Look for a very big head to roll," she said in a low voice, looking out the door of her glass cubicle to make sure that no one was watching.

"Here at Weldon and Stinchfield?" Gus asked.

"Oh, goodness no, not here."

Gus stared at her, knowing that more was to come. She mouthed but did not speak the two words, "Elias Renthal." If he had not been so stunned by the name she mouthed, he would have asked Beatriz Love if she knew Lil Altemus.

After he had said good-bye to her and thanked her for her help on the Jorgie Sanchez-Julia story, Gus, leaving, asked, "Does Elias Renthal know?" But Beatriz Love merely shrugged her shoulders. She had told him quite enough, far more than she intended, and she started putting Geraldine Sanchez-Julia's will back in the file folder.

"He's giving a ball this evening," said Gus.

"Oh, yes, I've read about the Renthals' ball in Dolly De Longpre's column," said Beatriz. "Didn't the Duchess of Richmond give a ball on the night before the Battle of Waterloo?"

All the way uptown in the subway Gus wondered if he should tell Ruby Renthal what he had heard. He felt very close to Ruby since the first night they met at Maisie Verdurin's party when she told him about her violent experience with Lefty Flint.

Late in the day he telephoned her.

"Oh, my God, Mr. Bailey. You're not backing out of dinner, are you?" asked the social secretary who answered the telephone. There was a note of hysteria in her voice. "Mr. and Mrs. Slatkin just backed out, and Mrs. Renthal is going to have a *fit* when she returns. It throws off the whole *placement*, and it's next to impossible to get anyone at this time of the day to fill in."

"Mrs. Renthal is not there?" asked Gus, surprised.

"No, the Renthals are attending a wake in Queens," said the secretary, in an exasperated voice that plainly said that she didn't understand what people like the Renthals were doing attending a wake in Queens, of all places, in the late afternoon of the evening of their ball when there were tables to be seated, decisions to be made, and a temperamental Mickie Minardos to be dealt with, not to mention Bobo, the hairdresser.

"Do you know what time they'll be back?" he asked.

"You're not backing out, are you?" she asked again, as if she could not deal with one more problem.

"No, no, I'm not backing out."

"Thank God."

"Would you have Mrs. Renthal call me when she returns? There's something rather important I must talk to her about," said Gus.

"Oh, Mr. Bailey, I really don't think it will be possible for her to call you when she returns. The calligrapher is going to have to do the new place cards when Mrs. Renthal finds someone to replace the Slatkins, and Mr. Minardos has a million problems for her to deal with, and, oh dear, Bobo, her hairdresser Bobo, is out of his mind with anxiety that she's not here, because he has to go from here to the Rhinelander to do the First Lady's hair. Oh, my God, I wasn't supposed to mention the First Lady. Forget I said that, will you, Mr. Bailey, so you see, it won't be possible for her to call you, but perhaps you can pull her aside during the evening and tell her whatever it is. Is that all right?"

"Sure," said Gus.

"I loved your article on the dictator's wife."

"Thanks."

WHEN RUBY returned home at seven, she called Justine right away and said, "You can't. You can't do this to me, Justine. I'll never be able to replace you at this hour." Poor Justine, who wanted to go more than anything in the world, begged Ruby's forgiveness but said there was nothing she could do, absolutely nothing, and was, when Bernie arrived home, still smarting from the ice-cold freeze in Ruby's tone of voice when Ruby said good-bye to her. She thought of calling back and suggesting Nestor and Edwina Calder as replacements, but then remembered that they were going to Maisie Verdurin's dinner before the ball. Then she thought of the Trouts, everyone's favorite poor couple, the Trouts, who could always be counted upon to change their own plans and substitute when there was a *placement* emergency, like the one she had just created. But then Bernie arrived home, and it was not a problem that she felt she could inflict on Bernie, who never had understood the importance of things like that, which was one of the things she most loved about him.

For a while the inevitable conversation they were both dreading, for different reasons, was postponed as they decided at what restaurant they would have dinner. Bonita, their cook, was off, because Justine had thought they would be dining at the Renthals', but the cook was off most nights, as Bernie and Justine had never, in the ten months of their marriage, dined at home unless they were having guests. Justine hated Joe and Rose's, which was Bernie's kind of restaurant. Too meat-and-potatoes for her. And Bernie hated Harry's, which was Justine's kind of restaurant. Too "Hi, darling," for him. In the end Justine suggested Clarence's, even though she had had lunch at Clarence's. It was easy, she said. Nearby. And, of course, there was never a problem of getting a table, even if the place was packed, because Justine was a particular favorite of Chick Jacoby's, and room was always made for Justine Altemus, which Chick persisted in calling her, even after she became Justine Slatkin, with or without a reservation. Besides, she said, Clarence's would probably be empty tonight, because everyone, absolutely everyone, was going to be at the Renthals' ball in their new apartment.

For a long time, during the salad and the chicken paillard, Bernie talked about Reza Bulbenkian, an Iranian American who had made a fortune in oil tankers in the Persian Gulf, and had moved to New York after the death of the Shah, where he had increased his fortune by buying up small companies who were likely targets for takeovers, in much the same manner that Elias Renthal was doing. Justine realized that the conversation about Reza Bulbenkian, whom Bernie had interviewed on television earlier that evening, was a way of avoiding the conversation about whatever it was that was so damn important they had to miss the Renthals' ball, but each of them clung to it desperately, as if what Bernie was saying really mattered.

"I've seen him. He has an enormously fat wife," said Justine, feigning interest in the conversation, while she kept staring at Yvonne Lupescu and Constantine de Rham, who were dining together in silence farther back in the restaurant. Justine wanted to tell Bernie to turn around and look at the outfit Yvonne was wearing: a red turban, red blouse, and red knickers with red bows tied at her knees, but there was something about Bernie tonight that made her think it was wiser to listen to him talk about Reza Bulbenkian, in whom she had no interest whatsoever.

Once, when she thought the moment had come for the topic at hand, which she still assumed to be his transfer to Los Angeles to become sole anchorperson of his own news program, she delayed the conversation by describing to him the latest news on the wonders of the Renthals' ball, descriptions of the dresses that her friends would be wearing, and an account, as reported by Bobo, of the terrible fights that had occurred between Mickie Minardos and Lorenza, hoping that he might say, still, this late, "Oh, hell, let's go," but he didn't.

"I'M SURPRISED to see the Slatkins here," said Yvonne Lupescu to Constantine de Rham. "Certainly they were invited."

Constantine, who had still not told Yvonne that he had been invited but she hadn't, postponed telling her, fearing her rage. Although he knew that she would never shoot him again, he feared that she would make a spectacle of herself, in her rejection, and do something untoward, like crashing the party, as she had crashed Justine's wedding. True to his word, Elias Renthal had left an invitation for Constantine with his secretary for Constantine to pick up. It was only for the ball. It had not been arranged for him to attend any of the ten big dinner parties that were being given before the ball, the two major ones being the Renthals' own dinner for forty in their dining room for the Earl and Countess of Castoria, their guests of honor, and Maisie Verdurin's dinner for sixty.

At home, his evening shirt was ready to be slipped into, the diamond-and-ruby studs and cuff links that Consuelo had given him for a wedding present in their proper holes. His white tie was even already tied and had only to be clipped on. His black silk stockings were in his black patent-leather evening pumps. Everything was in readiness. Only his fear of telling Yvonne that he was going off without her had to be dealt with.

"You've trimmed your beard, Constantine," said Yvonne, suddenly.

"Yes, yes, I have," answered Constantine.

"Have you had a manicure, too?"

"Yes, at the same time."

"Anyone would think you're going to the Renthals' ball."

"So likely," replied Constantine, nervously.

"I can't stand another evening of sitting home and watching television," said Yvonne, sulkily. Several times she had tried to get Justine's eye to wave at her, but Justine had not responded to her smiles.

"What do you have in mind?" asked Constantine.

"What about a movie?"

"Which?"

"I don't know which."

"Perhaps Chick Jacoby will have a newspaper," said Constantine, an idea beginning to form in his mind.

"Chick Jacoby is not here tonight," answered Yvonne, bitterly. "Chick Jacoby is at Maisie Verdurin's dinner before the Renthals' ball, at Maisie's table even, seated between Mrs. Frazier and Mrs. French."

"How in the world do you know all that?" asked Constantine.

"Maids," said Yvonne, wearily.

"There is a film on Fifty-eighth Street that I wouldn't mind seeing," said Constantine.

"Which?" asked Yvonne.

"I don't remember the name, but it's supposed to be terribly good." At last, he had figured out his plan.

DURING the grapefruit sorbet, Bernie told Justine that he wanted a divorce.

Justine, stunned, simply stared at her husband. She sat at the table for several minutes without saying a word and didn't even hear Michael, the waiter with the little ponytail whom she liked and regularly chatted with, when he asked her if she wanted regular coffee or decaffeinated. Instead, she stood up and walked through the restaurant, past the table where Constantine de Rham was paying his bill, to the ladies' room, where she threw up, rinsed out her mouth, reapplied her lipstick, removed and flushed down the toilet the seven rubrum lilies that Bobo had taken so long to set in her hair.

When she sat down again at her table, she said, quietly, "I haven't even written my thank-you notes yet."

"What thank-you notes?" asked Bernie.

"For the wedding presents."

"Oh."

"Is it Brenda Primrose?" asked Justine.

"Brenda Primrose?" replied Bernie, in a voice that stated the utter absurdity of the idea.

"Hubie told me he saw you dining with Brenda Primrose at an obscure restaurant in the Village."

"In the first place, Justine, how in the world would Hubie Altemus even know who Brenda Primrose was?"

"He didn't, by name. He recognized her from the wedding. He said she was beautiful with horn-rimmed spectacles. It was I who put the name to her. I told him she wrote your copy."

"She does not write my copy," said Bernie, annoyed. "I write my own copy. She does my research."

"Split hairs at this point. Is it Brenda Primrose?"

"It is not Brenda Primrose."

The waiter brought their decaffeinated coffee.

"Michael," said Justine, who had been raised to observe public appearance before all else. "Could you bring me some Sweet 'n Low?"

"Yes, Mrs. Slatkin," said Michael, taking a slightly moist packet from his shirt pocket.

"I never understand why Chick Jacoby is so stingy with the Sweet 'n Low," said Justine. Tears welled up in her eyes.

"Justine, your tears are falling in your grapefruit sorbet," said Bernie, glancing around to see if they were being observed.

Justine looked out the window of the restaurant until she was pulled together.

"It pains me if I have hurt you, Justine," said Bernie.

"Is your decision to leave me irrevocable?"

"Yes."

"Then let's not prolong this conversation."

"THIS IS the movie that you wanted to see?" asked Yvonne. "I thought you despised this kind of movie."

"It's meant to be awfully good, I hear," replied Constantine.

"I love horror movies myself," said Yvonne.

"Would you like popcorn?" asked Constantine.

"A big box," said Yvonne.

When he returned to their seats with the box of popcorn, Yvonne was already immersed in the film and only nodded her thank you when he handed her the box.

"I'm going to go to the men's room," he whispered to her, after looking at the film for ten minutes.

She merely nodded again, her eyes glued to the screen.

The theater was only a five-minute walk from his house on Sutton Place. He raced there, as fast as he could race, recovering as he was from the bullet wound in his stomach. It took him only minutes to change from his blazer and slacks to his tail coat and trousers. He buttoned his ruby-and-diamond studs and cuff links, snapped on his white tie, combed through his beard, eyed himself admiringly in the mirror, and left his house. He wanted to be gone from there in the event that Yvonne missed him in the theater and returned to the house herself to look for him. He had at least an hour and a half still before the ball started, and the problem now was where to wait until the dinner parties that preceded the ball were over.

"I'M JUST not happy, Justine," said Bernie. They were sitting now in the living room of their apartment, one of the few times since their marriage began that they had been home, just the two of them. He talked about political aspirations that he had, saying, truthfully or not, that his alliance with a family as rich and powerful as the Van Degans would be inconsistent with his own liberal views and that now, before children, the marriage should be terminated. Home, away from public view, Justine sat on the arm of a sofa, her mouth hanging open, in a near catatonic state. How, she wondered, had she not suspected that she was losing her husband.

"I love you, Bernie," she said, finally, as the tears started to pour out of her wounded eyes. "I love you with all my heart and soul and mind and body. Please don't leave me, Bernie. Please."

"Don't cry, Justine," said Bernie, when he saw the tears welling up in her eyes. "Please don't cry."

Bernie felt helpless with tears. Anger he could have dealt with, but not tears. Many women had screamed at him and called him terrible names when he broke off relations with them, and it was like water on his back. For the sobbing woman in front of him, who was his wife, whose heart he was breaking, he felt compassion. He put his arms around her, patting her more than embracing her, a signal of the ebbing of love that she did not understand.

"I love you so much," she said over and over, putting her tear-stained face next to his, as if her declarations could revive his lost ardor.

"I wish I knew the right words to comfort you," he said. While he was talking, she stared down at his hands. What beautiful hands he has, she thought. She could remember when those strong hands had fondled her breasts and between her legs, with the gentleness of a feather. She longed to touch the hairs on the back of his wrist. Her desire for him was so great she felt as if she were going to swoon.

"Are you all right, Justine?" he asked.

"What?"

"You look ill."

"Fuck me, Bernie," she whispered.

"Justine," he said, amazed.

"Please, Bernie. Please. Just one more time. Please."

"Justine, it's not going to do any good. It's over."

"I know, Bernie. Please. Don't leave me in this state. Just once. Please."

She began kissing the backs of his hands. She put her own hands on his chest and started rubbing his nipples through his shirt. She brought her hands down to his trousers. She wanted to rip them open and get to the part of him that she had dreamed about for the weeks that he had been indifferent to her.

"Justine, for God's sake. Don't do this to yourself."

She slid to the floor and threw her arms around his legs, pushing her face into the fly of his trousers. She looked up at him, tears streaming down her face. He could not bear to see her in such a state and felt pity for her. Slowly, he reached down and lifted her up by placing his hands under her arms and carried her to the sofa.

He raised her dress up to her waist and slowly pulled her pan-

tyhose down her legs to her shoes. When he placed his hand between
her legs, she was wet with desire for him. He took off the jacket of his
dark suit, unbuckled his belt, unzipped his fly, and let his trousers
drop to the floor. As Justine stared at his legs, he kicked off his
trousers and pulled down his undershorts, but he did not remove his
shirt or tie, shoes or socks. Standing over her, he allowed her to bring
his penis to erection with her hands and mouth, but he did not touch
her breasts or kiss her lips. When he was ready, he lifted her legs and
entered her, without speaking a word. He pushed in to the limit of
himself and then he partially withdrew, and then he pushed himself
in again, and again, and again, with long and even strokes. He did
not rush her. Sex was a thing he understood, and he withheld his own
climax until she had achieved hers, with gasps and muffled screams.
When his climax followed, he did not pretend to not enjoy the feeling
it brought, and Justine watched his face, his closed eyes, his slack
mouth, as he quietly moaned and flooded her insides with the seed of
a child. Finished, he did not immediately withdraw from her, but
remained inside her as she ran her fingers over his buttocks and down
between his legs.

She lay where she was as she watched him dress. She understood
the finality of his lovemaking and did not beg him again not to leave
her. Dressed, he talked briefly about his clothes, and possessions,
and when they should be picked up.

"Good-bye, Justine," he said, finally.

"Good-bye, Bernie," she replied. She stared after him as he
walked out of the living room, into the hall, and out the front door.
She did not move from her position as she listened to him ring for the
elevator. She heard the elevator arrive at their floor, heard the heavy
door open, heard the night elevator man say "Good evening, Mr.
Slatkin," heard Bernie reply, "Good evening, Willie," heard the elevator door close. Only then did she rise from the sofa. She walked to
the window that looked down on Park Avenue, hid a bit behind the
green drapery, and looked down to the street below. She watched him
come out from under the canopy of the building, saw him turn to say
good-night to the doorman and walk up Park Avenue to the corner.
She dropped the curtain, raised the window, and leaned out as she
watched him hail a cab, get in, and take off. She did not know where
he was going to spend the night. She only knew that it was not going
to be with her, that night, or ever again. "Good-bye, Bernie," she

said again, this time to herself. Walking back to turn off the lights
and puff up the cushions before Bonita, her maid, came in the morning, she saw the white stain, still wet, of Bernie's seed on the green
damask of her sofa.

IN THE Presidential Suite at the Rhinelander, the First Lady, exhausted from a visit to an orphanage in Harlem, a home for teenage
runaways in Bedford-Stuyvesant, the briefest, quickest lunch at Clarence's with Adele Harcourt, the *grande dame* of New York, an inspection of the AIDS ward at St. Vincent's Hospital, and an address
before the New York Council on Alcoholism, was awakened from her
rest by a call from a presidential adviser, telling her that it was inad-
visable for her to attend the ball that evening, if that was her plan, of
Elias and Ruby Renthal, as Mr. Renthal was the subject of a secret
investigation by the Securities and Exchange Commission into illegal
use of insiders' information.

MEANWHILE, at the other end of New York, another dinner was
about to take place, of a very different sort, but it was not without
social overlaps. In the weeks past, since his Easter encounter with
his mother, Hubie Altemus had absented himself from the world,
seeing no one except for several visits from his increasingly worried
sister, Justine. Juanito had taken over the management of the gallery
in SoHo, irritating the regular staff with his newly acquired authority,
but, for Hubie, the business was at least being seen to with his own
interests at heart. He had stopped returning telephone calls or seeing
friends.

On the night of the Renthals' ball, which he had declined, and
which he would have declined even if he had not been afflicted, he
felt a desire to see some friends and asked four gentlemen of similar
inclinations to dine with him at his apartment over the gallery. Hubie
was an excellent cook, and his little dinners were usually sought-
after invitations, for, although he chose to disassociate himself from
the upper-class world in which he had been raised, his china, his
silver, his napery, the table at which his guests dined, and the
Charles X chairs on which they sat bespoke another existence than
the corner of Houston and Greene streets would usually evoke.

The idea of the dinner party was, he knew, a mistake, almost from the beginning of the evening. Juanito, who had been most solicitous of Hubie's welfare in the past weeks, seized upon the dinner party as an excuse for a much needed night off for himself, and, dressed in jeans and leather jacket, with his diamond earring screwed into his ear, he departed the loft before the arrival of the first guest, Boy Fessenden, whom Juanito loathed, referring to him always behind his back as Girl Fessenden. Boy Fessenden had been a roommate of Hubie's at one of the many schools he had been asked to leave, and their friendship had survived, despite Juanito.

Opening the door, Hubie was able to read in Boy's eyes the extent of the devastation of his own features. He had learned to pass mirrors without looking into them; even shaving, he could now concentrate on his stubble and razor without examining his whittled-down, almost indented, cheeks that, in healthier times, he had often sought to reduce by dieting. He knew later, when he was in the kitchen, where he declined culinary assistance, that Boy and the others were talking about him in whispered tones.

"Oh, my God," said Robert.

"He must have it," said Herbie. It was the thing they all most feared.

"That's just the way Sam looked," said Boy.

The meal itself, excellent as always, was, however, a dispirited affair because death was in the air. Boy Fessenden, breaking one of the silences, said, "How sensitively you've cooked the fish, Hubie," and, briefly, they talked about the proper way to roast red snapper. Then Boy, a raconteur, set out to save the evening and made everybody laugh by retelling the story, with embellishments, of Hubie's encounter with the lifeguard at Bailey's Beach when they were both teenagers staying with Hubie's mother in Newport.

"What an exaggerator you are, Boy," said Hubie, laughing, as he got up to clear the dishes. "That wasn't the way it happened at all. You were just lucky that you didn't get caught."

He carried the dishes over to a tray on the sideboard. Ted, a singer, who was Boy's companion, rose to help Hubie. "No, no, Ted," said Hubie. "I can do it. I have it all down to a system."

In the kitchen the chill began to come on him. He sat down for a few minutes, fearing that he might faint. Then he got up and left the kitchen. The others, listening to another of Boy's stories, about two

men called Cecil, whom their friends called the two Ceciles, assumed that Hubie was going to the bathroom. In his bedroom, he lay
down on the bed and wished that Juanito was there, instead of out
tomcatting, which Hubie was sure he was.

"Where the hell is Hubie?" asked Boy fifteen minutes later, when
he had not returned. On the kitchen table was a chocolate cake and a
silver bowl filled with raspberries, blueberries, and strawberries.

"I thought he went to the bathroom," said Robert.

"I'll knock," said Boy.

The bedroom was dark when Boy went in.

"Hubie?" he asked. There was a note of fear in his voice at what he
might find.

"I'm here on the bed," said Hubie.

"What's the matter?"

"Can you get me to Saint Vincent's Hospital, Boy?" asked Hubie.

"Taxi or ambulance?" asked Boy.

"A taxi's okay," said Hubie.

"Why didn't you tell me, Hubie?" asked Boy.

"What good would it have done?"

"What about your doctor?"

"There's her number there. I tried to dial her, but I was too faint.
Dr. Alicia Montego," said Hubie.

"Dare I ask where Juanito is at a time like this?" asked Boy.

"Don't knock Juanito, Boy. He's been good to me lately. He needed
a night off."

"Should I call your mother? Or Justine?"

"They're at the Renthals' ball. You'll never reach them."

AS MICKIE MINARDOS was tied up right until the ball itself with
the last-minute preparations, Loelia Manchester was alone that evening. She had asked Gus Bailey to pick her up and take her to Ruby
Renthal's dinner for forty before the ball, but Gus had already been
asked for by Matilda Clarke and could not oblige Loelia. Dressed and
ready, she was planning to walk around the corner to the Renthals'
apartment when there was a knock on her door. A man, with a hearing contraption in his ear, whom she immediately recognized as a
Secret Service agent, told her that the First Lady would like a word
with her in the Presidential Suite on the floor above.

Inside the Presidential Suite, Loelia was surprised to find the First Lady still in her negligee and her hair not yet attended to.

"How pretty you look, Loelia," said the First Lady.

Loelia, complimented, smiled. "Thank you."

"I saw your mother today. Adele Harcourt had a little lunch this noon."

"Mother says unkind things about me these days," said Loelia.

"Not to me she didn't," said the First Lady.

"You're not dressed. Are you not going to the dinner first?"

"No. Nor the ball afterward."

"But why?"

"Oh, reasons."

"You mustn't miss this. You mustn't. Ruby will be crushed. At midnight, you know, ten thousand butterflies, live butterflies, just arrived today from Chile, all yellow and orange, are going to be released in the ballroom. It will be so divine. Please change your mind," pleaded Loelia.

"May I confide in you, Loelia?" asked the First Lady.

"But of course."

"I have heard there is a possibility that . . ." Alone, only the two of them in the room, she whispered in Loelia's ear what had been told to her earlier by the presidential adviser.

"Elias? Never!" cried Loelia, in total dismissal of the absurdity of the charge, as if the Pope himself in Rome had been accused of financial malfeasance.

"You're sure?"

"As sure of anything as I have ever been in my life," said Loelia. "I have never known a friend like Ruby Renthal. Not well born, perhaps, but a delight. She tells me everything, really the most extraordinary things, of extraordinary intimacy. If there were even a possibility of what you are suggesting, she would have told me."

"Perhaps she doesn't know. Perhaps Elias hasn't told her," suggested the First Lady.

"Oh, no, impossible. They have a marvelous marriage. Elias always says about Ruby, 'What a team we are,' and they are. They share everything."

The First Lady, who wanted to be convinced, was.

"I'm so happy to hear that. You know, she gave me those marvelous console tables, with the inlaid rams' heads, for the Green

Green Room of the White House, and I have a special affection for her myself," said the First Lady.

"You'll reconsider then?" asked Loelia.

"Perhaps I'll go for an hour, to see the butterflies."

"I'll come back for you at eleven, if you'd like. It's only around the corner."

THE RENTHALS hired the same red-and-white striped marquee, but covered on both sides, that Justine Altemus had used at her wedding at St. James's, so that their guests could pass into their building without the throngs who had gathered on Fifth Avenue to watch the arrivals of the fashionable folk being able to see the jewels that had been taken out of every vault for the party. It also shielded their guests' eyes from that part of the sidewalk where Julio Martinez had so few hours before fallen to his bloody death.

Whether the new apartment of the Elias Renthals was beautiful or not depended on the eye of the beholder, but it was deemed, by universal consent of the forty favored guests who were asked for the dinner preceding the ball, awesome and magnificent in size and contents. "Never have I seen such pictures," said Lil Altemus, who would have preferred to be in Rome visiting the Todescos, as she always was this time each year, but, alas, Laurance had requested that she postpone her trip until after the ball, and, always, all her life, she had accommodated her brother. Although Lil felt that her hostess had an excessive fondness for ancestral portraits of other people's ancestors—lords and ladies by Sargent, countesses and duchesses by Boldini, and an empress by Winterhalter that she had once seen in a museum—she could not help but be impressed.

"I'm surprised to see you here, Fernanda," said Lil to Fernanda Somerset, the mother of Loelia Manchester, who had only nodded to her daughter when they met in the elevator a few minutes earlier.

"I only came to see the furniture," answered Fernanda.

"How do you suppose these people collect so much in such a short time?" Lil said.

"When Mr. Duveen helped my grandfather collect, it took twenty years for the pictures alone," Fernanda Somerset replied. Then, holding her fingers in front of her mouth, she added, "Ezzie Fenwick tells me the curtains alone cost a million dollars."

"Imagine!" said Lil.

Everything had to move like clockwork that night. The dinner guests, asked for eight sharp, had to be in their seats in the dining room by eight forty, so they could be up and out, four courses later, before the first of the four hundred guests who would be arriving for the ball entered the apartment.

When dinner was announced, Lil looked about for Justine and Bernie, surprised that they were so late. She had heard from Bobo when he had come to her apartment to do her hair how pretty her daughter looked with the rubrum lilies in her hair, and she was eager to see herself how her daughter looked.

"I don't see Justine," said Lil to Ruby when Ruby came to tell them it was time to go into dinner.

"But she canceled at the last minute," said Ruby, surprised that Lil did not know.

"Justine? Canceled? I can't believe it," said Lil. "Bobo told me he set her hair only at five this afternoon."

"She canceled at six. I was at a wake at the time, someone who works for Elias, in Queens, and didn't hear until I got back. I've had such a hard time replacing them, but I finally got the nice Trouts to fill in."

Lil looked quizzical, wondering about Justine.

"Come along, Rochelle," said Ruby to Rochelle Prud'homme. "I'll show you where you're sitting." Although one of the dinner guests was still missing, Ruby, aware that precision was necessary to keep to the schedule of the evening, herded her guests to the dining room. Rochelle, feeling jealous of the magnificence of the Renthals' life-style, was already planning in her mind a party of her own that would rival the Renthals'.

Matilda Clarke, with Gus Bailey on her arm, wandered in silence through the rooms where she had once lived. It was a different kind of opulence than the opulence of Sweetzer Clarke's family, but even she would have to admit, if questioned, that it was an opulence to be reckoned with.

"How lovely you look, Matilda," said Ruby.

"A new dress for the occasion," said Matilda.

"I bought her that dress," whispered Rochelle to Ruby. "Otherwise she would have worn that damn black-and-white polka dot again. Terrible thing to go down the drain like the Clarkes did."

"Dinner for forty and everything matches," said Matilda to Gus, gazing around the dining room while looking for their seats, at the crystal and china and silver, all bearing the letter *R*.

Only a year before Ruby would have said, "I could have dinner for a hundred and everything would still match," referring to the Rothschild cache, but she had learned that Loelia Manchester would never have said such a thing, and now neither did she.

"You sit here, Rochelle," said Ruby, pulling out a chair for her.

Rochelle was concerned always as to where she would be seated, and an excellent seat at table could make her as ecstatic as a humble seat could make her miserable. Now her eyes darted around the dining room. Four tables of ten, she saw, with Lorenza's beautiful arrangements on each. She picked up the place card next to hers to see whom she was seated next to. Augustus Bailey, she read, written in a calligrapher's hand.

"Oh, no, no," she said to Ruby. "I don't want to sit next to a writer. They always want to do articles about me."

"You have the Honduran ambassador on the other side, Rochelle," answered Ruby. "You know Jaime."

"I feel a draft on my shoulders," said Rochelle. "I think I might be cold here from the air conditioning. Where's Elias sitting? I'll sit next to Elias. We're such old friends. I'll move Matilda over here where I was, next to the writer. She brought him anyway, didn't she? I'll sit next to Elias, and the ambassador's wife can go there."

"The Petite Dynamo has ruined my seating," said Ruby to Loelia. "Poor Elias. He begged me not to seat her next to him. Look, my God, the poor ambassador is now seated next to his own wife."

Although Ruby was desirous of becoming a member of only one set in New York, the set that she considered the best and most impenetrable, she, in turn, when she entertained her new intimate friends, always provided a celebrated person from the outside world to enhance the sociability of the evening. She liked hearing it said about her, "Last night I met the famous Dr. Priestly at Ruby Renthal's house." Her celebrated guest of that evening had, alas, not arrived.

Seated, finally, the thirty-nine of them, the waiters, in uniform and white gloves, began bringing in the caviar that made up the first course. Ruby engaged in animated conversation with her guest of honor Binkie Castoria on her right and, like the experienced hostess that she had become, signaled to a waiter to bring the Earl more caviar, for which she noticed he had an inordinate appetite, and, at the same time, with a gesture that indicated approval, let Maude Hoare know that her black dress, just arrived from Paris in time for the party, was perfection.

Arriving late, as she was famous for arriving late, entered the film star Faye Converse, ablaze with diamonds, and every eye in the dining room turned to stare at her. Faye, whose intimate circle of friends was of a more raucous variety than the refined friends of Elias and Ruby Renthal, played her role of movie star to the hilt, apologizing with the greatest charm to Ruby and Elias, both of whom had risen to greet her, as if they were the oldest friends, when, in fact, they were just meeting. A deal had been made, engineered by Gus Bailey, that Faye Converse would attend both the dinner and the ball afterward in exchange for a bountiful contribution toward the cure of the pestilence for which Faye worked so hard, although Elias was attributing to himself a nobility of purpose that was at odds with his true motive. Should his party be criticized in the press for its extravagance, he had in Faye the ready answer, that a contribution of enormous proportions had been made, as he intended to later point out in his speech, "toward a cure for the pestilence that is dwindling the ranks of the artistic community of the city."

Ruby took Faye's arm and led her to what was supposed to have been her place, on the left of Elias, but Rochelle Prud'homme, firmly entrenched in her usurped seat, showed no sign of surrendering it. Blocked by silence from Elias each time she attempted to engage him in conversation, Rochelle assumed that he was a nervous host, which was not the case, and she called across the table to Ezzie Fenwick, as if Ruby and Faye Converse were not standing there.

"The Duchess left me some gold plates," Rochelle called out. "What do you think I should do with them? Use them for ashtrays?"

"Or earrings," answered Ezzie, who had turned over his plate to examine the markings on the back. "China like this you only see today in the showcases of dukes' houses open to the public," he added.

"We've had a mixup with the place cards," whispered Ruby to Faye. "You were supposed to sit next to Elias, but someone, who shall be nameless, switched the cards."

"Sounds just like Hollywood," answered Faye, who couldn't have cared less. "That's what they do out there. Why don't you put me over there next to my friend Gus Bailey?"

When she was seated, Gus said to her, "It was to avoid sitting next to me that Mrs. Prud'homme switched the cards."

"How lucky for me," said Faye, as she picked up her napkin and looked around. When a waiter started to pour wine into one of the four glasses in front of her, she put her hand over the top of it to stop him and ordered a glass of water instead. "Who the hell are all these people, Gus?" she asked.

"To your right is Lord Biedermeier," said Gus.

"Oh, Lucien, how are you, darling? I didn't see you," she said with a laugh that indicated she had known Lucien way back when.

"Next to him is Janet Van Degan, as in Mrs. Laurance Van Degan, and next to her is Herkie Saybrook, and then—"

"Cute, Herkie Saybrook," said Faye. "My third husband looked sort of like Herkie Saybrook."

After the sorbets in assorted colors had been served, Elias rose and tapped a fork engraved with the letter R against a champagne glass engraved with the letter R, and the room was silenced. He thanked the Earl and Countess of Castoria, whom he called Binkie and Antoinette, for the marvelous friendship they had shared with Ruby and him, although, in fact, the friendship was of less than a year's duration, and he told an anecdote about a visit they had made to Castle Castor the previous winter where Ruby got lost in the halls finding her way to dinner. Elias spoke charmingly and received laughter and applause. Then the Earl rose and made a similar toast to Elias and Ruby, thanking them for their friendship and this marvelous party, with the ball still to come, which was being given in their honor. No mention was made in either toast that the Earl of Castoria was a member of the board of directors of Miranda Industries.

Then Elias moved across the room to the table where Faye Converse sat, and spoke about the great star's marvelous career and the forty pictures she had made.

"Sixty, not forty," said Faye, correcting her host, and everyone laughed.

"Isn't she marvelous?" said Maude Hoare.

Elias went on with his toast and told about the good work that Faye Converse was doing with the private time of her life, working to raise funds "toward a cure for the pestilence that is dwindling the ranks of the artistic community." With that, he presented her with a check.

Faye rose to great applause and thanked Elias and Ruby for the wonderful evening that was just beginning and for the check, which she then opened. "My God!" she said, "two million dollars!"

Again the dining room rang out with applause.

"We are an army fighting an enemy that has no allies," said Faye, as she became serious and started to talk about her mission.

"What's she talking about?" asked Fernanda Somerset, who was hard of hearing.

"AIDS," said Lil, mouthing but not speaking the word.

"I thought she said something about an army," insisted Fernanda.

"Look at Aline Royceton's teeth," said Ezzie.

"Still looks pretty, doesn't she?" said Rochelle.

"Who, Aline, for God's sake?"

"No, Faye Converse."

"The speech is too long," said Ezzie.

"Shh," said Ruby.

"How old do you think she is?" asked Rochelle.

No one in the room clapped harder than Lil Altemus at the end of Faye Converse's speech. "So marvelous," she said. Lil, whose own son was at that very moment, a mere sixty blocks to the south of her, being checked into St. Vincent's Hospital by Boy Fessenden, repeated to the Honduran ambassador what she had repeated to her daughter a few weeks earlier. "Bobo, my hairdresser Bobo, says there won't be a man left in New York to hem a dress or hang a curtain," she said, shaking her head sadly for those poor souls, as if it were a thing far removed from her own door and the doors of her friends.

Binkie Castoria, getting drunk, turned to ask Ruby what was this pestilence that was dwindling the ranks of the artistic community, and Ruby turned her attention to him. A waiter named Chet, from the catering service, while nodding a greeting to Gus Bailey, whom he knew from A.A. meetings, inadvertently collided with the waving arms of Ezzie Fenwick, who was keeping his table in convulsions of laughter with an imitation of a model on the runway at the showing of Nevel's new collection the day before, and the bottle of red wine, Lafite-Rothschild, that the waiter was carrying flew from his gloved hand and spewed its ruby content all over the white satin dress of Ruby Renthal. There was a gasp from the Earl, who liked being on the board of directors of Miranda Industries, as well as the other guests at the table, for the ball would shortly be starting, and they all turned to look at the unfortunate waiter whose face turned crimson with embarrassment.

"Oh, Mrs. Renthal, I can't believe I did that," said the waiter, who expected to be fired on the spot.

"Don't be upset," said Ruby, looking down at her ruined dress. "White is such a boring color." Chet, the waiter, looked at her with adoration. With that Ruby left the dining room to change, after asking her guests to go to the drawing room for coffee.

"How marvelous Mrs. Renthal is," said the Earl. "A duchess couldn't have handled that better."

Patriotic since her elevated position as a frequent guest at the White House, Ruby had recently abandoned the French *couture*, "given up the French," she called it, for its American cousins, like Nevel. On the advice of Ezzie Fenwick, who had the ability to minutely observe a woman's dress, tell at a glance if it was from the *couture* or ready-made, identify the designer, quote the price, and remember its distinguishing details days later, Ruby had ordered three different dresses for her great night when she told Ezzie she couldn't decide what to wear. Changing, she also changed her jewelry, her pearls and diamonds making way for her emeralds and diamonds. She remembered a line from a movie she had loved: "If you got it, flaunt it," she said to herself in the mirror.

RETURNED, redressed, Ruby looked better than ever.

Elias, taking her in, leaned down and kissed her bare shoulder.

"Elias, how sweet," said Ruby.

"You look good enough to eat," he said.

"Watch your language, big boy," she said, in her Mae West accent.

"I love you, Ruby Renthal," said Elias.

Ruby blushed prettily. "Ditto," she said.

"Who woulda thought, the two of us?" whispered Elias.

"Who woulda thought?" Ruby repeated.

Ruby, with Elias by her side, stood in the receiving line, greeting, by name, her four hundred guests, including the French ambassador, the Spanish ambassador, the British ambassador, and various members of the deposed royal families of Yugoslavia, Bulgaria, and

Rumania, who recognized certain of the pieces of marvelous furniture in the Renthal apartment as having come from palaces that had once been theirs. In the splendid crowd promenading from room to room, where gypsy violinists played, before descending to the ballroom, where a dance band played Cole Porter music, people who had seen each other as recently as lunch shrieked hellos like long-lost friends and exchanged kisses on each cheek. There were an abundance of social commentators, guaranteeing that the Renthal ball would be duly recorded for social posterity. Strobe lights flashed and the blinding lights of the television cameras went on and off as recognizable faces entered the marble front hall of the vast apartment. In addition to Dolly De Longpre, who was the only member of the press who had been invited to dinner, was young Florian Gray, as well as Mavis Jones, of the show-business columns, who usually did not attend the same parties as Dolly, nor Dolly the same parties as they, but the curiosity value of the Elias Renthals was such that all decided to overlook their differences and attend.

Ezzie Fenwick spoke to Ruby's maid, Candelaria, addressing her by name, establishing himself as a regular visitor to the household, known and smiled upon by its staff. Ezzie could hardly contain himself at the utter splendor of the Renthals' night. He made a rapid tour of inspection of the sit-out rooms, not knowing where to station himself to full advantage to witness the evening, before deciding on a position at the foot of the stairs leading into the ballroom, beneath a weeping willow tree, where he would not miss a single entrance. He was surrounded by women who clung to him to listen to his comments about everyone ("Just the nice Europeans, none of the trashy ones," he said) and compliment him on his pearl studs, as big as marbles, which all agreed, prompted by himself, stacked up to the pearls on any of the necks in the room. He greeted his particular friends, all women, with compliments on their dresses, and did not greet those he did not favor with his friendship. "Hello, Maude," he said. "Hello, Lil." "Hello, Dodo." "Hello, Rochelle." "Hello, Janet." "Hello, Matilda." "Hello, Maisie." "Hello, Adele. Marvelous, that dress." And they, in turn, all replied, "Hello, Ezzie," and kisses on each cheek followed.

"You know everyone, Ezzie," said Bijou McCord, the Texas millionairess who now sought New York recognition.

"Yes," replied Ezzie, beaming with pride and satisfaction for his high position.

Several times his brow furled with displeasure, as someone walked down the stairway whose presence on the invitation list had been unknown to him. The entrance of Constantine de Rham, about whose exclusion he had been particularly vocal to Ruby, came as a shock to him, and he instantly expressed the thought to his companions that de Rham had probably crashed, just the way Mrs. Lupescu, his companion, had crashed the wedding reception of Justine Altemus. "Elias will get rid of him, you mark my words," he said, but, at that moment, Elias, looking for Ruby, came upon Constantine and spoke a greeting to him, not a warm greeting, but the greeting of an important host to an unimportant guest.

Jamesey Crocus arrived with Adele Harcourt, whom everyone called charity herself, for all her good works for the city. Jamesey could always be pressed into service to escort Adele Harcourt, the *grande dame* of New York, and was inclined enough toward literature to have been asked to join Mrs. Harcourt's book club.

"My God, they got everybody," whispered Jamesey Crocus to Adele Harcourt, surveying the crowd through his spectacles, meaning that the *haut monde* had all turned out for the Renthals.

"*Tout* New York," whispered Mrs. Harcourt.

"What are you whispering about?" asked Ruby, walking by.

"I was just saying to Adele that we should read Trollope next in the book club, now that we've finished with the Russians," said Jamesey.

"I was saying what a marvelous job Mickie has done," said Adele Harcourt at exactly the same time.

Mickie Minardos's eyes were shining with the excitement of creativity fulfilled: a symphony composed, an epic written, a masterpiece painted. Compliments were being paid to him from everyone, even, he whispered to Loelia, who was bursting with pride for him, from Adele Harcourt herself. It was what he had always wanted, artistic recognition instead of shoe recognition. Modestly he brushed aside the compliments, without actually saying you-ain't-seen-nothing-yet, but thinking it, because, at midnight, during the waltzes, the spectacle would be enhanced when the ten thousand butterflies, yellow and orange, flown up from Chile only that day, were to be released to fly around the ballroom, in the bowers of flowers and in the weeping willow trees, as the final culmination of what he knew would be called forevermore the most beautiful party of the decade in New York.

"There can't be a yellow tulip left in all Holland!" cried Dodo Fitz Alyn Van Degan, looking at the ballroom.

"These people are spending a fortune to entertain us, and all they want in return is to be accepted by us," said old Ormonde Van Degan, who had been brought down on the freight elevator to see the ballroom before repairing upstairs, away from the music and the crowds, to enjoy a cigar with a few old friends he had spotted, while Dodo and Lil watched the spectacle and the dancing.

"It won't happen," said Lil to her father.

"Oh, yes, it will," said the old man. "It has happened."

Ruby and Elias then took to the dance floor, she with the Earl, he with the Countess, adhering to all the traditions, as if they had been giving grand balls all their adult years. People clapped, but no one clapped harder than Maisie Verdurin, her eyes glistening with tears of pride at the triumph of the Renthals, who had achieved business and social success without benefit of inheritance or heritage. "It's the American dream fulfilled," said Maisie, enthusiastically, to all around her as she continued to clap. Then Laurance Van Degan brought Faye Converse to the dance floor, and Jamesey Crocus followed with Adele Harcourt, and a Yugoslav prince with a Bulgarian princess, and then everyone was on the dance floor.

"Have you ever seen anything so beautiful?" asked Adele Harcourt.

"You've snowed us, Elias," said Janet Van Degan.

When Elias finally danced with Ruby, he thought that she had never looked more beautiful.

"We did it, kiddo," he whispered in her ear.

She smiled at him.

"We're a team," he whispered again.

"A team," she whispered back.

At that moment an ambassador cut in on Elias, but Ruby, before giving herself over to the ambassador, whispered again to Elias, "Don't forget, when the First Lady comes, you and I have to be at the front door to greet her and bring her in, and you have to have the first dance with her."

"I won't forget," said Elias.

"Don't go far. It's getting close," said Ruby.

IT WAS only in retrospect, when the people who had not been invited read about the party in the *News* and the *Post*, and in this case, even the mighty *Times*, which did not usually cover private parties, that the Renthal ball began to develop as a legend that would make it stand out in peoples' minds for years to come. "I read you were at the Renthals' ball," people said. "Tell me everything."

Only the pool room, or the room with the pool table, had been declared off bounds, because the pool table, which had once belonged to Edward VII, still had its original felt, and Elias worried that people might place drinks on it. While Dodo and Lil watched the dancing, Ormonde elected to enjoy a cigar in the company of Lord Biedermeier in a small upstairs room, adjacent to the pool room, usually reserved for cigar smoking and poker playing, which Ruby didn't allow in her main salons.

Lord Biedermeier, whose mind was always on books, even during social occasions, would have liked nothing better than to publish a biography of the Van Degan family, whose roots in the city and the nation—politically, socially, and financially—could be matched by no other family, and it was in this little smoking room that he broached the subject to the octogenarian Ormonde Van Degan, knowing that his cooperation in such a project might entice his son, Laurance, who was, on general principles, opposed to any form of publicity whatsoever, into agreeing to speak with the biographer he had in mind.

"You're looking particularly well since your marriage, Mr. Van Degan," said Lord Biedermeier, although, in fact, Ormonde Van Degan looked very much at that moment as if he were about to expire. The old man, who usually went to bed at eight, was exhausted by this late-night venture into society, which his son, Laurance, had asked him to attend, and his wife, Dodo, had begged him to attend.

"Who the hell are these people?" Ormonde Van Degan replied, his voice so faint as to barely be heard.

"What people?" asked Lord Biedermeier.

"Who are using my friend Sweetzer Clarke's apartment."

"Oh, I see," replied Lord Biedermeier, laughing. "Our hosts, you mean? Elias and Ruby Renthal. Elias Renthal is one of the richest men in the country."

"I miss Sweetzer. Damn fine sportsman. And a good shot, as he should have been; his mother was a Phelps. Gentleman, too. Some-thing Mr. Renthal is not," gasped the old man.

Lord Biedermeier thought it best not to pursue this avenue of con-versation and, instead, offered Mr. Van Degan a cigar, which had been the point of this visit to the smoking room in the first place. His cigars were from Cuba, by way of London, and he always felt proud when cigar smokers complimented him on their excellence.

"Cuba," he said, offering one to Ormonde Van Degan.

Ormonde Van Degan gestured to Lord Biedermeier to ready the cigar for him. When its tip was cut, he handed it to the old man, who placed it in his mouth.

"I've been thinking, sir," said Lord Biedermeier, as he lit a match and held it to Ormonde Van Degan's cigar for him to inhale on, "what a marvelous and distinguished family your family is and has always been in the history of this state."

"My father was the governor," whispered Ormonde.

"Exactly," said Lord Biedermeier.

"My uncle was the ambassador to France," he went on.

"My very point," continued Lord Biedermeier. "You must puff harder on the cigar, sir, for it to catch."

The old man inhaled the Cuban cigar.

"I thought that the time had come for a biography of your family, from the beginning, right up to the present," said Lord Biedermeier. "You see, Mr. Van Degan—"

As he coughed after inhaling so deeply, the old man's body was racked by a heart attack.

WHEN CONSTANTINE DE RHAM asked Lil Altemus to dance, Lil, remembering Consuelo, her greatest friend, replied, simply, "No," with no reason or excuse, although she was not dancing at the time, nor did she seem to have any prospect of a dancing partner once her brother, Laurance Van Degan, had taken her around the floor. Loelia Manchester also declined Constantine's invitation to dance, as did Mary Finch. Ruby Renthal, who had been a party to using Constantine's house on Sutton Place during her affair with Elias when he was still married to Gladyce, said, when Constantine asked her to dance, "Not now," pleading hostess duties, but Constantine understood her answer to mean not later either.

Looking for a place to sit, Constantine saw Laurance Van Degan place his hand over the seat of an empty gold chair at his table to indicate that it was taken, although it remained empty for the next twenty minutes. Finally, he spotted, sitting alone, a discredited Wall Street financier, Max Luby, an early business associate of Elias's, who had briefly served time for forgery, and took his place there by him. When Elias invited Max Luby to the party, Max, who felt uncomfortable in society, had said to Elias, "I won't know what to say to all those people," and Elias had replied, "Don't worry, Max, no one will speak to you anyway." He might have been a foreigner unable to speak the language for all the attention anyone paid him. Presently Max Luby and Constantine de Rham, each happy to finally have someone to talk to, were joined briefly by Gus Bailey.

"Are you enjoying yourself, Mr. de Rham?" asked Gus.

"To be able to say tomorrow that one had been here is what matters," replied Constantine, who was not enjoying himself.

"Mrs. Lupescu is not with you?"

"Alas, Mrs. Lupescu had other plans for this evening."

In a lower voice, Gus said directly into de Rham's ear, "I saw your friend, Feliciano."

"Yes, yes, I know. He called to check on whether you were good for that much money."

"And what did you tell him?"

"I said that you dined at some of the best houses in New York."

"That, we both know, is no guarantee of solvency."

"True, true, but it satisfied Feliciano."

Just then Ruby walked past and spotted Gus.

"Gus Bailey, do you mean to say you're not going to ask me to dance?" she said.

"I'm a lousy dancer, Ruby," answered Gus. Throughout the evening Gus had tried to find a moment with Ruby to tell her about Byron Macumber, and here it was.

"I never believe men who say they're lousy dancers. Come on." Ruby took Gus by the hand and led him onto the floor. They danced for a time in silence.

"What do you mean you're a lousy dancer? You're not a lousy dancer at all."

"Look who my partner is," said Gus.

The music changed. The beat became slower. Gus put his arm tighter around Ruby's back, and she moved into him, putting her cheek next to his. "I hear you called me this afternoon."

"I did."

"What about?"

"Where are you going to be tomorrow, Ruby?" he asked.

"Right here. Can you imagine what this is going to be like, taking this party down?"

"I want to see you tomorrow, Ruby. Just for fifteen or twenty minutes. Alone," said Gus.

Ruby leaned her head back and looked at Gus. He looked back at her. His face was serious.

"This is not party talk, I take it?" she asked.

"No."

"Lefty Flint?"

"No, not Lefty Flint. There's something I think you should know about."

"Tell me."

"Tomorrow."

"Three o'clock. Here comes one of those Albanian princes to cut in on you. Give me a hint, Gus, quick. You've got me curious."

"Byron Macumber," said Gus.

She thought for a moment but could not place the name and indicated this to Gus with a gesture. The prince cut in on Gus. "Byron Macumber, Byron Macumber, it's twilight time," she sang to the tune of the song the orchestra was playing, and the prince twirled her around.

"I'M JUST a simple guy from the Midwest. Poor family. Worked my way through school all my life, but in the few years I've been here in New York, I've learned a lot about people like you," said Elias to Loelia Manchester, as he danced her around the floor of his ballroom. Unlike Mickie Minardos, who went to great lengths to conceal his humble origins, Elias Renthal had taken to exaggerating the hardships of his background, in order to greater emphasize his spectacular rise in the world to the very pinnacle of wealth and power. "Look how even here, with the *crème de la crème* of the city gathered in my house, everyone breaks up into their own little subgroups. Over there, for instance, all those has-been royals that Ruby's so mad about, all sitting together at one table. And over there, under that weeping willow tree, there's all the Old Guard of New York, all together, Lil Altemus, and all the Van Degans, and Cora Mandell, and old lady Somerset."

"Old lady Somerset is my mother, Elias," said Loelia.

"Oh, so she is, so she is. No offense meant, of course. Have I put my foot in my mouth?"

"Not this week, Elias. My mother is cutting me out of her will."

"Oh, she'll come round in time, Loelia. With people like you, blood is thicker than water. Now look over at that table. You have to say about me that I am loyal to my old friends," said Elias, observing the lonely duet of Constantine de Rham and Max Luby. "I don't drop them like everyone else does when they take the wrong turns in life. There is Constantine de Rham, whom people no longer invite. And poor Max Luby, recently released from prison for that stupid forgery thing they say he did, but I don't believe it for a minute. Very few hosts would have these people, but I do."

"Perhaps you should think about having them on a night when people like us aren't here," said Loelia.

"I take it you don't approve of my friends," said Elias.

"I don't wish to have to dance with them," said Loelia.

WHEN LORD BIEDERMEIER walked, his posture stooped slightly forward from the waist. Now, in haste to reach Elias with the news, his pince-nez, which he wore on a black string around his neck, fluttered in front of him as he loped across the ballroom, hitting his chest and flying about in all directions.

"Such haste!" said Lil Altemus, pulling in the satin skirt of her elaborate dress, as he brushed by her.

"Ah, Lil," he said, stopping. "Forgive me." For an instant he considered telling Lil that her father had had a heart attack in an upstairs room, but at that moment Elias came up to them to ask Lil to dance.

"How kind, Elias," said Lil, getting up and handing her bag to Dodo to hold for her.

"I must first have a word with Elias," said Lord Biedermeier, trying to forestall the dance so that he could tell Elias that one of his most important guests, the father of the woman he was about to dance with, was possibly dying upstairs.

"No, no, not until after this dance," said Elias, taking Lil to the floor.

"This is so gay, Elias," said Lil, beaming graciousness, as she danced backward, leading.

For an instant, Elias looked at her. "I don't think that's quite the right word anymore, Lil," he replied.

"Oh, no, it's a word I simply refuse to give up. My friends all know I mean it in the old-fashioned way," said Lil. As they danced by Laurance and Janet Van Degan, both couples smiled and waved, duty being properly adhered to on all sides.

It was only when Elias returned Lil to her seat next to Dodo that Lord Biedermeier was able to pull Elias aside and whisper to him that Ormonde Van Degan had had a heart attack.

"It'll ruin the fucking party," said Elias.

"Yes," agreed Lord Biedermeier.

"And the First Lady's about to arrive," whispered Elias into his ear. Elias had been awaiting the arrival of the First Lady with the same secrecy and suppressed excitement that a newly rich English financier might await the possible arrival of a member of the Royal Family under his roof.

"No!" said Lord Biedermeier, who had not heard that the Renthals were to be so honored.

"You didn't tell anyone, did you, about the old man?" asked Elias.

"Heavens, no. I almost told Lil and Dodo, but you came along."

As the two men rushed off together, Dodo Fitz Alyn Van Degan rose and said, "But it's my turn, Elias. You promised to dance with me after Lil."

Just then Gus Bailey walked by, and Elias grabbed him by the arm and delivered him in front of Dodo Fitz Alyn Van Degan, with an elaborate gesture of affability to indicate an introduction without introducing him with words, as if he had forgotten Gus's name, which he had. His mime went further to indicate that the two should dance together and then he turned and rushed off with Lord Biedermeier.

"We met at Lil's at Easter," said Dodo.

"I remember," said Gus. "I'm not much of a dancer."

"I don't care," said Dodo. "I'd hate to have to say that I went to the

Renthals' ball and hadn't once danced. We don't have to be Fred and
Ginger, you know."

"That's true," said Gus, taking Dodo out to the dance floor.

UPSTAIRS, outside the small room used for cigar smoking and
poker playing, Elias and Lord Biedermeier looked in both directions
to be sure they were not being observed before opening the door.
Inside, Elias locked the door behind him.

"Where is he?" asked Elias.

"He was in that chair," said Lord Biedermeier.

"My God, he's on the floor," said Elias.

"He's dead," said Lord Biedermeier.

The two men looked at each other.

"It's going to ruin the party," said Elias.

"You already said that," said Lord Biedermeier.

"How about if we don't say a word until after the First Lady leaves,
and then you come up and discover him, and we'll call an ambulance
and get him down the freight elevator then," said Elias. "I mean, he's
an old man, for Christ's sake. It's not like a big tragedy."

"Okay," said Lord Biedermeier.

"Jesus Christ," said Elias. "He took a shit in his pants."

"Apparently, they all do," said Lord Biedermeier.

"GUS, HAVE you seen Elias?" asked Ruby, coming up to him and
Dodo on the dance floor. Ruby had changed again, into her third
dress of the evening, and she was bespangled with a new set of jewels, this time her rubies, in preparation for the imminent arrival of
the First Lady.

"I saw him go upstairs with Lord Biedermeier," said Gus.

"I'm sure he went up to smoke one of his damn cigars," said Ruby.
"Excuse me, will you, Dodo. I need to borrow Gus for a minute."

Ruby took Gus by the arm and walked with him toward the door.

"Go upstairs," she whispered in his ear. "Get him, will you, Gus?
The First Lady has left the Rhinelander and we have to be at the door
to meet her and bring her in."

"I didn't know the First Lady was coming," said Gus.

"Tell Elias to meet me at the front door."

ELIAS unlocked the door that connected the small room with the pool room beyond, and, together, the two middle-aged men carried the body of Ormonde Van Degan from one room to the other.

"Lift him up on the pool table," said Lord Biedermeier, sweating.

"That's an antique," said Elias. "That pool table belonged to Edward the Seventh."

"Put the carpet on the table, and we'll lay him on the carpet," said Lord Biedermeier. "And turn up the air conditioner."

"And lock the door," said Elias.

At that moment there was a knock on the door. The two men looked at each other, and Elias signaled to Lord Biedermeier not to reply.

Again there was a knock on the door.

"Elias," said Gus from the other side of the door. "Ruby wanted me to tell you that the First Lady is arriving and wants you to meet her at the front door."

"Holy shit," whispered Elias.

"We better get out of here," said Lord Biedermeier.

"Stinks in here," said Elias.

WHEN ELIAS and Ruby Renthal reentered their ballroom with the First Lady between them, amid musical flourishes from the society dance band, their four hundred guests rose to applaud. What each knew, even those, like Lil Altemus, who found it difficult to accept any of the New People, was that he or she was at the most important party being given in the country, or possibly the world, that evening, and that each was a part of it. The Renthals, whom no one had even heard of only a short time ago, had pulled off the social feat of the decade.

When the orchestra played "The First Lady Waltz," which Ruby had had specially written for the occasion, Elias took the wife of the President to the dance floor.

"So pretty," said the First Lady, looking about as she danced, at the weeping willow trees, and the orchids and tulips and lilies that filled the room.

"Just wait," said Elias, as he twirled her around. "More to come."

Nearby Mickie Minardos danced with Loelia Manchester, and not a soul who saw them could deny that they were in love. Nowhere was Mickie more at home than on a dance floor, and Loelia seemed to float in the air as she followed every intricate step he led her through. Loelia had never seen Mickie happier, receiving compliments from every direction on the beauty of his artistic designs.

"Is everything ready with the butterflies?" Loelia whispered in his ear.

"At twelve sharp," whispered Mickie back.

"Where are they?" she asked.

"Hidden in the clouds," he said. She looked up and saw the billowing clouds made of tulle and silk that swung back and forth on wires from the ceiling.

"You're a genius, Mickie," said Loelia.

Just then Ezzie Fenwick cut in on the lovers, and Mickie excused himself to see that his team of workers were at their stations to carry off the job when the hour came.

Although he was stout, Ezzie Fenwick was a superb dancer, and his little feet, encased in black patent-leather pumps with black grosgrain ribbons, could pick up the rhythm of whatever kind of music was played and twirl the prettiest ladies in New York, and very few were as pretty as Loelia Manchester, around the dance floor. When Loelia whispered to Ezzie during their dance, and made him promise not to repeat it to anyone, that the First Lady had been warned not to attend the Renthals' ball because Elias was under investigation by the Securities and Exchange Commission for financial malfeasance, Ezzie, a consummate actor, hooted with laughter and pretended to consider the matter just as absurd as Loelia considered it. But, at the same time, he had to admit, while not missing a samba beat, that Elias Renthal had accumulated one of the greatest fortunes in America in record time, and the White House would not willy-nilly give the First Lady such a warning unless there were some cause for concern. Although he enjoyed a reputation as a secret keeper, Ezzie Fenwick had never, ever, in his whole life, been able to keep a secret.

"And you know, darling Ezzie, when Ruby asked Mickie to design her ball, Mickie's first thought was, you guessed it, butterflies, and he said—"

Ezzie's need to repeat the news that he had just sworn never to repeat was so strong that he ceased to hear Loelia, to whom he usually listened avidly, going on and on about Mickie's accomplishments, a subject on which she was becoming quite boring, Ezzie felt. His nimble feet, so alert to all the latest dance steps, felt suddenly clodlike, his need to escape the dance floor and repeat Loelia's news was so great, even though he knew, from firsthand experience on such matters, that the person he found to repeat it to would swear to him never to repeat it, just as he had sworn to Loelia never to repeat it, and then not be able to contain himself from telling just one person, and that person would tell just one other person, and soon everyone would know that Elias Renthal was under investigation by the Securities and Exchange Commission, even while they were supping on his lobster and sipping his champagne.

"What a dancer you are, Loelia!" he cried. "I'm exhausted!"

Loelia laughed, and they left the dance floor hand in hand.

"That conversation was just between us, Ezzie," said Loelia.

"Oh, darling, my lips are sealed," said Ezzie.

At that moment Dolly De Longpre walked by. "Hello, Ezzie, darling," said Dolly. "Isn't this all too magical?"

"It's De Lightful, it's De Licious, it's De Longpre," sang Ezzie, twirling Dolly around, at the same time wondering if Dolly, to whom he sometimes told bits of gossip for her column, should be the recipient of his news.

"Oh, Ezzie, you're mad!" screamed Dolly, thrilled with his attention. "Help me, Ezzie. You're so good at these things. Exactly what color would you call the First Lady's dress?"

"Magenta," answered Ezzie.

"Magenta. Absolutely. I couldn't think of the word. I'm counting on you to call me in the morning, Ezzie," she whispered to him. "You always remember what everyone wore and who sat next to whom."

"Say, Dolly," Ezzie said in a confiding voice, so ecstatic with the treasure trove within him that he couldn't wait until morning to fill her in. Just then he looked up and saw Florian Gray, Dolly's young rival. Ezzie realized that Florian Gray, still making his name, would run with such a rumor, while Dolly, dear Dolly, everybody's friend, would cry, "Nonsense!" and dismiss the ugly tale out of hand, or, worse, would first call the White House to check out the story, or even, horrors, ask the First Lady herself if it was true, in a good-hearted effort to show that it wasn't.

Dolly turned to see who Ezzie was looking at and saw Florian Gray retreating toward the men's room. With a dismissive shake of her head, she said, "I can't imagine why Elias and Ruby asked him."

"Oh, Dolly, he's not worthy to kiss the hem of your garment," said Ezzie.

Wishing to talk with Florian Gray, but not wishing to be seen talking to him, especially by Dolly, Ezzie spoke hurriedly to him in the men's room and arranged a rendezvous in a small room on the second floor that was used for cigar smoking and poker playing.

When he entered the room ten minutes later, Ezzie found Florian already there waiting for him.

"Stinks in here," said Florian.

"Cigars, probably," said Ezzie.

"Let me open this window."

"You mustn't say that you learned this from me," said Ezzie in a lowered voice, although there was no one but the two of them in the small room.

"Yes?" said Florian, eagerly. The sheer beauty of the notion that Ezzie Fenwick, the clandestine supplier of society news to Dolly De Longpre, should be giving him what could only be a hot story was not lost on the youthful professional gossipist.

And then, as if thinking better of his rash act, Ezzie hesitated, but Florian prompted him on.

"You don't mean about the workman who was killed raising up the weeping willow trees, do you?" asked Florian.

"No, no, I didn't know that," said Ezzie.

"What then?" persisted Florian.

"Oh, listen, the waltzes are starting," said Ezzie, again regretting that he was here with Florian. "I specifically asked Ruby to set aside twenty minutes for waltzing, and she remembered, with all she has to remember. Marvelous woman, isn't she? I'll arrange for us to meet later."

Florian understood that Ezzie was having second thoughts about revealing whatever it was he was going to reveal and knew that, once lost, the moment would never be reinstated.

"You mean about someone having a heart attack?" asked Florian.

"Someone had a heart attack? Here at the party? No, I didn't know that. Who?" asked Ezzie.

"I haven't found out yet," said Florian.

"I must get back, really. They're going to release the butterflies, thousands of them, all yellow and orange, on the stroke of midnight. They've been flown here from Chile. We can't miss that."

"Tell me, Ezzie," insisted Florian.

"They're going to indict Elias Renthal for trading on insider information," whispered Ezzie, drawing closer to Florian to indicate the confidentiality of his information.

"No!" said Florian, eyes wide, knowing a scoop, a scoop of scoops, was coming his way, more important by far than yellow and orange butterflies flown up that day from Chile, the kind of scoop that might be front-page news, superseding not only his own column but the financial page of his newspaper as well.

At that moment the door of the small room opened, and Lil Altemus walked in, with Dodo Fitz Alyn Van Degan, looking for Ormonde Van Degan, whom they both felt certain would want to see the release of the butterflies before they took him home to bed. As if caught out in something nefarious, Ezzie and Florian leaped back from each other, blushing.

"Oh, excuse me," said Lil, with great ceremony.

"Quite all right," said Ezzie. "I was just giving this young man the names of the out-of-town guests he doesn't know."

"Yes, of course," said Dodo, with a wink.

"You haven't seen my father, have you, Ezzie?" asked Lil.

"He came up here for a cigar over an hour ago, and we can't find him," said Dodo.

"I haven't seen him," said Ezzie.

"Nor I," said Florian.

"What's in that room?" asked Lil.

"Where the pool table is," said Ezzie. "Apparently it's off bounds tonight. Elias didn't want anyone putting drinks on it. Old felt, or something."

"It's locked," said Dodo, who was trying the door.

"He must be in there. There's not another room in the house we haven't checked," said Lil. "Look in the keyhole, Dodo."

Dodo knelt down on the floor and squinted one eye, while placing the other next to the keyhole.

"Look! He's asleep, right on the pool table. It's too sweet," she said, with musical intonations in her voice, like a bird cooing. "Look, Lil, at your father."

"I'm going down to see the butterflies," said Ezzie.

"Me too," said Florian.

"Let me look, Dodo," said Lil, kneeling down to peek through the keyhole.

BY NOW all four hundred guests had heard about the ten thousand butterflies, yellow and orange, just arrived that day from Chile, that were going to be let loose at midnight during the waltzes to flutter about hither and yon in the bowers of flowers and weeping willow trees. Those nondancers who had been sitting out the evening in the drawing room and library in conversation, gossip, or cards, preferring the soothing strains of gypsy violins to the strident beat of society dance music, now descended the stairs into the ballroom, like New Year's Eve revelers awaiting the countdown until midnight.

Mickie Minardos, with Loelia Manchester by his side, issued last-minute instructions to his staff. Ruby and Elias, with the First Lady, the Earl and Countess of Castoria, and Faye Converse, grouped together in a trellised gazebo. Waiters in green jackets, designed by Mickie to blend with the flora, raced about replenishing champagne. Ezzie Fenwick was back on the dance floor, whirling Adele Harcourt about. Laurance Van Degan was dancing with Janet. The band played society music. Excitement was high.

The ballroom lights dimmed, and the partygoers gasped at the beauty as the regular lighting was replaced by pink-and-turquoise fluorescent light, giving the illusion of total fantasy. Then, with a pull of a golden rope, the clouds above burst open, and butterflies, thousands of butterflies, descended from the ceiling of the ballroom, fluttering here, fluttering there.

"Oh, heaven!"

"Divine!"

"Spectacular!"

"It's the most beautiful thing I've ever seen," cried Ruby Renthal. Ruby reached out and took hold of Elias's hand, and he, in turn, clasped his hand over hers. They looked at each other and knew that they had made it, as they always knew they would, but beyond their wildest dreams.

"Too marvelous for words," said the Countess of Castoria.

"Oh, look," said the First Lady, clapping her hands in delight.

Ezzie Fenwick, who knew beauty when he saw beauty, had tears in his eyes. "Divoon," he said.

People raced for the dance floor. Everyone wanted to dance. Abandon was the order of the night, as couples gave themselves over to the music and beauty of the Renthals' ball. The dance floor was full when the first scream came, from Rochelle Prud'homme, followed by screams from Matilda Clarke and Violet Bastedo, as the ten thousand butterflies, yellow and orange, flown up from Chile only that day, began dropping to their deaths, having been fried by the heat of the pink-and-turquoise fluorescent lights. Secret Service men rushed in past the dancers, who were now wiping dead butterflies from their hair and backs and shoulders, to rescue the First Lady before total pandemonium broke out.

"The *odor!*" cried Ezzie, waving his hand in front of his nose like a fan, as the dying butterflies kept descending.

"Turn out those fucking fluorescent lights!" screamed Elias.

"Don't say *fucking*, Elias," whispered an agitated Ruby into her husband's ear.

Mickie, nervous sweat pouring off his brow, pulled the switch that turned off the pink-and-turquoise fluorescent lights, and the ballroom was plunged into total darkness. Fernanda Somerset screamed. On the crowded stairway, an enormously fat Albanian princess fainted and, falling, knocked over several people.

"Turn on the ballroom lights!" screamed Elias.

"I can't find the switch!" screamed back Mickie Minardos.

"You ruined my party!" Ruby screamed at Mickie.

"How dare you yell like that at Mickie!" screamed back Loelia Manchester.

"Cobbler!"

"Twat!"

"Someone puked on my back," yelled Constantine de Rham.

"It was Binkie Castoria," said Jamesey Crocus.

"Adele Harcourt swallowed a dead butterfly!" cried Minnie Willoughby.

"Lights!"

"Lights!"

"Has someone called the police?"

"The phones are out!"

"Laurance, Father's dead on the pool table," screamed Lil Altemus.

"What do you mean, Father's dead on the pool table?"

"Let's get out of here!"

"The elevators don't work."

"The Greek shoemaker blew all the fuses in the building!"

"Who are these terrible people anyway?"

"I've only met them once before," said the Countess of Castoria.

"He's being investigated by the Securities and Exchange Commission."

"What do you expect from the kind of people who spend a million dollars on curtains?"

"Are those sirens I hear?"

"Is that police or fire?"

"Break the windows!"

"Not with that bergère chair, don't break the windows," cried Ruby.

By the time the police and firemen arrived, using the same cherry-picker crane that Julio Martinez had fallen to his death from the night before, the orchestra was playing "Nearer My God to Thee."

36

THE NEWSPAPERS reported, in addition to the death of Ormonde Van Degan, "whose roots in the city go back for generations," that there were two broken ankles, two broken arms, and a broken leg in the melee that had occurred when the power failed at the Elias Renthals' ball the night before, at which four hundred people, including the First Lady, had been present. The papers further reported that Adele Harcourt, the *grande dame* of New York, had very nearly choked to death on a dead butterfly but was resting comfortably in her room at Harcourt Pavilion of Manhattan Hospital.

"THEY'VE gone. They've flown the coop," said Ezzie Fenwick, over the telephone later that day.

"At least that saves us writing thank-you notes, or sending flowers, not that Ruby would ever want to see another flower again," said Matilda Clarke.

On the morning following the ball, the Elias Renthals left for Europe on their private plane, although no such plan had been in the making the day before. Later, people wondered if their flight was less for the embarrassment of the fiasco of their ball, which, knowing them, people like Ezzie Fenwick and Lil Altemus pointed out, they might have brazened out, than it was that Elias had heard the rumor at his own party of the investigation by the Securities and Exchange Commission of his financial dealings, and it was imperative for him to dispose of his extensive foreign holdings by transferring them to his wife's name before a freeze was put on his fortune.

"Today? We're going today?" Ruby had said, aghast, reported Candelaria, her maid, to Lourdes, Lil Altemus's maid. Ruby's eyes were still red and swollen from crying.

"Today," answered Elias. "In three hours, in fact."

"Elias," said Ruby, in a pleading tone. "I want to go. You know I want to go. I can't face anyone in this city, but I can't possibly be ready to go in three hours."

"Two hours and fifty-five minutes now," said Elias.

"But my clothes! My trunks! I can never get my things together for a two-month trip in that short a time," she said.

"Candelaria here," he said, pointing his thumb at the maid, "can pack up your stuff and ship it to you, and, in the meantime, buy new things there." Elias walked out of their bedroom and down the stairs. He was surprised in a minute when he heard Ruby following him.

"Is something going to happen, Elias?" asked Ruby.

"What do you mean?" asked Elias.

"Some sort of misfortune."

"Why do you ask that?"

"I feel it."

"Have you heard anything?"

"Look, Elias, don't play games with me. You told me we were a team, do you remember?"

"I remember, Ruby."

"A team means good times and bad times."

Elias walked into the drawing room and looked out the window onto Central Park. A weeping willow tree was being lowered on a crane outside his window from the ballroom above to the street below, as his party of the night before was being dismantled.

"Do you need money, Elias?" asked Ruby, following him into the room.

"God, no," he answered, with a laugh.

"I mean, I have all this jewelry," she said. She opened her black lizard jewelry cases, which she had brought downstairs with her and began taking out the pieces. "You can have all of this back, Elias. We can sell it. And there's all the money you signed over to me. It's yours."

"No, thanks, Ruby. I'm okay in the do-re-mi department, but I'll never forget what you offered."

"Tell me what's the matter, Elias. You're in trouble, aren't you?"

"Yes. Maybe."

"What did you do?"

"What a lot of other people have done before me, and a lot of other people will do after me."

"That's not an answer."

"I, uh, used, uh, insider information that I bought and paid for from young fellas in the brokerage offices who knew about mergers that were in the works."

"That's illegal?"

"Yeah."

"You knew it was illegal?"

"Yeah."

She breathed in deeply. "What do you want me to do, Elias?"

"Swear to my lies, if it comes to that."

It surprised Elias that Ruby's eyes filled with tears. The tears did not fill her eyes slowly, but sprang forth, as if he had slapped her. He understood that his wife's tears were not for his plight, which he knew she would see him through, but because he had asked her to lie for him. She walked away from him to one of the tall windows of their drawing room and looked out at Central Park across the street, where a bag lady began her preparations for the day on a bench on Fifth Avenue. Standing there, framed by the persimmon-colored damask curtains, with the fringe that had taken six weeks to be delivered from France, Ruby Renthal wept. When Elias walked toward her, to comfort her, for he loved her, she raised her hand to halt him, without turning, having felt his footfall on her Aubusson carpet that she bought from Justine Altemus Slatkin, that Lil Altemus gave Justine for a wedding present, that had come from the Van Degan house in Newport and had once been a wedding gift from the Belgian court to the ill-fated Empress Carlotta of Mexico.

ELIAS RENTHAL was a nonconfidential man, and, as a result, he had few confidants. One of the few was Max Luby, his crony from Cleveland. Elias had sometime back taken the stand at Max's forgery trial as a character witness. "Nonsense. Utter nonsense!" he had said in the courtroom. "If a man's gonna steal, he don't steal for a lousy ten thousand dollars, which is all he wrote the check for. If he needed ten thousand bucks, there were any number of people, myself included, who would have given him the money in five minutes. What it was is, quite simply, a case of temporary aberration." Although his logic was thought to have carried weight with the jury, Max still had to serve six months, but he was known to be grateful that such a great financier as Elias Renthal had come to his rescue in court and even invited him to his ball.

"Listen, Max," Elias said, in a confidential tone on his private telephone, after having received Max's consolation on the failure of the ball. He was sitting in the little room Ruby had arranged for him to smoke his cigars, the same room where Ormonde Van Degan had died the night before. "Ruby and I are taking off. There's a little heat on me, if you understand what I'm saying."

"Right," replied Max, in his perfect second-in-command voice.

"There's a few things I'd like you to do for me, and then maybe you can meet up with me in Paris in a week or so. Check out for me, in a discreet way of course, the consequences of canceling my pledges to the museum and the opera. I think I pledged ten million to each, over a seven-year period. Just in case there's a temporary cash-flow problem, I'd hate to be shelling out that kind of moola to some nonsense like the opera and the museum. They got money coming out their kazoos, those people."

"What about the Julio Martinez fund?" asked Max.

"Who the fuck is Julio Martinez?" asked Elias.

"The workman who was killed hoisting the weeping willow tree for the ball."

"Christ, I forgot about him."

"It was only yesterday, Elias."

"Gimme a break. I got a lot on my mind. Better stick with that."

"Right."

"Oh, and one other thing, Max," he said, butting out his cigar in an ashtray where a dead butterfly lay. "You better stop payment on that check I gave to Faye Converse last night for AIDS."

LOELIA MANCHESTER wished with all her heart that Mickie Minardos had not called Ruby Renthal a twat the night before when Ruby screamed at him that he had ruined her party. She hated the word, had never used it herself, and knew that it must have caused pain to Ruby, who had worked so hard to put her background behind her. Loelia liked Ruby and had enjoyed their friendship, although she understood that Mickie had made a resumption of it impossible. Loelia had never seen Mickie cry until the night before, when they returned to the Rhinelander. He had held it in, all during the elevator ride up to the thirty-second floor, not only because of the elevator man, whom they both knew, but because the Earl and Countess of Castoria were in the same elevator, returning to their suite on the same floor. Wearing several Band-Aids and still drunk, the Earl had laughed hysterically for all thirty-two floors every time he looked at Mickie, and the Countess, who had a dead butterfly in her chignon that she was unaware of, held her ripped dress together in the front. On parting, the Earl had made a Latin American farewell by yelling, "*Buenas noches, amigos,*" as the Countess led him to his room. "He's not Mexican. He's Greek, Binkie," she could be heard saying as they went down the hall.

Mickie cried like a child. He was an artist, he told her, not an electrician. How was he supposed to understand about amps and wattage and voltage? Hadn't he created the most beautiful party ever given until those motherfucking, cuntlapping, cocksucking fuses blew and wiped out in an instant his months of work? He sobbed uncontrollably. Loelia wiped his brow with a linen towel she had dipped into her scented rosewater.

They both knew they had to leave town, before the newspapers started to call. Loelia suggested Greece. "Good God, not Greece," said Mickie. "My family. Think what my family will say," and he started to cry again, as new rushes of shame that he had not thought about yet came to him.

"But I have the most marvelous idea," said Loelia, finally. "No one will find us."

"Where?"

"A clinic in Germany. Bavaria, actually. On Lake Tergernsee."

"Tell me."

"They give shots. Live cell shots from the fetus of unborn sheep. And it's restorative. It will be marvelous. We will be brimming with health. And feeling as young as my children, and no one will know where to trace us, and by the time we get back, everyone will have forgotten about the ball. You go to bed, my darling—I'll handle everything."

EARLY on the morning following the ball, Lil Altemus called her daughter, Justine. At first she did not notice that there was lassitude in her daughter's voice.

"Have you heard?" Lil asked.

"Heard what?" Justine replied.

"Your grandfather's dead."

"Poor Grandfather," said Justine, although there was no tonal difference in the weariness of her voice.

"That's all you can say? 'Poor Grandfather.' Like 'poor dog' or 'poor cat,'" said Lil.

"He was eighty-five, Mother."

"Eighty-four."

"Well, in that case, I'm utterly shocked."

"You sound odd, Justine."

"I can sound odd if I want to, without accounting for it."

"If I didn't know you better, I'd think you were drunk."

"You want to know something, Mother?"

"What?"

"I am drunk."

"This is no time for jokes, Justine. You'd better get right over here. We have things to decide, about the funeral and all."

"I can't."

"Yes, you can. Uncle Laurance just called, and he thought it might be nice if the younger generation, like young Laurance and Hubie and Bernard, of course, were pallbearers. I think it's a marvelous idea, don't you?"

Justine had hoped to not have to tell her mother that Bernie had left her, at least for the time being, because she was certain her mother would say, "I told you so," but the news of her grandfather's death now made that impossible.

"Listen, Mother," said Justine, about to reveal her secret, but she couldn't bring herself to say the words without crying. "Listen, I'll be over. Have Lourdes make me some coffee. There's something I have to tell you."

"I expected to see you last night. The world was there, except you and Bernard," said Lil.

Justine hesitated, again tempted to get the task over with on the telephone, but she still couldn't bring herself to say the words. "Bernie had to work," she said finally.

"Bernie always has to work. That doesn't usually keep you home."

"Headache."

"Not pregnant, are you?"

"Oh, no. Thank God."

"I thought you wanted a baby. Don't wait too long, Justine. Look what happened to Muffie Windsor, and she was only thirty-six."

"How was the Renthals' party?"

"You mean you haven't heard? My dear, I know it's awful to laugh, with my poor father lying in a casket at Frank E. Campbell's, but wait until you hear. You won't believe what happened. Now, don't call Violet Bastedo. You just get over here, and I'll fill you in. And call Hubie. You better get him here as well."

IT WAS a fact of Justine Altemus Slatkin's life that all the people she knew, and all the people her family and friends knew, lived within a thirty-block radius of each other in that part of the city known as the Upper East Side, and, just as in a small town, they were constantly running into each other in the streets and on the avenues in that small enclave.

Ezzie Fenwick happened to be in a taxicab going down Park Avenue at the moment Justine Altemus left her own apartment to walk the several blocks to her mother's apartment on Fifth Avenue and was witness to the fact that Justine took a swig from a can of beer she was holding. Later, describing the incident to a group of ladies he was lunching with, to rehash the events of the Renthal ball, Ezzie said that Justine's face looked like a fallen soufflé.

Justine, oblivious to everything around her, didn't see Ezzie leaning out the cab window, nor even notice Ned Manchester until he reached out and took her arm.

"Do you want to get a cup of coffee?" asked Ned.

"All right," answered Justine, listing a bit to the side.

Ned lifted the beer can out of Justine's hand and dropped it into a trash basket. They went into a coffee shop near the Whitney Museum.

"I know I look terrible," said Justine.

"Don't worry about it," said Ned.

"God, I hate beer. Bernie likes beer. I can't imagine why I drank it, let alone walked up Park Avenue with a can in my hand. You don't think I'm flipping out, do you?"

"What's the matter, Justine?" asked Ned.

When Justine looked over at Ned, she noticed that his hair was wet, as it always seemed to be wet when she saw him, and she assumed that he had probably just showered after playing squash at the

Butterfield. "My dog died," she lied, without even caring whether or not he knew that she didn't have a dog.

"What's the matter, Justine?" he repeated.

"Bernie," she replied.

Ned nodded but did not reply.

"Bernie's not even in love with anyone else, like Loelia was," Justine continued. "Bernie just doesn't want to be married to me."

Ned lifted up the creamer and asked her with a gesture if she wanted cream in her coffee and poured it for her, did the same with the Sweet 'n Low, stirred it, and placed it in front of her. "It's a terrible time, I know," he said.

"The incredible thing was I thought we were happy," she said.

"Drink your coffee," he said. "You'll feel better."

"I never knew you were so nice, Ned," said Justine, drinking her coffee.

"I've been through what you're going through."

"It's awful to feel like this," said Justine.

"All the little things in life that make a marriage work, like going to the movies on Sunday afternoons, or playing tennis together, or having dinner at home, just the two of us, we ceased to do," said Ned, about his marriage. "And then, along came the cobbler."

"I only cooked dinner for him once the whole time we were married, and that was when Bonita, my cook Bonita, went back to Honduras for her mother's funeral, and even then Bernie told me the dinner was lousy, and we ended up ordering in from Food-to-Go on Lexington Avenue."

"Have you told Lil?"

"I was on my way to see my mother when you were kind enough to take the beer out of my hand. I'd better go. She's waiting for me."

"Sorry about your grandfather. Matilda called me."

"Thanks, Ned."

On the street, Justine continued to her mother's apartment.

"Would you like to sign a petition to save the porpoises?" a man on Madison Avenue asked Justine, offering her a clipboard and a pen.

She seemed not to have heard what he said, although she was aware that he had asked her something. "What?" she said.

"Would you like to sign a petition to save the porpoises?" he asked again.

"No, actually I wouldn't," she said slowly.

The walk, only a few blocks, seemed endless to her. Within her, she ached.

A television news crew was outside the building where the Renthals lived, shooting footage of the weeping willow trees being lowered from the sixteenth floor to the street. Justine watched the procedure for a moment before moving on.

"Justine, are you all right?" she heard someone ask her.

Turning, she saw that it was Brenda Primrose, with a reporter's notebook in hand, making notes on the dismantling of the ball.

"Justine?" Brenda said again, taking hold of Justine's arm. Justine, usually so perfectly groomed, looked to Brenda like she had slept in the clothes she was wearing. Her hair was uncombed. A button was missing from her blouse. She smelled of beer.

"I'm fine," said Justine.

"You poor thing," said Brenda. "Is it your grandfather? We had it on the news that he died."

"Yeah," said Justine. "That's it. My grandfather."

"Do you need help, Justine? Where are you heading for?"

"My mother's."

"Where's that?"

"Two buildings down from the Renthals."

"C'mon. I'll take you there. Be right back, Charlie."

They walked for half a block in silence. Brenda thought Justine was crying.

"You guys must have been pretty close, huh? You and your grandfather? He must have been some guy," said Brenda.

At the entrance of her mother's apartment building, Justine turned to Brenda and said for the first time the words she would be saying for the rest of her life. "Bernie left me." Before Brenda could react, Justine turned and walked into the building.

IT WAS common knowledge that Lil Altemus thought her daughter had married beneath her, even though it was apparent, even to her, that Bernard Slatkin had not married Justine for her money. Nor could she ever say about Bernard that he had used her daughter for social advancement, because she knew that was not true. He had participated in Justine's social life in an agreeable and successful fashion, but her world held no particular fascination for him and his success in it was that he had remained a newscaster first and foremost.

However, when Justine informed her mother that the marriage was over, irreparably over, Lil, ever unpredictable, was enraged at the failure. Losing her son-in-law, she liked him better than she realized she had and felt sure she could reorchestrate the disastrous plans.

"Now, listen, please. What you're doing is overdramatizing an everyday marital situation. If anyone knows about these things, your old mother does. You've had a tiff, that's all. These things happen. It's a natural progression. The honeymoon is over. The marriage begins. He's simply flexing his muscles to show that he's the man in the family. He'll be back."

"No, Mother, he won't be back. I know him," said Justine.

The look on Justine's tear-stained face and the tone of Justine's heartbroken voice made Lil look at her.

"But what in the world has happened?" asked Lil.

"It was my fault. I tried to bring him into my life, which never really interested him, and I didn't make enough effort about all those news people."

"Oh, please," said Lil, dismissing her daughter's explanation. "Is there another woman?"

"I don't know."

"Matilda Clarke said he's a womanizer," said Lil. "Your Uncle Laurance even said he was a philanderer."

"Oh, please, Mother," said Justine, wounded by the thought.

"Where is that place his aunt and uncle live in New Jersey? Hackensack, is it?" Lil asked

"Weehawken," replied Justine.

"Exactly," said Lil, reaching for her book.

"Mother, please don't call Mrs. Slatkin. Please."

"Of course, I'm going to call her. Hester will understand that this simply must not be. Young people all have problems. They just have to be worked out."

"Then let me leave. I can't bear to hear that conversation."

"Have you called Hubie to tell him about his grandfather?"

"No."

"Do that now, and tell him to come right up here."

After Justine left her mother's room, Lil Altemus picked up her telephone book, looked up a number, and called Hester Slatkin, whom she had not seen or spoken to since the day of the wedding. A divorce after several years she not only could have tolerated but might gladly have accepted, but a divorce after a year she felt had an unseemly quality.

"We can't allow this to happen, Hester. We simply can't."

"When Bernie makes up his mind about something, Lil, he never changes it," said Hester. The coolness of Hester's answer surprised Lil, who had assumed she would be a willing ally.

"I should have objected, you see, right from the beginning," said Lil. "I should have said that it was all wrong, that it couldn't work. Because, you see, it's what I actually felt. But then I would have been the heavy. They would have said I was anti-Semitic, because that's what it would have come down to, but that never had a damn thing to do with it. I thought they were wrong together."

"Good-bye, Lil," said Hester Slatkin, with a tone of finality in her voice that indicated it would be their last conversation.

"THERE'S no answer at Hubie's, Mother," said Justine.

"Keep trying."

"There's no answer at the gallery either, and the machine's not on."

"I'll try," said Lil. She tapped the numbers out on her telephone.

"*Sí?*" came the answer after several rings.

"You see?" she said to Justine. "There is someone there. This is Mrs. Altemus speaking. Is my son there?"

"*No está aquí,*" said the voice on the end.

"It's that damn maid," said Lil to Justine. "Tell him his mother called. His mother. His *madre*. Do you understand? *Cinco, ocho, ocho.* What's the word for six, Justine, quick?"

"I don't know."

"Oh, never mind," Lil screamed into the telephone and slammed down the receiver. "Don't you miss maids who speak English? Do you remember when you were a little girl, all those marvelous Irish maids we always had? Kathleen and Maeve?"

"Oh, Mother, please," said Justine. "Let's not talk about Kathleen and Maeve, for Christ's sake."

"Really, Justine. There is no reason for you to take the Lord's name in vain. None whatsoever," Lil replied to Justine's outburst. She looked at her daughter. "You look terrible. Do you know that? Simply terrible."

"I'm entitled to look terrible. My husband left me. My brother has AIDS."

"He does not have AIDS! And don't you dare say that to a living soul!"

"I'm going to call Juanito."

"Juanito, Juanito. Who the hell is this Juanito I'm always hearing the name of?"

"He's the man Hubie loves, Mother."

"I simply loathe that kind of talk, Justine. Now go and pull yourself together, and we'll meet Uncle Laurance at Frank E. Campbell's and go over the funeral plans."

Lourdes, Lil's maid, came in to tell Lil that there was a man on the telephone to speak to her called Boy Fessenden.

"Boy Fessenden?" said Lil. "There's a name from the past. I haven't seen Boy Fessenden since that summer when he visited us in Newport. Do you remember?" She picked up the extension. "Hello, this is Lil Altemus. Yes, of course, I remember you. How are you, Boy? What a long time it's been. How's your mother? Do give her my love. Now what can I do for you, Boy? I must be quick. We've had such a sadness in the family. My father died last night. Eighty-four. Thank you. You're so kind, Boy. How can I help you? Hubie? No, I can't reach Hubie on the telephone. Or in the gallery. I want him to get right up here because we have to make plans for the funeral. What? . . . When? . . . Where?"

"What is it, Mother?" asked Justine.

Lil, ashen, handed the telephone to Justine. "You'd better take this, Justine. Boy Fessenden took Hubie to the hospital last night."

THAT NIGHT, after calling hours at Frank E. Campbell's funeral home, where the mayor, the governor, the board of directors of the Van Degan Foundation, the entire membership of the Butterfield, and several hundred family and business friends came to pay their respects to Ormonde Van Degan, Lil Altemus refused her brother's invitation to join him and Janet and Dodo for a late dinner at their apartment and returned to her own, pleading exhaustion. At nine thirty the doorbell rang and she let Bernie Slatkin in, whom, un-known to Justine, she was expecting.

"I don't understand how you can do this to my daughter," Lil said, after they were seated in the library, allowing no time for amenities, not even a condolence message from Bernie to her on the death of her father. Nor had she offered him a drink.

"It was my understanding always that you did not care for the marriage in the first place, Mrs. Altemus," replied Bernie.

Bernie's addressing her as Mrs. Altemus, instead of Lil, which she had requested him to do after the wedding, and which he had been eager to do at the time, was not lost on Lil. When she spoke, she called him Bernard, as she had always refused to call him Bernie.

"That was then. This is now, Bernard," said Lil.

"The marriage is over," said Bernie.

"But why?"

"Feelings change."

"So quickly?"

"It's over, Mrs. Altemus," Bernie repeated, as if to bring the matter to an end. "I do not see any point in prolonging a situation that is going to fail in the long run."

"I have to be quite frank with you, Bernard," said Lil, as if she were paying him a compliment. "I did think in the beginning that you might be using Justine to further your career, or you were interested in her money, but I know now that that is not the case."

"Never was," he said.

"Stay married to my daughter for four more years and then divorce, and I will make it worth your while."

Bernie, who did not usually smoke, leaned forward and took a cigarette from a box on a table by his chair, lit it, inhaled deeply, and smiled as he exhaled, shaking his head at her at the same time. He stamped out the cigarette in a Meissen dish, threw the stub in the fireplace, and rose. "I never understood people like you, Mrs. Altemus. I never will," he said.

"And what does that mean?" asked Lil, aware that she was not going to convince him to change his mind, as she had not been able to convince him to live in Justine's apartment in the same building she lived in, or to use Cora Mandell to decorate the new apartment he had insisted he and Justine move to when they got married.

"Stay married for four more years and then divorce, is that it? A five-year marriage is less of a flop than a one-year marriage. It all has to do with face, doesn't it, how it looks? Your daughter is far too good for such an arrangement as that. Good-bye, Mrs. Altemus."

"I never liked you, Bernard," she said, wanting the last word.

"I never liked you either, Mrs. Altemus," said Bernie, getting the last word.

"You're a womanizer," she hissed at him.

"That's right. That's what my problem is," he answered, staring her down. Lil registered surprise that he had not denied the accusation. "And I don't want a wife who is a tragic figure. 'Poor Justine. Her husband cheats on her.'"

"Get out."

"Remember this. I came by summons, not by choice."

THE WORD was out on Hubie Altemus's illness. The previous night, at Maisie Verdurin's, Ezzie Fenwick, who had heard that afternoon from Jamesey Crocus, who had heard from Juanito, whispered it to Maude Hoare, and Maude told Buster Dominguez, and Buster told Matilda Clarke, and Matilda told Gus Bailey, although there was no word on the matter from any of the members of the family.

The next day Gus was walking up Madison Avenue and passed Lil Altemus as she was coming out of the Wilton House Book Shop with a shopping bag in her hand. She looked as handsomely put together as always, but drawn.

"I'm sorry to hear about Hubie," said Gus.

Lil stiffened. It distressed her to think that people knew the news and were discussing it. A tear came to her eye. "I'm on my way to the hospital now," she said, indicating the bag of books she was carrying.

Their eyes met.

She mouthed but did not speak the word *lymphoma*, as if it were a release rather than a sentence. Gus understood that she was avoiding the subject that was so painful to her.

"How are you doing, Lil?" Gus asked.

"I'm all right," said Lil. "Really I am. I have been nipping a bit at the brandy and soda, but at least I'm no longer thinking of going out the window."

Gus, touched, reached out to take her arm.

"I couldn't figure out what to wear," she said, making a joke of it. "That's what saved me. Do you remember when poor old Mimi Chase wore a trench coat when she jumped, after they fired her from the magazine? I didn't want to wear a trench coat. I didn't ever have a goddamn trench coat, but I wouldn't have worn one if I had. Oh, Gus, it's been so awful. I don't know if I can live without him. No one understood it, I know, what we had, but I adored him. I absolutely adored him." She spoke of her son as if he were already dead.

IN THE several years they had been together, Juanito Perez had never been as kind to Hubie Altemus as he was in the months of Hubie's dying. Lying in bed at St. Vincent's Hospital, Hubie watched Juanito standing at the window looking out. Juanito was the only one now who could make Hubie laugh, telling his stories of the goings-on in the subterranean world that he still frequented, despite the dangers of the disease that was killing his lover. There were certain of their mutual acquaintances in the art world whom Juanito referred to with a gender switch, and it never failed to make Hubie laugh. That afternoon he was regaling Hubie with a tale concerning Jamesey Crocus, through whom he had met Hubie, and whom he always called Janie, or the furniture queen.

"So Miss Crocus kicks her train around and says, 'Those console tables are fakes, Ruby,' and walks out in a huff," finished Juanito.

By this time Hubie could only talk in a whisper. "You are awful, Juanito," he said, when he finished laughing.

As Juanito went on with his tales of the night before, Hubie watched him with affection. He wondered if Juanito's diligence in caring for him was because of the money he knew he was going to inherit, or because he really cared in return, but he decided not to allow it to occupy his mind for the time he had left, grateful that the caring existed at all, no matter what the reason. The only thing at that moment that bothered him was that his mother was coming to pay a visit, and he did not know if he had the strength to deal with his mother and Juanito in the room at the same time.

"Mother's on her way here," he said finally, hoping that Juanito would gather up his possessions and be off before her arrival.

"My mother-in-law here?" Juanito asked.

"Any minute," whispered Hubie.

"I've been dying to meet her."

"You're going to stay then?"

"Of course I'm going to stay."

"Juanito?"

"Don't ask me to go, Hubie."

"I'm not. When she's here, don't call Boy Fessenden Girl Fessenden, if his name comes up. Okay?"

"What do you think I am, from the slums?"

"Listen, one more thing."

"What?"

"Will you take off your earring before she arrives?"

"That's going to butch me up, is it, not wearing my earring?" asked Juanito, irritated, as he always was when Hubie acted embarrassed about him in relation to his family.

"No, that's not it," said Hubie.

"Then what? I like this diamond earring."

"That diamond was my mother's engagement ring from my father. She gave it to me when she thought I was going to marry Violet Bastedo."

Juanito and Hubie looked at each other, and both started to laugh. "That's the first good laugh I've had in weeks," said Juanito, unscrewing the diamond from his earlobe. He went over to Hubie and hugged him.

It was in this position that Lil Altemus saw them when she walked into the hospital room with her bagful of books. It was the first time Lil had seen Hubie since Easter night. He looked smaller to her, as if his face had shrunk. His teeth seemed bigger. His arms looked like the arms of an old man.

"Hello, my darling," said Lil, staring at him aghast.

"Mother, this is Juanito Perez. Juanito, this is my mother," said Hubie.

"Hellohowareyou?" said Lil, not looking at him.

"Ma'am," said Juanito.

"What a nice room, Hubie. My word, is that the World Trade Center out the window? Prettier from this angle than when you see it from Laurance's boat."

Neither of the young men answered her.

"Your grandfather's funeral was enormous, Hubie. You probably read about it in the *Times*. The governor. The mayor. All the Van

Degans. The church was packed. Young Laurance gave the most lovely eulogy. We all went up to Laurance and Janet's afterward. Not the governor and the mayor. Just the family, I mean." Even to herself, she sounded rattled.

"How's Dodo taking it?" asked Juanito.

For the first time Lil looked at Juanito.

"Dodo?" she asked, raising her eyebrows in exaggerated surprise.

"She buys my paintings," said Juanito.

"Oh."

"How is she?"

"Mrs. Van Degan is coping well under the circumstances," said Lil.

Juanito looked over at Hubie. He could see that Hubie was suffering, although Hubie managed to make a slight wink of reassurance.

"I'm gonna split, Hubie," said Juanito. "I'm sure you and your mother have things to talk over."

"When will you come back?" asked Hubie.

"I'll stop by tonight. Good-bye, Mrs. Altemus."

Lil nodded, occupied now with her shopping bag of gifts. She realized, as he was leaving, that she wanted him to stay, so that she would not have to be alone with Hubie. She wished that Justine was with her. She knew that she didn't know what to say to her own son, whom she loved, so devastated was she by his appearance.

"Did you see Justine?" she asked when Juanito had left.

"She was here earlier."

"How was she?"

"Drunk, I felt."

"Drunk? Justine? Never!"

"I repeat, drunk."

"That son of a bitch has left her."

"I never heard you say son of a bitch before, Mother."

"I've never said it before," she replied. "It's all so embarrassing." Lil looked down at her bag. The word *all*, Hubie understood, included him as well as Justine.

"Justine feels hatred for Bernard now," said Lil.

"I didn't get that impression."

"Oh, yes, hatred without limits."

"You weren't very polite to Juanito, Mother."

"I've brought you some books, Hubie," said Lil, putting the shopping bag from Wilton House on his bed. "Arthur thought you'd like the new book on the Princesses of Monaco."

"Arthur couldn't have thought that," said Hubie.

"No, I thought it. Do you remember when your old mother thought you'd be perfect for one of those girls? Can you imagine?"

Hubie looked at his mother and smiled.

"And the new magazines are all in there too," she said. "Now, I'm off." She was out the door.

Hubie started to drift off to sleep.

When he woke, he looked out the window at the skyline of lower New York, watching a barge go slowly by. On the bed he saw the shopping bag from Wilton House that his mother had left earlier. Unable to sleep again, he took out the magazines and the new book on the Princesses of Monaco, about whom he had no interest. Inside, at the bottom of the bag, he saw a dark brown plastic container. He reached in and took it out. Inside there were fifty Seconal pills.

Hubie reached down and undid the drawstring of his pajamas. For a while his hand rested on his stomach. Then he allowed his fingers to slide down between his legs, resting in his pubic hair. He moved his fingers around, massaging himself lightly. When his penis was semierect, he made a fist around it and pounded himself. For the two minutes and thirty-four seconds that it took to complete the act of masturbation, Hubie Altemus forgot that he was going to die at twenty-seven.

LIL ALTEMUS fainted when she left St. Vincent's Hospital. If her chauffeur, Joe, who had been with her for years, had not been there to rescue her, she might have been put into the same hospital where her son was a patient, but Joe understood her panicked look and delivered her back to her apartment on Fifth Avenue, where Lourdes cared for her, and Justine was sent for.

"I cannot bear it that that man is there," said Lil, resting in bed, about Juanito Perez.

"They're a couple, Mother," said Justine.

Lil shuddered.

"Under the circumstances, he has as much right to be there as we do," Justine continued.

When Lil was with her son, before his illness, and Hubie made what she thought was an inappropriate remark, such as Justine had just made to her, she would cover her ears and exclaim, "You know I can't *bear* that kind of talk!" Under the same circumstances, with Justine, Lil pretended not to have heard. It was a way she had of snubbing people who had gone too far.

"He makes Hubie laugh. He makes him forget that he's going to die," said Justine, who didn't care that she was being snubbed by her mother.

HUBERT ALTEMUS, the father of Justine and Hubie, always gave the impression, even in town, of a country gentleman. His tweed jacket fit too loosely on his lanky frame, but it was too loose by the mutual choice of its wearer and its wearer's tailor, and, to their refined tastes, altogether right. He had been summoned to town by his former wife, whom he had not seen since the day of Justine's wedding, to discuss the unraveling lives of their two children. Hubert did not enjoy going to Lil's apartment, where he had lived when he was married to her, nor did his present wife, Belinda, enjoy having him go there, so the lunch between the two was arranged for Clarence's, after he had visited Hubie in the hospital. They had, after desultory greetings, sat in silence until Hubert finished the first of the three martinis he intended to drink before they ordered lunch. As always, in the presence of her former husband, Lil, who rarely felt ill at ease, felt ill at ease and said to the waiter, Michael, with the small ponytail, who was always so nice to her daughter, "Will you take this thing away, please?" waving her hand over a vase of three pink carnations.

"Don't like flowers, Mrs. Altemus?" asked Michael, in his friendly way, obviously unaware that she had a dying son and a divorcing daughter.

"Yes, I do. I like flowers very much. I just don't happen to like those flowers," replied Lil.

With that Michael removed the offending vase.

"I cannot bear carnations," said Lil to Hubert, and Hubert nodded, knowing perfectly well that the carnations were not what was bothering her, that she was simply looking for something to find fault with to overcome her discomfort.

"Who was the guy with the diamond in his ear?" Hubert asked finally, not referring to Michael, who also wore a diamond in his ear, but to the man he had just seen in his son's room at the hospital, whose diamond earring was larger by far than Michael's.

"Pedro. Or Geraldo. Or some name like that," answered Lil, who often pretended not to know things she knew perfectly well, just as she now knew that her former husband was referring to their son's lover, Juanito Perez, or their son's catamite, as her brother Laurance, who was checking him out, referred to him.

"Who is he?"

"Justine says he is the man Hubie loves," answered Lil, looking away from Hubert as she said it.

"Jesus," said Hubert. He took a long drink from his martini and swallowed the olive at the same time. "If I didn't know better, I'd think that diamond in his ear was from the engagement ring I gave you when we got married."

"Oh, don't be silly," said Lil. At the same time she said the words, she realized that Hubert could be right, especially as she had given the ring to Hubie when she thought that he was going to marry Violet Bastedo, but that was not the subject that she wished to deal with now.

"When Hubie goes, Hubert, I hope you'll agree with me that there should be nothing in the obituaries about the cause of death," said Lil.

"Sure, Lil," said Hubert.

"Laurance can handle all that."

"I'm sure he can, Lil," said Hubert.

"It's Justine I really want to talk about, Hubert. What a crushed little creature she has become," said Lil, sipping a glass of white wine.

"She really loved that television announcer," said Hubert.

"I should never have allowed that marriage. Never. Nor should you have, for that matter," said Lil.

"Spilt milk," said Hubert, signaling the waiter for another martini.

"I don't particularly enjoy hearing that my daughter was seen walking down Park Avenue with a can of beer in her hand," said Lil.

"Do we know it's true?" replied Hubert Altemus.

"Of course, it's true. Ezzie Fenwick saw her himself."

"Of course it would be Ezzie who saw her," said Hubert, who had no patience for Ezzie Fenwick. "I'll talk to Justine."

"I want you to do more than talk to her," said Lil. "I want you to take her up to Bedford with you. Keep her there for a week or so. Make her ride and do all those things. She needs to get away from New York. She thinks everyone's talking about her. Everyone *is* talking about her."

"I'll talk to Belinda," said Hubert.

"Oh, we need permission from the former Miss O'Brien, do we?" asked Lil, who could never hear the name of Hubert's present wife without reacting adversely. She had once described Belinda O'Brien as the kind of woman who calls men at their offices.

"Ah, there's Belinda now," said Hubert, rising, with a look of pleasure on his face, and waving to his wife, who stood at the door of the restaurant.

"Belinda? Here?" asked Lil, gathering up her things.

"Yes, I asked her to meet me here." Belinda, waving back, smiled and made her way toward them through the crowded restaurant.

"I don't know how you could do this to me, Hubert," said Lil.

"Do what?"

"Ask that woman to come here to this table with everyone in the restaurant looking at us," said Lil.

"That woman has been my wife for twelve years," said Hubert, "and I don't see a single soul in this restaurant looking at us, except Chick Jacoby, who wants the table for Lord Biedermeier, who just arrived without a reservation, and, just to be perverse, I'm going to let Lord Biedermeier have a nice long wait."

"Hello, Lil," said Belinda, walking up to the table. Belinda Altemus, in her forties, was still pretty, although she had begun to put on what she herself called a few extra libs. Her face gave off a look of good humor, as if nothing bothered her. Her blond hair was what Lil Altemus called "touched up," and she wore what Lil called wet-looking lipstick.

"Hellohoware?" answered Lil, not looking up at her as she rose to leave. Hubert made no effort to detain her.

"You'll call me, Hubert, about the matter we discussed?" asked Lil.

"After I talk with Belinda," he answered.

Lil turned and walked out of the restaurant. Belinda and Hubert looked at each other. Hubert shrugged.

"I think she's still in love with you," said Belinda.

"Hardly likely," replied Hubert.

"Tell me something, Hubert. Did you ever love her?"

"Oh, I don't know. I probably thought so at the time. What it really was, I suppose, was the utter perfection of the union, smiled on by both sides." They both laughed. "Did I tell you today how beautiful you are?" he asked.

"Tell me that when you've had a few less of these," she said, tapping her very red fingernail against his empty martini glass.

Hubert smiled at her. "Want some lunch?"

"Sure," she replied, looking around the dining room. "How come we don't have any flowers on our table?"

HUBIE clung stubbornly to a life that had brought him little happiness. Justine, back from Bedford, visited him daily.

"Beautiful," he said about the large bunch of white peonies that Justine had brought him. "My favorite flower."

"I remember," said Justine.

"There was this guy in my class at Simsbury. Bobby Vermont. Do you remember him? He was Mom's friend Teddy Vermont's son by his third marriage. A sad, lonely guy at school. I probably would have become good friends with him if I hadn't been kicked out."

"I remember Bobby Vermont," said Justine. "He threw up at my coming-out party."

"Funny you should remember that. It's the first thing he said to me. 'Has your sister ever forgiven me for throwing up at her coming-out party?'"

Justine laughed. "What about Bobby Vermont?"

"I ran into him here at the hospital the other day."

"What's he here for?"

"Same thing I am."

"Oh, I'm sorry. Poor Bobby, but at least you have a friend here then."

"Had a friend. He died yesterday."

"Oh, dear." Justine turned away from her brother and placed the white peonies in a vase. "Mummy sends her love."

"Send her mine."

"She'd come, Hubie, but she couldn't cope after her visit. She doesn't mean anything. It's just that it's too much for her."

"The way I look, huh?"

"Yes."

"Doesn't matter."

"Of course it matters, but that's the way she is."

"You're not trying to explain my mother to me, are you?"

They both laughed.

"What are you going to do about your money, Hubie?" asked Justine.

"Leaving it all to Juanito," said Hubie.

"Don't."

"I didn't think I'd hear that from you, Justine."

"Hubie, it's ten million dollars."

"So?"

"Leave him five hundred thousand dollars. A million even. But don't leave him the whole thing. You know what Uncle Laurance will do. He'll take it to court. He'll call it undue influence on the part of Juanito. He'll expose everything there is to expose about Juanito: the drugs, those terrible bars he goes to. He'll find a way to prove that Juanito is the one who gave you the AIDS."

"It's not undue influence, Justine. No one is forcing me to do this. It's what I want to do. That's why I went to Herkie Saybrook to make out my will, rather than some gay lawyer in the West Village. Our own kind, that's Herkie Saybrook. You don't need the money. Certainly Mother doesn't need the money. Who else am I going to leave it to?"

"You could do something marvelous with it, Hubie. Give it to medical research, or something like that."

"I know," said Hubie, looking off at the river outside, thinking about what his sister was saying. "There's something in me that makes me want to get even with Uncle Laurance and young shitface Laurance. All my life they made me feel like I was nothing."

"Think about it, Hubie," said Justine.

Hubie looked at Justine and held out his hand. She took it and squeezed it. "What's with the television announcer?" he asked.

"Flown off to wherever it is they fly off to these days for a quickie divorce."

"Did you see him before he went?"

"Yes."

"How'd it go?"

"We did not go down Memory Lane, if that's what you mean."

317

"You taking it okay?"

"I loved him, Hubie. I really loved him."

Hubie looked at his sister. "One of the nicest things about you, Justine, is that with a mother like ours, you didn't get tough."

Justine started to cry.

"We're a pair, aren't we?" continued Hubie. "The rich Altemus kids, they used to call us, like we were something special. What happened to us, Justine?"

"I'm going to miss you, Hubie," said Justine.

Still holding her hand, Hubie drifted off to sleep. When he awoke, Justine was still there.

"You were right about the money, you know," he said. He could speak only in a whisper. "Can you get Herkie Saybrook to come down here? I can still leave Juanito well cared for, but the bulk should go to a hospice for all these guys here who have no place to go and no one to take care of them."

"I'll call Herkie," said Justine.

"Better do it quick," said Hubie.

She nodded. "Guess what, Hubie?"

"What?"

"I'm pregnant."

Hubie, dying, was still interested enough in life to be amazed. "By Bernie?" he whispered.

"Who else?"

"Does he know?"

"No."

"You going to tell him?"

"No. I don't want him back like that."

"Does Mummy know?"

"No."

"Are you going to tell her?"

"Not yet."

"Are you going to keep the baby?"

"Oh, yes, and I'm going to be a wonderful mother."

Hubie, tired now from the excitement of the conversation, could only pat his sister's hand in admiration.

"Want to know what I'm going to name it if it's a boy?" asked Justine. She knew Hubie was not strong enough to answer her, so she continued without an answer from him. "Hubie. Hubie Altemus Slatkin."

Hubie nodded his head and signaled for his sister to come closer. She put her ear near to his mouth as he said, "Hubie Slatkin. It has a certain insouciant charm." He smiled.

Later, leaving, Justine stopped at the door of the hospital room and looked back at Hubie. When he looked up at her, she said, "I've loved being your sister, Hubie."

Hubie understood that it was Justine's way of saying good-bye. He raised his hand and waved good-bye.

Justine nodded and looked away to avert a tear that was forming.

"I'm so proud of you, Hubie," she said.

That night Hubie died. Herkie Saybrook never knew that Hubie wanted to make a new will. Only Juanito was with him at the end, holding on to his slight body. The last words Hubie heard were Juanito crying, "Don't die, Hubie."

37

DESPITE the prominence of the family, there was very little made in the obituary columns, at the family's request, about the death of Hubert Altemus, Jr., the son of Mrs. Van Degan Altemus of New York City and Mr. Hubert Altemus of Bedford Village, New York, and the brother of Mrs. Justine Altemus Slatkin. If it hadn't been for Ezzie Fenwick, who read the obituary page before he read anything else in the newspaper, not just the prominent names in the news stories of the dead, but the long columns of names in the paid announcements, Hubie Altemus's passing might have gone undetected, as the family wished, until after the funeral, by which time Lil would have left for Europe.

Ezzie, a surprisingly early riser for one who spent every night dining out, called Matilda Clarke with the news, and then Maude Hoare, and then, in lieu of Loelia Manchester, who had still not returned from Europe, Loelia's mother Fernanda Somerset, and Matilda and Maude and Fernanda all made their six or eight calls, and by noon everyone who knew the Altemus and Van Degan clans knew that Hubie Altemus had died of AIDS, although that was a word not to be mentioned, under any circumstance, to family members, as the official story was that poor Hubie, who really never had much of a life, Ezzie commented over and over, had died of leukemia.

LEAVING Lil Altemus's apartment after paying a condolence call, Ezzie Fenwick ran into Cora Mandell in the lobby of Lil's building.

"Oh, Ezzie," said Cora. "I guess I'm going to the same place you're coming from."

"Rather a sparcity of merriment in that household at the moment," said Ezzie. "Not that it was ever a barrel of laughs at Lil's, or at any of the Van Degans', now that I come to think of it."

"Who's up there?" asked Cora.

"All the predictables. Aunt Minnie Willoughby. Matilda. Janet and Laurance. Dodo, and poor Justine. Get the pic?"

"Evangeline wanted to come, but she was too drunk," said Cora.

"Just as well. Lil has enough to contend with, without Evangeline," said Ezzie.

"How is poor Lil?" Cora repeated.

"Stoic. Absolutely stoic. Not a tear."

"Lil always does things so well," said Cora.

"I'm off to Sibila's cocktail party," said Ezzie.

MAKING her way down Madison Avenue to meet with Lorenza about flower arrangements for Hubie's funeral, Justine Altemus, who had decided to return to her maiden name, ran into Bernie Slatkin, who was on his way to interview Max Luby for a future television segment on Wall Street practices, although that subject did not come up in their brief exchange. If Justine had not been lost in thought and had seen the approaching Bernie before he saw her, she would have ducked into a shop in order to avoid the encounter, as it was the first time they had met since Bernie returned from his tropical-island divorce. In advance, she had agonized over how she would behave when that meeting came to pass. Seeing him, she dropped her eyes and hoped that he would do the same, until they had passed each other, but, alas, Bernie was not born for such subtleties of behavior.

"Justine," he said, reaching out to touch her arm.

"Oh, hellohoware?" she said, sounding more like her mother than herself, as she withdrew her arm from his touch.

"I'm so very sorry about Hubie," he said.

"Thank you," she replied. Her words were polite, but her tone was impatient, as if he were delaying her mission.

"I know what a wonderful sister you were to him," said Bernie.

"He was a wonderful brother to me," replied Justine. She made a gesture of moving on. Bernie looked at her, struck by the change in her. Gone was the lovesick attitude he had grown to despise. She had returned to the remote and distant heiress he had first spoken to in an elevator leaving one of Maisie Verdurin's parties. For an instant she looked beautiful to him again, and unattainable, or beautiful because she was unattainable. She met his eyes, as if understanding his thought.

There were things he wanted to know, even though he was no longer a member of her family: how had Lil taken Hubie's death, had Uncle Laurance been helpful, what had happened to Juanito? But he dared not ask the questions, and she, once so full of news for him on all the inner machinations of her family, provided no information. He knew that she had ceased to love him, that if he put out a hand to touch her, she, who had craved his touch to the point of humiliation, would reject him, first as a woman rejecting a lover, then as an upper-class woman rejecting an upstart.

Bernie Slatkin was a man who examined his feelings, right at the moment of experiencing them. Within him, he held on to a strange feeling that he did not recognize, not letting it escape until he understood it. What is this feeling, he thought? It was not a pleasant feeling. And then its meaning came to him. It was loss, he realized. He repeated the word to himself. Loss.

"Do you think in time we could be friends, Justine?" he asked.

"No," she replied.

"Why?"

"I wanted to stay married, and you didn't, so we didn't. Now you want to stay friends, and I don't, so we won't."

Bernie nodded. "You've gotten tough, Justine," he said.

"Don't you think it's about time?" she answered.

"When is Hubie's funeral?" he asked.

"Tomorrow."

"Where?"

"St. James's."

"Of course," he said. St. James's, where all the weddings, christenings, and funerals of the Van Degan family took place, and had always taken place. "What time?"

"It's private," said Justine. With that, she made her move and continued her way down Madison Avenue to Lorenza's small shop to discuss the flowers. Peonies, she thought. Just white peonies.

UNCLE Laurance made the decision that it would be far better for all concerned if there were no eulogy or hymns at the service, just the simple prayers for the dead, to be followed by cremation. Young Laurance, who would have been the logical person to make the eulogy, having been born the same year as his first cousin, was relieved by his father's decision, because he and Hubie had never, for an instant, enjoyed each other's company. Hubie's father, Hubert, was

offended that he was not consulted in any of the arrangements, although he would have arrived at the same decisions arrived at by the
Van Degan family. He did, however, in a show of assertion, let it be
known that he intended to have his wife, Belinda, by his side in the
family pew.

Lil Altemus, in the front row next to Justine, looked up at the rose
window that Alice Grenville had given the church in memory of her
son, and fanned herself with a letter she took from her bag. In the
extreme summer heat the black linen dresses and black straw hats
that she, Justine, Dodo, Janet, and other female members of the
family wore looked wilted, and perspiration scents could be detected
through deodorants, bath oils, powder, and perfume. "Wouldn't you
think they'd air-condition this church?"

"Yes, Mother," said Justine.

"The peonies are lovely," said Lil.

"Yes, Mother," said Justine.

"There's no one like Lorenza for flowers," said Lil.

"Yes, Mother," said Justine. She didn't tell her mother the idea for
the white peonies had been hers.

"Wouldn't you know Belinda would wear white instead of black?"
asked Lil.

"I think she looks very nice," said Justine.

"Make sure you ask Boy Fessenden back to the house afterward,"
said Lil.

"Yes, Mother," said Justine.

"And Gus Bailey. Didn't I see Gus Bailey? Sweet of Gus to come."

Juanito Perez walked up the center aisle to the front of the church
where the small congregation of mourners were gathered in the front
ten rows. He looked on both sides to see where to sit. Juanito nodded
to Lil Altemus who took no notice of him, nor did Hubert Altemus,
seated behind Lil and Justine with Belinda, when Juanito nodded to
him. Juanito was not one for going unnoticed and genuflected, in the
Catholic manner, and crossed himself in the abbreviated fashion of a
former altar boy, a point of his forefinger to his brow, his chest, his
left shoulder, and then his right. "Name of the Father, Son, Holy
Ghost," he could be heard whispering. Lourdes Perez, Lil Altemus's
ladies' maid and sometime confidante, had never until that moment
laid eyes on the lover of Hubie Altemus, and was aghast to realize he
was the runaway son of her brother, Duarte, in Puerto Rico. Lourdes

dropped her eyes and concentrated on her rosary, although she was in an Episcopal church.

"Who is that man with the diamond in his ear?" asked Lil.

"That's Juanito, Mother," answered Justine.

"What's he doing here? Who asked him?"

"You don't have to be invited to a funeral, Mother. A church is a public place. And he has as much right to be here as we have."

Dodo Fitz Alyn Van Degan, who could be counted on to annoy everyone in the family, waved a little wave at Juanito and signaled him to sit next to her, while Laurance and young Laurance and their wives looked straight ahead as if they were unaware of his presence.

Behind them all, Ezzie Fenwick, who never missed a funeral, and enjoyed social drama above all else, nudged Matilda Clarke and Cora Mandell not to miss the family snub of Juanito Perez.

"I do not want that man back at my house afterward, Justine," said Lil, measuring her words.

"I'm not going to tell him that, Mother," answered Justine.

"Tell Uncle Laurance to handle it," said Lil. "One thing, we'll never have to hear from him again."

"That's what you think, Mother," said Justine.

"What do you mean by that?" asked Lil. The minister, the Reverend Doctor Harcourt, Adele Harcourt's nephew, came out onto the altar.

"Hubie left everything to Juanito, Mother," said Justine, quietly, picking up the book of psalms in front of her in the pew.

"What?" said Lil, in a voice loud enough that all the Van Degans heard her. Then she lowered her voice to a whisper. "You must be mad. Hubie wouldn't have done anything like that."

"Will you please rise?" asked Reverend Harcourt.

Justine lifted up the book of psalms and did not reply to her mother.

"The Lord is my shepherd," said Reverend Harcourt, and the small congregation read along with him. Lil Altemus acted out giving her full attention to the service, but she was only half listening.

"DID YOU know Hubie Altemus?" Ezzie Fenwick asked Babs Mallett at Baba Timson's party.

"Yes," said Babs. "They lived near us in the country growing up."

"He died, you know."

"Yes, I know. Poor Hubie. Sort of a lost soul, didn't you think?"

"He didn't leave a thing to his family. Not even a memento."

"Oh, dear."

"All that furniture, all those pictures, and the silver were all Van Degan things his mother gave him. They say Lil is furious, all that family furniture going to that friend of his, Juanito *quelquechose*. Wears an earring."

"Oh, dear."

"Now, this is what I call a perfect *crème brûlée*."

"I DON'T understand how Herkie Saybrook could have allowed this to happen," said Lil.

"Allowed what to happen, Mother?" asked Justine, who knew perfectly well what her mother was talking about.

"You know perfectly well what I'm talking about," snapped Lil. "Those Charles the Tenth chairs came from the Altemus side via Aunt Minnie Willoughby. Imagine that ghastly Juanito having them."

Justine had heard the conversation over and over again since the reading of the will in Uncle Laurance's office. She had pretended not to hear when Uncle Laurance called Juanito "your brother's catamite."

"I've known Herkie Saybrook all his life," Lil continued, with or without a reply from Justine. "His mother and I came out the same year. He should have told us that Hubie was going to leave everything to Juanito whateverhisnameis, and we could have done something about it."

"It's what's called client privilege, I believe. Hubie hired Herkie. Hubie paid Herkie."

"But Herkie Saybrook is one of us," said Lil.

"So was Hubie, Mother," replied Justine.

Lil turned away from her daughter.

"I'll never speak to Herkie again," she said, after a moment. "I think Uncle Laurance should talk to him about this will. I also think Uncle Laurance should have him put out of the Butterfield. I never liked him anyway. Arrogant."

"You wouldn't have minded if I'd married him at one time, I seem to remember," said Justine.

"Let's not get into whom you should and should not have married, if you please. I can only concentrate on one thing at a time."

"What are you concentrating on now, Mother?"

"I'm concentrating on that horrible man with the earring performing unspeakable acts in Grandmother Van Degan's bed from the house in Newport."

38

THE RENTHALS took a cream-colored villa in Monte Carlo and chartered a yacht. They sailed to parties in St. Jean Cap Ferrat, and Beaulieu, and Villefranche, and Antibes. The kind of people they met had not heard of the impending investigation, or, if they had heard, didn't care, so pleasure-bent were they. Americans always took those things more seriously than they did. It was for the Renthals a period of calm before the storm.

At first Elias claimed to not take seriously the investigation by the Securities and Exchange Commission. He thought he was being persecuted by a self-righteous district attorney with political ambitions, hoping to bring him down simply because he was so rich. "I'm smarter than most of the people trading today," he said, "and all those SEC people can't stand that."

When Ruby read in the *Wall Street Journal* that Elias had been implicated by a young lawyer from Weldon & Stinchfield called Byron Macumber, she remembered the night of her ball when Gus Bailey had asked to meet with her the next day. "Give me a hint, Gus, quick. You've got me curious," she had said to him when the Albanian Prince had cut in on her. "Byron Macumber," Gus had replied. She knew now that Gus was trying to warn her. She also remembered that Byron Macumber had called once at the apartment when she was dressing for a party and Elias had acted strange when she told him, as if he didn't know who Byron Macumber was, when all the time they had been in cahoots.

Elias thought of himself as a member of the establishment. He pointed out his membership in the Butterfield. He pointed out his friendships with people like Laurance Van Degan. "People like that, you see, are not about to allow anything to happen to me," he explained to Ruby, pointing out that members of the establishment stood together. He pointed out the innumerable acts of charity he had performed in the past few years, all carefully recorded in the pages of the newspapers. "Maybe we should get that guy Bus Bailey to do another article on us, talking about all our charity work," he said, making a mental note to check on whether or not Max had stopped payment on the check to Faye Converse for AIDS.

"Gus," said Ruby.

"What?"

"It's Gus Bailey, not Bus Bailey," she said, quietly.

"Whatever. We could fly him over here in the plane."

"I don't think that's a good idea," said Ruby.

"Why not?"

"I don't think Gus Bailey's the kind of guy who's going to do a puff piece on us at this moment in time," she answered.

"What makes you say that?"

"Did you read this piece he wrote on Jorgie Sanchez-Julia?" She held up a magazine with a photograph of Jorgie Sanchez-Julia dancing with the clubfooted Geraldine.

"Jorgie Sanchez-Julia was a fucking gigolo who stole an old lady's money, for Christ's sake," said Elias, as if Ruby's reasoning was flawed.

Ruby stared at Elias, without answering, but the words, "You're a fucking thief who stole a lot more money, for Christ's sake," were in her thoughts.

Elias looked away, as if he could read her thoughts. "I'm going to call Laurance Van Degan right now to let him know I'll be at the Paris apartment all next week. We'll get this all figured out."

Miss Wentworth said that Mr. Van Degan was in a meeting and not available. When Elias called an hour later, Mr. Van Degan was still in a meeting and still not available, Miss Wentworth said. Elias left his Paris telephone number with Miss Wentworth for Laurance to call him there. Mr. Van Degan was out of the office when Elias called from Paris the next day. No, he could not be reached at home either. Mr. Van Degan was at the Van Degans' fishing camp in the Adirondacks. No, there was no telephone there, Miss Wentworth said.

RUBY, WHO had grown quiet and withdrawn, went where Elias planned for them to go, but she no longer arranged their social life with the passion she once had, as her passion for it had diminished, and her participation in it was obligatory rather than exuberant. Within her, she felt shame about the things that were being said about her husband, but, since Loelia, she no longer had anyone to

talk to or to confide in. It was now Elias who insisted on going every-
place, saying that it was important for them to be seen. Ruby was
content to follow Elias rather than lead him. Her sense of social
reluctance was favorably interpreted, especially by the grand ladies
she met who thought she was impeccably mannered.

At the hairdressing salon in the Hotel de Paris in Monte Carlo,
Ruby ran into Loelia Manchester. It was their first encounter since
the night of the ball. They exchanged greetings, like old friends who
had lost contact, but Ruby did not ask Loelia about Mickie, and
Loelia did not ask Ruby about Elias.

"Are you all right?" asked Ruby.

"Oh, yes, I'm fine," answered Loelia, smiling, but the smile covered a sadness. "And you?"

Ruby shrugged. "Fine, too, I suppose," she answered.

The two friends looked at each other, longing to talk as they used to
talk, to tell each other everything, but neither could make the suitable opening for such a conversation, at least in the hairdressing
salon of the Hotel de Paris in Monte Carlo.

"We went to this marvelous place in Germany," said Loelia, retreating into social conversation, and not mentioning Mickie by
name. "We had these wonderful shots. Live cells from unborn sheep.
So marvelous. Halts the aging process, you know. Goes right to all
the vital places, heart, liver, kidneys. Not that you would have to
begin thinking of things like that at your age, Ruby."

Ruby watched her old friend and noticed how rapidly she was
talking. She noticed that Loelia was wearing an excessive amount of
makeup so early in the day. To an observer, who did not know either
of them, it might appear that Ruby, in her expensive simplicity, was
the more refined of the two elegant ladies. Then, surprising both
herself and Loelia, Ruby placed her hand on Loelia's chin and lifted
it, turning her head to the left a bit. In the same way that poor dead
Hubie Altemus had once applied makeup to his face at his sister's
wedding to cover the blemish of his first lesion, Ruby saw that Loelia
Manchester had applied makeup to cover a black eye.

"I walked into a door at the Hotel du Cap," said Loelia, although,
even beneath her excessive base, a flush could be seen in her face.

"Will I see you at the collections?" asked Loelia. She meant in
Paris, at the *couture* showings, where the skirts were going higher and
higher and higher.

"No," answered Ruby, shaking her head. Her passion for high fashion, like her passion for social life, had diminished. She knew she would have no place to wear the short, short skirts that had become all the rage, even though she had the right kind of legs to wear them, because she understood she would no longer be invited when they returned to New York.

When they parted, with regret, for they missed each other, they made no plans to meet again.

"I SOLD the plane," Ruby heard Elias say to Max Luby on board their chartered yacht, as they sailed to Antibes to lunch at a fashionable house. Max Luby came to visit them regularly. "No point in having anything they can seize. Whatever flies, floats, or fucks, rent, is my new policy."

"How do I fit into that, Elias?" Ruby asked from her lounge chair on the deck, putting aside the book she had been reading. "Does that mean I'm rented?"

Elias blushed. "Just a figure of speech, Ruby," he said. "I meant the plane. I meant the boat. I didn't mean you."

Ruby lifted her hand. She was wearing the enormous diamond that Elias had given her at the time of their rise, the same diamond that Ezzie Fenwick had remarked upon at Justine Altemus's wedding reception, "If that rock is fake, it's silly. If it's real, it's ridiculous." With her thumb, she flicked the ring off her finger, and the huge flawless diamond fell into the Mediterranean Sea.

"Ruby, for Christ's sake!" yelled Elias, jumping up and looking over the rail to the sea. "Do you know how much that's worth?"

"Six million, two," she answered quietly.

Elias, red-faced and infuriated, grabbed Ruby by the arm and pulled her up from her chair and stared at her with the kind of withering look that in times past brought tears to the eyes of employees who worked for him. Unflinching, Ruby held his gaze for what seemed an interminable time, at least to Max Luby, who witnessed it.

"If you are thinking of hitting me, Elias, don't," said Ruby, in a tone of voice that he had never heard from her before.

Elias dropped her arm.

"Seven years ago, when I was still a stewardess, a guy in L.A. beat

me up. I said then, and I meant it, that if a man ever laid a hand on
me again, ever, I'd kill him."

"Jesuschrist, Ruby, I would never hit you," said Elias, collapsing
into a deck chair. "This whole thing is getting to me. I'm not myself. I
mean, I'm under such a terrible strain."

He put his head into his hands. Max Luby coughed.

"Get lost, Max," Elias said, and Max Luby, who understood Elias,
and had grown to love Ruby, gladly abandoned them to the conversation that both had avoided since their flight from New York. "What's
with you lately, Ruby?" asked Elias.

"You don't know?"

"You're not going to be broke, if that's what's worrying you."

"How like you to interpret my distress for my marriage, my husband, and our lives as bucks, Elias."

"What then?"

"I feel like you cheated on me with another woman."

"I never have. I swear to God."

"It's the same kind of betrayal. The mistake I made was thinking
you were brilliant, but you're just like a kid who cheated in school."

Elias flushed. Nothing Ruby said could have hurt him more. "I am
brilliant. There's no one who understands how to make money like
I do."

"You can tell that to the judge, Elias."

"Oh, Ruby, don't say that," said Elias, reaching for her hand.

She let him take her hand but did not return his squeeze.

"I'm not being a bitch, Elias," said Ruby. "I feel left out. You
treated me like a mistress, not a wife. Buy her a new fur. Buy her a
new jewel. If only you'd told me what was going on."

"And if you'd known?"

"I would have stopped you," she said. "It's as simple as that."

They looked at each other.

"Max explained it all to me," she said. "Something you haven't
bothered to do, about the Swiss bank in Nassau, and the fake name
on your account, my name, by the way, and paying off all those young
cheats feeding you information, like Mr. Byron Macumber, and I
could only think, why? What more did we need that we didn't already
have? We'd run out of new things to buy, and we still had more money
than anyone else, so for a lousy few more million bucks, we end up in
disgrace."

"Who said we're in disgrace?"

"Oh, Elias, please," she said. "Let us face up to the reality of our situation. So we're sailing on a yacht to Lady Montagu's lunch at her villa in Antibes, but, back there, in New York City, they're going to come after you and probably put you in handcuffs, just the way they put Byron Macumber in handcuffs."

"No way," said Elias. "Laurance Van Degan wouldn't allow that to happen."

"Laurance Van Degan doesn't even answer your phone calls anymore, Elias."

"He's in the Adirondacks, and there's no telephone at the fishing camp."

"I don't believe that somehow," said Ruby.

"He's my friend."

"Do you really think Laurance and Janet are still going to ask us to sit in their box on the opening night of the opera?"

"Of course," said Elias, expansively. "Laurance is a businessman. He understands. How the hell do you think old Ormonde's grandfather started the Van Degan fortune in the first place?"

"Not this way, I'm sure," replied Ruby.

He knew Ruby was right. He had not told her that Laurance Van Degan had been quoted in the financial section of the *Times* as saying, "I feel that Elias Renthal is insensitive to his fiduciary responsibilities to his policy holders." But he felt that she knew all those things.

"What do you want to do, Ruby?" Elias asked, wearily.

"I want to go back home. Whatever's going to happen, I want to let happen. Surely you've sold everything there was to sell by now."

"I thought you liked this kind of life. Lunch with the princesses. Dinner with the duchesses."

"Not anymore," said Ruby. "Not anymore."

THAT NIGHT, back at the rented cream-colored villa in Monte Carlo, Elias said to Ruby, "You never told me a guy beat you up in L.A."

"It's something I don't talk about."

"What did he do to you?"

"He knocked out a couple of teeth. He blacked my eyes. He fractured my jaw. He threw me down the stairs," she said, quietly, reciting her injuries like a litany.

"Jesuschrist."

She nodded.

"Did they catch the guy?"

"Not then."

"What happened to him?"

"He killed Gus Bailey's daughter."

39

SINCE his separation from Justine Altemus, Bernard Slatkin had made no attempt to keep in touch with any of the people he had met during the period of his marriage, which was one more indication to the Van Degan family that he had not tried to use them in any way, although it was rather a disappointment to Lil, who would have liked nothing more than to have labeled Bernie as an opportunist who had badly used her child for self-advancement.

One night on Park Avenue, late, after visiting his former apartment to remove the rest of his clothes, Bernie ran into Gus Bailey, dressed in black tie, who was walking home from another New York dinner party. The two men greeted each other warmly.

"I was sorry to hear about your divorce," said Gus.

Bernie shrugged. "These things happen," he said.

"I know," said Gus. "I wasn't a great success in the husband department either."

Bernie nodded.

"Going away?" asked Gus, indicating the luggage that Bernie had put on the sidewalk.

"No. Just picking up the rest of my clothes and junk that I left behind. Justine has put the apartment up for sale and wanted me to get everything out."

"Where's Justine moving to?"

"Back to her old apartment in her mother's building. She's really a Fifth Avenue girl, you know, cabbage-rose chintz, that sort of thing."

"Oh, Bernie," said Gus, reprovingly. "That's really not fair, is it?"

"No, you're right. It's not fair," said Bernie, kicking one of the pieces of luggage. "I'm just feeling ornery, or maybe guilty. Justine didn't even ask me to stay for a drink just now. I told her the station was sending a car for me to move the stuff, and she asked me to wait down in the lobby."

"She's hurt," said Gus.

"I know," said Bernie quietly. "Justine's a wonderful girl. Justine tried to make it work. It was my fault, not hers. I'm a slut, as you've probably heard. It seems to me half of New York has heard, thanks to my ex-mother-in-law."

Gus had heard. "I'm surprised I haven't been reading about you in Mavis Jones's column, taking actresses to opening nights."

"I've gone into the low-profile business," said Bernie, touching Gus's black tie. "Who's party are you coming from?" he asked.

"Let me see," answered Gus, figuring out the relationship. "Your ex-step-grandmother-in-law's."

"Oh, Dodo," said Bernie. "I always liked Dodo. Lil and Laurance treated her like she was a maid in that family, and then she fooled the two of them by marrying their father. Did you know she used to jerk old Ormonde off after showing him dirty videos that Hubie's boyfriend got for her?"

The two men roared with laughter. "Of course, I didn't know that, but it's a bit of information I'll store up here," Gus said, pointing to his head.

"Ezzie Fenwick always tells people that you're going to write a book about the bunch of them."

"Oh, yeah, I've heard he says that about me."

"Is it true?"

"Who knows? If I ever get the time."

"Here's my car," Bernie said. "Hop in. I'll give you a ride home."

"I HEARD you had a nice place," said Bernie, after they had settled in to Gus's apartment. "'Nifty,' somebody called it."

"Who'd you hear that from?" asked Gus, handing Bernie a drink.

"We have a mutual friend," replied Bernie.

"Who?"

"Ms. Myra."

"Ah," said Gus, nodding. "Nice lady."

The two men smiled at each other.

"And knows some nice ladies," answered Bernie. "Perfect for this interim period of my life."

"That's your low profile?"

Bernie nodded. "Ms. Myra told me you had a nifty place."

"On the other hand, Matilda Clarke says it's just the right degree of shabby," replied Gus.

"That's supposed to be a compliment, I guess," said Bernie.

"Absolutely. You're supposed to say thank you."

"I see." They both laughed.

"What a bunch they all are," said Gus.

"What a bunch."

Bernie got up and looked at the books in the bookcases. "Do you read all these books, Gus?"

"Most of them."

"I ran into Juanito Perez recently at a restaurant in the Village," said Bernie, picking up a book. "He's a rich guy now."

"According to Dodo, it kills Lil that Juanito got Hubie's money. She wanted to sue, but Uncle Laurance said the publicity would be terrible for the family."

"Did you go to Hubie's funeral?" asked Bernie.

"Yeah."

"I hear they didn't let Juanito come back to the house."

"True."

"Did you know that Lil brought fifty Seconals to Hubie on the one time she visited him in the hospital?"

"No, I didn't know that," said Gus.

"True. Left them in a bag of books from the Wilton House Book Shop. Juanito told me that. Juanito flushed them down the toilet."

"Jesus," said Gus. "Lil and Laurance still pretend Hubie didn't die of AIDS, and they expect you to believe them."

"The Van Degans are a tough bunch," said Bernie.

"They're all tough, those people," replied Gus.

"The Bradleys' cook jumped out a window on the day of my wedding, right around the corner from the Colony Club, and the Bradleys still came to the reception. Yvonne Lupescu shot Constantine de Rham in the stomach that day and crashed my wedding reception and caught Justine's bouquet." Bernie made a gesture that indicated madness.

"A workman fell out of a cherry picker raising a weeping willow tree up to the Renthals' apartment on the day of their ball, and the ball went on like nothing happened, after Elias paid off the workman's family," said Gus, carrying on Bernie's theme. "Ormonde Van Degan died at the ball, and they stashed his body on a pool table so as not to spoil the First Lady's entrance."

"There's a strong indifference to death around that group," said Bernie.

"There's a strong indifference to death everywhere, Bernie," said Gus.

"What's your story, Gus? There's more to you than this quiet guy whom everybody talks to. Some people say there's a mystery about you."

"There's no mystery about me, Bernie. It's just that no one ever asks me about me, and I don't volunteer."

"I'm asking you now."

"A creep came along and killed my daughter."

"I didn't know that."

"I don't go around broadcasting it, but it's why I moved here. To sit out the three years of the creep's sentence."

"And then what are you going to do?"

"I'm going to go back to where I came from."

"And do what?"

"I'm going to kill the guy who killed my daughter."

"Come on."

"I am."

Bernie looked at Gus, and Gus met his stare.

"I'm going to make me another one of these," said Bernie, holding up his whiskey glass.

"I'm going to call out his name. I'm going to say, 'Hey, Lefty,'" said Gus. "I want him to be looking at me at the moment. I want him to know it was me who did it."

Bernie, in the door of the kitchen, stared at Gus, not knowing whether or not he was being serious. "And then what'll happen?"

"Prison, I suppose."

"Prison?"

"Maybe that's when I'll have the time to write that book Ezzie Fenwick tells people I'm going to write," said Gus.

Bernie walked over to where Gus was sitting. "Gus," he said.

"What?"

"You don't really mean any of this, do you?"

Gus looked at Bernie for a minute and then smiled. "No, of course not," he said.

40

POOR HUBIE, people always said about Hubie Altemus, in re-
membrance, but his memory was already fading.

On several occasions Juanito Perez had tried to contact Lil after
Hubie's funeral, once by telephone, on the butler's day off, when
Lourdes had answered the telephone and hissed into the receiver in a
torrent of Spanish that Juanito was not to call back at la Señora Altemus's house *ever*, or she, Lourdes, would tell her brother Duarte in
Puerto Rico that his son was a *puto*. After that, Juanito wrote Lil on
two occasions, but each time his letter to her was returned by Lil's
lawyers, unopened.

"ISN'T IT marvelous the way Lil has handled the whole thing,"
people like Ezzie Fenwick and Matilda Clarke and Cora Mandell said
about Lil Altemus, whenever anyone spoke about Hubie's death.
They were referring to what her close friends called Lil's bravery in
the face of tragedy. However, in the bosom of her family, those closest
to Lil, like her daughter, Justine, her sister-in-law, Janet, her stepmother, Dodo, and her maid, Lourdes, knew that her grief, if grief it
was, had taken on another form, an abiding hatred for Juanito Perez,
whom she blamed for her son's death.

Sometimes in the night Lil would awaken from her sleep and remember family possessions she had given Hubie, that she hadn't
thought about for years, that were now in the possession of Juanito
Perez, and each time she would feel an anger so intense against
Juanito that she began to have heart palpitations. She became obsessed over the set of twelve Charles X chairs from the house in
Newport, that she had never cared for, that Aunt Minnie Willoughby
had given Hubert and her when they were married, and that Lil had
taken out of storage and given Hubie when he set up his own establishment. It mattered to her more than anything in the world that
those twelve chairs be returned to the family, as though honor was at
stake, although Justine didn't want them, and Lil had no room for
them, even if she had cared for them.

Lil had not forgotten, although she had never mentioned it, that her stepmother Dodo had offered Juanito a seat in her pew at Hubie's funeral, nor that Juanito had asked about Dodo when she met him in the hospital at Hubie's bedside, so she asked Dodo to go to handle the task of retrieving the twelve Charles X chairs from the despicable Mr. Perez. Dodo, who had been left independently rich by Ormonde, no longer did the family's bidding, as she had done for years when she was a poor relation, and flatly refused the commission. "I wouldn't *dream* of doing such a thing," Dodo said, in one of her increasing shows of independence.

When her mother asked Justine to undertake the task she refused. Then she added that she would have nothing to do with such an unappealing task even if she were not pregnant. Lourdes, Lil's maid who listened to everything that went on in the family, had never told Mrs. Altemus that Juanito Perez was the son of her brother Duarte in Puerto Rico. She was glad she had not confessed to the relationship, as she knew that she would have been assigned the unpleasant task of getting back the chairs.

It was Ezzie Fenwick, whom Lil had taken into her confidence, over lunch at Clarence's, who suggested that the perfect person to arrange for the return of the chairs was Jamesey Crocus. As everyone knew, Jamesey Crocus was thought to know more about fine furniture than any man in New York and had lately served as private curator to Elias and Ruby Renthal during their period of acquisition. Jamesey, on his part, liked nothing better than to be sent on furniture forays for families like the Van Degans and the Altemuses, which always resulted in increased intimacies with the grand families and invitations to even their small dinner parties.

JAMESEY CROCUS, getting out of the cab in SoHo, looked in each direction before entering Juanito Perez's building, in the manner he often adopted late at night when, after he had returned a fashionable dowager to her uptown address, he entered a low haunt in a different part of town that he did not wish to be spotted going into, for fear of lascivious stories being circulated about him. Buzzed in by an intercom, he walked up three flights of stairs after a sign on the self-service elevator informed him it was out of commission. Juanito was standing in the open door of the loft that had once belonged to Hubie

Altemus. Instantly, Jamesey, who had known Juanito before Hubie knew him, was struck by the change in his appearance. Although he was dressed casually, he was wearing a tweed jacket of excellent cut that Jamesey recognized as having been one of Hubie Altemus's and a blue shirt with a button-down collar open at the neck, in the manner that Hubie had always dressed. Jamesey looked at Juanito the way he had once looked at Ruby Renthal's console tables. Having money had eliminated from Juanito's face an expression that suggested furtiveness of character, a consequence of his extreme underprivilege, and replaced it with a look that brought out his good qualities. Only a cigarette hanging insolently from the corner of his mouth made him resemble the Juanito he had once known. For an instant they stared at each other.

"Very bad for you, smoking," said Jamesey, as a greeting.

"Don't see her for two years, and the first thing she says is, 'Very bad for you, smoking,'" replied Juanito, as if he were repeating this story to an audience. "Come in, Janie."

More than anything in the world, Jamesey Crocus, who moved in the finest circles, hated to be called Janie, but he said nothing. Inside, he looked around. The loft was, like Hubie, a combination of a life he left behind, but not completely, and a life he aspired to, but into which he never quite fit. A fire, going low, took the chill off the large room.

"How charming this is, Juanito," said Jamesey.

"I've kept everything just the same way Hubie had it," said Juanito.

"Oh, yes, of course," said Jamesey, who took this statement with a grain of salt. He had known Juanito to be promiscuous and notoriously unfaithful and doubted the sincerity of his maintenance of Hubie's home as a shrine. Jamesey expected Juanito to offer him a drink, so that time could be spent in friendly conversation before getting down to the purpose of the visit.

But Juanito did not offer him a drink. "To what do I owe the pleasure of this visit, Janie?" he asked.

"Mrs. Altemus, Lil, asked me if I would talk to you about some chairs that were left to you, a set of Charles the Tenth chairs," said Jamesey.

Juanito had not forgotten that his letters to Lil Altemus had been returned by her lawyers, unopened, a snub that still riled him.

"Those, you mean?" he asked, pointing over to the dining-room area. Around the table were eight of the chairs. Two more were in a group of furniture by the fireplace. One was at a desk. The twelfth was by a telephone table.

Jamesey peered ecstatically through his owlish spectacles at the magnificent chairs. Clasping his hands before his stomach, he breathed heavily in the manner that he always breathed when he looked upon a rare and beautiful object. "Oh, my dear, how perfectly gorgeous," he whispered, breaking his own rule never to allow a possible seller to think that his wares were too valuable. "Charles the Tenth," he said, in his instructor's voice, as if he were giving a lecture on furniture at the museum, "was the younger brother of Louis the Sixteenth, who, as you know, was beheaded during the Revolution. During his reign—"

"Whatever it is you're up to, Janie, it's not in my favor. That much I know," said Juanito, interrupting a history lesson in which he had no interest.

"Don't call me Janie," said Jamesey, through clenched teeth.

"Too familiar? Is that it? Am I overstepping? Excuse me, Miss Crocus. Is that better?"

Jamesey decided to let it pass. The possibility of an association with the Altemus–Van Degan clans was too attractive for him to risk spoiling it by becoming irritated with a man he still considered to be no more than a hustler. "You see, Juanito," he said, in a friendly tone, "the chairs belonged to Aunt Minnie Willoughby, and she gave them to Lil, and Lil gave them to Hubie, but Aunt Minnie always wanted them to stay in the family, as heirlooms."

"Aunt Minnie Willoughby," said Juanito, in an exaggerated pose of pensiveness. "Wasn't she the dyke?"

"Oh, no, no, that was Aunt Grace Gardiner," said Jamesey.

"I never could get Hubie's family straight."

Jamesey, who understood the genealogy of all the best families in New York, said, "Aunt Minnie Willoughby was on the Altemus side, and Aunt Grace Gardiner, who indeed was a dyke, now that I come to think of it, was on the Van Degan side."

"I really don't give a shit," said Juanito. "Now, what are you here for?"

"Mrs. Altemus wondered—"

"You can call her Lil," said Juanito.

"Lil, of course. Lil wondered if you would give the chairs back to the family."

"Have you told Lil that you're the one who introduced me to Hubie?"

Jamesey paused. "No, no, I haven't."

"I wonder if she'd still send you as her emissary if she was aware of that fact."

"I'm sure that if money was the issue, Mrs. Altemus would buy the chairs back from you," said Jamesey, evading the turn the conversation was taking.

"You forget, Janie. I got more money than I could ever spend."

"It's quite chilly in here," said Jamesey.

"Hard to heat these big lofts in these old buildings. That's why I keep a fire going. Let me build up the fire," he said. Juanito walked over to the fireplace. "Remember the time you paid me by check, and it bounced?"

"I made that check good," said Jamesey, indignantly.

"Only after I threatened to black your eye on your way to Adele Harcourt's book club," said Juanito. "Shit, I'm all out of firewood." He picked up one of the Charles X chairs, turned it over, and broke off one of the legs.

"Juanito!" screamed Jamesey, as Juanito fed the chair leg into the fire and then broke off another leg.

"What's the matter? There's eleven left," he said.

"Those chairs are priceless. Were priceless, I mean."

"Now you tell Lil for me, when you report that you failed in your mission, that if she had bothered to speak civilly to me in the hospital when Hubie was dying, or if she had offered me a seat in the church at Hubie's funeral, or if she'd asked me back to the house after the funeral with all the other mourners, or if her fucking lawyers hadn't returned my letters to her unopened, in which I offered to return these family heirlooms which I inherited, I would have given them back to her, but now I won't. Get lost, Jamesey, and stay lost."

41

AT THE END of summer, the Elias Renthals returned to New York. Ever since details of Elias's corrupt stock-trading practices were revealed to his stunned colleagues in the financial world, as well as to the public at large, Renthal, a man once celebrated for his financial acumen, was now reviled by many as a symbol of Wall Street greed. Those who had not been invited to the Renthals' ball now let it be known that they had declined the invitation, as if they had advance knowledge of the financier's dubious behavior and chose, for ethical reasons, to absent themselves from what was now referred to as a vulgar spectacle. No one had a word to say in Elias Renthal's favor, or a doubt of his guilt.

At the museum there was a collective sigh of relief that the board of directors had stuck to its guns and not made Elias a member, even after his pledge of many millions of dollars for the construction of a new wing, and persuasive arguments on his behalf by some of its most conservative members like Laurance Van Degan and Addison Cheney. At the time an alternate proposal had been forwarded, before the financial scandal, of course, that Ruby Renthal join the board instead of Elias, as her elegance was thought to be more acceptable to the membership than the still-rough-around-the-edges Elias. That plan, too, had now been dropped.

TO SEE Elias Renthal, however, in the weeks following his return, was not to see a crushed man. His business routines were followed the same as before, and, as was his practice, he continued to arrive at his office as early as six o'clock in the morning. He pored over financial publications, annual reports, and trade digests as avidly as ever, looking for investment ideas for his analysts to check out for him. His manner, which could be abrasive with subordinates who were not as quick as he in understanding market practices, remained as abrasive as ever. All of this was carried on with a sort of nonchalant attitude that belied the fact that investigators from the Securities and Exchange Commission were packing his files in cartons at the same time.

Nor was there any lessening of attentiveness in his manner of dress. He continued to order his suits, twenty at a time, from Mr. Sills, and his shirts and shoes from his shirtmaker and shoemaker in London, as if to show that all was right with his world, although there were those who wondered if he would not be in prison, in Allenwood, where his kind of felons were sent, by the time his suits and shirts and shoes, all of which took time, would be delivered to him.

It was not until after the taping incident, on a legally wired pay telephone in the office of the United States Attorney, that anyone made the connection between Byron Macumber's suicide the previous month and Elias Renthal. While Elias was still sailing the Mediterranean, an arrangement had been made between his lawyers and the office of the Attorney General to cooperate with their ongoing investigation by furnishing them with the names of his confreres in malfeasance.

WHEN ELIAS walked into the Butterfield for the first time after his return from Europe, he did not notice that the usually affable Jasper, at the desk in the front hall where members signed in their guests, did not return his greeting. Walking up the curved marble stairway, which he had planned to copy for the new stairway at Merry Hill, he passed Sims Lord descending at the same time. At the moment of passing, Sims Lord gave no indication that he realized another person was within inches of him on the stairway. In the bar, where nearly every table was occupied with groups of two, three, and four, a pleasant buzz of conversation filled the air as members, recently returned from summer holidays, were happily greeting each other anew and ordering drinks and lunch from the excellent kitchen, which boasted of serving the best food of any club in the city. But, on the entrance of Elias Renthal into the lovely paneled room, a silence rose that was almost audible as each person looked up at the stout man standing in the doorway. There were many in the room whom he knew, from the club, from business, and from society. He had dined with many of them at their houses, both in town and in the country, and many he had entertained himself, some as recently as at his famous ball at the end of the spring season. No one rose to speak to him, and he was aware that he must bear their cold looks and silence without seeming to notice them.

He walked to an empty table, waving with a nonchalant air to Herkie Saybrook and young Laurance Van Degan, who were playing backgammon a few tables away, but neither raised his eyes from their game to return the wave. After sitting for several minutes, he rang the bell on his table for service, although Doddsie, who was usually so prompt in taking orders for drinks, was standing at the bar in quiet conversation with the bartender.

"An old-fashioned, please, Doddsie, easy on the bitters, but ample on the fruit," Elias said in a hearty voice. "And gimme one of your menus at the same time. I suppose you've got the chicken hash today."

"Every day," replied Doddsie. He was not rude. Nor was he friendly. Elias noticed the change in attitude.

"I'll have the chicken hash," he said, ordering, as if he were in a restaurant.

"If you would write it on the pad," said Doddsie. He did not add sir, and the omission was not lost on Elias.

"Oh, yes, yes, of course." He picked up the pad and small pencil and wrote his order, although he could feel the beginning of anger. If he were in a hotel, he thought to himself, and treated in this manner, he would buy the hotel, and fire Doddsie, and, now that he thought of it, fire Jasper at the entrance desk downstairs as well. With Sims Lord, he could understand. They had had a business difference, although Sims Lord's version of the hostile takeover of his company by Elias Renthal was described by him in stronger terms than a business difference. He looked over at Herkie Saybrook and young Laurance Van Degan, still intent on their game of backgammon, and wondered if they had seen him or not.

He rose, old-fashioned glass in hand, and walked over to their table. When neither looked up, he stood next to young Laurance's side and watched the game for a bit.

"Hello, Laurance. Hello, Herkie," he said, when the game ended and Herkie was tallying the score.

"Mr. Renthal," Herkie and young Laurance said simultaneously.

"Mr. Renthal, indeed," said Elias, in an expansive manner, as if the young men were being formal with a respected elder. "You haven't forgotten, have you? It's Elias."

"We haven't forgotten, Mr. Renthal," said young Laurance. So saying, he banged on the bell on his table and called out, "Doddsie, I wonder if you could bring me the book with the rules of the club." While waiting, he continued to shake and roll his dice. When Doddsie arrived with the rule book, bound in blue, with green lettering, young Laurance said, in a voice heard throughout the room, "Will you look up and show me the page where it says that the Butterfield accepts members who wire themselves and entrap unsuspecting cohorts in order to lessen their prison sentences?"

Elias flushed scarlet.

Then young Laurance and Herkie rose and walked to the door leading to the dining room. "Are you ready for us, Doddsie?" Herkie asked.

"Indeed we are, Mr. Saybrook. Mr. Van Degan," answered Doddsie, back to his usual form. "There by the window."

Elias looked around the room and saw that the other members were staring over at the snub he had just received. When he caught their eye, they, in turn, held his for a moment and then looked away, except for Collier Stinchfield, of Weldon & Stinchfield, the old and respected law firm where Byron Macumber had been a junior partner. "Either that man leaves this club immediately, or I leave, and, if I leave, I will leave permanently," said Collier Stinchfield, his high aristocratic voice filling the room.

Elias placed his old-fashioned glass on the table where Herkie and young Laurance had been playing backgammon and walked toward the door where he had come in. By the entrance, he reached into a silver bowl and took out a handful of the Butterfield match books and stuffed them in his pocket. Walking down the marble stairway, he passed Laurance Van Degan coming up to have lunch with his son and Herkie Saybrook. Each met the other's eye, but neither spoke. In the downstairs hallway, Jasper did not look up as Elias Renthal walked by his desk and pretended not to hear the loud fart emitted by Elias at the front door as he walked out onto Fifth Avenue.

Instead of going back to his office, he decided to walk up Fifth Avenue to his apartment, have lunch there, and rest for an hour or so. On the marble-top table in the front hall, where the butler left the mail, he noticed an envelope from the Butterfield. Opening it, he saw that it was a letter from Laurance Van Degan, the president of the

Butterfield, signed and dated two days before, requesting his resignation.

He needed Ruby. He needed to talk to her. He was tired of keeping up the front he had been keeping up for the last several months. He was hurt. He was ashamed. He needed solace. He went up the stairs. The door of her bedroom was closed. He tapped on it. It was his lovemaking tap, a light drumming of the fingertips against the panel of the door.

"No," replied Ruby from inside, recognizing the signal. "Leave me alone, Elias."

RENTHAL SINGS! said the headline in one tabloid paper. ELIAS (DON'T-CALL-ME-ELI) RENTHAL PLEADS GUILTY TO ONE COUNT! said another. Variations on this theme were echoed in every newspaper and magazine in the land.

"I always said, but no one ever listens to me," said Lil Altemus, dining at Clarence's in a family group, "that people like that are to be avoided at all costs."

"Oh, shut up, Lil," said Laurance Van Degan, who had himself been the recipient of numerous advance stock tips from Elias Renthal and lived in fear that his name would be brought into the investigation.

"Laurance!" said Lil, hurt, looking to her sister-in-law Janet for solace.

"We've all got trashy friends," said Janet, mediating between brother and sister, "but we should choose our trashy friends with more care."

"Oh, Ruby's not trashy," said Cora Mandell, quietly.

RUBY MADE no attempt to contact any of her friends. She remained mostly in her room reading or talking with her maid, Candelaria. She gave up Bobo as her hairdresser, not wanting to be the subject of gossip that Bobo could pass on to his other clients who knew her, and found another hairdresser, as yet undiscovered by the fashionable world, who came to her apartment. Lorenza no longer came to do the flowers two days a week, because there were no more guests and the doors to most of the rooms in the large apartment remained closed. At night Ruby went downstairs to dine with Elias, but she no longer shared a bedroom with him.

"It's Mr. Renthal's snoring," Ruby said to Candelaria in explanation of Elias's move to another bedroom. "I can't sleep with his snoring." But Candelaria understood what was happening.

One evening, early still, she crossed over to the park side of Fifth Avenue and sat on the bench opposite her own apartment, where each night she watched a bag lady make her home. She looked up at her own home and could see the soft pink light cast by the lamps on her persimmon damask curtains and walls. Above, the leaves of the trees on her terrace blew in the twilight wind. She thought of herself in the days of her grandeur, when the whole city, or at least that part of the city that interested her, came out to dance in her ballroom. It was several minutes before she realized that she had begun to think in the past tense.

"*Señora?*"

Ruby looked. Standing there was Candelaria.

Ruby had always wanted Candelaria to call her madam, the way Loelia Manchester's maid called her madam, instead of *señora*, but she had never had the nerve to tell that to Candelaria. Now she was glad she never had, for what did it matter? What did any of it matter now?

"Yes, Candelaria?" she said.

"*Hace mucho frío, señora,*" said Candelaria.

"You know I can't understand you when you don't speak English," said Ruby, who had learned to speak French but not Spanish.

"It's getting cold, *señora*. I brought you a shawl."

"You are sweet, Candelaria. Sit down."

"No, no, *gracias.*"

"There's a woman who always sleeps here on this bench. I see her every night."

"*Sí.*"

"You know which one I mean?"

"*Sí.*"

"Later, when it's dark, I want you to bring her this," she said. She opened her bag and took out some money.

"Too much, *señora*," said Candelaria, looking at the two twenty-dollar bills Ruby handed her.

"No, it's not. Imagine what she must think looking up every night at where we live."

A jogger returning home from his run in the park walked rapidly by them. His face was pink from exercise, his hair wet, and his track clothes dripping. Had not Candelaria risen to leave at that same moment and collided with him, he might have gone on his way, not noticing Ruby Renthal, nor Ruby Renthal noticing him.

"I am sorry, *señor*," said Candelaria.

"No, no, it's my fault," he said, although it wasn't.

"Are you all right, Candelaria?" asked Ruby.

"*Si, si, señora.* Okay."

"Why, Mrs. Renthal, hello. We met at the Butterfield, on ladies' night. I'm Ned Manchester."

"Hello," said Ruby. "Of course. How are you?"

"Pardon my sweaty appearance."

"You look very fit and healthy to me."

"Do you often sit out here?"

"No. Never. I just had an urge to sit here and look up at my own house."

"Does it meet with your approval?"

"Too big, I've decided."

"Even the Clarkes used to get lost in that apartment, and they had the two boys," said Ned.

"I always wanted to have a child," said Ruby.

"And?"

"I guess it wasn't in the cards, even though I'm the mama type. When you're the third wife, the husbands already have their quota. How are your children?"

"They're well. Bozzie's going away to school. Charlotte says she wants to be an actress," said Ned.

"Oh, that should go over big with Grandmother Somerset," said Ruby, and they both laughed. Their eyes met. Ned liked the sound of Ruby's husky, fashionable voice. "You have a beautiful voice," he said.

"People say I sound like Loelia," Ruby answered. She spoke the name of his wife, for Loelia was still his wife, in a natural way, and he welcomed the openness of it, as everyone else he knew had gone to great lengths in the past year not to mention Loelia's name in front of him.

"You do," he said.

"When I first got to know Loelia, I used to imitate everything about her. Then it became natural. I'm what's called self-created." She laughed at herself and Ned joined in.

"Your looks are your own," he said.

"Had a little help there, too, my friend," she replied. "Oh, good heavens, the time," she said, looking at her watch. "I must go. Elias will be home."

"How is Mr. Renthal?"

"Let's just say he's been better," said Ruby. "We're in trouble. You've probably heard. I guess everyone's probably heard."

Ned nodded. "How have people been?" he asked.

"I don't know. I haven't seen anyone. I haven't called anyone."

"If you ever need anyone to talk to, I come by this way every night," he said.

"Thanks," she answered. She rose, shook hands good-bye, and left.

42

TIME WAS winding down for Gus Bailey. At some point along the way he stopped writing thank-you notes to his hostesses for the dinners he attended. Then he began declining invitations, first to one of Maisie Verdurin's dinners, and then to one at Violet Bastedo's, and then to Lil Altemus's. He had started to say, "I'll be away then," or, "I'm busy that night."

"They won't invite you anymore," said Matilda Clarke.

"I don't care," said Gus.

"Don't care?"

"I've seen enough."

Later, Matilda remembered that.

Bernie Slatkin ran into Gus Bailey at a restaurant in the Village and later told Brenda Primrose that he seemed distracted, as if his mind was on something other than what they were discussing.

Nestor and Edwina Calder came back from Hollywood, after shooting the mini-series of *Judas Was a Redhead*. Edwina and Nestor considered Gus one of their good friends, but, on the several times they called to invite him to dinner, he did not return their calls. People said Gus Bailey was spending more and more time by himself.

One night his telephone rang.

"Mr. Bailey?"

"Who is it?"

"You'll never remember me."

"Try."

"My name is Inez Peretti. We met once at—"

"At Ceil Somerset's. You're Ceil Somerset's psychic. Of course I remember you. Once I was going to call you, but I couldn't find the place card on which I wrote down your telephone number. I must have sent my dinner jacket to the cleaners, and they threw it out."

For a moment there was a silence.

"You're not surprised then to hear from me?" Inez asked.

"I'm not," said Gus.

"I got your number from Ceil."

"Fine."

"I feel like I'm always cautioning you."

"Yes."

"Last time I said you were going somewhere, and you said yes, you were going to Mary Finch's dance for Justine Altemus, and I said you were going somewhere before that, and not to go. Do you remember?"

"Yes."

"Did you go?"

"Yes."

"I feel that you are planning to do something."

"Yes."

"I feel revenge is in your heart."

"Yes."

"I wanted to warn you."

"Thank you, Inez."

43

"DO YOU have any kind of religious affiliation?" asked Henry Caldwell, Elias Renthal's lawyer.

"Why?" replied Elias.

"I thought we might get you registered in some sort of theological school between now and the sentencing. We can get it planted in the papers. All that stuff really goes down with the judges," said Henry.

"Christ, I haven't been to church since God-knows-when, except for a Catholic wake I went to out in Queens a while back with the Sorrowful Mysteries, but that don't count as church. Besides, it wouldn't look good starting up religion now at this late date," said Elias.

"But there has to be something of that nature you can do, Elias. Like good works."

Elias was impressed with the idea. "Good works, right. How about if I work with the homeless? That's the big deal these days. Dish out soup or cut up carrots a couple of hours each day over at St. Bart's? And it's right near the office."

"Terrific," said the lawyer. "Mavis Jones will run that in her column for sure."

DEALS had been arrived at, behind-the-scenes deals. For his cooperation in exposing other miscreants in the financial community with whom he had engaged in exchanging privileged information for personal gain, and paying a fine of $150 million, and divesting himself of his stock portfolio, Elias Renthal had had to plead guilty to only one criminal count, a single charge of stock fraud.

"I realize I've committed a very serious crime," said Elias Renthal, outside the courtroom, when the reporters asked him to make a statement. His lawyer tapped him on the arm to indicate that he had said enough, but Elias Renthal, even in adversity, was not one to be told when he had said enough. "I hope that by accepting responsibility for what I have done, I can make up for the anguish that I have caused my friends, my colleagues, and, most of all, my wife."

Looking at Elias, Ruby was unable to see his eyes. The lights of the television cameras reflected in the convex lenses of his gold-framed glasses and threw back the rays in iridescent circles. Elias had aged perceptibly in recent months. A blankness in his eyes and a permanent furrowing in his brows, and possibly his soul, bespoke shattered dreams and lost illusions.

"Poor Mrs. Renthal," said Bozzie Manchester, watching the evening news with his father. Ned looked over at his son and felt great affection for him, Yes, Ned thought, poor Mrs. Renthal.

IT WAS impossible for any observer not to notice the change in Ruby Renthal's status, but Ruby was, everyone said, a model of rectitude, standing by Elias's side on the several times he had to appear in court before his sentencing, in a silent but supportive stance, dressed simply but expensively, her hair pulled back, her eyes not hidden by dark glasses. She never failed to hold her head up for all to see, assuming an attitude that could not be misconstrued as arrogant, which it was not, nor overly friendly, as if she were courting the press, which she did not.

The press had grown fond of her, and respectful. Even when they called her Ruby, which they did when they wanted to get her attention to pose for pictures or to ask her questions, they called her Ruby with affection, although she never answered any questions, nor ever stopped to pose. On her fingers she wore no more than her gold wedding ring. On her wrist she wore no more than her gold Cartier watch with the roman numerals that had once belonged to the Duchess of Windsor, but no one knew that except Ruby.

"MY CLIENT is virtually penniless," Henry Caldwell had announced to the press over and over in the weeks preceding the sentencing, scoffing at reports that Elias had stashed hundreds of millions of dollars in Swiss bank accounts. Elias stood beside him, with a mournful expression on his face, but everyone knew that Elias Renthal was nowhere near penniless.

For propriety's sake, Elias, his lawyers, and his bodyguards squeezed into a Japanese compact car rather than his usual limousine to arrive at the courthouse on the day of his sentencing, in the hopes of conveying the impression to the reporters and photographers that his circumstances were reduced. They drove downtown in silence, interrupted only by Elias, who shifted his position uncomfortably in the crowded backseat, saying to no one in particular, "I've been in roomier women."

On that morning the newspapers were filled with remarks by business leaders on the about-to-be-sentenced financier. Sims Lord, who had personal reasons for loathing Elias Renthal, said in the *Times*, "It is impossible for me to admire people who rape the system and then get nothing but a slap on the wrist because they have entrapped their fellow partners in crime. I hope the judge throws the book at him."

Elias looked neither left nor right as he walked up the steps to the courthouse, flanked by his lawyers and bodyguards, ignoring the press as they yelled questions at him.

In the courtroom, there was not an empty seat. The sentencing of Elias Renthal was a media event, with press from around the world there to witness the great financier's downfall.

"Please rise," said the court clerk, as Judge Maurice McAuliff entered the courtroom.

Henry Caldwell pleaded that his client deserved leniency because he had exposed wrongdoing in ten major brokerage houses and had already paid a fine of $150 million. "A sentence in this type of case should not involve excessive incarceration," he said.

"It is unthinkable," argued the prosecutor, "that white-collar criminals can walk away by simply paying back what they have stolen in the first place."

Judge McAuliff, who was known to be lenient, listened to the arguments of both sides. "Your crimes, Mr. Renthal, are too serious to forgive and forget. It would be a terrible precedent for me to set in this court. The message must go out loud and clear that breaking the law is breaking the law," he said before passing sentence. "Criminal behavior such as yours cannot go unchecked."

Elias did not flinch when the judge sentenced him to five years in Allenwood, which meant, everyone knew, that, with good behavior, he would in all probability be released in two-and-a-half years. The judge was thought to have taken into consideration the work that Elias had done at a soup kitchen for the homeless at St. Bart's church during the time between his arrest and his sentencing.

IF BYRON MACUMBER had not committed suicide, and left two young daughters, Kimberly and Sharon, Ruby might have been able to forgive Elias, but even after she had made an arrangement through her lawyers that would guarantee the education of the little girls from her own money, the suicide haunted her.

On the night before Elias was to check into Allenwood, Elias and Ruby dined alone, except for Max Luby, in their magnificent dining room, beneath ancestral portraits, on exquisite plates, and drank vintage wines from glasses embossed with *R*'s by a now dead Rothschild a hundred years before. Each was glad to have Max there because they no longer knew what to say to each other. Later, leaving, Max, good old Max, as he had become known to Ruby and Elias, embraced Elias, and the two old friends from Cleveland looked into each other's tear-filled eyes as they nodded farewell.

Later still, walking by Ruby's bedroom, on his way to the bedroom that had become his since they returned from Europe, Elias tapped with the tips of his fingers on Ruby's door, not for an invitation to enter, which he no longer expected, but as a way of saying good-night for the last time.

"Come in," came Ruby's voice from inside, to Elias's surprise.

"Really?" he said, entering.

"Really," Ruby answered, smiling, patting the side of the bed next to her for him to get in. Whatever had happened, Ruby knew that Elias Renthal had taken her out of one life and made another possible for her, and for that she was grateful.

They spent the night together, as if they were the young stewardess and the middle-aged millionaire they had been when they first met and had dreams, all of which had been realized.

"I'M NOT going to keep the apartment, Elias," Ruby said, in the back of their limousine as they drove to the prison in Pennsylvania for him to begin his term.

"Why not? There's still plenty of money," Elias answered. Even on his way to prison for illegal use of money, he still thought of everything in terms of money.

Ruby shook her head. "Too big," she said.

"The Rhinelander?" he asked. "Why don't you move to the Rhinelander, like Loelia did? That might be nice for you until you find a new apartment."

"I thought I'd leave the city for a while," she said.

"Leave the city?"

"I'm going to move to Merry Hill. Or, should I say, Not-So-Merry Hill."

"You'll miss your friends out there."

"No, I won't." She hadn't seen any of her friends since she returned from Europe.

When the limousine arrived at the gates of the prison, a swarm of television cameras and newspeople were gathered. Ruby touched Elias's face. "I'm not going to get out, Elias," she said, pulling back into her corner.

"No, of course not," he answered.

"I'll send books, and magazines, and things, and call and write."

"I'm sorry, Ruby," he said. "I don't know the right words to tell you how sorry I am that I put you through all this."

"I know, Elias," she answered.

"You know I love you, don't you?"

"Yes, I know," she said.

"You didn't hate being married to me, did you?"

"Only when you peed in my bidet," she replied.

They both laughed. "I'm going to miss you, Ruby," he said.

For a few moments they looked at each other.

"Kiss?" he asked.

"Sure," she replied. He leaned over and took her in his arms and kissed her warmly.

"Remember the good parts," he said.

"I'm trying," she answered.

"Bye."

"Bye."

Elias knocked on the window of the limousine, and the chauffeur opened the door. Immediately the buzz of the media could be heard as they swarmed around the door of the car.

"Listen, Elias," said Ruby.

"What?"

"You were swell to me. I'll never forget that."

44

LIL ALTEMUS, ever perplexing, cried unconsolably for Bobo, her hairdresser Bobo, when he died, in a way that she had never been able to cry for her son Hubie. Justine felt, as did Dodo and Janet and Matilda, that the tears she shed for Bobo were the tears she had not shed for Hubie. "So young," she kept saying. "So young," although Bobo was ten years older than Hubie had been.

It was when Bobo, whom Lil always claimed to have "discovered," was dying, in the same hospital where Hubie had died, that Justine, visiting him with armloads of his favorite rubrum lilies, the kind he had once used to adorn Justine's hair, decided to take hold of her life and do something useful so that she would not end up like her mother, serving on committees. "The Van Degan women have always had a sense of their responsibility to the city," Lil would say over and over to Justine, but Justine had other ideas about her responsibility than serving on her mother's committees.

AFTER a gilded party chair collapsed under her weight during one of Maisie Verdurin's parties, Babette Bulbenkian, the immensely heavy wife of the billionaire Reza Bulbenkian, agreed to spend several months at a fat farm in Arizona. It was Yvonne Lupescu who had suggested the fat farm, which she called a diet farm, to Babette, telling her stories of wondrous weight reductions of friends who had gone there.

Returned, reduced, Babette pirouetted gracefully for her husband of thirty years, with the dainty mannerisms of a petite woman, to show off her weight loss of nine pounds and six ounces, a weight loss so insufficient to the amount she needed to lose that it was discernible only to someone as familiar with her body for as long a time as her husband was.

"Ah, yes, bravo, Babette," Reza said, clapping wearily for what Babette considered to be her triumph, and dreading the moments ahead of him. Reza had fallen hopelessly in love with Yvonne Lupescu, who had first caught his attention by complimenting him on the excellence of his toupee at another of Maisie's dinners, and, during his wife's absence at her fat farm, Reza had proposed marriage to her.

IN PRISON, Elias Renthal had disturbing dreams that caused him to awaken covered with sweat, but he could never remember what it was he had dreamed. He missed the silk pajamas and linen sheets that the maids at his apartment in town and his house in the country had changed daily for him. He complained about the rough and scratchy toilet paper and wrote Ruby to send him a carton of the two-ply variety she ordered in England.

At first he was assigned to the laundry detail and later, after some string pulling, to the library, although he knew very little about books, other than books about finance and investments. He exercised every day and began to lose weight. On the advice of his lawyers, he attended church services on Sundays and agreed to be interviewed in prison by Gus Bailey, whom he called Gus, not Bus, wanting to be pictured in as favorable light as possible, as if the prison experience had transformed him and the greed that had enveloped his insides had evaporated. He talked to Gus of wanting to help other people when he got out, specifically the homeless of the city of New York.

He learned to play bridge, writing to Ruby that he was becoming a regular Ezzie Fenwick of the bridge table, and had a foursome with a former congressman, in for accepting bribes, a former head of a rock-and-roll record company, in for dealing cocaine, and the former head of a cement firm, in for illegal payoffs. He continued to read all the financial papers and magazines. Barred forever from trading on the stock exchange, he took to making imaginary investments. He found that even without insider information, he could have made himself a very rich man.

In the days of his business triumphs, Elias had disdained reading social columns as too frivolous or too time-wasting, but in prison he regularly read the columns of Dolly De Longpre, Florian Gray, and Mavis Jones and became consumed with curiosity about the social life of people he had once known. "We would have been there," he thought to himself, or told his bridge group, reading about Ezzie Fenwick's birthday party at Clarence's, or Adele Harcourt's small dinner for the First Lady, or Lil Altemus's reception at her Fifth Avenue apartment for Placido Domingo after his concert at the Metropolitan Opera House. Elias was envious of their freedom to come and go, and saddened to realize that, even after he had atoned for his sins of greed, those people who had once been his friends lived in a world that would never be available to him again.

45

AFTER GUS returned to California, he took to stopping in at Peach's
house in the afternoons and sitting on the end of her bed. Sometimes
she thought he wanted to tell her something, but he never engaged in
anything more than desultory conversation.

One afternoon Gus thumbed through a magazine, casually reading
an article he had written on Elias Renthal in prison, while Peach
continued to look at her television set.

"Did you read this article I wrote about Elias Renthal in prison?"
he asked.

"Not yet. I will," she answered.

Gus sometimes wondered if Peach ever read the articles he wrote.
"As prisons go, that's the way to be in prison," he said. "I saw guys
jogging with Walkmans in their ears. No high walls, or barbed wire.
There's a painted white line, and the prisoners can't go beyond that,
and none of them do, because if they do, they're shipped right out to
a real prison, where the tough guys are, and there's no more jogging
with Walkmans in their ears."

Peach nodded and went on looking at television.

"Did I tell you I put the apartment in New York up for sale?" he
asked.

"I thought you liked that apartment," she said. "Doesn't it have a
terrace? I think someone told me that."

"I did like it, but I wanted to get my things in order."

"Good heavens. You're not thinking of committing suicide, or anything, are you?"

"No."

"We've had enough to deal with in this family, you know."

"I know."

"Why did you come back to California, Gus?" asked Peach, turning off the television set.

Gus shrugged. "Why not?"

"I don't call that an answer, when I've asked you a question." They
still talked like married people.

"I just decided that it was time to come back. I was gone for three years. I mean, this was home, wasn't it?"

"I thought you enjoyed New York. All those peculiar people you write about, like Elias Renthal and Jorgie Sanchez-Julia, and that ghastly dictator's ghastly mistress. I thought you liked all that."

"It was okay," Gus replied, not looking up from his magazine.

Peach looked at Gus. She was beginning not to understand her former husband, whom she had always understood so well.

ANTHONY FELICIANO told Gus that Lefty Flint was being released from the Men's Correctional Institute in Vacaville, California, on the thirteenth of the month. His sister Agnes Flint and his fiancée Marguerite Hanrahan were planning to drive to Vacaville and bring him back to Los Angeles. He was going to work as a bartender in Marguerite's bar in Studio City.

"What was his record in Vacaville?" asked Gus.

"A model of decorum. Read his Bible every day. The warden's favorite," said Feliciano.

"Where's he going to be living?" asked Gus.

"In West Hollywood. On Reeves—1342¼ South Reeves. You can't see it from the street. It's a little apartment over the garage behind an apartment complex."

Gus took out his wallet and removed a blank check.

"I want to pay up," he said.

"I'll send you a bill at the end of the month, like always," said Feliciano.

"No, I want to settle," said Gus.

"You're not firing me, are you?"

"No, it's just the end of the line."

"This is the time to keep an eye on him, now that he's getting out."

"I'd like to settle up," repeated Gus.

"I thought you wanted his hands crushed in a vise."

Gus laughed. "That was only a figure of speech."

"Shit," said Feliciano.

"What?"

"I'd lined up a great guy for you."

"What kind of great guy? A hand crusher?"

"Something like that."

"No, no, thanks," said Gus. "That sort of thing is not up my alley."
He moved toward the door. "Thanks very much for all your help."

"Listen, Gus," said Feliciano, stopping his exit.

Gus turned back to look at him.

"You don't mind my calling you Gus, do you?"

"Of course not."

"I read your article on Elias Renthal in prison."

Gus nodded.

"In case you're thinking of taking care of Lefty Flint yourself, the kind of place they'll send you to is nothing like the country-club prison that crook Renthal is in."

Gus looked at Anthony Feliciano for a moment, as if he was about to say something. Then he turned and left without saying anything.

AT A RED light on Sunset Boulevard, near the Beverly Hills Hotel, Gus looked into the light brown BMW in the next lane and saw Marv Pink behind the wheel. Marv Pink had been the defense lawyer who had managed to convince the jury that Lefty Flint had not committed murder, merely manslaughter, when he put his hands around Becky Bailey's neck for five minutes and strangled the life out of her. Marv Pink had on the same brown gabardine suit and brown tie with a single cream-colored stripe across the middle that he had worn during most of the trial. The feeling of revulsion that Gus always felt whenever anything to do with Lefty Flint intruded on his life came over him, but he continued to stare rather than look away, as if he were looking at a car wreck.

Aware suddenly that he was being stared at, Marv Pink turned and looked at Gus, whom he had not seen since Lefty Flint's sentencing three years earlier. The two men stared at each other from car to car. Marv Pink raised his hand in a gesture of greeting, and his iridescent cat's-eye pinky ring flashed in the California sunlight.

Gus Bailey did not give any indication of recognition.

46

WITHIN hours after Ruby Renthal put the vast apartment where she no longer wished to live on the market, the billionaire Reza Bulbenkian offered her twenty million dollars for it as a gift for his bride. Helene Whitbeck, the real-estate broker, said she had never had such an immediate reaction to an apartment in all her years in the business and thought that the famous ball of the Renthals had added to the cachet of the apartment.

After Bulbenkian divorced Babette, his wife of thirty years, at the same island resort where Bernie Slatkin had gotten his twenty-four-hour divorce, he immediately married Yvonne Lupescu, thirty years his junior, at a hastily improvised candlelit ceremony in the Lady Chapel of St. Patrick's Cathedral, which had been swathed in purple orchids and gardenias, Yvonne's favorite flowers, by Lorenza, for the occasion. Although the Cardinal did not officiate, because of all the divorces, he was present at the ceremony and at the small but lavish reception that followed at the Rhinelander Hotel.

Yvonne had hurried on the marital commitment, while Babette Bulbenkian was losing her nine pounds and six ounces at her fat farm in Arizona, following a confrontation scene between Reza and Constantine de Rham, who had burst in on the lovers in conjugal union in Constantine's house on Sutton Place.

Reza, in order to escape any unfavorable or even scandalous publicity, agreed to pay Constantine de Rham a sizable amount, after Constantine threatened to go to the police to tell them of Yvonne's part in his near fatal shooting.

Yvonne laughed and laughed. "It is simply this mad person's imagination, my darling," she said to Reza. "There is no truth whatever to what he says." However, she did not discourage her new fiancé from making his settlement on Constantine.

Reza's toupee was now gone. "I adore bald men," Yvonne told him. His teeth were now capped, also at the suggestion of his bride. Gone, too, were his black suits, replaced by smarter clothes made up in haste by Mr. Sills. Prodded by Yvonne, Reza made his offer for the Elias Renthal apartment, as soon as Ruby put it on the market, with a view to establishing himself and his new wife as top-flight social figures in the city.

"Look, Reza, we won't even have to change the drapes," said Yvonne, fingering the persimmon damask curtains of the drawing room, as if to prove to him early on that she was a woman who knew how to economize.

"Mrs. Renthal has marvelous taste," interjected Helene Whitbeck, the real-estate broker, who was showing the apartment.

Yvonne sniffed. "Ruby Renthal doesn't mean anything socially anymore," she replied.

The Bulbenkian purchase of the Renthal apartment came to naught however. The cooperative board of the exclusive building, embarrassed by the publicity brought on by Elias Renthal's financial disgrace, let it be known that the Bulbenkians would be turned down by the board if they should apply. Florian Gray printed in his column that the Bulbenkians had been turned down by the building.

"We'll sue," screamed Yvonne.

"Sue," replied Mrs. Sims Lord, who was the president of the co-op board and known to be fearless in her dealings with upstarts. It became known among the sort of real-estate brokers who dealt in dwellings for the very rich that the board wanted only people like themselves to live in that building from now on and had even voted to break up the enormous apartment into three smaller apartments, which people with lesser fortunes but more breeding than the Renthals and the Bulbenkians could afford. Or, as Mrs. Sims Lord said at a dinner that very night at Lil Altemus's, "We've had quite enough of the billionaires, thank you very much." To which Lil Altemus replied, "Hear, hear."

Undeterred by the rebuff, Bulbenkian purchased a house of embassy proportions that had long been shuttered on Park Avenue.

THE CROWDS turned out in record number for the three-day viewing that preceded the auction of the four thousand lots that made up the contents of the Elias Renthals' forty-one-room apartment on three floors that they had purchased from the estate of the late social figure Sweetzer Clarke. So great was the public interest in the magnificent possessions of the convicted financier and his elegant wife that lines formed around the block of the auction house on York Avenue, and people waited for as long as three hours to simply march by the treasures, while guards admonished them to keep moving so everyone would have a turn before closing time. The *New York Times* said, in its front-page coverage of the event, "The Renthals collected it all in record time. Now they will dispose of it in even less time."

Antiques dealers, private curators and museum curators, and collectors of eighteenth-century French and English furniture arrived in New York from London, Paris, and Tokyo for what had come to be known as the Renthal sale, in the way that their ball had come to be known as the Renthal ball. At night various charities took over the showrooms, and the rich of the city, unwilling to wait in line with the hoi polloi, paid hundreds of dollars each to view what the poor could see for free, with the certain knowledge that their admittance fee was going for a good cause. Ruby Renthal, who had become reclusive, declined to be present at any of the charity events.

"Oh, please, Ruby, come," begged Maude Hoare, who was chairperson for the evening benefiting the Hospital for Plastic Surgery.

"I can't. I'm sorry," said Ruby.

"You'd be an extra added attraction for the evening," said Violet Bastedo, who was chairperson for the evening benefiting Ballerina House, a home for indigent dancers.

"I'm sorry," said Ruby.

"Damn her," they both said later.

"Oh!" said Lil Altemus, covering her face with her catalogue, as she and Ezzie Fenwick jockeyed for position in front of Elias Renthal's pool table that had once belonged to Edward VII.

"What's the matter, Lil?" asked Ezzie.

"Daddy died on that pool table," Lil said, touching the faded green felt on which Ormonde Van Degan had expired on the night of the Renthal ball.

"Oh, right," answered Ezzie, whose eyes were eagerly scanning the crowd for people to wave to. He did not wish to be reminded that Lil and her stepmother Dodo had walked in on him passing information that Elias Renthal was under investigation by the Securities and Exchange Commission to the gossip columnist Florian Gray at almost the same moment that Lil had discovered her father dead on the pool table.

"Look, Ezzie, aren't those the console tables that Ruby gave to the

White House?" asked Lil Altemus. "Over there. With the rams' heads."

"They were returned to the Renthals by the White House," answered Ezzie.

"Because of the scandal, you mean?"

"Because they were inauthentic."

"No!"

"Yes. Jamesey told me."

They exchanged looks, as if to say, "What can you expect, from people like that?"

AT THE last moment, the auction was canceled. Reza Bulbenkian made an offer for the entire contents of the vast apartment. At a hastily called meeting between the auction house and Ruby Renthal, the decision was made to accept Reza Bulbenkian's offer. The auction house felt that the enormous offer made by the financier could very well be in excess of the profits from an auction of the possessions of a disgraced figure, and Ruby Renthal felt that it would halt the avalanche of publicity connected with the sale that put her name and photograph in the newspapers every day.

"How did you manage to halt the auction?" a reporter asked Reza Bulbenkian, at the news conference set up by the auction house and Reza to announce that the sale had been canceled.

"You can buy anything you pay too much for," said Reza, nodding his head, like a wise sage of finance.

The antiques dealers who had traveled to New York from around the globe for the sale hissed and booed the decision.

"I am so happy with Reza," said Yvonne Lupescu at the news conference, linking her arm in his and smiling up at him, as if saving the day. Unlike Ruby Renthal, Yvonne had no desire whatsoever to shun the press. She waved to the cameras. On her finger was a diamond the size of the diamond that Ruby had dropped into the Mediterranean. "Reza is the man I have been waiting for all my life." They hoped, she said, to be able to start entertaining in their new home in two weeks.

To her hairdresser, in private, she added, "He's rich. He doesn't drink and, thank heaven, he doesn't want to be beaten."

47

IN PRISON, it hurt Elias Renthal when he heard that his apartment had been sold, even though Ruby had told him on the way to prison that she didn't want to live there anymore. The apartment represented everything that he had ever strived for in his life, and he had always enjoyed the astonished looks on the faces of even the most established and wealthy visitors when he showed them through it. It hurt him even more when he heard that it was being divided up into three smaller apartments, making it forever irretrievable and squashing the daydreams he sometimes indulged in of resuming his former life after his release from Allenwood, a better and wiser man.

It enraged him that Reza Bulbenkian and his new wife, the former Yvonne Lupescu, should have purchased all the furniture and paintings that he and Ruby had collected so lovingly and that they were already starting to entertain on a lavish scale in their new mansion on Park Avenue, rivaling the life-style that the Renthals had made famous. Elias loathed Reza Bulbenkian and told his three bridge companions of crooked things that he knew Reza had done in business and gotten away with. Then he added, "so far," meaning that his practices would eventually catch up with him, too. The congressman, the rock-and-roll executive, and the cement-company owner laughed. They loved hearing Elias's stories. Elias also told them that Yvonne Bulbenkian used to be one of Ms. Myra's girls, before she took up with Constantine de Rham, and carried her whips in a custom-made Vuitton case. "Imagine, a former hooker running New York society," he said.

Most of all Elias missed Ruby. More than anything in the world, he wanted to make it up to Ruby for the embarrassment and the ostracism that he had caused her. He never remembered her as she was when he first met her, a pretty stewardess with a sassy manner. He thought of her coming down the stairway of their apartment on the night of their ball, dressed in white and wearing all her diamonds, and marveled each time he thought of her as the great lady she had become.

''MAX COMES to visit," Elias said to Ruby one day when she drove up from Merry Hill to see him.

"Good old Max," said Ruby.

"Max saw Loelia Manchester at the opera."

"Max at the opera? What next?" replied Ruby.

"He said he thought Loelia was unhappy."

"Heavens," said Ruby.

From the time of her arrival, Elias knew there was something on Ruby's mind, all during the time they were talking of other things, like Max Luby and Loelia Manchester.

"Elias," said Ruby, finally. "There's something I have to tell you."

"What's that, Ruby darling? Anything you want. Anything."

Then Ruby asked Elias for a divorce. She brought with her the papers for him to sign. Elias was devastated by Ruby's request but was not totally surprised. The congressman's wife had divorced him. The wife of the head of the record company had divorced him. The head of the cement company was already divorced. His hand shaking, he signed the papers.

"At least you didn't break the news to me through a lawyer," he said.

"You know I'd never do that to you, Elias," she answered.

"My friend the congressman read about his wife's divorce in the newspaper."

"Or that."

"I'll miss you."

"I know."

"Don't remember me badly."

"I won't. Count on that." Ruby took out a handkerchief from her bag and wiped a tear from her eye. Then she began gathering up her things and put the papers he signed into her bag.

"Well, good-bye," she said, rising at the end of the visit.

"We're allowed to kiss," said Elias.

"Oh, yes, of course." She smiled. As he leaned toward her, she averted her face a fraction of an inch so that his kiss landed on the side of her mouth rather than full on her lips, like a son at boarding school saying good-bye to a departing mother. Elias understood. Each avoided the other's eye. For a few moments they simply stood there.

"I read in Dolly's column that Loelia married Mickie," said Elias, wanting to forestall her departure.

Ruby nodded. "I read that," she answered.

"What do they call her now, Loelia Minardos?"

"Apparently."

"Don't sound so snappy as Loelia Manchester."

"I suppose not."

"You don't see Loelia?"

"No."

Elias nodded. "I wonder if she paid Ned all that money he was asking."

"No," said Ruby.

"How come?"

"Ned would never have taken money from Loelia. It was just to keep her from marrying Mickie that he asked for all that money. Now he doesn't care."

"How do you know?"

"That's what I heard."

LORD BIEDERMEIER visited Elias in prison and reported at a dinner party later that same evening, at Maisie Verdurin's house, that Elias had wept when he talked about the divorce. Feelings against Elias still ran high, and the consensus was that Ruby Renthal had done the correct thing.

"Ruby just dropped out of sight," said Maude Hoare. "I don't know a soul who sees her."

"Poor Ruby," said Aline Royceton.

"But why in the world did you go to visit Elias?" asked Maisie.

"Oh, I was always fond of Elias," replied Lord Biedermeier.

Lord Biedermeier did not say to the group at his table that he was hopeful of securing a second book from Elias, on the prison life of a billionaire, even promising him someone willing to make weekly visits to Allenwood to ghost-write it for him.

"A sort of *De Profundis*," Lord Biedermeier had said to Elias in the visitors' room, shifting his position to see him better through the mesh screening that separated them.

"A sort of what?" asked Elias.

"*De Profundis. De Profundis*," Lord Biedermeier said, clapping his hands in mock exasperation, as if everyone in prison would know about Oscar Wilde's final prose written during his incarceration. "Listen to this, Elias," he said, quoting, loosely, from Wilde's letter to Lord Alfred Douglas, that Lord Biedermeier had jotted down on the back of an envelope in the limousine on his way to the prison in Pennsylvania. "'I have disgraced my name eternally.'" Lord Biedermeier gestured toward Elias to show that he, too, had disgraced his name eternally. "'I have made it a low byword among low people. I have dragged it through the very mire, and turned it into a synonym for folly.' You see Elias, you could change folly to greed."

But Elias Renthal, whose name had indeed become a synonym for greed, could not think of *De Profundis* that day. Elias Renthal could only think that he had lost Ruby Renthal forever. He could only look blankly at Lord Biedermeier.

"Keep a journal, Elias. Write everything down, the day-to-day of what happens here. Get to know the most serious offenders. What a book it will make!" He clapped his hands, and his pince-nez fell off. "Start reading the Bible every day. You know the sort of thing, I-found-God-in-Allenwood. The public will eat it up, and everyone will be on your side by the time you get out. There's a whole great big life waiting for you out there. Oh, perhaps not with the Van Degans and that set, but there's other fish to fry in life than Laurance Van Degan who, by the way, in case you hadn't heard, had to resign as president of the Butterfield."

Elias looked up. "Because of me?" he asked.

"Apparently," replied Lord Biedermeier.

"Holy shit."

48

GUS MOVED into a hotel in Hollywood. He read books he had always meant to read. He watched videos of films he had wanted to see, but missed. He called none of his friends from the years he had lived in Hollywood, when he worked in films, and he did not frequent any of the restaurants where he was likely to run into people he knew. Several times a day he drove by the apartment complex in West Hollywood that blocked 1342¼ South Reeves from view from the street, but he never got out of his car. Every day he stopped in to see Peach, usually late in the afternoon. Every few days he went to the cemetery where Becky was buried and lay a rose from Peach's garden on her grave. Peach watched her former husband and worried that he might be having a nervous breakdown.

"He's out," Gus said one day, when they were staring at one of the afternoon soap operas that Peach always watched. He had come into her room and sat on the edge of the bed for twenty minutes before he said a word.

Peach didn't say, "Who's out?" even though they had not mentioned Lefty Flint's name since Gus returned to California.

"How do you know?" she asked instead.

"I just know."

"Did your private detective tell you?"

"He wasn't a private detective."

"I know he wasn't a private detective."

"I fired him."

"Then how do you know? Vacaville doesn't send out announcements."

"I saw him."

"You saw Lefty?" she asked. Peach looked at the back of his head. She picked up the tuner and turned off the television set.

"Where?"

"Carrying groceries out of Stop and Shop."

"Did he see you?"

"No."

"Was he alone?"

"No. Marguerite what's-her-name was with him. The bartender."

"Don't make me pull it out of you line by line, Gus. Tell me everything."

"They were laughing. They were enjoying themselves. I can't stand it that he should be happy, after what he did."

"Where did they go?"

"He has an apartment at 1342¼ South Reeves in West Hollywood. They went there."

Peach picked up a magazine from the bed. "Of all the cities in this country, why did he have to come back here where it happened?"

"Sometimes I wonder why we were never searched all through the trial when we went into the courtroom," said Gus. "It would have been so easy."

"What would have been so easy?" asked Peach.

With his forefinger and thumb, he imagined his Luger in his hand. He pulled his trigger finger and fired, making a *pow* sound with his lips at the same time. In his mind, his bullet hit its target.

Peach stared at him. Then she leaned over and picked up the telephone. "I'm going to call Detective Johnston," she said.

"Why?"

"I know that son of a bitch is going to come here. I know it. I've known it ever since he wrote me that letter from prison. I want them to put a guard on my house."

"He won't come here, Peach. I guarantee you that."

BY THE END of the first week, Gus had gotten the movements of Lefty Flint down. He knew the time of day Lefty Flint rose. He knew the diner where he had breakfast. He knew the laundromat where he took his washing. He knew he marketed at the Stop and Shop for only one day's provisions at a time, as if he were a temporary visitor. After lunch he drove Marguerite to her bar in Studio City and left her there. Sometimes in the afternoon he went to a film. He stayed by himself most of the time. At seven he went to the bar again and took Marguerite out to an early dinner at a restaurant near the bar. After dinner, he went to work as night bartender and stayed on duty until closing time. Marguerite often left between ten and eleven, either taking a cab home or getting a lift from someone she knew, but it was usually about two, after the glasses were washed and the tables stacked and the trash put out and the waiters paid, before Lefty Flint locked up and left the bar by the back entrance. There was a space by the trash cans where he parked Marguerite's Nile-green Toyota. Gus had twice tried the doors of the car, but they were locked. He had tried hiding himself behind the trash cans, but once he accidentally knocked one over. Afraid that the sound would attract attention, he had retreated to the street and walked away as fast as he could.

On an early morning, before anyone in the area of bars and restaurants was around to open the businesses, he made an inspection of the alley behind the bar. He found a place to stand on the far side of the alley wall, where, at night, he could not be seen but where he could see perfectly the back door of the bar, the trash-can area, and the place where Flint parked Marguerite's Toyota. He held up his hand, as if he were holding up the German Luger, and imagined pulling the trigger. The gesture and the *pow* sound he made had become a habit.

ON THE MORNING of the day that Gus planned to kill Lefty Flint, he went to Mass at a church he had never been to before. He sat in a back pew throughout the service without participating in it, like a street person seeking temporary shelter, neither reciting the prayers nor taking communion.

"What the hell are you doing here, Gus?" asked a voice from behind him as he was leaving the church.

Gus, surprised, turned. It was Faye Converse.

"What the hell are *you* doing here?" he replied.

"They've got a hospice here for some of my people," said Faye. "I come to visit from time to time. Brucie is here. Remember Brucie? My secretary. You met her on the plane."

"Sure I remember Brucie. How is she?"

Faye shrugged the shrug that said not good, or good under the circumstances.

"Give her my love."

"You look strange, Gus."

"How strange?"

"Not yourself. Haunted, sort of."

"How's this?" he asked, assuming a happy stance.

"Better. Better. I read your piece on Elias Renthal in prison. The son of a bitch."

"Why son of a bitch?"

"Did you know he stopped payment on the two-million-dollar check he gave me at the ball?"

"I don't believe it!" replied Gus, amazed, although he did believe it. It was the first time in weeks he had been interested in anything but Lefty Flint.

"Ruby made the check good, though," said Faye. "I liked Ruby. Terrible position she's in now."

"She's a class act, Ruby," said Gus.

"You never let me know when you're out here. How long are you staying?"

"I'm not sure."

"I'm having a party tonight. Come."

"Can't tonight."

"Yes, you can. What are you doing that's more important than a movie-star party at Faye Converse's?"

"I'm going to kill a guy."

"Well, come after you kill the guy," she said.

They both laughed.

LATER, on the evening of that day, Gus went to see Peach. He stood in the doorway of her bedroom most of the time, rather than sitting on the end of her bed, as he usually did.

"Did I ever tell you about this woman I know in New York called Ruby Renthal?" asked Gus.

"Whose husband is in prison for insider trading, that one?"

"That one."

"I don't know if you did or not. She gives parties and lives in that vast apartment. I've read all that."

"Her name used to be Ruby Nolte. She used to be an airline stewardess."

"Is there a punch to all this?"

"There is. About seven years ago, when she was still a stewardess, she got beaten up here in Los Angeles, by a man she was involved with at the time. The guy really bashed her face in."

Peach, interested now, looked at Gus.

"She was in the hospital for ten days. She wanted to press charges, but the guy warned her not to, and the guy had some tough friends, and so she didn't press charges."

"Yes?"

"The guy was Lefty Flint."

"Why did I know that was what you were going to say?"

"He's going to do it again. You know that, don't you?"

"Then call the police, Gus."

"The police can't do anything until after the damage is done."

They remained in silence for a few moments.

"I have to go," said Gus, finally, looking at his watch, as if he were on a schedule. He walked toward her bed. As usual, she was barricaded in it by her wheelchair and the long table covered with books and magazines. He undid the brake of her wheelchair and backed it out of his way, pushed the table to the side, and walked up to her. When he was by her side, he bent down and kissed her. In his gesture, she read farewell.

"S'long," he said.

"You sound like you're going on a trip," she replied.

"No."

"Are you all right, Gus?"

"Sure."

"You sound odd."

He looked at the woman he had been married to for so many years, and divorced from for so many years. Nearly bedridden, she had become accustomed to staring at a television set with picture but no sound when she did not wish to deal with the moment at hand in her life, but this time she returned her former husband's look. He felt a tremendous affection for her.

He turned and replaced the wheelchair in its correct position, braked it, put her table back in place, and walked out of her room, down her hallway to the front door. There, on a table, in a chipped porcelain bowl, was a bouquet of roses from Peach's garden, jammed together, in an arrangement that Lorenza, in the unlikely event she ever saw it, would disapprove of. Gus reached in and pulled out a yellow rose, open to almost full flower, and took it with him as he opened the front door and walked to his rented car parked in the driveway.

"Gus," called Peach after him, but he did not hear. In a louder voice, she called for her housekeeper. "Immaculata! Immaculata!"

Next to her bed, on the overcrowded table, she found her bell and rang it and rang it again.

"*Si, señora?*" said the older woman, shuffling into Peach's room in bedroom slippers.

"Stop him," cried Peach. "Outside. Mr. Bailey. Stop him."

Immaculata shuffled out of the room, unhurried, as always, down the hall to the front door, just as Gus's car was pulling out of the driveway. Alerted now to the emergency of the moment, she ran down the steps of the house, waving her dish towel in the air, but Gus did not see her.

HIS GERMAN Luger, cleaned and loaded, was in the glove compartment of his rented car. At eleven o'clock he drove to Studio City, being very careful to adhere to the posted speed limit, allowing other cars, going beyond the limit, to pass him. A car coming toward him in the opposite lane had on its bright lights, and he was momentarily blinded. He put his hand up to shield his eyes. As the two cars passed, he turned to curse the occupant, and his eyes locked for an instant with the driver's. He felt troubled, but he did not understand why.

He parked his car on a side street a block away from Marguerite's bar. He remained in the car until a quartet of noisy bar hoppers had turned the corner, and then he opened the glove compartment and took out the German Luger. He walked to the alley and took his place behind the wall. It was several moments before he realized that Marguerite's car was not parked in its usual place. An image of the car with bright lights flashed through his mind, and he wondered if he was now imagining that it had been Nile green. He walked out the alley to the street and turned the corner to where the entrance of the bar was. He had not been inside the bar since his brief encounter with Marguerite some months before. Entering, he turned away from the bar itself as if he were going to the men's room. Losing himself behind some patrons, he looked over at the bar. Lefty Flint was not tending bar.

"Help you?" asked a waiter with a tray of beer bottles.

"No, no, thanks," said Gus, making his way to the door.

Outside he ran the several blocks to his car. He drove to 1342¼ South Reeves. He parked his car on the street and walked down the driveway at the side of the complex, staying as close to the shrubbery as possible. Behind, the Nile-green Toyota was not in the parking place below the garage apartment. Upstairs, the venetian blinds were closed, but Gus could see light coming through the slats.

Frightened now, his heart beating fast, Gus mounted the rickety wooden stairway that led to the front door of the apartment. He looked but could not find a bell. He took the gun from his pocket and held it in one hand. With the other, he knocked on the door. There was no reply. He knocked again.

From within, he heard sounds. A shade covered the glass part of the door. He saw someone pull back the shade a crack and look out.

"Who is it?" came a woman's voice.

"I'm looking for Lefty," said Gus.

"You're too late," said the voice he recognized as Marguerite's. "Lefty's gone."

"It's Gus Bailey, Marguerite. We met once before," said Gus through the door.

She opened the door but left the chain on. "What do you want, Mr. Bailey?" she asked.

"Where's Lefty?"

"Gone. I should have listened to you, Mr. Bailey," she replied. "I guess you were trying to help me, but I didn't want to hear back then."

"Open the door, Marguerite. Let me in."

She took off the chain and opened the door. When Gus walked into the kitchen of her small apartment, he saw that her eye was closed, and her face had been beaten.

"Jesus," he said. "Come on with me. I'll take you to the emergency room at Cedars."

"I'm okay," she said. "I got off easy. It's not bad. I feel like such a goddamn fool. He just used me. I arranged for him to have a job when he got out, and a place to live, and he was all full of good intentions, and the parole officer thought he was all rehabilitated and on the straight and narrow, but working behind a bar was not exactly what he had in mind for himself. I thought the guy was in love with me, when I used to visit him in Vacaville, but the pickins are slim for guys in prison. They're not in great demand, if you know what I mean, and it's only some asshole like me, with my misguided sense of social consciousness, who would have thought that a man who strangled a woman and beat up other women was rehabilitated in three years."

"Where did he go, Marguerite?"

"You're just as big a fool as he is to go searching for him with a gun, Mr. Bailey," she answered.

"Tell me where he went," repeated Gus, insistently.

"Put your gun away, Mr. Bailey. He's gone. He's on a plane somewhere."

"Where?"

"He didn't confide in me. He just knocked me around a bit."

"Where do you think he went?"

"You weren't at the parole hearing, were you?"

"No. There was no point."

"There was some rich lady there who asked the parole board not to release him. He had a real grudge against that lady."

Gus stared at Marguerite. "What rich lady?"

"She's always in the magazines."

"You're not talking about Ruby Renthal, are you?"

"Ruby, that's right. Very high society."

Gus, listening, was stunned at what she said. "Ruby Renthal was at the parole hearing?"

"She asked the board not to release him."

"My God," said Gus.

49

ON THE DAY before she left New York for good, to take up permanent residence at Merry Hill, Ruby Renthal, in a nostalgic mood, paid a last visit to her apartment, which was shortly to be divided up into three smaller apartments. Wandering through the large empty rooms, she wondered if people would continue to refer to it as the Elias Renthal apartment, even after they were gone, in the way that people had continued to refer to it as the Sweetzer Clarke apartment for many months after she and Elias had purchased it, before it had become inalterably their own through its magnificent transformation by Cora Mandell, with the help of Maisie Verdurin and Jamesey Crocus. Only that day Ruby had seen a layout in the *Times Magazine* section showing Yvonne Bulbenkian lighting tapers for one of her parties in a pair of silver candlesticks that had only recently been her own, on a Chippendale dining table that had also been hers, beneath a portrait of King Boris of Bulgaria in hunting attire that had until their scandal hung in her own dining room. She felt no craving to own them again.

In her persimmon-lacquered drawing room, nineteen coats, or was it twenty, she wondered, the windows were bare, stripped of their elaborate hangings with the fringe from France that had taken weeks to come. She looked at the spot on the wall where her Monet of the water lilies, that she and Elias had purchased from Maisie Verdurin's wall on the night of her first party in New York, had hung, and the places on each side of the marble fireplace where her console tables with the inlaid rams' heads, from the Orromeo auction in London, had stood until she discovered they were fakes and donated them to the White House, which had returned them at the time of the auction, for reasons unknown.

In her ballroom, which she had not entered since the night of her ball, she stood at the top of the stairs, where she had received on that night, and remembered how it was in the magnificent hours before her world had begun to topple. She walked down the stairway and heard the music, the waltzes, and stood in the middle of the dance floor and closed her eyes as she remembered waltzing with Elias, with Mickie Minardos, with Gus Bailey, and her royal princes, from countries that no longer wanted them, who used to impress her so much. She looked up and could see the ten thousand butterflies, in the thirty seconds of their beauty, and hear the exclamations of joy from the mouths of her four hundred guests.

"Well, Ruby Nolte, as I live and breathe," came the voice that interrupted her reverie. She opened her eyes with a start.

Standing at the top of the short stairway leading to her ballroom was Lefty Flint. She watched him walk down the steps and across the dance floor to her.

"What are you doing here?" she asked, trying to keep the panic out of her voice.

"Paying a call," he replied. "You got yourself a gentleman caller, Ruby."

"How did you get in here?"

"I told them you were expecting me."

"But I don't live here anymore. How did you know I was here?"

"I got my ways." He looked around him, at the gold-and-white paneling of the room. "What do you call this room, Ruby? The ballroom? I didn't know people still had ballrooms. My, my. Imagine, having your own ballroom. You did good, didn't you, Ruby, for a stewardess? Look at you. Anyone who didn't know what I know about you would think you were one of the swells."

"Get out of here, Lefty, right now," she said.

"We've got a few things to go over, Ruby."

"No, we don't. We have nothing to go over."

"Oh, yes, we do. How fucking dare you come to my parole hearing and try to keep me in that place?"

"Obviously, it didn't have any effect."

"How could you do that to me?"

"I'd do it again."

"Listen, rich lady. I went to prison. I did my time. I have atoned."

"Only in your kind of circles, Lefty." Calm now, sure of herself, she met his eyes.

He looked at her. "You've changed," he said.

"You don't know how much," she answered. "If you have in mind to punch me out, I'd think again if I were you." She opened her bag and looked in it as if she were searching for her lipstick or compact. She lifted out her pistol and pointed it at him. "When my husband bought me this pistol, I thought it was the laugh of the year. He would say to me over and over, 'There are mad people out there, out to get people like us.' I never took him seriously about that, but now I see how right he was. I told you once. Now I'm telling you again. Get out, just the way you came in."

"Your husband in the slammer, that guy?" sneered Lefty.

"That guy," she answered, holding the pistol on him.

"Who stole all the money?"

"Who stole all the money," she replied.

"You're holding him up to me?"

"There's one big difference between you and my husband, Lefty. He didn't beat women or kill them. He can pay back the money. You can't give back the life you took. Wherever you go, people will say, 'He's the guy who strangled Becky Bailey.' You're a murderer."

Lefty said nothing. He moved toward Ruby.

"Get out of here, you son of a bitch," she screamed.

"Hold it, Lefty," came a voice from behind. Lefty turned quickly and faced Gus Bailey, standing on the stairs, his Luger drawn. During the split second before he fired, Gus remembered saying to Bernie Slatkin, "I want him to be looking at me at the moment. I want him to know it was me who did it."

Gus fired.

50

Men's Correctional Institute
Vacaville, California

Dear Peach:

My duties here, all manual so far, (although there is hope that a position in the library will open up soon, when Boyd Lonergan, who shot the jewelry salesman by mistake in the Tiffany's robbery, is released next month), have kept me so busy of late that exhaustion has kept me from writing sooner. Isn't it extraordinary that they should have sent me to the same place that they sent Lefty? Several of the inmates here remember him, and all of the guards. I'm pleased to say they remember him without affection. He told Boyd, with whom he shared a cell briefly, that he had beaten several women before he killed Becky.

For the first time in years, I feel calm. When I am washing clothes in the laundry, where I am currently assigned, or peeling potatoes in the kitchen, where I was assigned before, there is no longer a subtext of Lefty in my thoughts, as there has been for so many years. I keep thinking of all those nights in New York when I was talking about one thing and thinking about another.

How strange life is. If what happened had happened in the alley behind the bar in Studio City, the way I planned it, I would probably be here for twenty years. First degree, they would have called it. What ever possessed him to go to Ruby Renthal's house that day? How extraordinary that she was even there.

Do you know what I think, Peach? I think it's possible to be happy again. Even here.

With love,
Gus

51

EFFICIENT in her duties, Justine Altemus walked through the rooms and wards of St. Vincent's Hospital, as she walked through the rooms and wards of St. Clair's Hospital and Bellevue Hospital, bringing magazines and sweets to the victims of the disease that people called a pestilence, making telephone calls or writing letters for those who were no longer able to do such things for themselves. Steeled now, her duties before her emotions, she could smile and banter with the boys. "Hi, Justine," they would call out to her. "Hi, Billy," she'd call back. Or Phil. Or Christian. Or whomever. She knew all their names, and most of them knew hers.

"Hi, Justine," she heard someone say in the same bed where Phil, her favorite, had died a few days before.

"Hi," she called back brightly. She could see at once, whoever he was, that he was beyond caring for reading material or Hershey bars with almonds.

"Would you like me to write a letter for you, or call anyone?" she asked. He didn't answer. "I'd be happy to read to you. I have all the latest magazines."

"Don't recognize me, do you, Justine? Do I look that bad?" the patient asked. "I used to be a good-looking guy."

She knew that he was young, even though he looked old. His arms were like the handles of a broom. Then, on his earlobe, she noticed a diamond, the diamond that her father had given her mother in an engagement ring, and that her mother had given to Hubie when she had vain hopes that Hubie would marry Violet Bastedo, and that Hubie had given to Juanito Perez.

"Oh, Juanito," she cried, sinking to her knees by the side of the bed. She knew she would be asked to leave by the nurse in charge of the ward if she was seen crying, but she could not help herself, burying her head in the bedclothes to muffle the sounds. "I hadn't heard. I didn't know."

"Imagine, you crying for me, Justine," he said, with wonder in his faint voice.

"I'm sorry."

"I heard about this volunteer lady called Justine, real classy, everybody said, who comes here every afternoon, and I thought to myself, I bet that's Justine Altemus they're talking about."

"That's me," said Justine.

"You had a baby, I heard."

Justine smiled and nodded her head. "I called him Hubie. He's beautiful, Juanito."

"Got a picture?"

"Not here. Next time I'll bring you one," she said. They exchanged glances, each wondering if there would be a next time they would see each other.

"You're beautiful, Justine," said Juanito.

"Oh, no, I'm not," she replied. "Interesting looking. Almost pretty. Those are the adjectives that are applied to me, but it's sweet of you to pay me the compliment."

"Hubie always said you sold yourself short," said Juanito.

Justine smiled. "That's what Hubie used to say. You're right. I'd forgotten that."

"You seeing anybody since Bernie?"

"Not really. I'm turning into one of those women who call up men to take them places. I-have-two-tickets-for-the-theater-on-Tuesday- can-you-come?"

"One of these days you'll meet some nice doctor."

"You're different than I imagined you were going to be."

Juanito smiled. "I used to be a bum, but I classed up when I became a millionaire."

Justine smiled.

"There's a few things I want to tell you, Justine."

"What?"

"You know those chairs your mother wanted so bad?"

"It doesn't matter," said Justine.

"Charles-something chairs?" It was an effort for him to speak.

"Tenth. Charles the Tenth. Doesn't matter."

"No, you gotta hear this, Justine. Your Aunt Minnie Willoughby's chairs that your mother sent Jamesey Crocus to con me out of."

Justine nodded, knowing he spoke the truth.

"I left them out in the street one at a time, for those people who furnish their apartments with the discarded furniture they find on the sidewalk at night."

Justine started to laugh.

"Eleven poor people have got some pretty good chairs, if only they knew it," whispered Juanito.

"I think Hubie would have liked that, Juanito," said Justine.

"One more thing."

"Don't tire yourself, Juanito."

"About the money Hubie left me."

"Oh, I don't care about the money that Hubie left you. That was Hubie's money, and he wanted you to have it."

Juanito raised a hand to let him talk. "You have to know this. He wanted Herkie Saybrook to make a new will. He wanted the money to go to a hospice for guys without any money to die, to be able to die decent, but he died before Herkie could get here to make the change."

"It doesn't matter now, Juanito, really it doesn't, but you're nice to tell me that."

"But that's not it. I had Herkie Saybrook down to the loft before I got so sick they had to put me in here."

"Herkie? Why?"

"I know what you're thinking. I'm the first Puerto Rican Herkie Saybrook ever wrote out a will for."

She stared at him.

"I know you and your mother thought I was going to leave the money to a leather bar or something trashy, but I want to do with it what Hubie would have done if he'd lived a few days longer. It's all going, every cent of it, all those Van Degan bucks, to a hospice. Let me tell you something, Justine. Hubie and I may have had our problems, but he was the only person in my whole life who ever treated me nice."

"Oh, Juanito."

For a few minutes they remained in their positions, thinking their own thoughts. "Do you have any family you want me to get in touch with? That's one of the things I do."

"No," he said.

"Nobody?"

"There's an aunt, but she don't want to hear from me."

"A mother? A father?"

"My father kicked my mother in the stomach when I was a little kid, and she died. I grew up in a home for boys in San Juan. I don't even know if my father's alive or dead, and I don't care."

"Good lord," said Justine.

"That's the same thing Hubie said when I told him that story the first time. 'Good lord.' You swells all talk alike."

"Tell me more."

"I've led a dicey kind of life, Justine."

"What's dicey?"

"I used to hustle."

"That means doing it for money?"

"That's right. I knew from the time I was a teenager in that home that my looks were my only asset in life. There's not much I haven't done. Even porn, if you want to know the truth. After Hubie left me all that money, you don't know how proper I got. I mended my ways, and then I got sick. And here you find me."

"Oh, Juanito, I'm so sorry."

"I'm not afraid to die, Justine. I'm afraid of what happens between now and dying. I've watched some of these guys, what they go through. I don't know if I'm up to it. Hubie was a class act dying. I'm not a class act like Hubie," said Juanito.

"I think you're a class act, Juanito." She squeezed his hand.

Juanito squeezed hers back.

"Can I get you anything?" asked Justine finally.

"Just some water," he replied. "There's none left here."

"I'll fill the Thermos," she said.

When she returned a few minutes later, she poured him a paper cup of water and held it for him to drink. Then she puffed up the pillows behind his head. Juanito, sleepy now, smiled at her.

"I want you to have this, Justine," he said.

She looked at him. He reached out and took her hand. In it he placed the Altemus diamond.

IT WASN'T until she read it on the front page of the *Times* that Lil Altemus learned that Juanito Perez, the lover of her late son, had left his entire ten-million-dollar inheritance to a hospice for AIDS victims to be known as the Hubert Altemus, Jr., Hospice.

52

AFTER Gus Bailey went to prison, Ruby Renthal vanished from sight. The name Renthal was so well known and so associated with greed that even people in shops looked up and stared at her when she gave them her charge cards. She became altogether separated from the grand people who had once fought to sit at her table and to dance at her ball.

Ruby, however, in spite of the bad turns her charmed life had taken, was still the possessor of a large fortune, settled on her by Elias in their halcyon days. Her withdrawal from social life to a simpler existence in the country was from choice, not financial adversity, as many people thought. She enjoyed the quiet life, the country walks, and tending her garden. She saw a small group of country friends whose names never appeared in Dolly De Longpre's column, or Florian Gray's, and their sort of entertaining was of the last-minute variety, with dinner on trays in front of a fire, rather than with all the grandeur of her former life in New York society.

"The relief," she said to her maid, Candelaria, settling in to another quiet evening at home. She felt no yearning for the competitive life of charity events and nightly dinner parties and daily fittings that had consumed her for so long.

Ned Manchester, who lived nearby, taught her to play tennis and took her riding and eventually declared his love for her, but she resisted his attempts at love, although she was attracted to him. "I can't marry while Elias is in prison," she said to Ned. "I can't. He was too good to me. It would kill him."

Elias was still important to her, and she continued to visit him in prison, even after she divorced him. Their relationship, while not romantic, became as it had been in the beginning between them, before their financial and social fame.

Loelia Manchester, meanwhile, who had discovered that the object of her desire, Mickie Minardos, was not worthy of the sacrifices she had made for him, married him, at his insistence, although she no longer wanted to marry him. In the beginning, the romance of Loelia and Mickie had titillated New York society for about six months.

They were pointed out wherever they went. Photographers fought to take their picture. They were asked everywhere. Then, used to the sight of them, they ceased to fascinate. People began to wonder if Mickie wasn't a bit of a user, if Loelia wasn't drinking a bit too much, or if her last facelift hadn't been a ghastly mistake, with her popping-out eyes. On the rare occasions that Ned Manchester appeared in New York, at weddings, or funerals, or memorial services, people began to say how attractive he was, a gentleman to his fingertips, and hadn't Loelia been a fool to leave him for such an opportunist as the cobbler. Later they began calling her a damn fool, and then a god-damn fool. And then just poor Loelia.

Late in September of that year, Elias Renthal made several collect calls from Allenwood Federal Prison Camp in Pennsylvania. The first was to Max Luby. The second was to Laurance Van Degan. The third was to Ruby. Of the three, only Laurance Van Degan was haughty to him, although Laurance, like Max and Ruby, took the advice that Elias gave them from his confinement, for not one of them ever doubted that Elias was a financial genius. "Get out of the stock market," he told them. "There is going to be a crash."

53

"TALK LOUDER, Janet, or stop crying, or *something!* I can hardly hear you," Lil yelled over the transatlantic wires.

"It's Laurance," repeated Janet, for the third time.

"Oh, my God!" cried Lil.

The instant Lil Altemus heard of her brother's illness, from her tearful sister-in-law Janet Van Degan, she returned home from Rome, where she had been staying with her friends the Todescos, after what she always called her annual migration: Salzburg, for the music, Paris, for her fittings, and London, for the season.

In New York, she was met by Joe, her chauffeur, and a variety of officials from the Van Degan Foundation who had made arrangements to whisk her through customs without having to wait. She went straight from the airport to Manhattan Hospital, giving instructions to Joe as they drove to take her luggage on to the apartment on Fifth Avenue, to tell her maid Lourdes to unpack, to call Justine to join her for dinner, but not to bring the baby, and to return to pick her up at the hospital in an hour's time. It was not necessary for Lil to stop at the information counter to ask what room Laurance Van Degan was in. All the Van Degans, for as long as she could remember, during their illnesses, stayed in suite 690 of the Harcourt Pavilion of Manhattan Hospital.

When the elevator doors opened on the sixth floor, she was met by Miss Wentworth, Laurance's secretary, and even then, in her agitation and concern for her brother, Lil wondered anew why Miss Wentworth dyed her hair so very black.

"I hope your flight was satisfactory, Mrs. Altemus," said Miss Wentworth.

"Yes, yes, fine," replied Lil, walking down the corridor toward the room.

"And the customs?" asked Miss Wentworth, following, trying to keep in step.

"Yes, yes, fine. Right through. No wait. How is my brother, Irene?"

"Well," said Miss Wentworth, cautiously. "His mouth. You'll notice."

"These are pretty," said Lil in the sitting room of the suite as she entered, motioning to a large bouquet of roses. "There's no one like Lorenza for roses. Who are they from?"

"Mrs. Harcourt," replied Miss Wentworth.

"Sweet of Adele," said Lil. She took a deep breath, knocked on the door of the bedroom, and walked in at the same time. Laurance Van Degan was lying in the hospital bed. Laurance, so large, so imposing, so utterly aristocratic, looked small and frightened to her.

"Oh, Laurance," said Lil, as she bent down to kiss him.

"I've had a shitty little stroke, Lil," said Laurance.

Lil was startled. She had never heard Laurance say *shitty* before. His mouth, she noticed, had moved to the side of his face. He looked to her rather like their father, Ormonde, after his stroke.

"Oh, Laurance," she said again, and there was grief in her voice, for there was great affection between them. Her husband had failed her when he divorced her. Her father had failed her when he married Dodo and left her his fortune, even if it was only for her life use. Her daughter had failed her by making an inappropriate marriage, and then divorcing even more inappropriately. Her son, oh, dear, how her son had failed her. Only her brother Laurance had not failed her throughout their lives.

"Don't cry, Lil," said Laurance.

"It's so unfair, Laurance," said his sister.

"They say the mouth will go back in place in time," he said. His voice, coming as it was from a new position in his face, had a different quality, but its patrician intonations remained.

Lil watched him as he slowly lifted his left hand with his right hand and placed it on his stomach. When a nurse moved in to help, he waved her away with a slow shake of his head. "The left hand doesn't work too well," he said to Lil.

"It's that damn Elias Renthal who's responsible for this," said Lil. She could neither forget nor forgive that Elias Renthal's despicable financial manipulations had sullied the name of her brother, causing him to have to resign from the presidency of the Butterfield, which had broken his heart.

At that moment orderlies arrived.

"It's time, Mr. Van Degan," said the nurse.

"You caught me just as I'm on my way to therapy, Lil," said Laurance, slowly.

"Oh, of course, you're on your way to therapy. You know, Laurance, they do such marvelous things these days in therapy," Lil said, using the enthusiastic voice she used for invalids who couldn't move their arms. She didn't need to tell her own brother that she, as chairperson of the Ladies' League of Manhattan Hospital, had raised a million dollars at the spring dance for the Harcourt Stroke Center.

"Lil," said Laurance.

"Yes, my darling," answered Lil.

"Get out of the market," he said.

"Get out of what?"

"The stock market, Lil."

"Don't you even *think* about the stock market, Laurance. You think about getting well."

"There's going to be a crash. Get hold of young Laurance as soon as possible. He'll know what to do."

With that, the orderlies wheeled the bed out of the room.

"'PARIS isn't what it used to be. Six hundred dollars a night for a room at the Ritz, a *room*, my dear, not even a suite, and if you could have *seen* the kind of people," said Lil Altemus, with a shudder. "All those ghastly common women with their horrid little clipped dogs having lunch at the Rélais Plaza. Arabs everywhere you look. And the clothes are a disaster this year. Skirts up to *here*. I saw Loelia in Paris wearing one of those new dresses. She looked ridiculous, at her age, and she's had something else done to her face. She can't even smile anymore, her face is so tight. She sort of purses her lips, like this, look."

Every year for as long as she could remember, Justine Altemus had been listening to her mother say how awful the people were in Paris, how expensive everything was, and what a disaster the clothes in the *couture* were that year. Justine only half listened, making an appropriate comment from time to time, waiting for the moment when she could tell her own news.

"I have some news for you, Mother," she said, finally.

Lil realized that Justine was not interested in hearing about her trip. She rang her silver bell. "Parker," she said, when her butler appeared.

"Yes, ma'am."

"Will you tell Gertie that the vinaigrette has too much oil?"

"Yes, ma'am."

"But the asparagus is delicious. Perfection, tell her."

"Yes, ma'am."

"My dear," she said, when the butler had disappeared, "the Todescos' chef could make a vinaigrette sauce like you never tasted before. Something about egg whites, I think."

"Oh, Mother, so what?" said Justine, impatiently, bursting to tell her news.

Lil looked at her daughter with surprise.

"You've changed," she said.

"You haven't," replied Justine, meeting her eye. She remembered that Hubie used to sing, "It seems to me I've heard this song before," when their mother went on and on about the same things year after year.

Lil thought about making a retort to her daughter's rudeness, or what appeared to her to be rudeness, but decided to let it pass. "Do you know that your Uncle Laurance, even in the hospital, even with his stroke, is thinking about his family? Do you know what he said to me today? 'Get out of the market,' he said. As they were wheeling him to the stroke center for his therapy, he said, 'Get out of the market.'"

Justine nodded. "Young Laurance called me about that today," she said.

"Do what he tells you. Your Uncle Laurance always knows. Have you been to the hospital to see him?" asked Lil.

"I sent a note, and flowers," said Justine. "And I stopped by the apartment to see Aunt Janet."

"Janet's fallen apart completely," said Lil, who was proud of her reputation in the family for holding steadfast in crises. People still remarked about how bravely she had dealt with Hubie's death.

"Herkie Saybrook said that young Laurance said that Uncle Laurance didn't really want to see anyone until he moves a bit better. Bad for the business or something if everyone knows his mouth is on the side of his face and his left hand just hangs there," said Justine.

"Still, you should have gone. You're not just anyone. You are his niece, after all."

"I will, when he can move better," replied Justine.

"In no time, he'll be as good as new. The Harcourt Stroke Center at the hospital is the best in New York, and I'm proud to say that I personally am responsible for raising a million dollars for it at the annual spring dance at the Rhinelander."

Parker cleared away the asparagus plates and reappeared with plates for the main course.

Lil placed her hand on her plate to see if it had been properly warmed.

"Herkie said—"

"Herkie, Herkie, Herkie. How many times are you going to tell me what Herkie Saybrook said?" Lil had still not forgiven Herkie Saybrook for writing Hubie's will. "The sole looks marvelous, Parker. Tell Gertie perfection."

"Yes, ma'am."

"Herkie's on the board of the hospice, and I see him at the meetings, and we talk."

Lil shook her head impatiently. The hospice. The Hubert Altemus, Jr., Hospice. She could not bear that her son's name was connected to it. She believed that the money should have been contributed anonymously, if it had to be contributed. She could not bear also that her daughter worked there with such passion.

"How long are you going to continue working there? Hasn't this Nurse Edith Cavell performance gone on long enough?"

Justine stared at her mother. "As long as they need me," she answered, evenly.

"What about your child?"

"My child, as you call him, has a name, Mother. He's called Hubie, after my brother, or your son. He's a year old and you've never called him by name once that I can recall. 'Your baby,' you say, or 'your child.' Never Hubie."

"That's not a very attractive tone of voice, Justine."

Justine did not reply.

"How is, uh, little Hubie?" Lil asked. The name pained her.

"He walks. He talks. Most grandmothers would be ecstatic to have such a divine creature, but, then, you're not most grandmothers," said Justine.

"What's that supposed to mean?"

"Oh, Mother, let's not fight. You're just back. Uncle Laurance is sick. I'm being cranky. And I have something important to tell you."

"You're not getting married again, are you?" she asked, excitedly. "If you want to make your old mother happy, that's what she wants to hear."

Justine shook her head. "No, I'm not getting married."

"Are you in love then? Oh, how marvelous, Justine. You have been holding out on me."

Justine shrugged. "I have what's called the occasional suitor. Herkie Saybrook takes me out to dinner, and would take me out more if I gave him a bit of encouragement, and there's a doctor I met at the hospital who's attractive, and I see him from time to time, but I'm not planning to get married, at least not right now. If it happens, it happens, but it's not my priority. I like the work I do at the hospital, and I'm good at it, and the patients like me and ask for me, and it has given me a great deal of satisfaction. And, Mother, I've been asked to be the executive head of the hospice."

"Is that what your news was?"

"Yes, Mother, that's what it was. I know it's not in the same league of importance as the Todescos' chef's recipe for vinaigrette sauce, or the length of Loelia's skirts."

"Please don't be sarcastic, Justine. If that's important to you, then it's very nice, but I would like to point out to you that all the Van Degan women have always felt a responsibility to the city of New York."

"Yes, that's what I feel, Mother."

"I'm not finished, Justine. I think that perhaps where you can be of greater service to the city is if you come on the board of the Van Degan Foundation. I'll talk to Uncle Laurance tomorrow when I go to the hospital."

"I don't want to be on the board of the Van Degan Foundation, Mother, and I am very much aware that the Van Degan Foundation does many good things for the city, but I have found something in my life that is really important to me."

"Hmm," said Lil.

"Mother, all my life I've been identified as Laurance Van Degan's niece, or Mrs. Van Degan Altemus's daughter, or, worse, the Van Degan heiress, as Dolly De Longpre always calls me in her column. Now I'm Justine Altemus, all by myself, without even the terrible word *socialite* in front of it, because no one knows I'm Uncle Laurance's niece, or if they know, it's not any more important to them than it is to me."

"I think we'll have coffee in the library, Parker," said Lil. "And bring some cookies for those naughty doggies, will you? And tell Gertie the eggplant soufflé was yummy."

For a moment after Lil sat in her regular seat in the library, Justine thought her mother was going to cry. Then she lifted her face and looked at her daughter. "Why don't they call it the Juanito whateverhisnamewas Hospice, rather than the Hubert Altemus, Junior, Hospice?" asked Lil.

"Good-bye, Mother," said Justine. "I'm going home to my baby."

"You're not staying for coffee?"

"No, I'm not staying for coffee."

Justine rose and walked out of the room and out of the apartment.

54

THE PREVIOUS day the stock market had fallen five hundred and eight points, exactly as Elias Renthal had told Ruby, and Max Luby, and Laurance Van Degan it was going to do, and exactly as Laurance Van Degan had told his sister, Lil Altemus, it was going to do, and a mild hysteria swept the lunch crowd at Clarence's where all the familiar faces were occupying all the best tables, and people were waiting three deep at the bar for the familiar faces to finish their chicken paillard and decaffeinated cappuccino and leave, but no one wanted to leave that day.

"How come Elias Renthal called Laurance Van Degan from prison with a tip to get out of the stock market?" asked Constantine de Rham. Everyone knew that Laurance Van Degan had felt that his sterling reputation had been tarnished in both the business and social community by his endorsement of Elias Renthal, especially at the Butterfield, and had publicly turned his back on Elias Renthal during the months of his disgrace.

"Listen, Constantine, Elias Renthal is first and foremost a businessman, and he probably wants to keep a finger in the pot. He'll be getting out of prison in a year or two," said Lord Biedermeier. He removed his pince-nez and cleaned the lenses with a napkin, so that he could survey the crowd at Clarence's. He noticed that despite the economic hardships that might be coming on the nation, the restaurant was filled to capacity. He noticed also that, because of his luncheon companion, Constantine de Rham, people who might ordinarily wave hellos to him, like Lil Altemus, chose not to cast their eyes in his direction.

"I thought he couldn't trade anymore. I thought he was barred for life," insisted Constantine, who enjoyed other people's ill fortune.

"You're right, he can't trade, and he is barred for life, but that's not to say he can't get someone else to trade for him. Max Luby, for instance. Max trades; Elias calls the shots."

"He won't be giving any more society balls," said Constantine, with grim satisfaction.

"No, he won't be giving any more society balls, and he won't ever get inside the front door of the Butterfield again, even as a lunch guest, but when he makes a new fortune, and he will, people will start seeing him again. Even Laurance Van Degan. They'll have lunch, at some obscure place, and pretty soon everyone will have forgotten. It's the way of the world."

Constantine wondered but did not say that no one had ever taken him up again. It was as if Lord Biedermeier read his thoughts. "Even you, Constantine. People will see you again. Write a book."

"About what?" asked de Rham.

"Playboys, my dear Constantine, are very fashionable this year. There is an enormous interest in Ali Khan and Rubirosa, and you are their heir. Look at the Monaco Princesses. The public can't get enough of them. That is why I thought that you perhaps would want to talk about the accident in Paris when that beautiful young girl lost her head. And all the rumors that have plagued your life," said Lord Biedermeier.

"But those rumors were utterly false," said Constantine, indignantly.

"It doesn't matter," replied Lord Biedermeier.

"They were never proved."

"It doesn't matter. People who haven't spoken to you in years will be all too glad to have you to dinner again if you have a hit book. All this happened years ago when you were very young. You didn't understand what you were getting into. Think about it. The public loves reformation."

"But I don't know how to write," said Constantine.

"The least of our worries. If you could read the marvelous manuscript Elias Renthal has just handed in about life in prison, and he didn't have to write a word of it. I simply sent an author to visit him once a week in Allenwood, and they talked and talked. It will guarantee him acceptance when he gets out of prison."

"Hmm," said Constantine.

RUBY RENTHAL was the first to say that only her dentist or her gynecologist could entice her to make the trip to town, for semiannual checkups, and it was the former who brought her to the city on the same day that Gus Bailey returned to New York. They met in the waiting room of Dr. Chase's office.

"Gus, my God!" said Ruby, surprised when Gus walked in.

"Hello, Ruby," replied Gus, as surprised as she. For an instant they looked at each other. When she held out her hand, he took it and leaned to kiss her on the cheek.

"I didn't know you were out."

"Just. The courts don't take your first shooting seriously these days," he said.

"Oh, Gus, don't joke."

"I'm not joking. It's the truth. I got less time than Elias."

"I wrote to you," she said.

"I know."

"You didn't answer."

"I thought I'd brought you enough notoriety already."

"Gus, for God's sake, you saved my life."

"I didn't really. You had a gun."

"Let me tell you something about that famous gun, Gus, and I don't mean that it used to belong to Queen Marie of Rumania. I always carried it because Elias wanted me to carry it, but what Elias never knew was that it was never loaded. I couldn't bear the idea of carrying a loaded gun."

Gus looked around him in the waiting room, aware that other patients were looking at them.

"Have you already been to the doctor, or are you going?" he asked.

"What do you have in mind?" she answered.

"A little lunch maybe?"

"You've got me."

"Let's get out of here."

Without a moment's hesitation, Ruby called into the receptionist's office and said, "Tell Dr. Chase I'll call back for another appointment."

"But he's ready for you, Mrs. Renthal," said the receptionist. "Mrs. Lord is just leaving."

"I'll call back," she repeated, taking her mink coat off the coat rack and following Gus out the door.

In the elevator, she said to him, "I watched you on television."

"A ghastly kind of fame, isn't it?"

"At least he didn't die."

Gus nodded. "Do you know what I think, Ruby?"

"What?"

"I think at that last second when my eyes met his, that Becky, from wherever she is, pushed my arm just enough to the side so I didn't kill him."

"Looking after her father, you mean?"

"Right, that wasn't the way. I realized it as I was pulling the trigger."

"You're not sorry it turned out this way, are you?"

"Not anymore. I was obsessed for three years with that man. Nothing mattered but that I kill him. That was all I could think of. That obsession has lifted, thank God."

"How much time did you serve?"

"I got a year. I served nine months."

"Do people talk to you?"

"I don't know. You're the first person I've seen. But I don't care if they don't. It's time for another beginning."

"Good for you, Gus. I'm a great believer in new beginnings."

They looked at each other.

"Do you see Elias?"

"Oh, sure. I go to visit."

"Do you see the old crowd?"

"Heavens, no."

They laughed.

"How about Clarence's for lunch?"

They laughed again. "Perfect."

"LAURANCE knew all this was going to happen," said Lil, who was lunching at the window table with her friends Matilda Clarke and Cora Mandell and Ezzie Fenwick, who had just told them about the fight over money at the Bulbenkians' house the night before. "Laurance has been saying for some time that the market was at an unsustainable high level." Lil Altemus quoted her brother more than any person in her life. She spoke with the ease of someone whose fortune would remain intact throughout any financial crisis. "Laurance got out of the market a week ago, and, of course, I did too, and so did Justine."

Ezzie, who had lost money, at least on paper, was testy that day and spoke of canceling a trip to Egypt that he had planned. When Michael, everyone's favorite waiter at Clarence's, placed his plate in front of him, Ezzie lifted his dark glasses and examined the plate with his good eye, which was not the eye that looked like a poached egg.

"I want tartar sauce with my crab cakes," said Ezzie, loudly. "That's not tartar sauce. That's mayonnaise."

"We're out of tartar sauce," replied Michael, with the courtesy and tact with which he was known to deal with difficult customers.

"Out of tartar sauce? How can you be out of tartar sauce?" asked Ezzie, raising his eyebrows in assumed exasperation.

"We are," said Michael.

"Then tell the chef to make some more, or send to the market and buy some more," ordered Ezzie.

"Yes, sir," said Michael, retreating to report to Chick Jacoby the latest incident from the quarrelsome Ezzie Fenwick.

"*Never* let them have the last word," said Ezzie, as if giving his friends a lesson in deportment, before resuming his account of the Bulbenkians' fight, which Lil had interrupted.

It was then that the reclusive Ruby Renthal, so long out of sight, and the just-released-from-prison Gus Bailey walked into Clarence's, without a reservation. "My dears, you will not *believe* who just walked into this restaurant," said Ezzie, all good humored again. Ezzie's companions, and everyone else in the front part of the restaurant, where all the good people, as Ezzie called them, sat, turned to look at the curious duet who stood quietly just inside the door waiting for Chick Jacoby to hurry forward to greet them.

"You watch," said Ezzie, in his nasal voice. "Chick will move Lord Biedermeier and Constantine de Rham over to his own table, as if he's giving them a big treat, and put Ruby and the jailbird there."

Of the three women with Ezzie, only old Cora Mandell, who had decorated the spectacular Renthal apartment, waved a greeting. Ruby smiled back but made no attempt to speak to the others, as she sat at the table just vacated by Lord Biedermeier and Constantine de Rham.

"Talk to me, Gus," Ruby said.

"About prison?"

"Make any friends there?"

"I wrote a book there."

"Ezzie Fenwick always said you were going to write a book."

"For once he was right."

At that moment Matilda Clarke appeared at their table.

"Gus Bailey!" she said.

"Hello, Matilda," said Gus, rising.

"Ages," she said.

"Ages," replied Gus. "You know Ruby."

"Hellohoware?"

"Well, Gus, tell me everything," said Matilda.

"I've been in prison."

"Oh, I know. I think you're a national hero."

"No, I'm not."

"Listen, Gus, Maisie Verdurin is having one of her dinners on Thursday, and it might be her last for a while, because no one's going to be buying paintings for a while, with the crash and all. Would you like me to arrange it so we can go together?"

"Can't on Thursday," said Gus.

"Then come to the country for the weekend. I've got Justine Altemus and Herkie Saybrook. They're an item, I hear, although Lil denies it vigorously. He's so much better for her than the TV announcer. Sweetzer always said, 'Stick with your own kind,' and he was right. You've simply got to come, Gus. We're going to Rochelle's on Saturday night."

"Can't this weekend," Gus replied.

"Not off on one of your mystery trips, are you?"

"No, my mystery trips ended with the bullet I put in Lefty Flint."

"Oh, I get it," said Matilda. "Branching out? New directions? That sort of thing?"

"Something like that," answered Gus.

"Well, all right," she said, shrugging her shoulders. "Us single ladies do what we can." She moved back to Ezzie's table.

Gus and Ruby looked at each other.

"You did that well, Gus," said Ruby.

"I can't get back into all that. I never fit in in the first place," said Gus. "It just kept my mind off what was going on in my life that I couldn't do a damn thing about at the time."

"What are you going to do now that you're back?" asked Ruby.

"I'm just here to sell my place, go to the dentist, close out a chapter. I'm moving on."

"Where?"

"Maybe just a block away. It doesn't matter. All that I know is that this ain't it."

Michael, the waiter who served the front part of the restaurant, came up to take their orders. "Welcome back, Mr. Bailey," he said.

"Thanks."

"Nice to see you, Mrs. Renthal," he said.

"Thank you, Michael."

"Let me tell you the specials for today."

Ruby and Gus looked at each other.

"Listen, Michael," said Gus.

"Yessir."

"We're not going to stay."

He looked over at Ruby. She was smiling at him.

"Why are you smiling?"

"That's just what I was going to say," she said.

Ruby rose from her seat. She looked over to Chick Jacoby at the bar and blew him a kiss. Then she walked out the door, followed by Gus.

For a while they walked down Lexington Avenue without speaking. At the corner of 72nd Street, Gus raised his hand and signaled a taxi. When the car stopped in front of him, he turned to Ruby and they looked at each other fondly.

"S'long, Ruby," he said.

"Bye, Gus," she answered.

"Will you be okay?"

"Oh, sure. And you?"

"Sure."

"Luck."

"Same."

As Gus got into the taxi, Ruby turned and walked across the street.